D0742272

The Honest Folk of Guadeloupe

Also by Timothy Williams

The Honest Folk of Guadeloupe

Timothy Williams

Published by
Soho Press, Inc.
853 Broadway
New York, NY 10003

Library of Congress Cataloging-in-Publication Data
Williams, Timothy.
The honest folk of Guadeloupe / Timothy Williams.

HC ISBN 978-1-61695-385-0
eISBN 978-1-61695-386-7
1. Police—Guadeloupe—Fiction. 2. Murder—Investigation—Fiction.
3. Guadeloupe—Fiction. I. Title.
PR6073.I43295H66 2015
823'.914—dc23   2014021690

Map of Guadeloupe: © istockphoto

Printed in the United States of America

10 9 8 7 6 5 4 3 2 1

Aux anciens étudiants de l'Université de l'Express:

Claude
Patrice
Laurent
Roland
Bernard
Éric
Kamel
Yves
Pierre
Serge
Chantal
Madly

et à la doyenne de la faculté de pharmacologie,

Éléonore

The Honest Folk of Guadeloupe

Pointe
Allègre

Port-Louis

Sainte-
Rose

Petit-Canal

Le Moule

Deshaies

GRANDE-TERRE

Marigot

Saint-Martin
(Guadeloupe)

Philipsburg

Saint-Maarten
(Neth.)

La Désirade
(Guadeloupe)

Pointe des Châteaux

Saint-Barthélemy
(Guadeloupe)

Pointe-à-Pitre

Saint-

Pointe-Noire

Le Gosier

Sainte-
Anne

François

Gustavia

Petit-Bourg

Îles de la Petit Terre
(Guadeloupe)

Basse-Terre

GUADELOUPE

Capesterre-Belle-Eau

Basse-Terre

Trois-Rivières

Saint-Louis

Marie-Galante
(Guadeloupe)

Grand-Bourg

Capesterre-Belle-Eau

Îles des Saintes
(Guadeloupe)

I

Madame Dugain

Wednesday, May 16, 1990

"You're looking for me?" The woman was attractive, but her face appeared tired, the eyelids dark. There were wrinkles about her soft brown eyes. She placed a pile of exercise books on the table beside her handbag.

"Madame Dugain?"

"Yes, I am Madame Dugain. I teach French and Latin. Your child is in which class?"

Anne Marie moved toward the table. "It's about your husband."

For a moment the expression went blank, devoid of emotion, while the eyes searched Anne Marie's face. "I have already made a statement to the *police judiciaire*." Madame Dugain drew a chair—a school chair with a steel frame and a plywood seat—toward her. "Several statements." She leaned wearily against the backrest.

Anne Marie sat down on the other side of the table. On the formica top there were a couple of tin lids that had been used as ashtrays.

The far wall was covered with pinned-up notices concerning the different teaching unions. Beneath the drawing pins, the paper rustled relentlessly; the doors to the staff room were wide open and a mid-morning breeze kept the air cool. Through the shutters, Anne Marie could see a flame tree that had started to blossom.

"My husband is dead—isn't that enough?"

Anne Marie nodded sympathetically. "He died under strange circumstances."

"He was hounded to death."

"I don't think anyone hounded your husband."

Madame Dugain shook her head. "I'd rather not talk about these things."

"I understand."

The eyes flared with brief anger. "You understand?"

The two women were alone in the silent staff room of the Collège Carnot.

(Somewhere children were singing. In another building a class burst into muffled laughter.)

"I know how painful it is to lose someone you love." Anne Marie held out her hand. "I'm Madame Laveaud. I'm the *juge d'instruction.*"

Madame Dugain took the proffered hand coolly, keeping her distance. "I really have nothing to say to an investigative magistrate or indeed to anybody else."

"I asked the head mistress for permission to speak to you."

Madame Dugain folded her arms against her chest. She was wearing a dress that went well with the brown, liquid eyes. A necklace, matching gold earrings. Black hair that had been pulled back into a tight bun. Her lipstick was a matte red.

"On Saturday, April twenty-first, three officers of the *police judiciaire* visited your husband in his offices in the Sécid Tower. They had a search warrant and they were seeking information concerning accusations made against your husband—"

"Everybody accused Rodolphe."

"Accusations that as director of the Centre Environnement, he had been misappropriating funds."

"My husband's not a criminal."

"Your husband received money from the government—from the Ministry of Employment—in order to recruit and train young people under the Youth Training Scheme. There were six young people working for him at the institute. Their salaries, funded entirely with government money, were paid into the Institute's account."

"I know very little about my husband's financial affairs."

"Your husband's accused of employing two of the young people in his small business in Abymes and paying them with the government allowances."

"I've given the police as much information as . . ." She bit her lip. "My husband would never have taken money that wasn't his."

Anne Marie touched Madame Dugain's arm. "Given the circumstances, I don't think any good can be achieved by continuing with the enquiry."

The corners of her mouth twitched. "My husband and I were happy. We'd been married for seventeen years. You don't think my children and I have suffered enough?"

Somewhere an electric buzzer sounded, followed almost immediately by the sound of scraping chairs and the scuffling of feet as the pupils left their desks at the end of their lesson.

"Just supposing that your husband was guilty of these accusations . . ." Anne Marie shrugged. "A fine—twenty thousand, thirty thousand francs. Not a lot of money—not for your husband."

Madame Dugain flinched.

"He could've paid that sort of money," Anne Marie said.

"Rodolphe was innocent."

"It's not for thirty thousand francs that an influential and well-respected member of the community decides to do away with himself."

2

Fait Divers

France Antilles, April 23, 1990

Mr. Rodolphe Dugain, better known to most television viewers as Monsieur Environnement, died on Saturday, April 21, of multiple internal injuries after throwing himself from the fourteenth story of Sécid Tower block in central Pointe-à-Pitre.

If the rumor had been circulating for some time that the police judiciaire *were making enquiries into the Centre Environnement, the sudden and untimely death of Monsieur Dugain, one of the major and most respected figures in the cultural Who's Who of our* département, *seems to have taken Guadeloupe by surprise. The shock can be still felt in the University, where Monsieur Dugain held a lectureship in natural sciences, as well as in the corridors of the RFO television station, where he regularly broadcast his popular nature programs.*

On Saturday morning, three officers of the Service Régional de la Police Judiciaire presented themselves at the offices of the Centre Environnement. According to eyewitnesses, Monsieur Dugain appeared his normal, jovial self, not allowing his good humor to be affected in any way by the presentation of a search warrant. According to sources, he offered a drink to the three men. Then, while the officers were looking for documents and other information—the nature of which as yet has not been revealed by the parquet—Mr. Dugain managed to slip from the room. Once on the far side of the steel front door, he locked it, making prisoners of the police officers. Taking to the stairs, Mr. Dugain climbed from the third to the fourteenth floor of the tower block. On the top floor, he made his way to the observation window and from there jumped to his death, landing on a car parked on the sidewalk of the Boulevard Chanzy. Mr. Dugain died immediately on impact. The vehicle was badly damaged and several people were taken to the nearby Centre hospitalier, *suffering from shock.*

A crowd of onlookers soon gathered around the macabre spectacle. Yet again in Guadeloupe, the lamentable behavior of rubbernecks and passersby hindered the fire and ambulance services in the execution of their duty.

Mr. Dugain, who was a Freemason and an ex-secretary of the Rotary Club, was born in Martinique 57 years ago. He leaves a wife and their two children, as well as two children from an earlier marriage.

There will be a memorial service at St. Pierre and St. Paul on Tuesday at ten o'clock. The inhumation will take place at the municipal cemetery at midday.

3
Public Trial

"My husband is dead."

"I need to know why he died."

Madame Dugain raised her eyes. "Is that important?"

"You said he was hounded to death by the police."

"The police, the media, whoever else—it doesn't matter. Not now."

"It matters."

A moment of hesitation. "You don't believe my husband was innocent?"

"Innocent or guilty, suicide is not a normal reaction."

"The SRPJ threw him from the fourteenth floor."

"Unlikely."

Madame Dugain allowed her shoulders to sag. Then she took her bag. "I must be going." She stood away from the chair. She was in her late thirties, with a trim, girlish silhouette and attractive brown legs. She ran a hand through her hair.

"Unlikely the *police judiciaire* should want to murder your husband."

"It's been nice meeting you."

"When somebody's pushed through a window, the victim hits the ground close to the building. The car on which your husband landed was nearly four meters from the entrance to the Tour Sécid."

Madame Dugain stared in silence at the clasp of her handbag.

"Nothing else you can tell me?"

"Else in what way, *madame le juge?*"

"Anything worrying your husband?"

A hard laugh. "His name in the papers? The accusation of embezzlement? The police coming to search his offices? Worrying my husband? What more do you want, for heaven's sake? His probity, his reputation—his very life were being called into question. His dignity was being put on trial. No, not a trial. A public lynching without trial. The telephone never stopped ringing."

"With a good lawyer . . ."

"Rodolphe was innocent."

"With a good lawyer, he could have—"

"My husband did not need a lawyer. He needed to be left alone, he needed to not be dragged through the mud. The mud his enemies wanted. That the police wanted. And that's what you've got now. You're satisfied, aren't you?"

"Satisfied?"

"Rodolphe's dead."

Anne Marie caught her breath. "Who are these enemies that you talk about?"

"I've nothing further to say."

"Why don't you want to help me set your husband's record straight?"

"You couldn't care less about my husband's reputation."

"I care about the truth."

"Your truth." Madame Dugain turned and walked out into the sunshine, the handbag held to her body. Her heels clicked on the stone paving of the courtyard as she passed beneath the flame trees.

4

Les Seigneurs de Saint-Domingue

"Liliane Dugain's my cousin."

It used to be the *lycée*. Then, in the mid-sixties, a new school complex was built at Baimbridge on the edge of the city to accommodate the increase in the number of pupils. Consequently the old colonial Lycée Carnot, with its courtyard, its mango and flame trees, its airy, wooden classrooms, stranded in the heart of Pointe-à-Pitre, was transformed into a *collège*, a junior high school.

The two women walked out of the staff room and across the yard, between the trees. A breeze rustled through the leaves, and the pendulous mangoes swayed gently at the end of their long stalks. Other mangoes had fallen to the ground and split their bruised skin.

(Anne Marie was reminded of her school years in Algeria.)

"I got the impression she was more angry than upset."

The headmistress shrugged. "Liliane had been married long enough to know what Dugain was like."

There was surprise in Anne Marie's voice. "He was fond of women?"

"You know a man who isn't?"

Anne Marie glanced at Mademoiselle Salondy as they stepped into the school building. "That's why you never married, Lucette?"

"One of many reasons." The headmistress put her finger to her lips and nodded to the closed doors of the administrative offices.

The muffled sound of a typewriter.

They went up the wooden stairs and entered an air-conditioned room. A photograph of President Mitterrand hung on the wall between a poster of the Declaration of Human Rights and a calendar from a local garage. The cables leading into the light switches were unconcealed and had been tacked into the wall with staples. A telephone on the large desk, and beside it, a plastic cube containing various pictures of Lucette Salondy's relatives. In a small glass jar stood a solitary anthurium.

"Madame Dugain's your cousin?"

"Sit down, Anne Marie." Lucette Salondy had a smile that formed wrinkles at the corner of her bright eyes. "Who isn't a cousin on this island?" She was a large woman whose dress could not hide matronly hips. In her youth, she had been very beautiful.

"You know her well?"

"I taught her. Liliane's more than twenty years younger than I am and when I came back from France in sixty-six she was doing her philosophy baccalaureate. A bright girl, and the youngest in her class." She tapped the desk. "That was when the *lycée* was still here, before they built the concrete jungle on the ring road."

"I shouldn't discuss things that have been told to me in confidence."

"Then don't."

"Liliane Dugain was acting out a role—that's the impression I got."

"Liliane's too old to act."

"My looking into his death doesn't seem to interest her."

"She needs to be left alone."

"That's what she said."

"The women in Guadeloupe hide their suffering."

"Here at school, do you ever talk to her?"

"My prison." The headmistress gestured to the office, the walls painted the pale grey of France's tropical public buildings and beneath the opaque louvers, the potted dieffenbachia, leaves yellowing at the edges. "My job's to sign bits of paper or phone the *rectorat* in Martinique. No time for idle chat—there are at least three new teachers this year whom I've never spoken to." She pulled a blue cardigan from the back of the chair onto her shoulders. "Headmistress? I'm just a cog in a big, faceless administration. A factory, an educational factory. The gentlemen of Martinique fail to understand our problems here."

"The gentlemen of Martinique fail to understand the good folk of Guadeloupe?"

"You're learning your West Indian culture!" The headmistress clapped her hands in pleasure. "*The noblemen of Saint Domingue, the gentlemen of Martinique and the honest folk of Guadeloupe.* Two centuries after the independence of Haiti, the honest folk of Guadeloupe run around in SUVs while Saint Domingue's aristocrats cut cane in our fields."

Anne Marie smiled. "Despite the gentlemen of the *rectorat* in Martinique, you have time to talk with me, Lucette."

She stretched a plump arm across the desk and squeezed Anne Marie's hand. "I rarely manage to get out of this office."

"You've just been out."

"Because I wanted to talk to my sister-in-law before she scurries back to the *palais de justice*."

"Not your sister-in-law, Lucette. I'm your sister's sister-in-law—remember? You still have your beach apartment in Le Moule?"

"I just don't get time to go there. My weekends are taken up with administrative work. Perhaps when I retire . . ."

"I don't think you'll ever retire, Lucette."

The large woman sighed. "It was Dugain's second marriage, you know."

"They weren't happy?"

"Liliane married someone who was seventeen years older than her. That kind of age difference's common here in our islands, but Liliane's an educated woman and she wanted a companion, a friend. In the end she married somebody who could've been her father. She wanted equality and found a man who never treated her as an equal. Someone who gave her two lovely daughters but who went elsewhere for his pleasure."

"Other women?"

"You sound surprised, Anne Marie."

"Not the sort of thing you expect."

"What would you expect?"

"When there's a big age difference, aren't men supposed to lose interest in philandering?"

"Are they?"

"Or so I am told."

"Perhaps French men—but not here," Lucette Salondy said, folding her arms. "Dugain appeared on television—he was a public figure, the kind of person to appeal to women, to our groupie psychology. We're all attracted by the dominant male." She clicked her tongue, as if reproaching herself for something. "Dugain didn't go out of his way looking for women—but they were there."

"Who?"

"There are always women."

"Who?"

"Even a headmistress and a spinster locked away in her office gets to hear things." She got up and went to a small filing cabinet. She turned the key. "Care for a drink?"

"No thanks."

"I often wonder how you manage to stay so slim, Anne Marie. So slim and so young." Lucette Salondy poured a thimbleful of white rum into a small glass. From a small refrigerator, she took a slice of green lime. "Worry about my figure at my age?" She sipped and winced. "The great thing about being old is you don't have to try to please any more, and it's only when you've stopped trying to please men they actually start to notice you. Not for your body, for your figure, for what you can do in bed—they actually notice you for what you are." She smiled wistfully. "I was thinking about your husband only the other day, Anne Marie."

"My ex-husband."

Another sip. "How's your son?"

"Who were Dugain's women?"

"Tell me about Fabrice, Anne Marie. We were all sad when he moved on to the *lycée*."

Anne Marie flushed. She was about to say something bitter, but instead she chose to relax. She allowed herself to sit back in the tubular chair. "Wind surfing, most of the time. And probably about to repeat his *première scientifique* at the *lycée*. Fabrice's pretty hopeless at school."

"He can't be too hopeless if he's in *première scientifique*. Always top of the class here. A lovely boy."

"English is the only thing he's willing to put his mind to. He's stubborn and never wants to be helped."

"Stubborn like his father."

Anne Marie looked at her hands. "If Fabrice's not interested in something, then he just can't be bothered."

"Like his father."

"He spends his time watching the American channels on the satellite dish. Understands everything in English—but refuses to work at school. I mustn't complain too much—he's very affectionate and dotes on his little sister."

Lucette Salondy's face broke into a broad smile. "And Létitia?"

"The apple of her mother's eye."

The headmistress took the plastic cube and pointed to a photograph on one of its faces, a photograph taken outside the church in Pointe-à-Pitre. Children in white dresses, holding flowers and squinting into the sun. Létitia stood in the center of the group. Her dark hair hung in short, beribboned plaits. The soft brown skin of mixed parentage. She looked at the camera with her head to one side. Inquisitive, self-assured eyes. She was holding a bouquet of flowers.

"The apple of her aunt's eye, too. An aunt who doesn't get to see her enough."

"Létitia loves church—goodness knows why. Perhaps it's the dressing up she likes." Anne Marie touched the cube with her finger. "I thought I was too old to have a second child, and when I found out about Létitia . . . It wasn't the happiest of times. I thought about an abortion. When I now think I could've spent the rest of my life without Létitia . . ." Anne Marie looked up at the older woman. "You could've had children, Lucette."

"Instead I've got an entire school. Before long, you'll be sending Létitia to us—only by then, I'll be retired."

"You love this job too much to retire."

Somewhere a bell rang.

"Why are you interested in Liliane Dugain, Anne Marie?"

"It's her husband's death I'm interested in."

The headmistress folded her arms. "He killed himself—jumped from the top of a building."

Anne Marie remarked, "There are a lot of nasty rumors."

"Rumors concerning the *police judiciaire*?"

Anne Marie gave Lucette Salondy an unblinking stare.

"Dugain had a lot of enemies, Anne Marie."

"Arnaud doesn't believe it was a suicide."

"Who's Arnaud?"

"You don't know the *procureur* of Pointe-à-Pitre?"

"Not his given name . . . It's Arnaud?"

The room seemed to chill suddenly. Lucette Salondy held her glass motionless in mid-air. With the other hand, she pulled the cardigan tight against her large shoulders.

"Dugain had a mistress?"

"You really want to know?"

"It's my job."

"Perhaps you ought to change jobs."

Anne Marie pointed to the poster on the wall. "There's no republic without justice."

"I thought it was me who was supposed to teach philosophy."

"And there's no justice without truth."

A laugh lubricated with white rum.

"Never underestimate the *lycée* in Sarlat." Anne Marie grinned with pleasure. "I won the *prix d'excellence.*"

"You must've been teacher's pet." The headmistress put down the glass and took a pen from the mahogany inkstand in front of her. "Everybody knew it was a mistake. Liliane should never have married Dugain. Few people will miss him. Not even his groupies. " She jotted something onto a scrap of paper. "In your position, I'd forget about justice and I'd certainly forget about *Monsieur Environnement.*" She folded the piece of paper twice, firmly, as if she wanted to have nothing to do with its written contents. "A womanizer and a fraud."

"You're not in my position." Anne Marie took the slip of paper, without glancing at it.

"But like you, I'm a woman."

5

Trousseau

Trousseau had been putting on weight.

"They told me downstairs you were here, *madame le juge*."

Lucette Salondy smiled brightly. "Please enter."

Trousseau took a hesitant step into the office. He held a briefcase under his arm, and beneath the white shirt, the narrow shoulders ran down to a bulging belly that pushed at the cracked crocodile belt of his trousers. His eyes darted from one woman to the other. He smiled nervously and straightened his tie. "I wouldn't have . . ."

"Come in and sit down, Monsieur Trousseau." Anne Marie gestured him to the chair beside her. "Nobody's going to hurt you. Just two old ladies chatting."

"Bit of a hurry, *madame le juge*." He stood with his dark hand on the handle of the open door. "I've just come from the *palais de justice*."

"Monsieur Trousseau, you know Mademoiselle Salondy?"

He moved reluctantly toward the desk and shook the outstretched hand, while his eyes remained on Anne Marie. "There's a plane waiting for you, *madame le juge*. At the airport."

She laughed. "My children are waiting for me."

"You're wanted in Saint-François."

"On Wednesdays I have lunch with my children. You know that, Monsieur Trousseau. This afternoon I'm taking them to the beach."

"It's urgent."

The laughter left her eyes. "Why a plane, Monsieur Trousseau?"

He smiled nervously and edged back toward the door.

"And to think that I chose this job." Anne Marie looked at Lucette Salondy. "A functionary of the state," she sighed before getting wearily to her feet. "Come and see the children soon."

Lucette held Anne Marie's hand. "I'm retiring at the end of the year. An old woman, thirty-seven years a teacher. I'll have plenty of time to visit you then."

Trousseau pulled at the dark tie again. "The *procureur* insisted on an escort."

"Give my love to the children, Anne Marie. Kiss the lovely Létitia."

"If the *procureur* ever allows me to see them."

The two women embraced and Lucette Salondy squeezed Anne Marie's hand.

6

Gendarme

The officer helped Anne Marie from the military helicopter and accompanied her to the waiting car—a dark blue Peugeot that glinted in the sunshine. Trousseau followed, muttering to himself and wiping his forehead with a handkerchief.

"We'll be there in a few minutes." The *gendarme* spoke with an educated accent. He belonged to the generation of West Indians that was now beginning to reach positions of authority. There was about him the faint odor of expensive *eau de cologne* and self-assurance. Anne Marie got into the car and he closed the door behind her. He went around the back of the vehicle and climbed in from the other side. A smile played at the edge of his lips.

Trousseau sat beside the uniformed driver. He held the battered attaché case on his knees. He was now wearing his threadbare jacket.

"To the Pointe des Chateaux." The *gendarme* removed his *képi*. He had a high forehead and short, curly hair that had begun to recede. He was good-looking, but slightly chubby. "Capitaine Parise," he said.

"Anne Marie Laveaud."

The lips broke into a wide smile. "I've heard much about you." He held out his hand; Anne Marie noticed a gold wedding ring. "A pleasure to meet you, *madame le juge*."

The car took the road from the small airport, went past the Méridien hotel and the bright flags flapping from the high staffs, and out onto the road toward the Pointe des Châteaux.

Tourists were swinging golf clubs on the green of the nearby course. Caddies lolled in the limited shade of the motorized buggies.

The sky was cloudless, the sun directly overhead. The car was air-conditioned and the windows tinted. Only the slightest hint of humming as the Peugeot traveled eastwards. Thin dancing mirages played on the surface of the tarmac. "I don't envy you."

"What?"

"The Dugain business." His eyes ran over her face. "You're making a lot of enemies within the SRPJ."

"Why the helicopter, *commandant?*"

Parise coughed. "The *procureur* wanted you here as soon as possible. I'm afraid you're going to be rather busy. Good thing it's not the high season."

"High season?"

"The high season for tourism."

"Does that matter?"

Parise glanced at Trousseau's neck. "A nurse, *madame le juge*, aged twenty-three or twenty-four. She was on holiday here."

The unmarked Peugeot went past the new restaurants—low, concrete buildings with grey-green corrugated roofs—specializing in lobster, conch and other seafood. The restaurants were doing brisk business beneath the midday sun. Rented cars with their stenciled plates were parked along the narrow highway.

Another day in this tropical paradise.

"A tourist from Paris. Raped and then murdered, *madame le juge.*"

In the cool air of the car, Trousseau was humming softly.

7
Jacuzzi

(Jean Michel used to call it their Jacuzzi Beach. "*One of those places where families go on weekends. The rest of the time, it is deserted—apart from the occasional fisherman.*")

When Fabrice was little, Jean Michel would drive the family down here. They would picnic and later Jean Michel would go off swimming with his goggles and snorkel. The surf was not ideal but a few meters into the sea there was an outcrop of rocks where the waves broke, forming a natural tub into which the foaming current swirled, massaging the body. Nine, ten years ago—before the divorce, before Létitia.

A blue van was pulled over onto the shoulder of the road. On the roof, the light turned slowly. Other vehicles were parked under the trees, between the road and the white beach.

The sun was overhead, hot and implacable. It was almost one o'clock as Parise helped Anne Marie out of the car and they walked to where the *procureur* stood talking to a couple of men in green fatigues.

An intercom rasped unpleasantly and one of the men, dark aureoles of sweat beneath his arms, spoke into a microphone.

Easterly trades blew in from the sea and rustled at the branches of the sea grapes. There were picnic tables made of unvarnished timber that had been anchored to cement blocks with steel pins to prevent termites eating into the woodwork.

The *procureur* kissed Anne Marie on both cheeks. "Sorry about this, Anne Marie." He shrugged apologetically. "And on a Wednesday."

"Where's the body?"

"Monsieur Trousseau said you were busy." He used the *tu* form.

"An investigating magistrate's always busy."

"He also said you were taking lunch with your children . . ."

"A mother's always busy," Anne Marie said. "The maid knows how to heat something up."

The *procureur* was a tall man, with sandy hair and stooped shoulders. He wore white cotton trousers and black shoes. He held a cigarette in his hand; a box of Peter Stuyvesant was visible through the fabric of the shirt pocket. He was sweating; there were beads of perspiration on the freckled forehead.

He took Anne Marie by the arm and led her toward the beach. Underfoot the hot dust became fine, white sand.

"I used to come here with my husband."

Stakes had been driven into the sand; red and white police ribbon stretched from one stake to the next, curved and flapping in the breeze.

"A fisherman leaves his boat here. He got back from fishing just after dawn and he saw something under the bushes." The *procureur* put a hand to his eyes and pointed toward a tree on the beach's edge. "Didn't give it a second thought—until he returned to the beach at ten o'clock. Dogs were everywhere and when he realized they were mauling a corpse, he alerted the *gendarmerie* in Saint-François."

The glare from the sand was painful. "Where's the body?" Anne Marie took a pair of sunglasses from her shoulder bag.

The *procureur* stepped over the ribbon and then helped Anne Marie. His hand was damp. The wind ruffled his wispy hair.

"At the morgue."

"Then what am I doing here?"

"I was in Le Moule and so I got here almost immediately with Docteur Malavoy." He kneeled down in the shade of the tree and touched the sand. "The *gendarmerie* have done all the scene-of-the-crime stuff. No traces of blood." A hand to his forehead. "I wanted to pack everything off to the lab as quickly as possible."

"Without a corpse there's not much point in my being here."

"In this heat, it was best to get the body to the hospital as soon as possible."

"Tell me about the victim."

"Evelyne Vaton, resident of the fourteenth *arrondissement*."

"A tourist from Paris?"

The *procureur* nodded. "Twenty-four years old and unmarried. Mademoiselle Evelyne Vaton, a nurse by profession. The only personal belonging we've found so far is a bikini."

"How do you know who she is?"

"Through Hertz, the car rental people," the *procureur* said. "She hired a car for a week and when she didn't return the car on Monday night, the rental firm contacted the family she was staying with."

"Monday?"

"She should have handed it in the day before yesterday."

"The car's been found?"

"A Fiat Uno." He made a vague gesture toward the Pointe des Châteaux, just visible beyond the low shrub that ran along the beach to the east. "Left it in the Pointe des Châteaux parking site."

"The Pointe des Châteaux's three kilometers down the road from here. It's a pretty long walk to this beach." Anne Marie gestured to the police vehicles. "She could've parked here."

The *procureur* shrugged. "The sandwich woman says she noticed that a white Fiat was the only car at the Pointe des Châteaux when she went home at seven o'clock last night."

"Last night? When was the girl murdered?"

"We've got the signs of decomposition."

"When did she die, Arnaud?"

"According to Docteur Malavoy, Evelyne Vaton was probably still alive at midnight on Sunday." He glanced at his watch. "More than sixty hours ago."

"Just last night the woman noticed the car?" Mockingly, Anne Marie counted off two fingers. "After two days?"

"Her name is Olga and she takes Mondays off."

"The body's only found now? When it's started to decompose? More than two days on the beach and nobody saw the body?" Anne Marie could feel sweat trickling down the insides of her arms.

"The murderer hid the body." The *procureur* added inconsequentially, "She was naked."

"You said there was a bikini, Arnaud."

"The bikini was half buried in the sand."

"It may not have been hers. Two days on the beach—you don't think the dogs would have got to her?" Anne Marie exhaled noisily.

The *procureur* gave a thin smile. "All the signs of rape, Anne Marie."

"Why didn't the dogs run off with her clothes?"

"The fisherman found the bikini over there." He gestured toward the sun-bleached timbers of an old fishing boat, ten meters up the beach. He rubbed his chin. "Bruising of the thighs and on the lower abdomen." He added, "If it's not her bikini, it's quite a coincidence. It's her size and it's new. Nothing else on this beach but washed up tires and tin cans."

"Top or bottom?"

"What?"

"It's a bikini top or bottom?" Anne Marie asked testily.

"Bottom," the *procureur* said.

Sweating in his dark suit, the case under his arm, Trousseau stood on the hot, shadowless beach. Anne Marie wondered whether he could hear what was being said. She also wondered why he did not move out of the sun into the shade of the sea grape trees.

Arnaud was saying, "Everything's been sent off to the Institut Pasteur. Flesh rots fast in this climate."

8

Golf

"I can count on your discretion, Anne Marie?"

"You always have."

"One of your many virtues." The *procureur* nodded. "You're also very efficient."

She let her head drop back onto the upholstered headrest and stared at the roof of the car. "Arnaud, the *gendarmerie* knows exactly what to do."

"I want you to deal with this."

Anne Marie asked, "This girl's death is so important?"

"More important than the Dugain dossier. You're wasting your time and making a lot of enemies among the SRPJ."

"You gave me the Dugain dossier, Arnaud. Remember?"

He smiled grimly. "You really think I was expecting you to follow it up?"

"I'm not a mind-reader."

"You're best rid of it."

"How am I supposed to know what you want?"

"Not what I want—it's what the politicians want."

"The politicians want me to drop Dugain?"

"A nest of vipers." A sigh of exasperation. "Anne Marie, I'm not a free agent."

"The word's to lay off the Dugain dossier?"

"The murder of a tourist is of paramount importance." He tapped the steering wheel in emphasis.

"Who's to tell me this Vaton murder isn't a nest of vipers?"

"A white girl, Anne Marie. And a tourist." He took the pack of Stuyvesant from his shirt pocket and pushed the lighter into the dashboard. "It's very important."

"Put Monneron on it."

"It's you I want, Anne Marie. I want you and the *préfet* wants you."

"Anybody'd think I was pretty and unmarried."

He ignored her. "Murder in Guadeloupe rarely goes beyond the family. A jealous, drunk husband who takes a machete to the mother of three of his seven children. This is different." The *procureur* drove the Volkswagen Golf in a jerky, undecided manner, his hands making sharp tugs at the wheel, while his foot hesitated between the brake and the accelerator. "The industry's only just getting back to where it was before Hugo."

"Murder Incorporated?"

He glanced at her unhappily. "You're being facetious."

"Tired, Arnaud. Middle-aged and tired."

He smiled as he lit the cigarette. "You're looking marvelous."

"That's not what my mirror tells me. I could do with a shower. And some sleep."

"Time you got married again."

"A forty-two-year-old woman—who's interested?"

"I'd be."

"Don't be silly." She turned her head on the headrest and closed her eyes. "What about Hurricane Hugo, Arnaud?"

He took a hand from the wheel and lightly touched her cheek. His fingers smelled of nicotine. "You're a complicated woman. I like you, Anne Marie. You know that."

"You call me away from my children and fly me over to Saint-François just to talk about my private life, Arnaud?" A small laugh, her eyes closed. "Let's stick to business. And whatever happened to your lady friend from the checkout desk at the Bonheur des Dames?"

The hand returned to the steering wheel. "Bonheur des Dames?" Very slowly the *procureur* inhaled on the cigarette.

"Put Monneron on it—he's better than me when it's political."

"Bombs and terrorism for nearly ten years. Then just when it looked as if Guadeloupe had at last found tranquility, last September we get the worst hurricane in recorded history. Winds at three hundred kilometers an hour—it didn't do the hotels any good."

"It's the tourist industry you're worried about?"

"Lots of things I'm worried about." The finger returned to her cheek.

Anne Marie opened one eye.

"I can take you to lunch somewhere, if you wish."

"My children are waiting for me."

He blew out cigarette smoke. "Bring the children."

For a moment, Anne Marie bit her lip in thought.

"Well, Anne Marie?"

"It's a long time."

"You need a man in your life."

"Three days, Arnaud. If Evelyne Vaton was dead for nearly three days, why didn't anybody see her? You're not telling me the fisherman was the only man to go onto that beach."

"That's what you've got to find out and fast."

"Fast?"

"Tourism's the only industry that brings in any money on this island."

"Monneron's good and you won't have to waste money on taking him to lunch."

"You're good, Anne Marie." He grinned. "It's your female intuition. And you know how to deal with the press." His voice softened, after a brief hesitation. "These are all things we can discuss over a meal."

"Not a good idea, Arnaud."

"You need a good man."

"I need a headache?"

"Not all men are rats. You can't forget your ex-husband, can you?"

She looked at him coolly. "Nor, it seems, can anybody else." She removed his hand from her face. "But thanks for the invitation."

For the rest of the way back to Pointe-à-Pitre, Anne Marie dozed off, despite the jerky driving, a smile on her lips, the smell of nicotine in her nostrils.

The *procureur* remained silent.

9

Mobylette

Béatrice put Létitia to bed and then went to her room. Fabrice was doing his homework on the veranda. He was sprawled across a hammock, listening to heavy metal on his Walkman.

Anne Marie sat down in front of the television. She had gone back to the *palais de justice* and got to the beach just as Fabrice was rolling up the sail. Anne Marie was now tired, too tired to read the magazines that had piled up, unopened, on the bookcase. She watched the bright screen and the advertisements unthinkingly. A couple of times she glanced at her watch. An untouched glass of *rhum vieux* stood on the armchair beside her.

She did not want to think about work.

The Dugain dossier was in her attaché case. It could wait until tomorrow. She would take the *procureur*'s advice. Why bother, why make enemies? Anne Marie yawned. "Poor Arnaud," she said to herself.

A dog barked somewhere beyond the cemetery and other dogs answered in antiphony.

The advertisements came to an end and the announcer, smiling and uncomfortable beside a vase of studio anthuriums, announced the evening link-up with Antenne Deux in Paris.

The phone rang.

France—perhaps she ought to return. Soon Fabrice would be at university; and it was time Anne Marie thought about her career.

Eleven years as *juge d'instruction* in the same backwater. *Colonial backwater*, as her husband always used to say. She shook her head. Time to move on, to go to Brittany to be with her sister.

She picked up the receiver on the fourth ring.

"Anne Marie? Hope I'm not bothering you."

"I was about to go to bed." She stifled another yawn. "Who am I speaking to?"

"Eric."

"Eric?"

"Eric André of the Tourist Bureau."

"Of course." She smiled and put her head back against the armchair. "How are you?"

"Off to New York at the end of next week. We're expanding the Guadeloupe office on Broadway."

"And the family, Eric?"

"Perhaps we could go for a meal."

"We?"

"You and I."

"A meal with a married man?"

"A business lunch."

"Eric, how's your wife?"

"In Paris—with the children."

"On holiday?"

"In a manner of speaking." She heard him catch his breath. "Anne Marie, I'd like to speak with you confidentially. Are you free tomorrow?"

"It wouldn't have anything to do with the Pointe des Châteaux?"

From beyond the house, on the far side of the mangrove and the endless chirruping of the night toads, a noisy Mobylette scooter went past, heading toward Sainte-Anne.

The dogs were still barking, call and answer.

"I thought it'd be a good idea if we could talk, Anne Marie."

"Eric, I have a job to do."

"So do I, Anne Marie."

"I'll let you get on with yours."

"Half past twelve at the Tribun. I've booked a table."

"You're very sure of yourself."

"Very sure of my sister-in-law."

"The ex-sister-in-law of your wife."

A brief laugh. "Half past twelve at the Tribun. I'm counting on you." Eric André hung up.

The receiver still in her hand, Anne Marie closed her eyes.

For a few minutes, unaware of the noise and flickering image of the television, she thought about Eric André.

She went to bed without touching the *rhum vieux.*

10

Palais de Justice

Thursday May 17, 1990

"So much for discretion."

Trousseau was smiling and he ran a finger along the line of his moustache. With the other hand, he handed Anne Marie the newspaper.

She sat down at her desk, and yawned. "Another day."

"I like the red shoes. As always you're looking marvelous, *madame le juge.*"

"I bought them in Caracas." She placed her bag in the drawer and glanced at the headlines: YOUNG TOURIST RAPED AND MURDERED. Beneath, in smaller print, WOMAN'S MUTILATED CORPSE DISCOVERED NEAR THE POINTE DES CHÂTEAUX.

A passport photograph, badly reproduced and badly printed.

"Not very good for the tourist trade," Trousseau said.

"Not very good for anybody."

Anne Marie liked her office—the same place she had been given when she had first arrived in 1979. It was little more than a cupboard, just big enough for her desk and the *greffier*'s, a couple of filing cabinets, a floor of polished mahogany and a small sink. It was at the top of the *palais de justice* and the gentle winds came through the open shutters and pushed against the lace curtains. The same Chantilly lace that she had bought in Paris before sailing out to the Caribbean with her husband and son.

Anne Marie leaned her elbows against the desk and glanced out over the vivid red of the corrugated roofs of the nearby bank and the old Chamber of Commerce that had been converted into the Tourist Office. Ship masts, bare without their sails, rocked to the movement of the green sea within the small port.

Pointe-à-Pitre.

In the distance, standing out in clear relief against the sky, La Soufrière. The mountain range filled the horizon and the volcano, with all the intricate detail of its eroded flanks, its gullies and its tropical vegetation, rose up above everything else until its summit was lost in a dark crown of clouds.

After all these years, the view still managed to impress her. "Those curtains are dirty. They need changing." She turned to look at her *greffier* sitting behind the Japy typewriter. "Well, Monsieur Trousseau? Apart from the newspaper?"

"Two faxes, *madame le juge.* Not sure they're any use." He paused, nodded toward to the *France Antilles.* "Our local paper seems to have more information than Paris." He stood up and moved round the desk. Taking the paper and holding it at arm's length—his long-sightedness had notably worsened over the last two years—Trousseau read aloud, his voice nasal:

"The young woman, Evelyne Vaton, had been in our *département* for less than ten days. She was staying with the family of a doctor friend from a hospital in Villejuif, outside Paris. Monsieur and Madame Lecurieux of rue de la Manufacture in Basse-Terre, both retired schoolteachers, whose daughter is a doctor in the hematology department at Villejuif, said the young woman was charming and very friendly. Evelyne Vaton arrived on Saturday, May fifth, and spent her first week in Guadeloupe visiting the Basse-Terre region. Last Saturday morning she shopped in the town of Basse-Terre and went to mass in the evening. After an early breakfast on Sunday morning she had taken the hired car, announcing her intention to visit the Pointe des Châteaux. She bid her hosts goodbye for the last time at seven o'clock Sunday morning. They were never to see her again."

Trousseau ran a finger along the side of his nose before continuing.

"The police are now reconstructing the events of the last day. It is believed that the young woman was murdered at about midnight, Sunday."

"That's all?"

Trousseau nodded. "The same photo as in the dossier."

"Show me the faxes, would you?"

He handed her the two sheets of flimsy thermal paper.

"The girl's mother will be coming this evening on the early flight from Paris. She's required for a formal identification of the corpse."

"Somebody'll have to pick her up at the airport. Can you see to it, Monsieur Trousseau? And a room in a one of the better hotels in Gosier."

"Madame Vaton won't make it in time for the autopsy this afternoon."

"Get hold of the Lecurieux people. I'll have to see them." She made a short note on the small Air France calendar.

"Of course, *madame.*"

Anne Marie coughed. "Monsieur Trousseau?"

Trousseau glanced at her inquiringly. "Yes?"

"I'm still waiting for you to tell me about the man."

"What man?"

"What does he want?"

Trousseau frowned.

"The man sitting outside in the corridor. I'm not supposed to be seeing anybody this morning, am I?"

Trousseau shook his head. "He was here when I arrived at half past six."

"Call him in. There's work to do on this Pointe des Châteaux dossier." Anne Marie added, "Damn it."

II

Green

The eyes were staring at her.

The man held a leather case under his arm. He was dressed in green. Green trousers, a safari shirt with epaulettes and short sleeves, a green *foulard* tied at the neck. Grubby green canvas shoes. He entered the room walking slowly with a slight stoop of the shoulders.

"Please be seated."

He did not smile. The eyes were close together and deep set; they looked at Anne Marie attentively, glinting slightly in the oblique light.

"*Monsieur?*"

He sat down and crossed his legs. He placed the case on the floor, then folded his hands on his lap.

"You wished to see me, *monsieur?*"

A small smile, revealing narrow teeth. "I met the girl."

"Which girl?"

He had the pale, yellow skin of the *metis*: some black blood, a lot of white blood. "The murdered nurse." He nodded toward the open newspaper on the desk.

"You can help me?"

"Why do you think I've been waiting here?"

"That's very good of you." They stared at each other. The man hardly blinked.

"With your approval, then, there are a few questions about yourself that I'll need to ask." Anne Marie took a note pad from the second drawer. She also took the recording machine. As she uncapped her pen—a Mother's Day present from Fabrice—she raised her head. "How did you know I'm dealing with the case?"

He raised his shoulders. "I asked downstairs."

"At seven in the morning?"

"Last night."

"You should've gone directly to the police."

"I'd rather see you than the police." He turned to look at Trousseau, who had closed the door and returned to his seat behind the Japy typewriter. "You want me to leave?" The man bent over to pick up the suitcase. Anne Marie noticed a hole in the green ankle sock.

"You say you saw the nurse?"

He sat back in the chair. A long, ringless finger started tapping nervously on his knee. "That is why I am here."

"When did you see her?"

"You know who I am?" He nodded toward the notepaper beneath Anne Marie's uncapped pen. "Name, address, date of birth, mother's maiden name, social security number?"

"I know how to do my job." Anne Marie faced the unblinking eyes.

"I have better things to with my time than sit waiting in the *palais* . . ."

She smiled. "I didn't know you were waiting for me."

His lips tightened as if in recognition of an apology, but still the eyes did not blink.

"Your name and your date of birth please, Monsieur Desterres. And your mother's maiden name."

"You know my name but do you know my social security number?"

Trousseau chuckled from behind the typewriter.

"Yes, I know who you are, Monsieur Desterres." Anne Marie raised her hand and gestured vaguely to beyond the roofs of the city. "You own a small restaurant near the beach Tarare, a few kilometers from the Pointe des Châteaux."

The eyes remained on Anne Marie. "Five kilometers from the Pointe des Châteaux—and a kilometer from where the girl's body was found."

"I've seen your posters, Monsieur Desterres. You're an ecologist, I believe, and you've run in various municipal elections."

"Unsuccessfully."

"The crowd is fickle, Monsieur Desterres."

"*Mobile vulgus.* Fickle and very stupid."

"Tell me about the unfortunate girl."

He picked up the leather case and unzipped it. "She came to my restaurant on Sunday morning. At Tarare."

"At what time?"

"Mid-morning—about ten o'clock."

"You're certain it was the nurse you saw? Evelyne Vaton?"

"Tarare's a nudist beach." The sallow face was motionless. "She was very pale."

"Lot of pale women about."

"I can recognize a tourist."

"Not very brown myself."

"You are not getting the most out of your Caribbean posting."

"I never get time to get out of the office." Anne Marie glanced through the window. "How d'you know it was Evelyne Vaton?"

"We talked. She called herself Véli—but I know it was her." He took a square photograph from his bag and slid it across the table. "And because of this."

12

Mère Nature

She had been to Tarare several times, accompanied by her husband. It was not far from the Jacuzzi Beach, but on the other side of the Pointe des Châteaux isthmus. Jean Michel enjoyed swimming naked in the blue, translucent water, yet he had never managed to persuade Anne Marie to remove all her clothes. "That's what comes from growing up in a Muslim country," he would say, laughing.

"That's what comes from being an investigative magistrate."

Despite the entreaties, her husband would have never accepted her skinny dipping in the turquoise waters of the Caribbean. Anne Marie picked up the photograph.

She had not been back in years—Fabrice insisted on going to good windsurfing beaches; Tarare was too sheltered—but she recognized the shack-like lean-to that had been converted into a restaurant. It was made of half-timbers and was painted white. The roof of corrugated iron was in need of fresh paint. There were several wooden tables and plastic chairs on the open, concrete apron.

The restaurant was called Mère Nature and specialized in fresh fish or seafood.

No diners were visible in the photograph, and to judge from the harsh light and the short shadows, the photograph must have been taken toward the middle of the day.

Anne Marie wondered whether Desterres was able to make a decent living from the restaurant. She knew that he came from a rich mulatto family that had made money by importing agricultural machinery from England at a time when English engineering had a reputation for reliability.

As if reading her mind, Desterres said, "Low season at the moment. On weekends, customers turn up around midday. In a couple of months there'll be all the *Négropolitains* . . ."

"*Négropolitains?*"

"Blacks living in the *métropole*, who come back from the mainland for their summer vacation."

She studied the three people in the photograph. "This is Evelyne Vaton?"

Desterres stood staring at the camera, with his arm over the shoulders of the girl, a possessive smile on his narrow face. Evelyne Vaton wore a pair of plastic sandals and a pink bikini bottom. She was short but had a pleasant well-formed body, narrow hips and large breasts. She smiled cheerfully at the camera, her face partially concealed beneath a baseball cap. Because the photograph had been taken from at least four meters, it was difficult to make out the facial details.

"Who's the man?"

"He was with her. Called himself Richard."

Richard was on the other side of Evelyne Vaton. He stood with his arms crossed against a dark, broad chest. He had fine features and a long, straight nose.

"An Indian," Desterres said.

Richard was wearing bathing shorts. Tall but putting on weight at the waist. A reflex camera hung from his neck against the bare chest.

"What does he do?"

"Works in a bank. The girl was asking him questions about getting money wired from France."

"Who took the photo?"

"The self-timer."

"You seem to have hit it off with them."

Desterres shrugged, indifferent to the implied flattery.

"Was Evelyne with Richard?"

"I got the impression they'd met fairly recently, perhaps even on a beach."

"What sort of person is this Richard?"

Again a movement of the shoulders. "He was afraid I was moving in on his girl."

"Vaton was his girl?"

"I didn't ask."

"What were they doing at Tarare?" Anne Marie asked.

"They'd been to the Pointe des Châteaux, but Evelyne was interested in swimming and the currents at the Pointe were too strong for her. Richard brought her to Tarare, hoping no doubt to get her undressed." The immobile face broke into a wolfish smile that disappeared almost immediately.

"You saw the girl's car?"

"She had a car?"

"A hired Fiat Uno. You didn't see it?"

"The parking area's at the top of the cliff. You can't see anything from the beach."

"You didn't accompany them to the car park?"

"When they left?" Desterres shook his head. "I had to prepare lunch."

"When did they arrive at Tarare?"

He glanced at Trousseau. "It must've been just before eleven that I saw them swimming and when they came out of the water, I explained it was a nudist beach."

"Richard didn't know that?"

"Both were wearing swimsuits."

"She was not wearing a bikini top." Anne Marie tapped the photo.

"Precisely."

"There was nobody else around?"

Desterres hesitated for a moment. "A couple of men who normally come in midweek, but they were on the other side of the trees." He added, "Two men who were more interested in each other than in a topless female. The people who come to Tarare are the sort of people who like to sleep in on the weekend. They don't get down to the beach until after twelve."

Anne Marie nodded. "Richard's a native of Guadeloupe?"

"I think so."

"Whose idea was the photograph?"

"It was me who suggested it—the girl had a camera."

"And the other photos?"

"What photos?"

"She took more than just this one photograph, Monsieur Desterres?"

"The girl kept them."

Anne Marie pointed to the photograph. Desterres was wearing the same clothes that he now wore. To protect his face, he also had a peaked cap. "What's that, leaning against the bar? Looks like a rifle."

"A gun for the rats and the mongooses."

"Having trouble with vermin?"

"Human vermin." Seeing Anne Marie's surprise, Desterres remarked, "We live on an island of thieves. People can be very jealous of success in Guadeloupe, particularly if like me you're light-skinned. I have a business to run. I know just how much I can count on the police. Sometimes I spend the night in the little back room, just to be sure that nothing gets stolen."

"What was the relationship between this Richard and the girl?" Anne Marie asked neutrally.

"What do you mean?"

"She liked him?"

"He was interested in her—but most men in Guadeloupe are interested in young girls. Particularly if they're single and if they are from France."

"How old would you say he was?"

"Richard? Thirty-eight, forty." A pause. "Or perhaps a bit older."

"What did you talk to the girl about?"

"I talked to the girl and I talked to the man."

"You're not interested in young, single women?"

"Not when they're already accompanied." The cold, deep-set eyes stared at her.

"You're married, Monsieur Desterres?"

"How does that concern you?"

"Kindly answer my question. Are you married?"

"I do not live alone."

"What did you talk to the girl and Richard about?"

"They wanted something to drink, and I served them Coca-Cola. Later I sat down and we made small talk."

"Coca-Cola?"

"I suggested a punch or a planter—but the girl was off alcohol and the man went along with her to be polite. We chatted about what to visit, what to see in Guadeloupe. The place used to be very beautiful but it's been raped, pillaged, transformed into a concrete suburb."

"The girl was interested?"

For the first time since entering her small office, Desterres smiled with genuine amusement. "I told her about the tropical rain forest, the coffee plantation, the mongooses and raccoons. About Marie-Galante and La Désirade. I gave her the addresses of a few good restaurants."

"Monsieur Desterres, did you get the impression Evelyne Vaton knew anybody here in Guadeloupe?"

"Why d'you ask?"

"Women are more often the victims of violence from people they know, close family and friends, than from strangers. Evelyne Vaton may've been murdered by somebody who knew her—somebody who was expecting her."

"She knew Richard." Desterres added, "They left together."

"What was she carrying?"

A moment's pause. "A beach bag. And before leaving, she put shorts on. Shorts and a T-shirt."

"Did Evelyne say if she knew anyone else in the *département*?"

"She was staying with the parents of a friend of hers."

Anne Marie nodded.

"I invited them to stay for lunch. The French girl was pretty and Richard seemed good company, even if he was a bit too introverted for my taste. Evelyne Vaton chatted readily, so I invited them to taste some fresh conch, but the girl couldn't stay." He rubbed his chin. "She was meeting people for lunch."

"What people?"

"No idea." Desterres shrugged the epaulettes of his safari shirt. He sat forward in the chair and picked up the attaché case. He slowly opened it and, like a reluctant magician producing a rabbit from a top hat, Desterres withdrew a piece of pink material. "She left her bikini top on Tarare beach."

13

Lafitte

Lafitte's smile was apologetic. "I'm sorry the *gendarmerie* wasn't informed."

The *gendarme* standing at the window said, "We're supposed to be collaborating." He spoke without looking at Lafitte.

"Precisely," Anne Marie commented, turning from one man to the other. "Supposed to be collaborating and whether you like it or not, gentlemen, we shall be collaborating. Each of us works for a different ministry and we may not always have the same goals, but we all want the culprit brought to justice as soon as possible. There's a lot of pressure on us." She leaned forward in her chair. "An hour ago Desterres came here to see me of his own accord, Capitaine Parise." Anne Marie put her hands on the table and speaking slowly, faced Lafitte. "This enquiry's going to be done by the book. No arrests simply because that's what the public wants. When we arrest the culprit, it'll be because you and I have built up a watertight case." She paused. "I hope that's clear."

The yellow skin of Lafitte's face seemed to tinge with a blush. He glanced at the *gendarme* before turning to Anne Marie. He coughed. "*Madame le juge*, Desterres has a record."

"What record?" Anne Marie asked sharply.

"Attempted rape in 1983, *madame le juge*. Let off with a warning. Extenuating circumstances, no doubt."

"Attempted rape?"

"Two years later he was accused of having sex with a girl under the age of consent."

The lace curtain danced with the wind; somewhere along the docks a car hooted angrily.

"Again let off with a caution. Desterres has friends in the right places."

Lafitte set his arms on her desk, the open newspaper beneath his elbows. "Desterres's father was a rich man. One of that mulatto class that's done almost as well as the *békés* and the businessmen from Martinique. The father sold off the machinery business before dying last year and now Desterres's going to have to fend for himself. The restaurant at Tarare doesn't make money."

"You think Desterres's coming to see me was preemptive, Monsieur Lafitte?"

"No one is guilty until proved so."

Lafitte was a few years older than Anne Marie. His skin had taken a jaundiced tint, with the wrinkles of years spent in the tropics. The sandy hair was short and brushed back. He spoke with the hint of a northern accent. From Roubaix or Lille. He had entered the police after a brief career as a professional cyclist and later he had captained a veteran team. Until his promotion to the Service Régional de Police Judiciaire, he had appeared boyish, but since his return to the Caribbean after a couple of years in Limoges he had been putting on fat. No more cycling. There was a jowly look to the face and the dark chin was beginning to sag from too much rum.

"You think it's possible Desterres tried to rape the girl?" Parise asked, turning away from the window.

"We have no proof of rape." Lafitte threw a hurried glance at the *gendarme*. "For the moment, Desterres is the only lead we have. A restaurant little more than a kilometer from where the victim was found. And a record." Lafitte added, "He's the last person to have seen the girl alive."

"You don't have yourself photographed by the woman you intend to rape," Parise said.

"You don't always know yourself you're going to rape somebody."

"Most sexual violence is carried out by somebody within the family," Anne Marie said flatly.

Parise turned toward her and grinned. "I'll remember that when serving Sunday dinner."

Anne Marie looked at Parise. "In fact the last person to have seen Evelyne Vaton alive is this man Richard."

"Supposing Richard actually exists."

"He's in the photograph," Anne Marie remarked as she tapped the Polaroid.

"That doesn't mean Richard was with the girl and it certainly doesn't mean Desterres's telling the truth."

"We'll know that as soon as we've located Richard." Again Anne Marie tapped the picture with her pen. "No proof of rape, Lafitte?"

"The autopsy's this afternoon."

"You'd better take this bikini top to the Institut Pasteur. Desterres left it." She held up a plastic envelope. Anne Marie shook her head unhappily. "A woman with no belongings? Whatever happened to the other Polaroids and the rest of her swimming stuff? Didn't she have a tote bag, suntan oil, towels? I'm told women carry a lot of clutter. Did she really leave nothing in the hired car?"

"Nothing was left in the car." Lafitte shook his head. "I've sent a couple of men to take prints but the Hertz people hired the car out yesterday afternoon."

Parise sat down at her desk beside Lafitte. He coughed. "*Madame le juge*, we've had a few phone calls to the incident room in Saint-François. People saying they saw the white girl."

"And?"

"She's not the only young female tourist in the Saint-François area. Several callers saw a Fiat Uno. Every call's recorded, but at the moment, we don't have any leads, beyond a couple of people who say they saw a topless white girl at the Pointe des Châteaux before ten o'clock on Sunday morning. A woman who was by herself, sitting on the beach." Parise's intelligent eyes looked at Anne Marie. "In Saint-François, the hotels and the restaurants don't want anything happening to the flow of satisfied tourists."

"Anything happening to the flow of cash," Lafitte remarked.

Anne Marie tapped the desk like an irritable teacher calling for order. "The *préfet* told the *procureur* yesterday in no uncertain terms that he wants results. Which can only mean one thing."

"Political interference."

"Precisely, Monsieur Lafitte." Anne Marie nodded grimly. "And when you get politicians interfering into an enquiry, nobody's backside is safe."

Lafitte grinned sideways at the *gendarme*. "How do you fancy Wallis and Futuna?"

"No South Pacific, Monsieur Lafitte," Anne Marie said. "Don't count on retiring to some tropical paradise."

"Guadeloupe's a tropical paradise."

"Not for the Vaton girl. And not for us."

"*Gwada—pa ni pwoblèm.*"

"No." Anne Marie shook her head vehemently. "There are a lot of problems in Guadeloupe."

Again Parise coughed and lowered his hands onto the creased trousers of his uniform.

"Until we have the murderer behind bars, the three of us'll be seeing a lot of one another." She gave a taut smile. "I know the *gendarmerie* in Saint-François is taking this seriously." She looked at Parise before turning her glance to include Lafitte. "You know the snares of the press, and so both police forces will observe complete silence when in contact with the outside world. By the outside world, I mean the written and spoken press. In particular RFO."

Parise nodded.

"Let the *gendarmerie* get on with their enquiry—Saint-François's their territory, but I'll also need all the expertise of the SRPJ." This time a brief nod toward Lafitte. "Collaboration's the keyword, *messieurs*. However"—she held up her hand and tapped her chest—"it's me who's in charge of this enquiry."

They looked at her in silence.

"Our respective standpoints don't always coincide and it's only normal we shouldn't always see eye to eye. But our ultimate goal—yours, gentlemen, and mine—is a common goal. Therefore we collaborate." She paused. "Do I make myself clear? For now, all other enquiries go onto the back burner."

"Including the Dugain dossier, *madame le juge*?" Lafitte grinned.

She said, "The *procureur*'s under pressure from the local assemblies. And the local assemblies are under pressure from the *préfet*."

"And the *préfet* no doubt is under pressure from Paris."

"Nobody wants embarrassing questions in the United Nations about French colonialism. Even if things've changed these last ten years and with decentralization, France prefers to let the two local assemblies get on with their business." She paused. "Whoever calls the tune, it's us who must dance."

"The polka?"

"*Zouk*—hot, fast and sweaty. A relentless Caribbean rhythm." She smiled. "I'll need to be kept posted. I'd like you to report here at seven thirty in the morning. In person, on a daily basis." Again Anne Marie paused. "Capitaine Parise will be working out of Saint-François—the *procureur*'s no objection to my entrusting this enquiry to the *gendarmerie*." She looked at Parise. "But I repeat I am coordinating and it's back to me here in Pointe-à-Pitre that you'll report."

Parise nodded.

"I'll be needing all the support of both the *gendarmerie* and the SRPJ so we'll be seeing a lot of each other—perhaps too much. I trust we can put aside professional rivalries, petty animosities and everything else to get this murder cleared up before it goes cold on us. For everybody's sake."

Again Parise and Lafitte nodded. Two schoolboys, Anne Marie thought, wincing inwardly.

"I'll be standing in on the autopsy." She lowered her voice. "Not something I relish, but I've informed the *procureur*. Perhaps you could accompany me, Monsieur Lafitte."

"A pleasure, *madame*."

Anne Marie wondered if she detected sarcasm in his voice.

"Capitaine Parise, please get this photograph distributed and a search put out for Richard. Richard works in a bank, but it might also be a good idea to put pressure on your informers in the ghetto."

"The SRPJ has informers in Boissard. We don't go in for that sort of thing."

"Perhaps you should." She clicked her tongue sharply, in the West Indian manner. Turning back to Lafitte, Anne Marie went on, "Boissard, Pointe-à-Pitre—see if you can find anything there, Lafitte. Anybody mysteriously scratched, grazed or covered in blood, any external bruising that could be the result of the victim putting up a fight."

"In the ghetto?" Lafitte asked in mild surprise.

"Use stick and carrot."

"A reward?"

"Whatever gets results." She coughed. "Then, gentlemen, I think—"

Lafitte said, "I've brought Desterres's dossier, just as you asked."

"If he's got a history of sexual violence, it'll be useful to know how he operates. For the moment, let's do nothing more provocative than keeping a tab on him. A man like Desterres can always afford lawyers—and it's best to keep lawyers at arm's length as long as possible."

Parise said, "A man who's got money can always buy women—he doesn't need to rape them."

"But he has in the past. Go to Tarare. He gave me his address in town—but Desterres said he often sleeps at Tarare rather than driving back home to Pointe-à-Pitre. Check his car."

"I'll need a warrant."

"You'll have your warrant," Anne Marie said.

14

Court Bouillon

He did not wait for Anne Marie to be served, but sliced the *boudin* and began to eat.

"*Bon appétit,* Eric."

He nodded. The air was very chilly in the dining room and the table Eric André had reserved was just beneath the air conditioner. Anne Marie shivered.

The waitress set down plates of salad and for the next half hour, Anne Marie and Eric ate in silence, apart from an occasional remark concerning the food. Eric had ordered a court-bouillon of fish with lentils and rice. From time to time he rubbed the fish with sliced pepper.

Anne Marie took the *plat du jour* of octopus, which she found too salty. The white wine was palatable.

"Not the best food in the world," Eric admitted as he stirred his coffee. "This place has the advantage of doing real Creole cooking rather than the bland compromise you get in a lot of the hotels."

"You hope to get the tourists down from America and Canada?"

"It's precisely the bland, Coca-Cola variety of food they prefer."

Anne Marie's coffee was served in a cracked cup. "Why did you want to see me, Eric?"

"Always nice to see my sister-in-law, Anne Marie."

"Eric, I used to be your wife's sister-in-law but that was before the divorce."

He seemed surprised. "I'm not divorced."

"Before my divorce, Eric."

He wiped his lips with the stiff white napkin. He had a high fore-head and he had started to go bald. He had the brown eyes that Anne Marie liked in West Indians. Yet despite the firm jaw and the brown eyes, Eric irritated her. Perhaps, she told herself, she knew too much about him.

He had nice, long hands.

"You still see your husband, Anne Marie?"

"You invited me here to talk about my husband?"

He lowered his shoulders in apology. "I want to talk about you."

"About me, Eric? Or about the Office of Tourism?"

"Office of Tourism?" He wrinkled the skin of his nose—a strangely boyish gesture.

"That's what you're in charge of, isn't it? Americans and Canadians are no longer going to visit this island now a tourist has been found raped and murdered on the beach."

"Anne Marie, the majority of non-French tourists are from the EEC. More Italians and Germans than Americans. The Americans prefer Hawaii."

"Why the lunch?" Anne Marie sighed. "Somehow the entire island knows I've been given the enquiry. And what's worse, the entire island knew long before I ever did."

"Why are you French women so aggressive?"

"Thanks, Eric, for the lunch. It was very good, I enjoyed the octo-pus, thank you, and I enjoyed the wine. Now if you think you can influence me, I'm afraid—"

"I'm not trying to influence anybody." He held out a silver case. "A cigarette?"

"I must be going, Eric."

"I need to talk to you."

"We've already talked."

"Anne Marie, you're not making this easy for me."

She looked at her watch. A Kelton, nearly twelve years old, but with the new strap, it was now quite fashionable. Very retro, very *tendance.*

"Why so aggressive? We may no longer be family, Anne Marie, in the strict sense of the word . . ."

She bit her lip. "I'm not sure men know the strict sense of the word family."

"We're friends." His hand touched hers.

"I'm never friends with a married man."

His laughter surprised her. It also surprised several other diners who turned their heads. "You think I'm trying to seduce you?"

"Where's your wife?"

"In Paris." He lit the cigarette. The flame of the lighter flickered. "She's in Paris with the children."

"And you're getting divorced?"

Eric made a gesture, lowering his hand. "Keep your voice down." He glanced at the other diners before shaking his head. "We've decided on a short separation to get things into perspective."

"You want perspective? Go to the art gallery." She made a sound of irritation. "Perspective's what you wanted to see me about?"

"Of course not."

"Eric, I must be going—there are things I've got to do."

His eyes carefully scrutinizing her face. "You know I'm going into politics?"

15

de Gaulle

"That surprise you?"

"Politics? And the Office of Tourism, Eric?"

"I'm hoping to get onto the Conseil Général. For way too long it's been a fief of the Socialists and the Communists. What the *département* needs is a modern, capitalist approach to our problems."

"You want to give up your job?"

Eric ignored the question. "The left's held sway for too long; they've stifled any enterprise. If this island's to get anywhere, it must stop turning to France for handouts. Since Hurricane Hugo, things've only gotten worse. We're like whores, always asking for more money— but at least whores work. They put in the mileage even if they are lying on their backs. They earn their keep while we overseas French, we do nothing other than fret over our mixed identity. Are we blacks or are we French? We're spoilt children, always asking for pocket money for our champagne habit and trips to Paris. Except we're no longer children and it's up to us to produce our own pocket money. Thirteen percent, Anne Marie—that's how much our exports cover our imports. Thirteen percent—and the Socialists begging for more money. It's time we assumed responsibility."

"You know of a politician who doesn't want greater local responsibility?"

He shook his head. "You don't have much respect for politicians?"

"I've worked with them."

"We must run our own island."

"You mean independence?"

"I never said that," he retorted. "Without France, Guadeloupe's not going to achieve anything. Certainly not yet. We haven't got the know-how, we haven't got the managerial experience." He ran the point of his tongue along his lips. "I'm a Gaullist; there's no alternative to being French. But at the same time . . ."

Anne Marie shook her head. "You really did invite me here to talk politics."

Realizing his mouth was still open, he put his hand to his face and rubbed his chin before asking, "Why are you so aggressive?" Eric André had difficulty in concealing his irritation. "I wanted to see you, Anne Marie, because perhaps there are some things you don't fully appreciate . . ."

"About de Gaulle, Eric? I grew up in Algeria, remember."

"Things you don't completely understand. That you could . . ."

Anne Marie was smiling. "Yes?"

"You could put yourself in a situation that would be far from satisfactory."

"You're talking in riddles, Eric."

"I'm trying to help you."

"When I needed help, it was not forthcoming. Not from you, nor from the rest of my in-laws."

"That's not what I meant."

"I've managed to get on famously without your help."

"Stop being so stubborn, Anne Marie. You white women are all the same. I thought you were different—you've been in Guadeloupe now for ten years and you've done useful work. You're stubborn, Anne Marie—too stubborn."

"I get by."

"You must be careful."

"You want me off the Pointe des Châteaux affair—is that it? The Tourist Office wants me to keep the lid down?"

He laughed, but there was no humor in his eyes. What Anne Marie saw was male pity and chose not to hide her anger. "I mustn't frighten off the Italian and the German tourists, Eric? They might head off to Hawaii and eat all that bland American food. That would throw discredit on your Tourist office."

She dropped her napkin onto the table and pushed her chair back, ready to leave.

He caught her wrist. "As a relative, I want to help you."

"Eric, we're no longer relatives."

"Several people—people who don't know you and I are in any way related—several people are more than unhappy about what you're up to."

She stood up. She had started trembling.

"People who can make life miserable for you."

She laughed incredulously. "It's not miserable enough?"

"Forget Dugain, Anne Marie."

"Dugain?"

"You can't do any good. Not now. The man's dead and gone."

16

No Man's Land

Carême, the Lenten drought, was now over and it had started to rain.

The rain cooled the air, but Anne Marie felt hot and sticky, with her blouse clinging to her back. She crossed the road, her eyes on the sudden torrents of swirling water that ran across the asphalt and fed the rising puddles. An Opel hooted at her, and she had to step back fast. Its spray flecked her skirt and drenched her shoes—red shoes bought in Caracas.

She walked across the no-man's land between the road and the new multi-story car park. The white earth was wet but hard underfoot. Rain battered onto her umbrella as Anne Marie hurried toward the courier office.

The octopus lay heavy on her stomach.

Twenty years earlier, when Anne Marie, young and newly married, had visited Pointe-à-Pitre for the first time, this part of the city had been a ghetto of wooden shacks lined haphazardly alongside the ditches where mosquitoes and glow-moths danced to the rhythms of tropical poverty, and where late at night the trucks collected buckets of malodorous night soil. In time, the mayor had had everything pulled down, replaced by the new town hall, the post office and the social security buildings, concrete tokens of France's determination to modernize the long forgotten colonial backwater.

("*After a century of doing it wrong in Algeria and Indochina,*" Jean Michel said.)

Two young boys cycled past her. They wore baseball caps, shouted gaily to each other and were impervious to the rain that drenched their clothes. Each boy carefully balanced his machine on the rear wheel, while the front wheel was held in suspension in the damp air. The tires left tracks that were immediately washed away by the incessant rain.

They grinned, their smiles lit up by perfect white teeth. The rain ran down the glowing skin of their young faces.

For some reason this stretch of land, glistening now in the grey light of the afternoon clouds, had been left, overlooked by the politicians and the developers. Surrounded as it was by high rises, office blocks, the ugly parking lot and the walls daubed with impenetrable curlicues of graffiti, Anne Marie could have been in the suburbs of Paris or Lille.

The sweat trickling down her back and the monotonous croak of the frogs reminded her she was in the tropics.

"Continental Couriers Inc. *Expédition vers les Etats Unis, la Métropole et l'Europe.*"

Anne Marie pushed open the glass door and entered the office. The air was chill. She closed her umbrella and wiped the dampness from her face as she looked around.

"Can I help you?"

"I am looking for Madame Théodore."

The woman stood up. "I am Madame Théodore."

Average height, navy blue slacks, a blouse, a red and white scarf slipped through a gold ring at the neck. She set a half consumed cigarette in the ashtray and moved round the desk. She smiled. "You seem surprised." Long hands and varnished nails.

Anne Marie returned the smile. "I wasn't expecting a white woman. And you're not wearing a wedding ring."

"Because I'm no longer married, Madame . . ."

The two women shook hands. "Madame Laveaud. I should like to talk to you."

"About sending a parcel to Miami or Tokyo? Or perhaps you want something to be in Paris by tomorrow morning. Because if you do, you've come to the right place and to the right person, but at the wrong time." Madame Théodore glanced at her watch. "You've just missed the last Paris flight. Mid-morning Monday is the best I can now do." She nodded to the low chair in front of the desk. "Please be seated."

Anne Marie sat down and set her elbows on the edge of the table. Madame Théodore sat down opposite her, returning the cigarette from the ashtray to her mouth.

"No parcel, I'm afraid."

"A letter?" The grey eyes twinkled. "A flat rate up to two US pounds."

"I'm an investigating judge."

"How exciting."

"Mainly routine, and it can be depressing."

"Change jobs."

"It's not always depressing."

A cough followed by a gesture of the right hand. "Join me in the wonderful world of private enterprise."

"Not as easy as it sounds, Madame Théodore, when you live by yourself and you've got two young children to bring up. There are certain advantages to being a civil servant." Anne Marie sneezed.

"Bless you."

"Wet feet from walking in puddles." She added, "And I've ruined my best Italian shoes from South America."

"Use a car and you won't get your feet wet."

"I don't enjoy driving in town."

"Then it won't be you I give a job to. Being a courier means driving back and forth between here and the airport—and spending most of the time in traffic jams. I've gotten to the stage where I have to smoke if I can't get a decent intake of petrol fumes."

There were filing cabinets, a fax machine, a photocopying machine and on the wall, a large, framed map of the world. The office was on the ground floor. Venetian blinds of coarse brown linen protected the office from the glance of passersby along the arcade outside. The carpet was synthetic, green and badly stained by the passage of feet.

Anne Marie's umbrella had left trails of water.

"Madame Théodore, I haven't come here to ask you for a job."

"I guessed that."

Anne Marie sneezed again.

Madame Théodore exhaled smoke through her nostrils. "You're not going to arrest me?" The eyes flickered.

"Not for the time being."

"How can I help you, *madame le juge?*"

"With information."

"What sort of information?"

"Monsieur Dugain. He killed himself by jumping from the top of a building and I want to know why."

"Dugain?" Madame Théodore looked away. "I only know what I've read in the papers."

Anne Marie sneezed again. "You weren't his mistress, Madame Théodore?"

17
Vitamin

Blood had gone to her face and neck. Madame Théodore stubbed her cigarette in the overflowing ashtray, stood up and went to the door. She turned the key, then pulled the blinds, cutting out the grey light of the wet afternoon. She switched on the neon, which flickered hesitantly before filling the room with its impersonal whiteness.

"You are very direct." She took another cigarette and lit it. She did not sit down. "Dugain's mistress?" She shook her hair. She wore it in short, permanent waves, without any attempt to hide the greying streaks.

"You did know him, didn't you?"

"Knowing someone doesn't make me his mistress." She breathed on the cigarette. "Where do you get your information?"

"Monsieur Dugain didn't kill himself just because he'd been embezzling. I want to know why he died during a visit from the *police judiciaire*." Anne Marie sneezed.

"Take some vitamin C if you've got a cold coming on." There were small wrinkles at the corner of her mouth. Late forties, early fifties; her skin was not soft. Too much sun, perhaps, or too many cigarettes and too much work.

"I was hoping you could help me." Anne Marie sneezed again. "Yours, his or anybody's private life is of little interest to me personally."

"You surprise me." Madame Théodore leaned against the desk with her arms folded in front of her. A few flakes of ash had fallen onto the blue serge of her slacks.

"I'm not very curious."

"First time I've heard of an investigating judge not being curious."

"You talk to many judges?"

A mocking curve at the corner of her lips. "What on earth makes you think Dugain and I were lovers?"

"I have a certain idea of justice."

"Of course."

(Once, Anne Marie had seen a young Arab—fourteen or fifteen years old—in the middle of Boulevard Foch. The boy had unfurled a French flag that he had smeared with excrement. Then, relying on the protection of his young age, he had set fire to the cloth of the flag, which, imbibed with petrol, was soon burning like a torch.

On a nearby balcony, a Frenchman had taken a rifle and had shot the boy through the head. Anne Marie could recall the sound of the man's laughter. She could remember the headless child lying on the surface of the road.)

"I grew up in Algeria—my family left Oran in 1958, when I was still an adolescent. What I saw there made me decide on a career in law."

"Noble feelings." The blush had disappeared and a cloud of smoke masked the eyes. "That's why you ask me who I go to bed with? I fail to see the connection."

"I wish to save you any embarrassment." A smile. "You must know there's a rumor about Dugain's death."

"I gave up paying attention to rumors a long, long time ago."

"A rumor the *police judiciaire* were responsible."

Madame Théodore shrugged. "The papers say Rodolphe committed suicide."

"You knew Rodolphe?"

"Not in the way that you think."

Again Anne Marie sneezed.

"Who didn't know Rodolphe Dugain, *madame le juge?*"

Despite the air conditioning, Anne Marie now felt hot. She ran a hand across her forehead. There was a tickling in her nose.

"Some coffee?" Madame Théodore's features were still taut but the corner of her mouth softened, turned upwards in a smile. "You need a towel for those wet feet of yours." She moved away from the desk and went to the door. She put up the closed sign. "I might just have some vitamin tablets. And . . ."

"Yes."

"Never buy cheap shoes, not even in South America. It's a false economy."

18

Divorce

"I have children. Two very lovely little boys. And I left them." She held the coffee mug between her hands. "No doubt I should've felt guilty. Everybody wanted me to feel guilty yet I didn't feel anything. Not at the time." She took a sip. "I had no choice."

"After how many years, Madame Théodore?"

"The comedy had being going on far too long."

"You still see them?"

"I swear that at the time I didn't feel any guilt." Madame Théodore paused, glanced at her hands, at the steaming coffee. "What's done is done. There's no new deal—not for a mother."

Anne Marie repeated the question, "You see your boys?"

"The little one's suffered and Jérôme is still not ready to forgive me."

"One morning you walked out?"

"In a manner of speaking." Madame Théodore laughed to herself. "If walking out can take three years. For three years I had this thing buzzing round my head and in the end, I knew it was either divorce or madness. I had to protect myself." She shrugged. "Don't try to understand—because you can't."

"He had other women?"

"I don't need sympathy. I made my decision and I must live with it. Divorce or madness—or perhaps both." A smoker's laugh.

"Why did you leave your husband, Madame Théodore?"

"You need to know? That part of your job?"

"Since you're talking about it . . ."

"All part of your not being curious?" She looked defiantly at Anne Marie.

"You're not the only person who wants to do the right thing—and spends the rest of her time being plagued with remorse that only pretends to go away but's always there, every night, lurking beneath the pillow."

The sound of footfalls outside along the covered walkway, beyond the beige window shades. Passersby.

"Some things you cannot admit even to yourself." Madame Théodore opened the lid of the packet that lay on the desk, and took another cigarette. She used a matchbook advertising CONTINENTAL COURIERS INC. The flame of the match danced at the end of the new cigarette.

"Another woman?"

"My ex-husband didn't need women. If he did, perhaps I wouldn't've felt the need to escape."

"Why did you?"

"Escape from perfection." She lit the cigarette. "He even washed the dishes, you know."

"That's when you got involved with Dugain?"

"Axel was perfect and he didn't want fighting in front of his children. Not ours—his children. Ever the intellectual, he was determined to understand me. When what I most needed was his anger. Perhaps what I needed was violence. Anger's a form of love, but instead Axel tried to understand. So cool, so detached, so wonderfully reasonable and he tried to analyze."

"You left your husband for Dugain?"

"I thought I made myself clear."

"There was an affair?"

"I'd love to know who told you I was his mistress."

Anne Marie shrugged.

"This is a small island—and nothing goes unnoticed. A couple of times Rodolphe Dugain and I went to a restaurant together. He was married and so I could never be his mistress. There was never anything like that between us. Even if, like all the men here, he wanted to think he was irresistible to white women."

"Your husband's white?"

She nodded. "White—despite his skin. White, French and perfect. A marvelous, wonderful husband. That's why I liked Dugain. He had his faults and perhaps I should have hated him. In many ways I did hate him." She paused, breathed heavily on the cigarette. "But in his own way, Dugain was all right." Again she made her rasping laughter. "You can understand that, can't you? There was nothing about him that could've interested me."

"Position and wealth? Power?"

"I wasn't running away from one nightmare to get involved with another—from one father figure to another. At least Dugain was human. Egotistical, dishonest, an eye for the main chance—but human. With him, I never felt I had to be perfect."

"Your husband's older than you?"

She held Anne Marie's glance. "He was born old."

"How did you meet Dugain?"

"It doesn't matter—suffice it to say that in his way he was nice to me. In his way."

"In what way?"

"You're no longer sneezing. I told you the vitamins were effective."

"In what way did Dugain help you?" Anne Marie put the mug of coffee—weak and instant—down on the cluttered desk.

"He had friends—and I needed a place to be by myself and to do a lot of thinking. The kind of thinking I'd never had the time to do in thirteen years of marriage."

"A long time, thirteen years."

"You're telling me?" The laugh in her throat caused the silk scarf to bob. "I married late—at thirty. I thought I wanted children."

"And Dugain?"

"Through a friend of his, Rodolphe Dugain got me a little apartment in Gosier as well as this job. It was the job—the responsibility, the right to be in charge—that really saved me from going mad. Or perhaps just the fact of getting out of the house. I was never meant to be a hausfrau." She added, "I grew up among boys—three older brothers."

"You saw Dugain often?"

"From time to time he would come and see me."

"You played Monopoly?"

She glanced briefly at Anne Marie and the knowing, worn face softened. "I've no illusions about men, West Indian or European, here or anywhere else."

"Spoiled and selfish?"

"They give little and they always want something in return."

"That's what they say about us."

"My ex-husband—his love of me, his love of the children is selfishness—a very subtle, very cruel form of selfishness, despite the exterior of perfection."

"What did Dugain want from you?"

"Not Monopoly." Madame Théodore breathed on the cigarette; the tip glowed. "No bed, no sex. He wasn't getting it. He knew he never would and so he never asked." She inhaled. "Perhaps that's why we became friends. He needed to be admired by intelligent women, and without quite knowing why, I got to like him, I got to know his faults . . ."

"A womanizer?"

"He liked to think so." Madame Théodore shrugged. Smoke danced in her eyes, causing them to water. "Rodolphe did something my husband never learned to do. Rodolphe listened to me." She brushed at her watering eye, caught in the cigarette smoke. "Unlike my husband, Rodolphe Dugain was not perfect. Far from it and, believe me, I found that very, very reassuring."

19

Hospital

"Bouton makes my flesh creep."

The sensation of heaviness in her belly had grown. She should never have eaten the octopus and now Madame Théodore's coffee had only made things worse. Anne Marie felt angry and unhappy. She also felt helpless. Her feet were wet and she had started sneezing again. So much for the vitamins.

The tang of ascorbic acid lingered at the edges of her tongue.

Lafitte did not reply. He parked the car at the back of the hospital, near the concrete tonsure of the helicopter pad. It was late afternoon; to the west, the last streaks of color were being drained from the overcast sky. The rain had stopped but puddles in the tarmac threw back the reflection of the hospital lights.

"Bouton must be a zombie."

"He does a good job, *madame le juge.* You know that. Given the woefully small sum he's paid for each autopsy, you should be pleased he's a zombie. Only two qualified pathologists in the *département* and the other doctor refuses to do anything for the *parquet.*"

"A zombie."

"A motivated zombie."

Anne Marie glanced at Lafitte and silently wished Trousseau were with her. Trousseau never pretended to be reasonable.

The damp tarmac was carpeted with flame tree blossom.

They stepped through the sliding doors of the main entrance, to be met by the cold, antiseptic smell of the building. One or two patients shuffled aimlessly about the foyer. They all wore identical tartan slippers.

Anne Marie followed Lafitte down the two flights of stairs into the basement. Her shoes were silent on the rubber floor. She had difficulty keeping up with her companion.

"It'll soon be over, *madame le juge*," Lafitte said and grinned over his shoulder.

They came to the hospital morgue.

The grey door was not closed. Lafitte waited for her. Anne Marie brushed past him, not bothering to knock.

"Ah, *madame le juge*." Dr. Bouton stood up as she entered the room. Light twinkled in the steel frames of his round glasses. He held out his hand, which Anne Marie shook with neither enthusiasm nor warmth.

It was a small, windowless laboratory. Most of the floor space was taken up by two tables made of dull, glinting steel, each with a perforated surface. At the end of each table was a sink. Above each table hung a stainless basin attached to a weighing scale.

Anne Marie could feel her belly lurching.

Overhead, the banks of neon gave off a shadowless light. Dr. Bouton had not yet switched on the long-armed directional lamp that was set directly above the steel tables.

"You have news for me?"

Bouton smelled of ammonia and coffee. He smiled a thin smile. "How's the little girl?"

"Little girl, Docteur Bouton?"

"Your daughter."

Anne Marie had difficulty in repressing a sneeze. "Létitia's doing very well. The *procureur* informed me he'd like me to be present for the autopsy."

"Létitia—such a pretty name. And what a lovely child."

"I'm ready when you are, Docteur Bouton."

"There's no rush." He picked up his paper cup from where he had placed it on the table.

"The sooner . . ."

"Please sit down, *madame le juge*." He gestured to two hard chairs placed against the walls of glazed tiling. "Like some coffee? Or perhaps something a bit stronger? You look as if you've got a cold coming on."

"I've been drinking coffee all afternoon." Anne Marie glanced at her watch. "It is nearly half past five . . ."

"Some vitamin C, perhaps? Or if you care for it"—he winked—"I have some firewater in my drawer. For medicinal purposes, you understand."

Anne Marie asked brusquely, "What have you been able to find out about the girl so far?"

"Once upon a time, Mother Mortis had four daughters—Algor, Livor, Pallor and Rigor." Bouton opened the bottom drawer of a filing cabinet and took out an opaque bottle. It was half-full.

"Neither Monsieur Lafitte nor I are thirsty," Anne Marie said.

He held up a finger. "To calm your nerves."

"Tell me what you've found out about the nurse."

"Monsieur Lafitte, a little something to keep the demons away?"

Lafitte eagerly took the paper cup Dr. Bouton gave him.

"Evelyne Vaton?" He pronounced the name as if testing it for poetic resonance.

"Precisely."

"Algor mortis, livor mortis, pallor mortis and rigor mortis," he repeated. He turned and pulled a wooden stool toward him. He was wearing loose corduroy trousers. Because of the chill air, he also wore a cardigan with a heraldic badge at the breast pocket. His lab coat and cap hung from a hook on the back of the door. Dr. Bouton had a thin face. His skin was waxy and was pulled tight across the bones of his skull.

"You now have established time of death?"

"You will recall that I was not called to the scene of the crime." He sounded slightly peeved. "I have Malavoy's report to go on and as usual, Docteur Malavoy's done a professional job." He looked up, but not at Anne Marie. "At the scene of the crime, the medical examiner found no foreign bodies other than sand and insects on the corpse. Everything washed away by the rain and several days' exposure to the elements. A very professional job in all senses."

"Professional?" Following the doctor's glance, Anne Marie turned. She had not seen the other man who was sitting quietly in the corner of the room, on a low wooden stool, like a child who had been reprimanded. A West Indian in his early sixties, with a bald head. He was wearing a suit and staring at the ground. Anne Marie had met Dr.

Malavoy on several occasions; on each, he had struck her as excessively shy.

Dr. Bouton was saying, "Anal or vaginal reading of body temperature is subtracted from the normal body heat of thirty-seven degrees centigrade. You then divide that by one point five and you get a rough idea of the number of hours the person's been dead. Obviously deducing the time of death through algor mortis is rough and ready—and there are variables. Here in the tropics, a body will cool more slowly than in Europe or North America. On the other hand, the body was exposed on an open beach, with a cool easterly breeze. Also there are differences due to body size. Docteur Malavoy put the time of death at somewhere between eleven o'clock on Sunday night and one in the morning. This would be reasonable. I got back from France last night and didn't get to see the girl until this morning." He gestured with his thumb toward the grey metal door in the far wall, and beyond it to the morgue. "My colleague was not available."

"Why not?"

Dr. Bouton shrugged. "Very strange when you recall time is of the essence in an autopsy. This will be mentioned in my report, you understand. More than three and a half days have elapsed since the presumed time of death. Absolutely imperative a body should be examined with speed. When a body dies, some cells live on. It's their chemical activity that causes a stiffening of the muscles. By now . . ." He clicked his tongue in irritation. "By now there can be no sign of rigor mortis."

Anne Marie nodded.

"I'd go along with Docteur Malavoy."

Malavoy had got up from his stool and approached the others in silence. He said nothing and did not offer to shake hands. He was wearing a black bowtie.

"Between eleven Sunday night and one in the morning of Monday?"

Dr. Bouton smiled magnanimously. "Give or take twelve hours."

"And livor mortis?"

"Always in a hurry, *madame le juge.*" There was irritation in his urbane voice. He stood up and went to the wall-phone. "Bring me number two, Léopold. I'll be starting the autopsy in five minutes." As he placed the receiver back in its cradle, he said over his shoulder, "Postmortem lividity appears to coincide with the photos I have."

"Which means?"

"The body, once it was abandoned, was not moved."

"When was the body abandoned?"

"At death—or soon after."

"And the dogs the fisherman saw pulling at the corpse?"

Again the blank look—the clever schoolboy amazed at his teacher's obtuseness. "I wasn't aware of tooth bites indicating the intervention of a dog."

"The fisherman was lying?" She glanced at Lafitte who stood with his hip against a wall table, near a camera. The camera had elongated bellows and was attached to a sliding steel rod. Lafitte stood with his arms crossed, a notebook in one hand, a ballpoint pen in the other. Like Anne Marie, he was not dressed for the chill air of the laboratory. His face had acquired a yellowish tinge in the bright neon light.

Lafitte caught her glance and wrote something in his notebook.

"Wouldn't dogs have altered the position of the corpse?"

"Understand, *madame le juge*, that I've no more than glanced at the cadaver. In a few minutes, while taking a much closer look . . ."

"In your opinion, once the body fell to the ground, it remained there until it was discovered?"

"An opinion, *madame*, based on little more than the ME's preliminary report and a superficial glance. A superficial glance at the body and at the *in situ* photographs."

Dr. Bouton was interrupted by the arrival of a young assistant. Léopold wore a lab coat that set off the dark skin and regular features of his boyish face. His hair was cut flat, to resemble the deck of an aircraft carrier. He walked with a spring in his step. He shook hands with Anne Marie and Lafitte cheerfully, a twinkle in his eye, and then crossed the room and opened the door to the morgue.

Dr. Bouton went to the sink and scrubbed his hands before putting on his white coat and the round cap.

Anne Marie glanced through the open door, down the long walls of stainless steel lockers. She bit her lip. Each locker was large enough to contain a wheeled stretcher.

"Sure you wouldn't care for some medicine?"

"Docteur Bouton, I'd like all samples you take signed and countersigned. If there's going to be a trial, I don't want our work thrown out for the lack of a signature. And perhaps I could sign the *procès verbal* now."

"Something to drink? We're going to be here for a least an hour . . . if not longer." He added smugly, "I like to do a thorough job." He returned the opaque bottle to its cupboard. When he stood erect again, he held out a blanket. "For the cold air, *madame le juge.*"

An Air France blanket. It was bit grubby and could have done with cleaning but Anne Marie was grateful for the warmth it afforded her. Her damp shoes were now deformed.

In a matter-of-fact voice, Bouton said, "I don't envisage any real difficulties so perhaps you'd like to put on a mask now. And some of this beneath the nose—it can lessen the odor."

She took the stick of Vick's vapor rub.

Lafitte took another sip of Bouton's spirit.

"A few abrasions and bruises, particularly in the genital area and the thighs," Dr. Bouton said.

Lafitte looked up from the notebook. "You've already got an idea of how she was killed?"

"Cause of death?" Dr. Bouton raised an eyebrow, and Anne Marie was reminded of the day he had told her she was pregnant with Létitia. He laughed a dry laugh and then turned as the assistant energetically wheeled the stretcher into the laboratory.

There was a body bag in thin nylon, a zipper running down the front. Léopold opened the fastener and the sound grated on Anne Marie's ears.

Dr. Bouton rolled a fresh pair of plastic gloves over his dry fingers and he stretched his arms. Like a pianist, Anne Marie thought, before a concert.

"I regret not having been able to get down to Saint-François. Sand samples fail to show the presence of blood. The amount of blood spilled can tell you a lot about the nature and the timing of a wound." He faced Anne Marie, the percolator in a gloved hand. "Sure you wouldn't like some coffee?"

The laboratory assistant shifted the body from its bag onto the autopsy table. Bouton switched on the overhead light while with the other hand he refilled his cup of coffee. He drank thoughtfully, his eyes hidden behind the glint of his glasses. "Poor thing."

Léopold opened the evidence case and produced the seven Polaroid photographs of the body as it lay on the beach at Saint-François. He ordered them in two neat rows on the tabletop so that Dr. Bouton could refer to them. Next Léopold set out a series of wooden spatulas, plastic jars, glass slides.

Plastic bags for the internal organs.

The laboratory seemed very chilly and Anne Marie sneezed behind the gauze mask.

Looking up at her and smiling, Léopold said, "Bless you."

"Poor thing," Dr. Bouton repeated to himself. He peered into the dead face before testing the microphone of his recorder.

The body was no longer human; it was a dark grayish blue and the inert limbs had nothing to do with the young woman who had once been alive and well and healthy.

Twenty-four years old and still alive last Sunday. Until around midnight.

Dr. Bouton finished his coffee. "A white girl?" He checked the label attached to the large toe of the cadaver.

"I beg your pardon, doctor."

"Coarse hair, dark nipples." He bent forward. "And prominent, rounded buttocks. Are you sure that Evelyne Vaton's a white woman?"

Anne Marie stepped forward hesitantly. She looked down at the round face. It was grey. The two breasts, pretty and firm in the photograph, now sagged slightly to either side of the body. Coarse hairs around the nipples. "She was born in Paris."

"Less white than you are." The doctor glanced at her, before turning back to the corpse. "There's West Indian blood—or perhaps North African." He turned on the cassette recorder. He coughed before announcing, "Docteur Jean Louis Bouton, at the University Hospital of Pointe-à-Pitre, pathologist to the *parquet*, in the presence of the investigating judge Madame Laveaud and police officer Geoffroy Lafitte . . ."

Léopold was carrying a circular saw. The teeth of the blade were sharp and spotless. He grinned brightly as he plugged the lead into the wall socket.

20

Lipstick

"I can't stand him."

"Who?"

"I'm sure he's a nice man. That's what's so awful. Lafitte's always very nice with me, always has been." She laughed. "I try not to hate him."

"You've no reason to dislike him, *madame le juge*. A good police officer and a good man."

"An ageing boy scout who's taken to rum."

It had been raining again and the wheels of the Peugeot hissed along the drive to the airport. Above the double row of palm trees, the low clouds caught the lights from the landing strip. The illuminated Air France livery—red, white and blue—of a jumbo's tail-plane rose above the terminal building.

"He's so earnest."

"Lafitte managed to sit out the autopsy." Trousseau grinned. He ran a finger along his moustache. "And you didn't."

"Not much fun when Docteur Bouton starts cutting through the skull." Anne Marie bit her lip.

"You should never have gone to the morgue in the first place—it wasn't necessary."

"The *procureur* wanted me there." Anne Marie shook her head, as if trying to rid it of a bad memory. "Poor cow."

"Vaton? She's dead."

"So young." Anne Marie added, "Bouton thinks she's part West Indian."

"She looks white in the photograph."

"Hard to tell from the photograph. She may be North African."

"Lot of West Indians get taken for Arabs in France—and they don't like it." Trousseau laughed. He pulled over and parked illegally in front of the departure lounge, beneath the wet fronds of the palm trees. "Desterres said she was white."

An overweight policeman, his plastic raincoat glistening, saw Anne Marie and gave an almost imperceptible nod of recognition.

"We shouldn't be too long, officer," Anne Marie said as she climbed out of the car. After the chill air, the exterior was hot and humid. She could feel the damp climbing her legs, into her clothes.

The man saluted. Unexpectedly, the dour face broke into a grin. "No problem, *madame*," he said in Creole, with a wink. He had the round features and soft complexion of a young girl.

Trousseau got out of the car, still carrying his attaché case but not bothering to lock the doors.

The first Boeing from Paris had already landed.

"Bouton couldn't find a cause of death." She guided Trousseau gently by the arm as they cut across the road, past the laurel and hibiscus bushes. "He hadn't found anything by the time I had to leave. I think he was embarrassed. Wouldn't look at me, just the occasional remark into the tape recorder. I could feel him getting annoyed. Very proud of his forensic skills, our Docteur Bouton."

"She was raped?"

"No sign of penetration."

"And the bruising around the belly?"

"Bouton says it occurred after death." They entered the airport hallway. "If the Institut Pasteur can't find the cause of death, it'll mean sending tissue to Paris."

"Hopefully that won't be necessary."

"Let's hope we can identify the killer first."

Trousseau laughed again and in that moment, Anne Marie realized just how fond she had grown of her *greffier*. She touched the dark, gnarled skin of the Indian's hand. "Thanks for being here tonight, Monsieur Trousseau."

For some reason he took offense. "I never had to become a *greffier*.

I own good land in Guadeloupe and in France. The day the revolution comes . . ."

"I know, I know." Anne Marie nodded vigorously. "You'll be on the first plane back to France. Your wife— you've already told me—your wife is a white woman and your children are all studying in France. And there's no need for you to stay in Guadeloupe once the independence people get hold of power."

Trousseau went into a sulk. He hugged the attaché case to his chest and watched the new arrivals waiting to collect their baggage. "Revolution," he muttered under his breath.

Four hundred or so passengers barged and pushed as they retrieved their luggage from the moving belt. There were many West Indians, overdressed and glad to be home, relieved to have been delivered safely from the sky. The majority of the passengers were off-season tourists from France, pink faced and uncomfortable in the sudden heat and humidity of the Caribbean. The jackets and long sleeved shirts seemed out of place.

"They're all crazy."

Trousseau did not look at her. "Who, *madame le juge*?"

"I can understand tourists in winter, but why now? May's the best month of the year in Europe."

"Low season prices."

"When I was growing up in the Dordogne . . ."

Trousseau turned to look at her, his face lit up by a bright grin. "I thought you were from North Africa, *madame*."

"We *pieds-noirs* got kicked out of Algeria. When I was growing up in Sarlat—"

"Madame Laveaud?"

Anne Marie was interrupted by a jovial man from the Frontier Police who saluted her, his eyes partially under the peaked cap. He was holding a walkie-talkie. "Bertillon's getting your woman off the plane." He beckoned and led them to his office on the main concourse. The air was frigid. He did not remove the cap, merely pushed it back, and Anne Marie wondered whether he was bald. On the desk, beside a pile of Haitian passports lay an unopened copy of *L'Equipe* that had come in on the Paris flight.

The officer gestured to a couple of seats and then sat down himself. He turned his attention to the newspaper.

Anne Marie and Trousseau waited five minutes. The walkie-talkie, as if bored by the inactivity, suddenly began to beep. The officer got up. He nodded at Anne Marie and simultaneously slipped the cap back down over his eyes. "Here they come."

Shuffling through customs without being stopped by the men in khaki, an elderly woman was accompanied by a female police officer. The young woman, in uniform slacks and shirt, a holster at the wide hip, recognized Anne Marie and nodded. She neither smiled nor saluted but simply said, "Madame Vaton."

Anne Marie held out her hand to the older woman. "You have no baggage, Madame Vaton?"

Without permission and without another word, the two Frontier officers went off together, returning to the office and *L'Equipe.*

"I am Madame Laveaud."

The white woman took Anne Marie's hand. A soft, almost bone-less grasp. Her eyes were bleary, as if she had been crying. The vivid lipstick was badly smudged at the corner.

Anne Marie continued, "I am the investigating judge and this is my *greffier,* Monsieur Trousseau. I'm most grateful to you, Madame Vaton. This must be an ordeal for you and I realize you must be very tired. My *greffier* and I will drive you to the hotel immediately. Unless of course you'd care for something to eat?"

"The first time I have ever been in an aircraft." Her voice was thin and had a marked Paris accent.

Madame Vaton had taken off her pale raincoat. She was wearing a loose-knit beige cardigan, a rumpled skirt and shoes with corduroy uppers. She held her suitcase close to her body. In her other hand, she had several magazines, *Jours de France* and *Paris Match.* Her skin was pale. Fresh powder freckled her face. The *eau de cologne* was strong.

"You'd like to go to the hotel?" Anne Marie asked, holding back the desire to sneeze.

The older woman nodded.

"No other baggage, *madame?*" Trousseau spoke in a soft voice as he took her raincoat from her. Anne Marie took Trousseau's attaché case.

"No point in bringing a lot of clothes." Madame Vaton looked at Anne Marie; she had pale blue eyes. "I'm not on holiday, am I?" Her eyes were bright and questioning. "They'll give me breakfast in the hotel?"

They made their way through the arrival hall. Noisy, rhythmic music came from one of the airport shops. Already the large hall was filling with people who would be flying to Paris in one of the evening Boeings.

Several people, waiting to be called to the departure lounge, were carrying bunches of anthuriums and other tropical flowers. At the newsstand a mulatto girl with green eyes gave Trousseau a wave and a grin. He chose not to see her, his attention taken up in helping the older woman.

Overhead, the slowly swirling fans moved through the sluggish air. The dry season was over.

"They'll give me breakfast?"

"Of course you will have breakfast."

"I'm returning to France tomorrow. It seems a bit strange to . . ."

"Tomorrow? You can stay in the hotel for several days, if you so wish. I imagine you're tired. With the time lag of six hours . . ."

"Stay in the hotel?" The woman sucked at her lip. "That'd be very nice." She walked slowly and leaned on Trousseau's arm for support. Anne Marie noticed swollen veins beneath the thick, skin-colored stockings.

"After the long flight you must want to sleep. Then in the morning, there'll be somebody to fetch you and we can see about all the formalities." Anne Marie tapped the woman's arm reassuringly. "There's no hurry."

They moved out of the terminal into the damp night. Trousseau directed her toward the car. The policeman in the plastic raincoat had disappeared.

"It's very warm, isn't it?"

Trousseau replied, "You soon get used to that. It's like the cold in Paris for us West Indians."

"That noise? What's that noise? There." Madame Vaton held her pale head to one side. "A kind of chirping."

Trousseau ran his finger along his moustache. He smiled. "Frogs, *madame.*"

"They make that din?"

"After a while you no longer notice it."

"How horrible!"

Trousseau opened the door of the Peugeot and helped Madame Vaton into the back seat. "Like the sound of the traffic in Paris."

"Frogs? It certainly doesn't sound like frogs." She must have been about sixty years old. Her white hair had been recently permed. She smiled at Anne Marie. "There was so much to eat. They keep waking you up to give you more food. And to think that I'd always been frightened of taking the plane." Madame Vaton's smile broadened. "I really enjoyed the journey." A glance at her watch. "Eight hours? The time just flew by."

Anne Marie got into the front seat beside Trousseau.

The car pulled away from the curb. Trousseau had closed the windows to the warm, humid air.

"The hostesses were very nice."

Anne Marie found the woman's *eau de cologne* overpowering.

"One hostess kept bringing me food and drink. Lovely girl. Very attentive and very black."

Anne Marie sneezed all the way to the hotel.

21

Bed

"A woman's pubic hair is normally coarser than a man's."

"Go to sleep, Anne Marie."

"You always say that, Luc."

"You worry too much."

"Have you ever been to an autopsy?"

"It's over—forget about it."

"You ever been?"

"Why do you think I became a pediatrician? Try and get some sleep."

"I can't."

"At least let me sleep."

"Sleep if you want to."

"Not with you tossing and turning beside me. Worrying and fidgeting and sneezing."

"I took something to stop the sneezing."

"And just for once, Anne Marie, turn that light off."

"I always sleep with the light on."

"Just once, as a favor, Anne Marie."

"Luc, I'm hot and I can't sleep."

"I can't turn the conditioner up any further. Take a shower. Close your eyes. Breathe deeply and relax."

"I've got a bad cold coming. I don't like these hotel beds."

"We could've stayed at your place."

"With the children?"

"Take another aspirin, Anne Marie."

"Thanks for the sympathy."

"Stop thinking about the autopsy."

"Why did you become a pediatrician, Luc?"

"The one branch of medicine where the patients survive."

"It's true, isn't it?"

"What?"

"The difference in pubic hair—between men and women."

"I don't know."

"But you're a doctor, Luc."

"Then I must've forgotten. Funny, things I did in third year anatomy—I forget about them at this time of the night."

"It's not the autopsy."

"You're an investigating magistrate, you're not expected to stand in on every postmortem."

"The *procureur* wanted me to go."

"If it was so important, why did you walk out halfway through?"

"Sometimes you can be very unfeeling."

"You're stopping me from sleeping, Anne Marie."

"I worry about Fabrice."

"Go to sleep."

"I worry about my son."

"There's nothing you can do. Not in the middle of the night."

"I think I'd better get back to the house."

"You're blackmailing me."

"Why can't we ever talk, Luc?"

"Now?"

"You never want to discuss anything."

"I have a job to do, too."

"Sex's all you care about and once you've got what you want, you go to sleep."

"I blame my biological clock but you see, I'm not a civil servant. I've got an important meeting tomorrow. I'd like to get some sleep."

"Fabrice comes home from school and tells me he's been kicked out of his English class."

"You were never kicked out by your teacher when you were at school?"

"I was only too glad to be able to go to school. Education wasn't compulsory in Algeria—at least, not for everybody."

"A goody-goody."

"The English teacher's written he's insolent and aggressive."

"Who on earth could he have inherited that from?"

"Fabrice's never aggressive at home, and he's good at English. He spends his time watching the American channels on the television."

"See the teacher."

"I am bogged down with work."

"You want a good job—or you want to be a good mother?"

"I've got so much to do."

"Work of your own making."

"What does that mean?"

"If you work so hard at the *palais de justice*, it's because you want to. Because it keeps you occupied, Anne Marie. That's why you go to the damned autopsy—and everything else. Because it keeps you from asking yourself questions."

"Thanks for the sympathy."

"Questions about yourself and about your life. You put it all out of your head. The other investigating judges don't have anything like your workload. Look at Monneron."

"That's not true."

"You went to your postmortem to show you're better than everyone else. A woman but better than all the others. You went because you like to feel that without you there's no justice."

"The *procureur*'s breathing down my neck for results. Since they found the girl . . ."

"Let the *gendarmerie* get on with it. You're always saying it's the police's job to do the initial work. The *gendarmerie* and your alcoholic chum Lafitte. Take some time off, for heaven's sake. Go and see about your son. And then perhaps you'll let me sleep."

"Luc, there are times when I feel . . ."

"Not tonight, Anne Marie, not tonight. There's nothing you can do for Fabrice tonight. He's a sweet kid and I'm fond of him, even when he sits looking at me and he's not listening to a word I'm saying because he's got his Walkman on full blast. Go to sleep. In the morning, you can drop by at the *lycée*. Speak to the teacher, find out what's going wrong."

"Why doesn't Fabrice talk to me about it?"

"For somebody who's dealing with men all day long, you're not very good with male psychology."

"Kind words."

"He's turning into a man."

"So what?"

"Anne Marie, you don't like men."

"What entitles you to say that?"

"You think Fabrice doesn't realize that?"

"You can be a bastard, can't you, Luc?"

"Sleep, Anne Marie. You need the rest."

"Just listen to me for once. I would like to get Fabrice to talk but he doesn't want to. This last year he's been drawing away from me. If he had a father . . ."

"Anne Marie . . ."

"I'm a woman. There are things I can't do. I know I'm not always getting through to Fabrice."

"You're using your emotional blackmail."

"Blackmail on who?"

"Anne Marie, we've been over this before."

"What blackmail?"

"I am not the boy's father."

"I've never asked anything of you. I don't even ask for warmth or affection."

"You want me to go?"

"I don't ask for warmth and affection because I know I won't ever get them. Not from you, Luc."

Outside, along the beach, beyond the hum of the air conditioner, the frogs were croaking their private monody.

"You're a married man and even if you don't love her, you'll never leave her."

"Say the word, Anne Marie, and I'll get a divorce. As strange as it may seem, I love you. Even in the middle of the night when you start talking about pubic hair."

"You'd never leave your wife."

"You want to quarrel? Three years now I've been asking you to marry me but you don't want to live with me, share your life with me.

To be together, we have to hide away in a hotel yet you expect me to be a father to your children."

"Who's quarreling?"

"You want to quarrel at one in the morning? In a hotel. Here in Saint-François?"

"It's you who's quarreling."

"Go to sleep."

"I'll go to sleep and perhaps you'd better get your clothes, Luc. I'm sure your sweet little wife's missing you."

22

Canine

Friday, May 18, 1990

"Good morning, Monsieur Trousseau."

He fumbled with the newspaper behind the desk, stood up and shook hands with Anne Marie. "Good morning, *madame le juge*." His breath smelled of fish sandwich. He gave her a lopsided grin.

"Today's agenda?"

"Lafitte and Parise are already here."

"Please call them in."

"Lafitte was saying they haven't got any trace on the Indian."

"Indian?"

"Richard—the Indian with the Vaton girl in the photo." He tapped the newspaper. "Strange." Trousseau then clumsily folded the newspaper and dropped it on top of his Japy typewriter. He was holding a ballpoint pen that he clipped to his tie. Trousseau left the office.

Anne Marie looked down on her desk.

(She had left the hotel at half past one in the morning and, getting home, had taken a pill to help her sleep. Now she was rested and was no longer sneezing. She felt unexpectedly relaxed even though Fabrice had not uttered a word during the drive into Pointe-à-Pitre. He had not answered Anne Marie's questions but sat beside her looking out at the long, slow traffic jam. Létitia, her nose to the rear window and giggling, had not stopped chattering the whole drive. She was looking forward to the school outing to the mangrove the following week. Anne Marie had promised to let her wear her green dress.)

Without sitting down, Anne Marie put her Texier bag in the desk drawer, unlocked the metal cupboard and took out the beige dossier: Pointe des Châteaux. Before opening it, she went over to Trousseau's narrow desk and glanced at the *France Antilles.* "Strange," she repeated to herself, imitating Trousseau's nasal intonation.

On the front page, the headlines announced that the murderer of the Pointe des Châteaux had yet to be identified. The article indicated that the *gendarmerie* and the SRPJ were working together but despite their collaboration, and despite the growing anxiety among the population at large for such a heinous crime, no lead had as yet been found.

The Polaroid of the Indian had been enlarged and was printed at the foot of the front page. DO YOU KNOW THIS MAN? The picture was blurry.

Absentmindedly, Anne Marie flicked through the other pages— the film and television programs, the world price of sugar, a new home for handicapped children at Gourbeyre, the syndicated news from France. She was about to fold the newspaper when her attention was caught by two strokes lightly marked into the margin with a red pen.

YOUNG MAINLAND FRENCH WOMAN, THIRTY, ATTRACTIVE, WELL EDUCATED, SEEKS FRIENDSHIP, VIEW MARRIAGE WITH WELL EDUCATED WEST INDIAN GENTLEMAN, 35—50. ONLY SERIOUSLY INTENTIONED NEED APPLY.

MARTINIQUE WOMAN, TWENTY-SEVEN, LIGHT SKIN, STRAIGHT HAIR, SEEKS AFFECTIONATE MALE, AGE AND COLOR OF NO IMPORTANCE, VIEW FRIENDSHIP, PERHAPS MARRIAGE. BOX 257.

"Very strange."

When she heard the sound of footfalls in the corridor, she swiftly returned the newspaper to its place on top of Trousseau's typewriter.

The *greffier* entered, accompanied by Lafitte and Parise.

The two men shook hands with Anne Marie.

Parise looked as fresh and neat as ever. His khaki clothes were crisply pressed and short hair still damp. He held his *képi* under his arm. He gave her a bright smile, the corner of the soft eyes wrinkling with pleasure. This early in the morning, his aftershave was strong and not unpleasant.

("You don't like men," Luc had said.)

"What news do you bring me, gentlemen?" She had returned to her desk. "Perhaps Monsieur Trousseau would care to fetch some coffee."

Trousseau left the office, tucking the newspaper under his arm.

Lafitte's eyes were puffy. "I have Bouton's preliminary report, *madame*."

"Why preliminary?"

His hand shook slightly. He placed the type-printed sheets on the desk in front of her. His smile was crooked. "You were at the autopsy, *madame*."

"Can't truthfully say I was following. Once Bouton started using the saw on the girl's skull, my attention began to wander."

Parise asked, "How's your cold now, *madame*?"

"Clearing up, thank you." She sniffed. "At least, I hope so."

"You should ask Monsieur Trousseau for a natural remedy. He knows about that sort of thing."

"It wouldn't be the first time he's tried to poison me with guava peel and *bois bandé* bark. I'll stick to aspirin and vitamins." She looked back into Lafitte's puffy eyes. "What does Docteur Bouton say, Monsieur Lafitte?"

Lafitte ran a finger down the first page of typescript. "Bouton suspects cardiac shock. We're waiting on the blood and toxicology tests from Pasteur. As yet, Docteur Bouton cannot come to a firm conclusion. Nothing really wrong with the girl. No external wounds, no cutting, stabbing or battering. Nothing wrong with her health. No hardening arteries, no internal problems. Or at least, nothing Docteur Bouton can identify. There just don't appear to be sufficient traumata to cause death—not in a healthy young woman."

"Cardiac arrest caused by drug abuse?"

"No signs of injection or scabbing due to a syringe; likewise, the nasal cavities appear healthy."

"She didn't sniff cocaine."

"Apparently not."

"Then why cardiac shock?"

"Bouton says we must wait for results. There are in fact various punctures and tears in the skin, but Bouton says these were caused after death and attributes them to animals."

"Then he goes along with Malavoy?"

"If Vaton was murdered on the beach—which is not impossible, since algor mortis would suggest the body was not moved after death—it seems strange scavenging dogs didn't do more damage to the corpse. Very little more than superficial scratching."

"I once ran over a dog," Parise remarked, looking down at his long fingers, "and when I parked my car, my own dog never stopped howling—he could smell carrion on my car wheels. Intimation of canine mortality." He shrugged. "Possible the girl's corpse gave off an odor that kept scavenging animals at bay."

"Possible—but unlikely in Docteur Bouton's opinion," Lafitte said coldly.

"Perhaps the body was in the sea and got washed up."

"No seawater was found in the lungs, which makes drowning unlikely. No salt deposits on the skin, although admittedly it rained several times on Tuesday. Nor is there any trace of blood on the beach. No traces beneath the fingernails, no sign of a struggle."

"Vaton had been swimming." Parise raised his hand. "It'd explain why she was naked."

"You checked the bikini bottom?"

"Would appear to be the same bikini that Desterres left with you." Lafitte nodded. "We're waiting for the lab to get back to us for hairs or saliva traces."

"On a bikini?"

"The bikini that Desterres gave you had been washed. Because of the skin contact, the bottom might give us useful information."

"Desterres washed the top thinking the girl'd come back—that's what he told me."

"He's lying, *madame*," Lafitte said sharply. "Why wash a bikini top that belonged to a passing tourist?"

"I'll ask him."

"The bikini's all we've got to go on," Lafitte said.

Parise spoke. "We've had a couple of calls from people who say they saw a topless girl on the beach at the Pointe des Châteaux. They said they saw her between nine and ten o'clock."

"By herself?"

"It's not a nudist beach and local people don't like women going topless there. West Indians aren't prudish but we don't appreciate the provocation of Europeans exposing their bodies. There are frequent pilgrimages to the calvary and children don't need to see naked women." Parise nodded. "She wanted to go swimming in the sea at the Pointe des Châteaux but she left after somebody warned her of the dangers."

"Of not wearing a bikini?"

"Of swimming there. There's a very strong undercurrent and it is probably the most dangerous beach in Guadeloupe—because you can be pulled by the undertow out to beyond the barrier reef. Then you're lunch for the sharks."

Lafitte coughed.

"I think we'll have to send the bikini—top and bottom—off to Paris." He shrugged. "Which means more delay. Pasteur normally does our forensic work on unnatural deaths but Bouton isn't optimistic. Our good pathologist's baffled."

Anne Marie frowned. "I find it hard to believe nobody saw the corpse on the beach over a sixty hour period."

Parise said, "Few people go to that beach during the week—not even the fishermen."

"Apart from the bikini, there really doesn't appear to be much to go on." Anne Marie turned back to Lafitte. "What signs of sexual activity?"

"According to Bouton, there's slight bruising around the genital regions, but again, the bruising most probably came about after death."

"Excluding sexual violence as a motive?"

"There was no struggle. There are, however, several superficial cut marks on the lower abdomen possibly caused by a blunt knife or cutting edge. Bouton says the murderer may have been trying to make it look like a sex crime." Lafitte looked at the typewritten notes. "No bruising, no irritation on the walls of the vagina or anus. Docteur Bouton finds no signs of forceful penetration, no saliva, no tooth bites." Lafitte hesitated before adding, "The breasts are not bruised."

"So?"

"When struggling with a woman, the rapist knows that the breasts are the most sensitive part of a woman's body."

"Are they?"

"It's an erogenous zone."

"For the rapist or for his victim?"

Lafitte began to blush.

"And sperm?"

A shrug.

"Well?"

Lafitte's blush grew deeper. "Bouton took smears and is waiting for results."

"Can sperm stay alive inside a dead body?"

"All depends on the time of death, but we can't be very optimistic. Bacteria producing lactic acid prevent the growth of pathogens in the vagina. It has a low pH and is a cleaner orifice than the mouth."

"It has to be," Anne Marie remarked drily.

Parise smiled and Lafitte hesitated before adding, "Vaton was not a virgin—according to Docteur Bouton she was sexually active."

"She was a nurse, not a nun, Lafitte."

"Vaginal scarring which Bouton sees as evidence of genital herpes. He thinks we can dismiss rape, *madame le juge*."

"So Desterres's off the hook?"

"Let's wait for the blood test results from Pasteur," Lafitte said. "Until we get hold of the Indian, Desterres remains the last person to have seen her alive."

Trousseau arrived with the coffee.

"And Desterres doesn't have an alibi."

23
Paraboot

Trousseau had gone to fetch Madame Vaton at the hotel in Gosier and Anne Marie found herself alone with Lafitte. In the sunlight outside the *palais de justice*, his skin had an unhealthy tinge. There were dark rings beneath his eyes and although he kept his hands in the pockets of his light cotton trousers, he could not relax. "We've got another forty minutes. Why not go for a drink, *madame*?"

"We've just had coffee."

"Perhaps something stronger. I don't enjoy the morgue."

"Docteur Bouton will let you drink his firewater, no doubt."

The sky was cloudless. After an early shower, the morning air was still cool, the surface of the sidewalk still wet. Anne Marie had wanted to walk to the hospital. It would take time and save her having to wait for Trousseau and Madame Vaton in the morgue.

"We've got to be at the hospital by nine."

"Then take a taxi, *madame*."

"Exercise will do me some good." She was wearing Paraboot shoes today, inelegant but practical, with thick soles.

"Exercise?"

"Didn't you use to cycle, Monsieur Lafitte?"

Lafitte shrugged and fell reluctantly into step beside her. He carried a leather case. He was peeved and Anne Marie smiled to herself.

"It's the bikini that baffles me." They went past the church, past the newly renovated flower market and onto the boulevard. The morning rush hour—parents taking their children to school—was over, but there were still a lot of cars.

"Why, *madame le juge*?"

"A bikini top—the one thing she's not wearing in the photograph. And it's the only piece of evidence we have."

A buxom woman, in the blue uniform of a traffic warden and with an umbrella under her arm, showed Anne Marie a golden-toothed smile.

Lafitte chose to dawdle as they went past a dark bar giving off the heady emanations of rum, molasses and freshly ground coffee. He took a cigarette from the packet in his shirt and stopped to light it.

Anne Marie, waiting for him, said, "On the other hand, I really can't see much point in bringing Desterres in."

Lafitte inhaled, then quickened his pace. "Desterres's not telling everything he knows."

"Unless he killed the girl, what else can he know?"

"He came to see you, don't forget. And he had the bikini top he'd carefully washed."

"Bouton's evidence goes against it being a sex killing."

"Perhaps it wasn't a sex murder."

"The only reason we're interested in Desterres is precisely because he has a record of sexual aggression. If he didn't rape her, what could possibly be Desterres's motive?"

"The fact she wasn't raped doesn't mean the murderer didn't want to rape her, *madame le juge*."

"Trousseau thinks Desterres could have lost his head over a sexy girl?"

"Desterres or any other West Indian male." He pulled the cigarette from his mouth. "Though Vaton doesn't appear particularly sexy."

"A nice body, Monsieur Lafitte."

"More important, she's white."

"She wasn't white." Anne Marie resumed her walking.

"Nobody'd notice the difference. Light-skinned enough to pass for white—and that's all that matters. Let's hang onto Desterres, *madame le juge*, until we've got other leads. Desterres's alibi for Sunday evening is far from watertight—he claims he was at his restaurant, but it'd already closed and there's nobody to corroborate his whereabouts. We don't know where Richard is so let's make do with the lead we've got. At least we can be seen to be doing something."

"Not the prime goal of my job," Anne Marie remarked tartly.

Lafitte snorted tobacco smoke. "You know what Trousseau's like."

"Trousseau?"

"He's got a thing about white women."

"Everybody on this island has a thing about white women."

"Trousseau's an Indian, and Indians don't like blacks. There's always been rivalry between the two races, ever since the landowners brought coolies in from India after slavery was abolished. Indians tend to marry among themselves—or with a white, if they get the chance. That's why Trousseau married his French woman."

"Not because he loved her?"

Lafitte smiled mirthlessly. "That's why he's now divorced."

"Divorced? Monsieur Trousseau never told me that."

Lafitte took a long, deep breath on the Bastos cigarette before throwing the stub away. "Trousseau keeps his cards close to his chest."

"Most men do."

Lafitte raised an eyebrow and the corner of his mouth simultaneously. "You don't have many illusions, *madame le juge.*"

"I was married for twelve years."

"Judging from the photo, Vaton wasn't sexy—despite what Trousseau might say. White, black or brown—Desterres can pick and choose. He's got money. He can find better than Vaton any day."

"You can't know what she was like in bed."

"Once you put the lights out, *madame le juge*, all women are the same in bed."

"You don't have many illusions either."

"When you get to my age . . ."

They crossed the road. A Polo coupé went past and hooted. Beside the middle aged driver sat a black girl, straightened hair blowing in the wind. Bright lipstick, bright teeth. Lafitte put one hand to his shield his eyes and with the other, he waved. "The sly old bastard."

"Who?"

"Jean Claude Pichon gets them all," Lafitte said admiringly. "Pichon used to be with Renseignements."

"You don't think Desterres's guilty?"

"He's got enough money and enough power to get what he wants."

Anne Marie glanced at him. "You don't have a great deal of esteem for women."

"Because I say women are attracted by money and power?" They had come to the rue Vatable and had to step past a couple of women who were selling bananas and mangoes from their curbside stall. Their huge chests battled with stretching, grubby T-shirts. The women shared an ancient weighing machine and jabbered in a falling English patois. *"Nice Dominica lime, darlin'."*

"I am a realist and I have unlimited esteem for the power of money."

Anne Marie said, "Desterres's twice been accused of rape."

For a fleeting moment, Lafitte looked her in the eye. "I wouldn't take those rape things too seriously. Could've been a girl trying to get even, trying to get her own back for promises Desterres had reneged on. To get a girl into your bed, you've got to promise her a white wedding—even if she's already got a kid."

"A misogynist."

"Misogynist? Desterres is a fornicator. He can afford to be—he's got money and he's not married. I'd love to be a misogynist like him."

"You really do sound like a misogynist, Monsieur Lafitte. You don't much like women, do you?"

"Why do you say that? I've always respected you. I've always admired you, *madame le juge.*"

"You don't like women, you don't like blacks, you don't like Indians. It's hard to see just who does meet with the Lafitte seal of approval."

He did not reply as he walked along beside her. With his hands in his pockets, the case tucked beneath his arm, he stared at the sidewalk that had begun to give off steam in the morning heat.

"Is there anybody you actually like, Monsieur Lafitte?"

Silence.

"Well?"

"Are you interrogating me, *madame le juge?*"

"Anybody who meets with your approval?"

"I admire you."

"Apart from me."

"My wife is West Indian."

"Your wife?"

He nodded, still not looking at her.

Anne Marie smiled, visibly softening. "We've worked together on and off for nearly ten years, Monsieur Lafitte—and I always thought you were a bachelor. You've not once mentioned your wife."

"I keep my private life and my job separate."

"You must introduce us."

"A girl from Sainte-Anne."

"Black?"

He grinned. "After a while, you don't notice."

"Even if you don't turn out the lights?" She touched his arm. "You must have beautiful children."

"No children, *madame le juge*."

They had reached the end of the Chemin des Petites Abymes and were within sight of the hospital.

"If Desterres was motivated by sexual desires, why do you want me to hang on to him?"

"Desterres's a politician. Politicians are all congenital liars—otherwise they wouldn't be politicians. When somebody like Desterres comes to see you at seven in the morning and volunteers information, you know he's protecting himself."

They laughed. As Anne Marie stepped from the sidewalk, Lafitte held out his arm to give her support. The policeman's gentleness surprised her.

24
Sunkist

"I see no reason for the SRPJ to be hostile." She screwed the top back onto the spray and slipped it into her bag.

"I like your perfume, *madame le juge*."

They were sitting on a bench outside the hospital. The concrete slab was cold beneath her Cacharel skirt. Lafitte had placed the attaché case between his feet. One hand was in his pocket, the other held a packet of cigarettes.

They watched the arrival of taxis in front of the main entrance. Although it was still too early for visiting hours, several people, well-dressed and unsmiling, arrived carrying flowers.

"Anything's better than Vicks vapor rub." She clicked her tongue in irritation. "Why the hostility?"

Lafitte had taken out a cigarette. "*Madame le juge*, I don't know anybody at the SRPJ who's hostile. I don't know anybody, either, who sees the need for your enquiry."

"Dugain committed suicide at a time that three SRPJ officers were searching his offices."

"So what?"

"No witness to his death. There are people who question the truth of the police allegations."

Lafitte squinted, his head to one side as the cigarette smoke rose. "People believe what they want to believe. That's something that you learn about Guadeloupe."

"My job's to get to the truth."

"You question the honesty of the SRPJ?"

She allowed herself a smile. "I've never questioned your honesty, Monsieur Lafitte, if that's what you mean."

"Once you've got the Vaton killing cleared up . . ."

"Cleared up?"

"Once you've got it sorted out to your satisfaction, you intend to resume your enquiries into Dugain's death?"

"Not a question of resuming—it's a question of priorities." She looked at him quizzically. "Why d'you ask?"

Here, on the top of the hill, the wind was stronger; the palm trees creaked in the humid morning breeze. Pleasant weather at a pleasant time of the day. She dreaded returning to the hospital basement. Her sensible shoes felt damp although they were quite dry.

"Why do you ask, Monsieur Lafitte? Are you worried?"

He played nervously with the packet of cigarettes in his hand. "Dugain was a bastard. Better that he's dead."

"There's something bothering you?"

He threw the stub away and ground it out against the tarmac with the heel of his shoe. "You."

"I bother you?"

Lafitte grinned, but the squinting eyes remained small and cold. "Worried for you, *madame le juge*, because over and above the professional relationship between us, I've always considered you a friend."

"You're very kind."

"A friend with whom I've been able to work over many years."

"You worry about me?"

"You're not aware who Dugain was."

"You knew him, Monsieur Lafitte?"

"You can only make enemies here. Enemies and a lot of trouble for yourself."

"I think you're trying to frighten me."

"Dugain was a shit of the first order."

"Answer my question—did you know him?"

"Never met him."

"Then what's the problem? I really don't understand."

"Lose a lot of friends by making unnecessary enquiries into his death." Lafitte set the crumpled cigarette packet on the bench. *"Madame le juge . . ."*

"My friends are of my own choosing." Anne Marie stood up and took a couple of steps forward. She could feel herself trembling. She stopped just short of the flowerbeds and a row of bedraggled poinsettia. A couple of empty cans of Sunkist lay on the fissured earth.

"I'm trying to give my advice, *madame le juge.*"

"Everybody's merely trying to give me advice." She turned to face him. "I take my own counsel. I know where my duty lies."

Lafitte stood up. "Not as an officer of the SRPJ but as a friend . . ."

"A friend?"

"Madame le juge . . ."

She could feel his warm alcohol breath and cigarette smoke on her skin. For a moment she thought he was going to touch her and she shivered.

Anne Marie was relieved to catch sight of her *greffier* coming up the hill in the Peugeot.

"Here comes Trousseau." She tried to make her voice cheerful. "Perhaps, then, Monsieur Lafitte, we can at least get the formal recognition of the corpse out of the way."

25

Chamonix

"Always was an inquisitive child, our Evelyne. Never could mind her own business." A proud smile. "Curious and inquisitive—just like her father. Always asking questions, always getting into trouble."

"Her father's still alive?" Anne Marie asked as together the two women went down the stairs.

"Never knows how to keep her mouth shut. Just like her father." She added, "He's dead now."

"West Indian?"

"What?"

"Your husband was West Indian, Madame Vaton?"

"His family was from Basse-Terre." The woman nodded. "Gérard grew up in Marseilles."

"When did you last see your daughter?"

She frowned. "How d'you say she got herself killed?"

"She was murdered."

"Yes, I know that." No attempt to hide her irritation. "But how was she murdered?"

"We think it was cardiac arrest. Perhaps suffocation."

"Nothing ever wrong with her heart." Madame Vaton was indignant. "Who'd want to murder my daughter? A lovely girl like Evelyne."

"Precisely what we're trying to find out. That's why I am personally so very grateful to you."

The older woman stopped walking, her head tilted to one side. She smiled. "Only too pleased to be of help. You're a kind person."

Despite the oppressive *eau de cologne* that Madame Vaton was wearing, Anne Marie took her by the arm. The two men followed Anne Marie and Madame Vaton into the building. They slowly went down the stairs to the hospital morgue. "When did you last see your daughter, *madame?*"

"Some time ago."

"Can you remember when?"

"My little girl no longer lives with me. I still keep her room ready—just in case."

"In Paris?"

"I live in the fourteenth *arrondissement* but Evelyne never stays. Not now that she has a place of her own near the hospital."

"Your daughter visited you?"

"She used to." A hesitation, a hint of regret. "She was always closer to her father than me. And since Gérard died . . . But she rings. At least once a week, she makes a point of phoning. She's a good daughter at heart, our Evelyne."

"At heart?"

"We all have our faults, don't we?"

"You've seen your daughter recently?"

"At Christmas." Madame Vaton nodded like a thoughtful bird. "And she came again in February. That's right, it was in February, because she said she was going for a week to Chamonix."

"Alone?"

"With a friend." Madame Vaton hesitated an instant. "My daughter said she was going skiing with a friend."

"A friend—or her boyfriend?"

"I've never met him." Madame Vaton shook her head vigorously. "A lovely girl—but she keeps her secrets. I suppose she gets that from me. I like to talk and I like being with people—that's why I became a hairdresser. I like the contact with people but I always feel some things are best kept to yourself. What do other people need to know about me? About my life? It's not that important, after all. You understand that, don't you?"

"You have the name of the boyfriend, Madame Vaton?"

Again she shook her head. "You know, I don't like to interfere. She's a big girl now—a grown woman."

"What—if anything—did your daughter tell you about him?"

"Jean Philippe or Jean Marc or Jean Michel—she must've mentioned his name, but it wasn't very serious between them. She said he was a nice boy. A young girl, she'd just qualified as a nurse, our Evelyne, she didn't have time for men. Just like me—I didn't get married until I was thirty-five." The woman shrugged. "I probably never would have if I hadn't met Vaton. We were working on the same ship, you know. He was near retirement, we met and then we went to live in Paris."

"Evelyne was your only daughter?"

"I come from a big family and I spent most of my childhood looking after my brothers and sisters. Just the one daughter—that was enough."

"Why did you become a hairdresser?"

"It's important to look your best, isn't it?"

"You never wanted to have other children?"

"Having children?" she said, as if it were the first time the idea entered her head. "There are so many other things in life that are just as important for a woman, I'm sure you'll agree." A pause as she reflected on her own past. "I was thirty-five when I had Evelyne." A nod of the head. "I can't complain. Evelyne's a good child. Headstrong and inquisitive—but a good child who loves to help people. That's why she became a nurse. I left home and went out to work because it was a way to escape. But Evelyne . . ." She shook her head. "Always wanting to help people. So unselfish." A reflective pause. "My daughter's dream was to become a doctor. But that costs a lot of money and we couldn't keep her at school for ever, could we?"

"This man—Jean Pierre or Jean Marc—did he work at the hospital with her?"

"No idea." Madame Vaton shrugged again. "My daughter doesn't talk about that sort of thing."

"Her private life?"

"Sex, sex, sex."

Anne Marie smiled politely. "I beg your pardon."

"There really are more important things in life than sex. Everybody seems to be obsessed with sex nowadays. You look at the television, you see the young people, you'd think sex's all that mattered in life. There are other things."

"Very true." Trousseau smiled.

The woman beamed at him happily.

"What other things, *madame?*"

"Jesus."

"I beg your pardon."

"Jesus," she said. "Our Redeemer."

Lafitte held open the door and they entered the morgue.

26

Sheet

"Bless you."

Anne Marie sneezed a second time.

"Bless you," the woman repeated and tapped the back of Anne Marie's hand affectionately. "I hope I don't catch your cold. I always catch something when I travel. Last year I went to Venice and came back with a shocking flu. I didn't like Italy. You know it? Not at all civilized and very dirty and there was orange peel in the canals." Madame Vaton chirped, "I must say, it's a lot nicer here. This is my first time in the West Indies and my husband would be terribly jealous if he were alive to see me in Guadeloupe. Always jealous of me, Gérard was—always jealous, and yet he liked to stay at home. Thirty years traveling the world and then he'd scarcely leave the house. Preferred to be with his little girl." The eyes were bright like a bird's. "Such lovely weather, isn't it? You're so lucky to live here. And so many lovely flowers. He'd have liked this, my Gérard. Always talking of coming back one day to his Guadeloupe."

The smell of the morgue. Anne Marie could feel a tightening in her stomach. "Your husband grew up in Basse-Terre?"

"He grew up in Marseilles but he traveled the world, did Gérard. He was with CGM—French Line. But he came to his island only a couple of times. South America, yes, and Australia. But Guadeloupe only twice in more than thirty years. Perhaps better that way—he might've met a local beauty and settled down here. I must say, these dark girls are so very pretty."

Trousseau said, smiling, "A lot of pretty women in France."

Anne Marie found herself impressed by the courtesy of Trousseau. He was polite and thoughtful and he did everything to put Madame Vaton at ease. He now gave her a helping arm as they approached the viewing window.

"Such nice people and my husband always said so. He said that in Martinique the girls are even prettier. Black as ebony, of course, but pretty."

"Your husband chose the prettiest of them all, *madame*," Trousseau said.

Anne Marie held the inside of her wrist to her nose—First, van Cleef and Arpels. The smell of flowers, of life.

"Instead he chose me." The gay laugh seemed out of place in the morgue. The woman looked earnestly at Anne Marie. "I was his second wife, you know. He was nearly sixty when we married. I don't think he regretted it—I hope not, I tried to be a good wife. Gérard always dreamed of coming to the Caribbean—it had been his dream since childhood." The woman laughed again. "How he'd love to be here."

The sweat was drying on Anne Marie's skin and she found herself wanting to sneeze again. She fumbled with a vitamin tablet in her bag.

"If he could see me now, he'd be green with envy."

Behind the glass, there was the whine of a motor and the corpse, lying beneath the sheet, was hoisted slowly into sight.

"Of course, the death of his daughter would be a terrible blow. He loved our Evelyne. Gérard loved our daughter more than he loved life itself."

"Bouton's done a good job." Lafitte, standing close behind Anne Marie, whispered in her ear, his breath bitter with smoke and rum. "Bit of an artist with the scalpel."

Léopold, the assistant, loomed from behind the glass wall and pulled back the sheet covering the corpse. He glanced at Anne Marie. Beneath the flight deck haircut he winked conspiratorially.

"I was at work most of the day. I met my husband when I was at sea—but I got too seasick and so we went to Paris where I got a job in a hair salon. Had the little girl and then went back to work. Evelyne was just a little thing and Gérard'd stay at home and play with her. Nearly sixty-five years' difference between them—and they were like brother and sister." The woman shook her head. "Now they're gone." A sigh. "There's only me."

The doctor had reshaped the face; the eyes were closed. Although the features were lopsided and the skin was waxen, it was as if the dead woman had just fallen asleep. Anne Marie wondered if Bouton had used makeup. There was a scarf around the top of the head, hiding the line of incision.

Anne Marie glanced unhappily at the socket in the wall. No sign of the electric saw. She shuddered and took a small step back, again breathing at the scent on her wrist.

Lafitte and Trousseau remained at Madame Vaton's side, afraid perhaps she should fall. Instead she chatted continuously. From behind, Anne Marie watched the woman's face. Madame Vaton pulled her cardigan tightly to her shoulders—it seemed to be growing colder by the minute in the basement—and frowned.

"I'm not looking forward to this," Madame Vaton said. Then there was silence.

On the far side of the glass, Léopold stood beside the corpse. His hands were crossed in front of his white laboratory coat. In one hand, he held a comic book. Remembering it, Léopold put it down somewhere out of sight. He grinned sheepishly.

Madame Vaton turned her head round to face Anne Marie. "Where's my daughter?"

Anne Marie stepped forward.

The woman's face had suddenly turned very pale, as if at last she realized where she was. "You told me they'd murdered my daughter."

Anne Marie gestured to the other side of the glass.

"My daughter." Again the woman shook her head. "Where's my daughter? Our Evelyne?"

Trousseau held her arm with both hands. His weathered face was drawn and pale.

"This is not our little girl."

"Not Evelyne Vaton?"

"My child has soft, white skin." Like a fluttered bird she shook her head. "I've never seen this unhappy creature before. Never." Madame Vaton pulled anxiously on the cardigan and started to cry. Small, round tears.

27
Accountancy

Trousseau drove.

Madame Vaton had overcome her emotion and now sat in the back of the Peugeot, looking out at the passing countryside, the cardigan folded on her stockinged knees. In her left hand she held a small leather-bound volume.

They took the busy ring road, went past the university—now being repainted an improbable bright pastel—and headed along the riviera toward Gosier and the hotels.

Anne Marie did not speak. She had nothing to say and despite her cold, she could no longer stand the woman's sweet perfume. Anne Marie held her wrist to her nose; the van Cleef and Arpels seemed to have lost much of its effect.

"The poor, poor thing," Madame Vaton said. "Who could've done a thing like that to a young girl?" She had a handkerchief in her right hand, but was not crying. Since leaving the morgue she had found time to repair her makeup and renew the lipstick along the thin lips. "My Evelyne's a naughty girl, not to keep in touch. Headstrong, just like her father." She added, "The Lord loves Evelyne and He loves me so I knew He would not take her from me. He doesn't need her—not yet."

"You've no idea where your daughter is?" It was Trousseau who spoke. He half turned his head, taking his eyes for a moment from the road, from the black tarmac.

"She's here somewhere." A pause. "Evelyne must be in Guade-loupe."

"What makes you so sure, Madame Vaton?" Even interrogating her, Trousseau was uncharacteristically gentle. "You say she never told you she was coming to the West Indies."

"It was her dream—just like her father." A thoughtful pause. "Madame Laveaud's shown me the photograph."

"You're sure it's your daughter? The photograph's not very clear."

"Not the sort of thing I approve of, that kind of nakedness on the beaches. Certainly not at her age. There's a place for everything—and on the beach there are young children and it's wrong to shock them. I belong to an older generation, that's what Evelyne always says. There are things I don't really understand about this modern world."

Trousseau smiled without taking his eyes from the road.

"The photo certainly looks like our Evelyne."

"Looks like her—but it could be the girl in the morgue," Trous-seau remarked, briefly glancing at her over his shoulder. "Do you have in your possession a photograph of your daughter that you could give us?"

"Give you?"

"To be on the safe side. It was your daughter who was reported missing, it was your daughter who hired the car. So when she turns up, we want to be sure it's her."

"I have a picture . . . it's at the hotel. But you must promise to give it back. It's a very lovely photograph—taken at La Baule several years ago. The summer before my Gérard died."

"A recent photo?"

"People used to think we were sisters—even if I'm a lot broader across the beam than her. And I didn't have her until I was thirty-five."

"The person in the Polaroid doesn't look like you at all. Your daughter's white, Madame Vaton?"

The woman gave a high-pitched giggle. "What a strange question!"

"Would you care to answer my strange question?"

It was a few minutes after eleven o'clock and children were return-ing home from primary school for lunch. They walked by the roadside, their clothes bright, their satchels perched high on their backs. Away from Pointe-à-Pitre, ribbons and plaits appeared popular among the rural schoolgirls.

"Is your daughter white? Your husband . . ."

"Somewhere, perhaps, my dear husband had Negro ancestry but it was nothing to be ashamed of. He was from Guadeloupe and he had lovely skin."

Trousseau drove carefully. "You weren't surprised your daughter had come to Guadeloupe without telling you?"

"Ever since she was little she talked about coming to her father's island."

"She didn't tell you before she left?"

"My little girl can be secretive—that's something she gets from me."

"There are relatives? Your husband was from Basse-Terre. Is it possible she's gone to stay with people from your husband's family?"

Perhaps Madame Vaton did not hear Trousseau's question; perhaps she chose to ignore it. "With the Lord's help, I know she'll turn up. It's happened before. She'll turn up, alive and well."

"She has relatives in Guadeloupe?"

"Not that I know of."

A row of banana trees ran alongside the road, their green leaves shifting with the breeze of the passing cars.

Soon the Peugeot came to the cemetery where a group of boys was intent on throwing sticks into a mango tree; to take better aim, they stood out on the roadway, indifferent to the hoots of the traffic.

"Happened before?" Anne Marie had come out of her reverie. "What happened before?"

"A cemetery?" Madame Vaton pointed. "Is that a cemetery?"

Trousseau smiled. "Here in the islands, the cemeteries are often bigger than the towns. Probably something to do with our voodoo past."

"I wouldn't like that."

"We're on this Earth for a short space of time. Death is forever so we take it seriously."

"Madame Vaton." Anne Marie did not attempt to hide her irritation—as much with Trousseau as with the woman. "This isn't the first time your daughter's disappeared?"

"Voodoo?"

"Please answer my question. Your daughter's disappeared before?"

"Several times." Madame Vaton looked sideways at Anne Marie. The thin lips had tightened. "Nothing to worry about. I never believed she was dead. I knew Our Lord wouldn't take my little angel from me." A tight smile. "In my heart I knew she was alive, even when the two policemen came to my house." She touched her forehead. "And to think it was only two days ago."

Trousseau turned right off the riviera and headed toward the center of Gosier, past the Total garage.

"When was the first time?"

Madame Vaton lowered her voice, "When she pretended to run away from home."

"Where did she go?"

"Evelyne was sixteen and under the pressure of exams. Evelyne is such a perfectionist. She gets that from me."

"When did she run away?"

"It was before her Brevet but we soon found her—or at least the police found her."

"Where was she?" Anne Marie asked, resenting the sweet *eau de cologne*, resenting the woman's deliberate obtuseness and her synthetic emotions. "Where was she?"

"Staying with a teacher—a woman teacher of bookkeeping. Stayed with her for nearly a week before we found out where she was. I was almost out of my mind from worry and when they found her, the police weren't at all happy."

"What made her run away?"

The voice was now a whisper. "The police were convinced she was a . . ."

"Yes, Madame Vaton?"

"That she was a . . . lesbian."

Trousseau turned in his seat and for an instant forgot about the other traffic, about the children playing at the roadside.

"I never believed it, of course." Madame Vaton reverted to a conversational tone. "When Gérard retired, there was his pension, but that wasn't enough. Not for a family, not to pay for her school things. I had to go out to work. I did a lot of overtime—it would pay for the clothes. Clothes and the other innocent pleasures in life." The face broke into a pleasant smile. "I must say, *madame le juge*, that you have a lovely skirt."

"Thank you."

"Evelyne always said I worked too much. Wanted me to stay at home—but I couldn't afford to. She likes to be spoiled, to be pampered by me. That's not a good thing." A sigh. "I tried not to give in—for her sake. Evelyne didn't always understand it was for her good. When she went to Church on Sunday, it was important she should be well-dressed. As pretty as a picture. I tried to do my best, I tried to do what was right. I was a good mother and I brought my daughter up to be a good Christian."

"Your daughter's a lesbian?"

"A lesbian? Of course not. What on earth makes you think that?" She laughed with amusement. "The teacher of bookkeeping was a lesbian. Or perhaps she wasn't. It didn't really matter either way, because our Evelyne's a good girl and she doesn't need any of that. She's not interested in sex with women—or with men. Perhaps when she was younger—it's a stage they all go through, isn't it? But now she's very sensible." Madame Vaton raised the leather-bound book. "Too much talk about sex nowadays."

Trousseau nodded. "Undoubtedly."

"Evelyne was studying for her Brevet and the police said the woman'd tried to seduce other young girls, too, so we decided, Gérard and I, we decided not to bother with pressing charges. Best all around to let the matter drop. And of course, Evelyne got her exam. Clever girl, Evelyne. Clever and hardworking." Madame Vaton added, "I like to think that she gets that from me."

28

Allude

Anne Marie climbed back into the car

Trousseau had straightened his tie. "Back to town, *madame le juge?*"

"You've got the photo?"

Trousseau was sweating and he ran a handkerchief across his brow before handing Anne Marie a manila envelope. "Hot, isn't it?"

"Take your tie off." She took the envelope he held out. "For once, you could take off your jacket."

Trousseau clicked his tongue as he slid behind the wheel of the Peugeot.

"Can we go now?" Anne Marie said tersely.

"Why the hurry?"

"Turn the conditioner off."

Trousseau appeared offended. "Where to?"

"And open all the windows, for heaven's sake. Get rid of that smell of perfume. I think I'm going to vomit."

Trousseau did as he was told. He yanked the car into gear and looped round in front of the hotel. The wheels screeched on the hot concrete.

"That better, *madame le juge?*"

"Sorry to be so abrupt. Forgive me." Anne Marie felt guilty. "I didn't mean to be aggressive."

He drove in silence.

"And thanks for accompanying her, Monsieur Trousseau. I didn't feel up to it."

"Madame Vaton was excited at the prospect of lunch. Said she'd heard so much about breadfruit, she was dying to try it."

Anne Marie shuddered. "You've looked at the girl's photo?

"A Christian woman," Trousseau said.

"Madame Vaton?"

"You don't like her, *madame le juge?*"

"I can't stand her."

"Lately there haven't been many people you can stand, *madame le juge.*"

"As I get older, I get more intolerant."

"You're a lot older than you look because quite clearly you can't stand me." He caught his breath. "I do my best."

"It's the heat, Monsieur Trousseau. The heat and that woman's dreadful *eau de cologne.* I know I'm . . ." She ran a hand through her hair. "I'm fed up, Monsieur Trousseau, fed up with the morgue and with this wretched enquiry—I hate murders. So sordid and sad."

Trousseau glanced into the overhead mirror and accelerated. The stone walls to the hotel gardens were covered with unkempt, blossoming bougainvillea. "I'm simply a *greffier, madame le juge.* I try to do my job to the best of my ability."

"You were very good. I truly admire your diplomatic approach, Monsieur Trousseau. You understand white women."

The face clouded. "White women, black women, oriental women— *madame le juge,* I really don't choose to distinguish." He grimaced. "The Creator made us all equal, you know."

"I appreciated your asking all the questions." Anne Marie added, "Perhaps we ought to change jobs, you and I."

"A nice lady."

"You liked her?"

"Back to Pointe-à-Pitre?" Without waiting for a reply, without stopping at the stop sign, Trousseau pulled the car out on to the main road, turning left toward the city.

"You liked Madame Vaton?"

Trousseau said nothing.

"There are times when you amaze me."

"Amaze you? I don't see why. To me Madame Vaton seems a good Christian woman."

"Can I invite you for lunch? I'd appreciate your company."

"I don't see what pleasure a *juge d'instruction* could possibly find in my company."

"Lunch and later a drive into the country. A long drive to Saint-François."

"It's Friday afternoon and you're seeing the *procureur*."

"Not often we're together, Monsieur Trousseau, and I value your opinions."

"Will the *procureur* appreciate your absence?"

"Your company and your opinions." Anne Marie had slid the photograph from the envelope. "Let me worry about the *procureur* while you worry about the driving."

"Saint-François it is, then." Without waiting for a reply Trousseau cut across the road, turned in the forecourt of the garage and headed back in the opposite direction. Five minutes later they reached the *route nationale* and he spoke again. "Left or right?"

"To Saint-François."

"I do as I'm told and I mind my own business."

"You're a good man, Monsieur Trousseau, and you know I've always respected your opinion."

In the photo, mother and daughter were on the beach at La Baule. Behind them, L'Hermitage Hotel. A photograph that made Madame Vaton appear younger. She wore a cotton frock. Her daughter was in a swimsuit. The photograph had been taken too far from the subject for the facial details to be clear.

"About the same height as the girl in the morgue."

"Her daughter's alive and she knew that," Anne Marie said. "She was not behaving like a woman who's just lost her only child."

"Our Lord had told her. She's a deeply religious woman."

"She makes my flesh creep."

Trousseau ran a finger along his moustache. "Like Docteur Bouton?"

"At least Docteur Bouton hasn't got religion—even if he does make my flesh creep."

Trousseau tugged at his tie. "I know a lot of people who could benefit from religion. People who ought to be a lot more charitable."

"If you're alluding to the fact that my maiden name is Bloch, Monsieur Trousseau . . ."

"Jesus came to earth to save sinners."

"Let me remind you that I'm Catholic. Like my mother, God rest her soul, I'm a baptized Catholic."

"Too many sinners who don't want to be saved."

"What is that supposed to mean?"

"Our Savior came to wash away our sins."

"You sound like Madame Vaton."

"A Christian lady."

"Vaton's religion's not sincere."

"The day of reckoning will soon be upon us—and then perhaps you'll see the need for religion, *madame le juge.* You will have ample time to regret not paying more attention to the word of the Holy Scriptures." He again pulled at the knot of his black tie. The short end, Anne Marie noticed, was frayed.

"Monsieur Trousseau, I respect your religious beliefs. I respect other people's opinions—but Madame Vaton's not sincere."

"You've no right to say that, *madame le juge.*"

Anne Marie savored the air rushing through the window, pulling at her hair. With a sudden, inexplicable lack of decorum she kicked off the ungainly shoes, raised her legs and set her feet under her thighs on the back seat. In the mirror Trousseau raised a disapproving eyebrow.

Anne Marie set her fist under her chin before continuing. "From the moment she gets off the plane, it's as if she's on holiday. Even in the morgue, for goodness sake. The Club Mediterranée. Her daughter's dead and she's enjoying herself!"

"She knew her daughter wasn't dead."

"Excited at the thought of eating breadfruit."

"You're forgetting her husband's originally from Guadeloupe."

"She's not human."

"If Evelyne Vaton's not dead, Evelyne Vaton must be alive."

"If she's not dead, she's alive." Anne Marie started to laugh.

"And if Evelyne Vaton's alive, she's going to turn up." He gestured over his shoulder to the photograph on Anne Marie's lap. "When Evelyne Vaton turns up, you'll know whether the mother was lying."

"An unidentified corpse in the morgue—and because of the Hertz car, everybody thought it was Evelyne Vaton. We've shown our incompetence—and we're no nearer to solving who killed the woman."

"Incompetence?" He ran his finger along the line of his upper lip.

"Precisely, Monsieur Trousseau—incompetence. I should've checked with the people she was staying with in Basse-Terre."

"Why bother when the mother was flying from France for the autopsy?"

Anne Marie shivered unhappily. "Some mother."

"I wouldn't use the word incompetence." Trousseau shrugged. "Everybody thought it was Vaton's body—including the prime suspect, Desterres. There was the photo and there was the bikini. You were fed the bait."

"Bait?"

"You rose to it, *madame le juge.*" Trousseau started laughing to himself, showing his teeth in the mirror. "Nothing to be ashamed of."

"I don't see what's funny. What bait, Trousseau?"

"Evelyne Vaton's bikini. Someone wanted you to think it was Evelyne Vaton dead on the beach . . ."

29

Sandwich

The heat at the Pointe des Châteaux was tempered by a strong sea breeze, coming from Africa, south of the Sahara. It blew and tugged at the Cacharel skirt, pushing it against her thighs. Her feet were hot in her sensible shoes.

Anne Marie approached the snack van. She walked slowly, enjoying the wind, enjoying the magnificent view. The most easterly tip of the island, Pointe des Châteaux had a ruggedness reminiscent of the Brittany coast: Pointe du Raz, Ouessant, Molène. Here the Atlantic and the Caribbean clashed, sometimes angrily. Today the turquoise sea was no more stormy than the placid blue sky. The water was not threatening; the sea gently threw its low breakers against the coral sand.

A beautiful beach, but dangerous. There were red flags flying permanently, warning people not to bathe. Occasionally a surfer ignored them, wanting to enjoy the thrill of the waves crashing landward. He ignored the warning at his own peril: a treacherous undercurrent could easily drag him way out beyond the barrier reef. Beyond the protection of the reef to where the man-eating sharks infested the warm sea.

Trousseau was parking the Peugeot, trying to find some shade in the low scrub. The wind was too strong for the vegetation to grow beyond shoulder height.

It was past midday and the sun was directly overhead, at its zenith and beating down on the shadowless beach, on the smooth sand, on the whitened flotsam of polished branches, tires and rusting cans.

There were few tourists about.

As soon as Anne Marie moved into the lee of the dunes, sweat started trickling down her body. At least, she told herself, she had got away from Madame Vaton's *eau de cologne.* She took deep breaths of sea air, heavy with the tang of salt, iodine and seaweed. Anne Marie was no longer sneezing.

SANWICHS' OLGA had been painted onto the van, an aging Iveco, gnawed at by rust, by the salty air and the humidity. Anne Marie moved into the shadow of the overhanging flap.

"*Bonjour, doudou.*"

A woman sitting behind the counter stood up and smiled at Anne Marie. She was in late middle age, with chubby features and brown skin freckled around the nose and cheeks. There was lipstick but it had been applied carelessly. "What would you like, *doudou?*" The woman pointed to a slate advertising Orangina where the prices of food and drink had been chalked up in an unlettered hand. She dabbed at her cleavage with a Kleenex.

"Lovely fresh sandwiches, *doudou.*" She gestured to a glass cabinet containing sliced baguette. On the top of the cabinet, an opened can of Sovaco butter attracted the attention of a solitary fly. "Chicken, mackerel, cheese, tomato, ham, egg . . ."

"What sort of cheese?"

"Emmenthal or Vache Qui Rit. Of course, I can do a hamburger or a *croque-monsieur.*" She pointed to a couple of grubby cookers, smeared with grease. She was a buxom woman. She wore a T-shirt that said ORANGINA. Beneath the T-shirt, a sturdy brassiere; below the brassiere, patches of sweat.

Anne Marie said, "Make that Emmenthal."

"Two cheese sandwiches, then, *doudou?*" A small fan was attached to the open side of the van and the woman set herself in its breeze. "For you and for your gentleman friend?"

Anne Marie turned, following the woman's glance. In jacket and tie, Trousseau approached the van. From out of the trunk of the Peugeot, he had produced a black umbrella, which he had opened and now held above his head, protection from the midday sun.

"Monsieur Trousseau," Anne Marie called out. "What sort of sandwich would you care for?"

"Monsieur Trousseau?" The woman in the van had bent forward and was peering toward the oncoming *greffier*, a fleshy hand to her eyes. "Looks to me for all the world like Alphonse."

"Alphonse?"

"I always thought Alphonse was in France."

Trousseau walked with his head down, in the shadow of the umbrella.

A chuckle. "It's a small world, after all these years."

"Monsieur Trousseau?"

The woman cackled her amusement. "My word, Alphonse's aged a lot, hasn't he?" There were large patches of sweat beneath her arms. "And he's got a belly, I see. The girls loved him twenty years ago."

"You know Monsieur Trousseau, *madame*?"

"I know Alphonse Ayassamy." She put her head back and the damp neck rippled as she laughed. "God's gift to women. Back in the days when he was the Nat King Cole of Capesterre/Belle Eau." The various gold necklaces danced on the dark skin. "He left enough with a gift of his own—of the squalling, crying kind."

Trousseau heard the woman's laughter, looked up and tilted the angle of the umbrella. He changed direction and headed for the plastic chairs set out on the sand. There were several tables, each protected by a large blue parasol flapping in the sea breeze. Trousseau sat down with his back toward the van.

"God's gift to women," the woman repeated and again she trembled with amusement. "Congratulations, *doudou*." Olga—if that was her name—had coarse, short hair that had been straightened and dyed red sometime in the last month. The color was disappearing to reveal greying strands at the root. "I heard Alphonse'd married a white woman from the mainland." More throaty laughter. "I only hope he looks after the children."

"I am Madame Laveaud. I am the *juge d'instruction* for Pointe-à-Pitre."

"I nearly married him." A click of the tongue. "I thought back in those days an Indian was more reliable than a black." She suddenly clapped her hand to her mouth and several gold teeth. "No better, no worse. I learned that the hard way. They're all the same—but we can't do without them, can we, *doudou*?"

"Monsieur Trousseau works for me."

"Alphonse has done well for himself—a lovely lady like you."

"Monsieur Trousseau and I are colleagues," Anne Marie said coldly. "We're not related."

"A white wife. And a lot younger than him, I bet. You two must have lots of lovely children with nice hair? I just hope, with you being French, he's reformed his ways." A big wink of the watery eye. "I hope he's zipped up that fly once and for all." She called out in a deep, masculine voice, "A cheese sandwich, Alphonse?"

Trousseau did not move.

"My *greffier* and I are making enquiries into the death of the unfortunate girl who was murdered."

"To drink, *doudou?*"

"I beg your pardon."

"Sunkist, Krony, Coca, Kroenenburg, Heineken, Pepsi, malt beer, Perrier, fresh passion fruit, cane juice, grapefruit, soursop, starfruit—made this morning. What would you like to drink, Madame Ayassamy?"

Anne Marie held up her hand, turned and walked across the burning sand, approaching Trousseau, who sat with one hand on his attaché case, the other holding the umbrella. He had neither undone his tie nor removed his jacket. He stared in front of him, toward the calvary set atop the Pointe des Châteaux promontory. "A fruit juice and a sandwich, Monsieur Ayassamy?"

"I thought you were taking me to lunch."

"I need to talk with this woman." Anne Marie leaned forward. "She seems to know you."

Trousseau did not react.

"Calls you Alphonse."

"I've never seen the old harpy before. And God willing, I shall never see her again."

"Alphonse Ayassamy." Anne Marie began to laugh. She laughed till the tears came down her cheeks. She forgot about the sun reverberating off the sand, she forgot about the nauseous *eau de cologne*. She even forgot about the morgue.

30

Tarare

"Alphonse suits you."

Despite the oppressive heat, there were clouds lowering in the north, heading fast toward the Grands Fonds and beyond.

"You invited me for lunch, and in return for driving you, I get a Sunkist and a sandwich."

"I didn't know your family name was Ayassamy."

"I should have stayed in Pointe-à-Pitre where I could've bought my own Sunkist. I hope you asked for a receipt."

Anne Marie shook her head.

"Back to town, *madame le juge?*"

"Now I'm going to take you to lunch. At Mère Nature—Desterres's restaurant."

Unsmiling, Trousseau nodded, put the Peugeot in gear and they set off toward Saint-François. Anne Marie insisted Trousseau keep the windows of the Peugeot open and the air conditioning off. She was now cheerful; Olga's good humor had been contagious. Her belly muscles ached from too much laughter.

"It was there on Sunday night."

"What, *madame le juge?*"

"The Fiat Uno—the Hertz car Evelyne Vaton hired." Anne Marie allowed herself a cheerful giggle. "Your friend Olga's a very interesting woman."

"I know nobody by that name."

"She knows nobody by the name of Trousseau."

"Which can only mean we have never met."

"She was adamant, insisting you were a lady's man."

"I'm a happily married man."

"Before you ever married."

"My wife's a white woman. Whiter than you. And unlike your obese black friend, in my household we speak French."

"I believe you, Monsieur Trousseau."

"If ever I were to have married a Negro woman—a highly unlikely possibility—there are hundreds, nay thousands of women who would have caught my glance before that . . . before that harpy."

"Who mentioned marriage, Monsieur Trousseau?"

"She's mad."

"She knows a lot about you."

"She knows nothing about me—and neither do you. Must I remind you yet again my private life is my own affair? It's not because I work for you, *madame le juge*, or because there's always been a spirit of collaboration between us that you should feel entitled to pry into my private life. I'm an Indian and a *greffier* and I mind my own business. Those pleasures of the flesh that you allude to exert no charm for me. I've been married to a very beautiful woman for more than twenty years and it's certainly not with some sweaty woman, some Creole-speaking virago selling hot dogs, some toothless old harridan that I'm likely to seek carnal satisfaction."

"She was not necessarily sweaty twenty years ago. In those days she had all her teeth. And twenty years ago you weren't married."

"I don't wish to continue this conversation, *madame le juge*."

Anne Marie was still grinning but she adopted a placating tone. "Don't get upset."

"I've shown you unstinting loyalty."

"The woman must've made a mistake."

"If I had known it was your intention to make lewd and unjustified allegations about my private life I would've stayed in Pointe-à-Pitre. Madame Laveaud," he continued, his eyes on the road, his features drawn, "I'm not some West Indian who considers all white women as fair game. I've always shown you respect—because you are my hierarchical superior, because you are a good and efficient investigating magistrate. Above all, I have shown you respect because I admire you."

He ran his finger along the edge of his mustache. "It would be a great shame if many years of fruitful collaboration and friendship should come to naught simply because you give credence to the ravings of an ignorant old gossip—*une vieille macrelle.*" He tapped the steering wheel. "You shall let the matter drop."

Anne Marie turned her head to look out of the window. She did not want Trousseau seeing her, for she could not control the smile that pulled at her lips, she could not control the wrinkling of her eyes, the laughter within her chest that still wanted to work its way out, that caused her muscles to ache.

They followed the Saint-François road. The hedges were a riot of flowers, bougainvillea, laurel and allamanda. The flame trees were in dazzling blossom.

They went past the old sugar plantation that had been renovated, past the new apartment blocks, past the American hotel.

"If we're going to eat, I don't see why you tried to make me eat one of her greasy sandwiches."

"To get her to talk."

Clouds were scudding in from Désirade, driving inland.

"And what did she say?"

"That the car was there on Sunday night. She remembered seeing it there."

"I thought it was on Tuesday night."

"That's what the *procureur* said but she was quite certain. A shame you were sulking."

"I was not sulking, *madame le juge.*"

"You would have heard her testimony."

Trousseau remarked coldly, "Judging from her absurd allegations, your black woman would appear a highly unreliable witness."

"Perhaps the car was broken into."

"That's not what Hertz said."

"There's a lot of theft at the Pointe des Châteaux—Olga said as much. If the car was broken into, that'd explain why there were no documents."

"But the car wasn't broken into. And anyway, the Vaton girl's not dead."

"She doesn't seem to be alive, either."

They followed the long beach of Salines, visible through the low shrubs, and the waves breaking against the cays. After another kilometer, they saw the first sign for Tarare, for the nudist beach and the restaurant Mère Nature.

"Are you hungry, Monsieur Trousseau?"

"I was until your friend destroyed my appetite with her base allegations."

No longer able to hold in her laughter, Anne Marie pretended to sneeze.

31
Mother Nature

They turned off the hot main road onto an unsurfaced track. The car bounced on its high suspension. Dust swirled upwards and reluctantly Anne Marie had to ask Trousseau to close the windows and turn on the cooler.

They traveled through the low brush at little more than ten kilometers an hour for over five minutes. Nobody was in sight.

They came to the open parking space.

"We'll get out here."

The ground was hard, dry and uneven beneath the thick soles of her Paraboots. They set off on foot toward the beach. Trousseau had insisted upon taking the umbrella, but rather than giving shade, it prodded at Anne Marie's face, uncomfortably close to her eyes.

A sign announced Tarare beach and invited visitors to remove their clothes.

Trousseau straightened his tie, allowed himself a sly grin, and they went down the steep incline that led to the beach. From time to time he held out his hand to offer support. Anne Marie noticed, not without pleasure, that her *greffier* was considerably less agile than she. After a while, he closed the umbrella and used it as a stick to give him balance.

Out of the wind, the air was close. Insects danced in Anne Marie's eyes and there was a pervasive odor of rotting plants and dead cactus.

Suddenly the path opened out and they came on to the crescent beach, brilliant beneath the overhead sun. With relief Anne Marie rediscovered the breeze. Sweat ran down her back and her linen blouse clung to her skin.

"Very quiet." Trousseau wiped his face with a handkerchief. He had dropped umbrella and attaché case to the ground.

With its palm trees, Tarare could have been the picture of tropical paradise in a tourist brochure. The sea was calmer than at the Pointe des Châteaux. It was a bright blue, becoming turquoise over the sand, then turning darker where the coral outcrops lay beneath the surface, a magic patchwork of kaleidoscopic greens and blues. The Caribbean as the postcards liked to show it. Even the lapping of the waves against the sand was perfect.

Gwada, pa ni pwoblem.

The restaurant was as Anne Marie remembered it; a wooden building surrounded by tall palm trees, their trunks painted white up to a meter from the sand.

On the wooden veranda stood half a dozen tables. They were bare. The door to the kitchen was closed and bolted. The only living thing was a solitary cat that eyed the two functionaries of the state with indifference.

There were living quarters at the back of the restaurant—a small bedroom with an outside sink and cracked mirror.

"I think we've come at the wrong time, *madame.*"

She remarked, "We can have a look around, can't we?"

"And I get no meal?"

"Forgotten the Sunkist, Monsieur Trousseau?"

While Trousseau sat down wearily at one of the tables, the closed umbrella between his legs, Anne Marie wandered off along the beach.

The water looked so limpid, so inviting, that she was tempted, out of the view of her companion, to go for a dip. But, as she reminded herself, not only was she without a costume, but she did not have anything to dry herself with. Without fresh water to rinse her body, the salt would be sticking uncomfortably to her skin for the rest of the afternoon.

She took off her shoes and sauntered along the beach. From time to time, the warm water ran up to her feet. Rediscovering an old friend. She felt a strange happiness at being here, at not being in

Pointe-à-Pitre, not being in her office, not being at the morgue. She started to whistle and had gone some seventy yards when she heard a movement to her right. She stopped.

Anne Marie saw a low sea grape, but apart from that, nothing. No movement.

She glanced back at Trousseau. He had lowered his head onto the table as if trying to doze. "Alphonse," she said, smiling to herself. Anne Marie resumed her whistling.

"*Bonjour!*"

In front of her stood a tall man with his arms crossed against a dark, broad chest. Tall but beginning to take on flesh at the midriff. He had fine features and a long, straight nose. A reflex camera hung from his neck. He held out his hand.

"My name is Richard."

A bright, white smile but the eyes were bloodshot. The man had not shaved in several days.

Apart from the camera, Richard was as naked as the day he was born.

32
Chair

She felt like a schoolgirl playing hooky.

"Take the umbrella."

Anne Marie shook her head and got out of the car. "Trousseau, get this man to the hospital as fast as you can and then get hold of Bouton."

So much to do and yet Anne Marie did not want to return to Pointe-à-Pitre. Not yet. She would get a taxi back to town, or failing that, would wait for one of the rural buses.

She waved but her *greffier* was sulking—for the last half hour he had been saying he was hungry. Without looking at her, he released the clutch and set off toward Pointe-à-Pitre, accompanied by Richard, immobile in the back seat. The tires screeched on the tarmac road.

There was something terribly pathetic about Richard, Anne Marie thought. He did not look at her, he did not turn his head on the fleshy neck. Lost in his thoughts, indifferent to what was happening around him.

She walked toward the wooden fence.

Loud music came from a radio. There was a gate in the fence that was ajar and as she stepped into a small garden, Anne Marie was surprised by the abundance and brightness of the flowers. So green. The dry season was long over here in the Grands Fonds.

Dark clouds had come scudding in from the east and the sky was now turning grey with the threat of rain in the afternoon. The green and mauve leaves caught the luminescence of the overcast sky and reflected it with a sullen intensity.

The music grew louder.

Anne Marie made her way down the path to the shack, pushing back ferns, tall grass and the branches of a pepper tree. Thanks to the dry air of the Pointe des Châteaux, Anne Marie felt a lot better. Yet the memory of Madame Vaton's perfume lingered in the pit of her belly. Anne Marie would soon have to return to the morgue. She could feel a lump swelling in her chest.

(In all her school years, in Algeria as at Sarlat, Anne Marie had never once played hooky. She could hear Luc's voice, "You've always been a goody-goody." She smiled guiltily to herself.)

The door to the shack was open. Anne Marie went up the wooden steps. "Anybody at home?" She knocked at the jamb, leaning inside.

The interior of the shack was clean, the music noisy.

A bare floor, walls of unvarnished planks and a table of molded orange plastic. A couple of matching seats had been taken from a car. A vase beside the radio contained dried bullrushes. The room was empty, but there was another open door that gave on to the back garden.

The music came to a stop as a local disc jockey chatted with a woman who had phoned in to request, in banana French peppered with Creole, a record: Zouk Machine. The radio screeched strident feedback.

Anne Marie stepped into the house and she noticed an exotic smell that took her back to her childhood in North Africa.

"Looking for me?"

A young woman's face appeared at the rear door. An oval, pretty face, bright eyes, dark skin and hair plaited into long, parallel rows.

"Madame Augustin?"

The woman smiled. "Mademoiselle Augustin." She came up the plank steps into the room. She was wearing a skimpy cotton halter and khaki shorts. She wore sandals; there was mud on her feet. The skin of her legs was perfect except for a vaccination mark at the thigh. In her hand she held several green limes. "I'm Marie Pierre Augustin. Who are you?"

"Madame Laveaud. I'm an investigating judge."

"Investigating what?"

Anne Marie ran a hand along her forehead. "I wonder if you could give me a drink of water? Would you mind if I sat down?"

The young woman laughed a nasal laugh. "Of course not." She spoke French with the intonation of the Paris suburbs. Drancy, Aubervilliers, Saint-Denis. Postal code 93.

"Perhaps I could also ask you to turn down the radio—I'm hot and sticky. Finding anywhere in the Grands Fonds can be so difficult . . . even with a map."

"You don't like music?" The girl rolled the limes onto the table. She switched off the radio and went with a light, youthful step through the doorway into the kitchen. Kitchen, living room and another room— the bedroom, no doubt—were separated by hardboard walls that rose to a height of a couple of meters. No ceiling. Above the walls, four sloping sheets of corrugated iron formed the roof of the shack.

Anne Marie lowered herself onto one of the car seats. The smell seemed stronger.

An entire side of the living room was filled with leather bags—small heaps of shopping bags, handbags, men's bags—that were kept in plastic wraps. There were little tags. Stretching her arm, Anne Marie took a bag and looked at the price tag. The figures were in a currency she did not recognize; the writing looked Spanish.

Anne Marie raised one of the bags to her nose; it had the rich odor of oiled leather.

The girl returned, holding out the glass. She said, nodding to the handbag in Anne Marie's hand, "Just got back from Brazil."

"I need to ask you a few questions." Anne Marie drank some water. "Nothing very serious, *mademoiselle*."

"I hope not." The girl's mouth smiled a pretty smile.

"I've always dreamt of going to Rio."

"I spent three weeks there." She gestured to the articles on the floor. "On business."

Anne Marie held up her hand. "I'm not from Customs."

"We paid customs, *octroi de mer*—the lot."

"I really couldn't care less—provided it's not cocaine from Latin America." Anne Marie took another sip of water, her eyes on Marie Pierre. "I've a son at the *lycée* and like most parents, I have an obsession about drugs."

"Drugs?" The young woman shook her head. "I stick to lemongrass tea from the garden." She made a gesture toward her garden.

The sky had darkened.

33
Incense

It was the same incense her grandmother always used to smell of.

"You'd care for something to eat?" Marie Pierre was sitting crossed-legged on a rug. She kept her back upright and her hands were placed on her knees. "There are lentils in the pot."

Anne Marie shook her head. "You're very kind."

"I am a vegetarian. Or perhaps you'd care for a yogurt."

It had started to rain. There was a short silence as the two women listened to the first patter of raindrops on the roof. Then Anne Marie asked, "What made you become vegetarian?"

"I believe in harmony."

"Hard to believe in harmony when you've seen an autopsy." Anne Marie changed the subject. "Why the leather goods, Mademoiselle Augustin?"

"We wanted to set up a little business. Selling handicraft, authentic souvenirs—that sort of thing. Ponchos, panamas."

"We?"

The frown returned to the smooth skin. "Why are you asking these questions? I've already told you the *octroi de mer*'s been paid on everything."

Anne Marie cast a glance round the room. The furnishings were functional and the place was clean. There was none of the untidiness that came from two people living together. "You're married?"

"Used to be."

"And now?"

"I have a friend. Do we make love? Is that what you mean?"

"It's not my wish to pry."

"What do you want?"

"You talk about 'we.'"

"I'm not ready for another marriage. There are a lot of things to do in life and I'm not yet ready to settle down, serve one man and have children. Cook three meals a day." She shook her head. "Each thing in its own due course."

The patter on the iron roof became more insistent.

"How long have you been together?"

"What's that got to do with you?"

"I'm curious." Anne Marie gave an apologetic smile.

"Why?"

"All part of my job." Anne Marie did not wait for a reply. "You said you used to work in a shop."

A nod. Anne Marie saw hesitation in the girl's eyes.

"You worked for Monsieur Dugain, didn't you, Marie Pierre? Along with another girl, you informed the work inspectorate you were being paid with government apprenticeship money."

"I've answered enough questions about Monsieur Dugain."

"He subsequently died in mysterious circumstances."

"I didn't know he was going to kill himself. I just wanted to be paid decently. I wanted my social security payments. There was nothing personal against Monsieur Dugain. I liked the job."

"He flirted with you?"

"I never said that."

"What was your job, Marie Pierre?"

"Monsieur Dugain has a health food shop in Abymes."

"What did you do there?"

"Working there I decided to become a vegetarian. Agnès and I were sales girls." She shrugged. "Dugain wasn't paying our health contributions."

"Whose idea was it, your seeing the work inspectors?"

"I was fed up with being screwed by that man." She paused. "Agnès's boyfriend's an accountant."

"And?"

"Olivier said Dugain was not paying us, but the government was giving him money for us. That working in Dugain's shop was part of the training program and that we could complain to the inspectors because he made us do a lot more than the contract stipulated. We never got any training."

"You threatened him?"

She looked down at her hands, at the long fingers and the specks of deep red nail varnish. "Agnès wanted to have a baby. She needed health coverage to pay for the doctor."

"How did Dugain react?"

The falling raindrops became more angry, faster. Wind blew at the open doors and water darkened the wood of the threshold.

"They said he jumped from the top of a building." Marie Pierre nodded to an old television set that stood on a molded plastic stand. Her eyes reverted to Anne Marie.

"How did Dugain react when you threatened him, *mademoiselle*?"

"I'd left the shop in February, long before he killed himself." She tilted her head to one side. "How was I to know he was going to kill himself?"

"How well did you know Dugain?"

"He helped me when he gave me the job."

"You didn't like him?"

With her regular features and her perfect skin, she reminded Anne Marie of an African goddess carved in a black hardwood.

The girl rose from her cross-legged position and went to close the door. Rain fell onto the back of her hand and glistened there.

"He harassed you?"

For a moment she stood in the doorway, her back to Anne Marie, as she stared out into the small garden. Without turning, she said, "I can't answer your question."

"Why not?"

"Nothing's free in this life."

"That sounds to me like an answer."

"Please." Marie Pierre closed the door and pulled the wooden bar into place. It was now dark. She turned on the electric bulb, which gave a tungsten glow to the small room. Rain had fallen onto the bare skin of her shoulder. "I don't want to talk about him." A plaintive tone to her voice. "Please."

"Were there many people who disliked him?"

She laughed. "He was fat and ugly and overbearing and he smelled of aftershave he picked up in Unimag. Or in the Prisunic. He was tightfisted and he bought whatever was cheapest. We worked hard, Agnès and I; we got on well together, we liked the job and we felt we were doing something useful. And he screwed us—he screwed us and he screwed the government." A click of her tongue. "He used all these long words and he thought he was clever, teaching at the university, but he was just a jumped-up mulatto from Martinique who drove around in a big Mercedes Benz. And between his fat legs . . ."

Anne Marie frowned. "Jumped-up?"

"He thought we were little girls who could be used and abused."

"Marie Pierre, why didn't you leave?"

"I needed the money." The young woman shrugged. "With thirty percent unemployment, you think I could walk out, just like that?"

"You could've complained to the ANPE."

She gave a toothy grin. "I wanted to get even with the bastard."

"For exploiting you?"

"All we'd done is ask for a raise. He found a pretext. Said we were not courteous, that we didn't now how to deal with the public, and he gave us the sack. That's when I went to the Inspectorate."

"Where does Agnès work now?"

"I haven't seen her in a long time."

"Good friends?"

"We used to be. She's got her life to lead—and so have I."

"Her family name?"

"Loisel—Agnès Loisel."

"Where can I find her?"

The question irritated her. "She was working in a hotel in Gosier but I haven't seen her recently. Somebody told me she went to Paris."

"And her boyfriend?"

"They're not together."

"I thought you said she wanted a baby."

"She didn't talk about anything else."

"You know his name?"

"Olivier. Why do you want to know?" Marie Pierre's face had hardened.

"Perhaps Monsieur Dugain was murdered."

"Nobody liked Dugain." She folded her arms. "I'm glad he's dead."

"Not a nice thing to say."

"Dugain was not a nice man."

"Did you sleep with him?"

"That's none of your business."

"Nobody deserves to be murdered, Marie Pierre. Not even Dugain."

"Perhaps you'd like to leave."

"How did you meet him?"

Marie Pierre breathed deeply before answering. "Through a contact."

"What contact?

"A friend."

"Who, Marie Pierre?"

"A man who runs a restaurant near the Pointe des Châteaux."

"Desterres?"

The African princess did not try to conceal her surprise. "You know him?"

34
Neurosis

"I'm very angry."

"Of course you're not, Arnaud."

"Don't tell me whether I'm angry or not."

She held up her hand. "I don't see how you can be angry with me."

"For God's sake, Anne Marie. I'm not going to come looking for you again. Don't you realize?"

"I was about to call for a taxi."

"My blasted phone hasn't stopped ringing in the last four hours. I've just been speaking with the *préfet*'s secretary."

"So?"

"The *préfet* is out for blood."

"You look anemic enough."

"I find you amazing." He lit a cigarette, his hand trembling. "Where've you been all day?"

"I've just got back from the Grands Fonds."

"Where?"

"Bouliqui."

"What on earth were you doing there?"

"Arnaud, there's not much I could've done in Pointe-à-Pitre."

"I gave you the murder case—the *préfet* insisted—and you're traipsing in the Grands Fonds. The wrong corpse, the wrong name and you go off into the boondocks. The island is in crisis, a collective neurosis about a murderer at large on our beaches, murdering the tourists, and you go wandering off into the Grands Fonds." He banged his hand against the steering wheel. "Bouliqui? Tell me I'm dreaming."

"Wake up, Arnaud."

"You're in charge of the whole enquiry and you can stop being flippant. Your attitude's far from helpful."

"No need to shout, Arnaud. Sign of moral weakness—and I'm not deaf."

"I'm not shouting."

"You're shouting, Arnaud."

"I'm very angry."

"You have no right to be angry. Parise and Lafitte—"

"Anne Marie, you're responsible. You shouldn't have allowed any autopsy before identification."

She turned away, looking out of the car window. "Madame Vaton lives in France—there wasn't time and the body had started to decompose. There could have been sperm, for heaven's sake."

"Was there?"

Anne Marie shook her head. "It was lucky Bouton was back from France . . ."

The *procureur* placed his hand against his forehead. "Are you serious?"

Anne Marie turned to look at him. "Melodramatic gestures don't become you, Arnaud."

The *procureur* was a tall man, with sandy hair and stooped shoulders. There were beads of perspiration on the freckled forehead. He said, "I thought I could count on you." He put a cigarette to his mouth while the other hand remained on the steering wheel. "Why are you wasting your time and mine in the Grands Fonds?"

"I've got a cold coming and the morgue . . ." Anne Marie let her head drop back onto the upholstered rest. "I took Madame Vaton back to her hotel. And then went to Tarare beach."

"In the Grands Fonds, working no doubt on the Dugain dossier."

"You gave me the Dugain dossier, Arnaud." A smile she could not hold back.

Very slowly he inhaled on the cigarette. "It's not a joke. We're talking about your career—and mine."

"What do you expect me to do? The only thing we can do now is go back to the beginning."

Smoke came from his nostrils. "Bouliqui," he muttered under his breath.

"I'm not at my best in the morgue, Arnaud . . . Twice in less than a day."

"Three times." The *procureur* grimaced. "We're going to the hospital now, Anne Marie."

"Jesus Christ," Anne Marie said under her breath.

He frowned. "I thought you were Jewish."

"Not the first time you'd be way off base. Send Parise or Lafitte."

"You're coming with me, Anne Marie."

"No."

35
Préfet

"I need an arrest, Anne Marie."

"I don't see how we can arrest anybody without knowing who the victim is."

"Arrest Desterres, for heaven's sake." He nodded and the reflected afternoon sunlight of a passing car illuminated the angular face. "We've got to be seen to be doing something."

"Did you know that Desterres and Dugain were friends?"

"Don't talk to me about Dugain."

Anne Marie used her schoolteacher voice. "There's no way I can connect Desterres with the death of the unidentified girl who's now in the morgue."

"There's the bikini—follow it up."

"Ninety francs in any Prisunic." She went on, "We were assuming the victim was Vaton. We were wrong."

"Where is this damned Vaton girl if she's supposed to be alive?"

Anne Marie shrugged. "She hired a car, left it at the Pointe des Châteaux last Sunday and hasn't been seen since. Because the victim's more or less of the same age, I assumed the dead girl was Vaton. I also assumed the dead girl was white."

"She's what?"

"You're just as much to blame as I am."

"The corpse isn't white?"

"Next time, Arnaud, I'd like you to come to the autopsy."

"What color, Anne Marie?"

"Mixed blood, probably a local woman—pale skin, but she's not European. Docteur Bouton thought she might be from North Africa."

"That's your fault, Anne Marie."

"There are times, Arnaud, when you are truly pathetic. When you sent the helicopter for me, you told me the girl had been identified as Vaton."

"That is absurd."

Anne Marie caught her breath. "Arnaud, there's no point in arguing. We're checking with Air France, Air Guadeloupe and the other airlines to see if a Vaton has left the *département* over the last four days."

"Good."

"By the way, we found Richard, the Indian."

"Congratulations."

"I hope you're not being sarcastic. Richard was probably the last person to see the dead woman alive—that is, if it is the dead woman in the picture and not Evelyn Vaton. According to Desterres, the woman in the photo left Tarare beach with him."

"Where was your Richard?"

"At Tarare, at the Pointe des Châteaux. He was wandering around in a bit of daze."

"I thought you were in the Grands Fonds."

"Your worst problem is you never listen, Arnaud. I don't think Richard's slept for several days. Or washed. He came up to me and I recognized him from the photograph. He was completely naked."

"I hate to think what you recognized."

"Name's Ferly and he works in a bank. I can't get a straight answer out of him."

"Now you know how I feel, Anne Marie."

"He seems to be amnesiac. Trousseau ran him back to the hospital."

The *procureur* clicked his tongue. "It's not the Vaton girl I'm concerned about. It's the dead woman."

"For all you know, I've found the murderer," Anne Marie replied hotly. "I needed to talk to the woman who has a snack bar at the Pointe des Châteaux." Anne Marie added, "The murder and the disappearance of the Vaton girl are connected. If we can get hold of Vaton, then we'll have an answer."

"Find her, Anne Marie."

"What do you think we're trying to do?"

"A little less than nothing."

"I never asked for this job." Anne Marie could feel the blood rising to her face. "We'll be a lot closer to closing this case once I've spoken to this Richard."

"Don't go prancing off into the Grands Fonds again."

"You don't know what I was doing in the Grands Fonds, Arnaud."

"I know you weren't looking for the murderer."

"Perhaps Richard's the murderer. What more do you want?"

"I want the *préfet* off my back, Anne Marie. There's a dead tourist whose name I don't know lying in the morgue."

"You want a miracle?"

"The *préfet* wants a miracle, the public wants one. I want a miracle and beatification."

They had reached the edge of the city. "You want my resignation too, Arnaud?"

"No need to overreact."

Anne Marie folded her hands on the Texier bag. "I'm beginning to get fed up."

"You're the only one who's fed up?"

"Fed up with you."

"Stop acting the temperamental female."

"Fed up with you, fed up with the SRPJ, with the *gendarmerie*. I'm fed up with the honest folk of Guadeloupe and if you want me to resign, you only have to say the word."

There was a long silence.

"Say the word, Arnaud."

The Volkswagen slowed and the *procureur* clumsily changed gear. It was not until after the sharp curve near the university that he glanced at her. His face had softened. The line of his eyebrows was raised in sympathy. "I need you, Anne Marie."

"I can do without your bullying me."

He touched her knee. "Anne Marie, I must have an arrest."

"That's not my job."

"When are you going to interrogate this Richard?"

"That depends on the doctors, Arnaud."

"Then haul Desterres in again. That's not much to ask you, is it? Haul Desterres in again but without his lawyers. With a bit of luck, perhaps you can get a confession out of him."

36
Courtesy

Yet again Anne Marie was impressed by Trousseau's courtesy. He was polite and thoughtful. He did everything to help the old gentleman. Trousseau proffered his arm for Monsieur Lecurieux to lean an unsteady hand on.

The woman smiled and shook her small head. "In his own time."

Madame Lecurieux had a thin face, grey hair hidden beneath a madras scarf and bright hazel eyes. She must have been over seventy years old, but she walked erect. She moved slowly, her shoulders held back. She gave the impression of dignity, a retired schoolteacher who had lost none of her authority or her desire to set a good example.

(Anne Marie was reminded of her husband's grandmother, who had been so kind to Anne Marie in the early years of their marriage, who had gone out of her way to help the young outsider feel at home in a West Indian family. M'man Jeanne herself had given birth to five children but had never been married; Gaston, the man she had shared her bed with, the man who was Jean Michel's grandfather, had gone on to marry Ondine, a light-skinned mulatto from Martinique.

M'man Jeanne had died the day after Hurricane Hugo at the age of ninety-two. Anne Marie had not been invited to the funeral—Jean Michel's family still held Anne Marie responsible for the divorce. When Anne Marie had belatedly heard M'man Jeanne's obituary over the radio, she had sent a wreath, lit a candle and cried.)

"This way, *madame*."

Madame Lecurieux was followed by her husband.

The man wore a suit and in the same hand that held a walking stick, grasped a cream colored panama hat. It looked new, with its longitudinal crease and its broad black band. A necktie and a stiff wing collar, the formal wear of his youth. A pair of rimless glasses were perched on the ridge of his nose. With the passage of time, the unforgiving steel had carved a niche into the golden flesh. His skin was now creased by age and freckled with cancer. His head was ringed by a crescent of white hair. The dome of his head was bald.

He followed his wife toward the observation window, leaning on Trousseau's arm.

The *procureur* had been sitting beside Anne Marie. Arnaud now stood up and approached the elderly couple. They shook hands.

The *procureur* ran a hand nervously through his hair. "Most appreciative, Monsieur and Madame Lecurieux."

On the other side of the window, Léopold nodded toward Anne Marie and gave his conspiratorial grin. He was holding an *Akim* comic book in his hand and Anne Marie wondered if it was the same as yesterday. A slow reader.

Yet again the corpse on its gurney was hoisted into view.

"This is where we came in." Anne Marie this time controlled her emotion. Forewarned, she had sprayed her wrists with van Cleef and Arpels and placed a shawl over her shoulders. She did not sneeze but kept her eyes on Madame Lecurieux, whose taut features were brightened by light from the far side of the thick glass.

The eyes did not blink; they stared at the corpse as Léopold pulled back the covering sheet.

"Monsieur and Madame Lecurieux, do you recognize this body? Is this the young woman who was staying with you in Basse-Terre?" The *procureur* hesitated, very embarrassed. He said less formally, "Please take a careful and close look. Do you know this young woman?"

Monsieur Lecurieux tapped his wife gently and reassuringly. Behind the glasses, his old, weary brown eyes were damp with tears.

37
Ylang ylang

It had been raining in Pointe-à-Pitre and the tarmac glistened.

"I will get somebody to run you back to Basse-Terre."

"There's no need." Madame Lecurieux shook her head. "We're staying with my brother."

"It's very kind of you to have driven up from Basse-Terre. You're quite certain it's Evelyne Vaton?"

The old woman bit her lip. "She's my daughter's friend. We didn't see very much of her—other than at meal times. Most of the time she was off visiting places or in her bedroom. But yes, that's her."

"Evelyne Vaton?"

Madame Lecurieux nodded. "In death . . ." She did not finish her remark.

"In death a corpse gets darker," Anne Marie explained. "We failed to notice she was West Indian—everybody thought she was white." Apologetically, she added, "Docteur Bouton thought she was from North Africa."

Anne Marie had sent Trousseau on to wait at the main entrance. She wanted to be alone with the couple; there were questions she needed to ask.

Night had fallen and the wind was cool and pleasant. It rustled through the high palm fronds.

"The dead woman probably stole Evelyne Vaton's driving license."

"She's not Evelyne Vaton?"

"No." Anne Marie said. "She was pretending to be. She stole the driving license and credit card that she used to hire her car from Hertz."

"Pretending to be my daughter's friend?"

"I don't know how else to explain it." Anne Marie shook her head. "Did she talk about your daughter to you?"

"She didn't talk very much at all."

"But she did talk to you?"

"About Guadeloupe. About her holidays here."

"You ever sense she didn't know your daughter?"

"Not really."

"You realized she was of mixed blood?"

Madame Lecurieux laughed. "Her backside's not a white girl's."

"Steatopygous." Anne Marie smiled. "The sort of backside that men like."

"I don't have to tell you why."

"Evelyne Vaton's mother was here this morning." Anne Marie gestured toward the hospital behind them. "It's not her daughter."

"If it's not Evelyne, who is it?"

"Somebody pretending to be Evelyne Vaton." Anne Marie paused. "As a result of her pretense, she got herself murdered."

Monsieur Lecurieux had difficulty in walking and they made their way slowly down the hill toward the boulevard, now busy with the weekend traffic. The hospital rose up like an illuminated castle behind them. There was the heady perfume of ylang ylang in the wet air. Monsieur Lecurieux leaned on his tipped walking stick.

"When will you return to Basse-Terre, Madame Lecurieux?"

"Why was the poor thing murdered?"

To her surprise, Anne Marie found herself relieved—even pleased to be in their company. There was something reassuring about the old couple, human and authentic. Madame Lecurieux reminded her of M'man Jeanne.

"Why was the poor thing murdered? You didn't answer my question, *madame le juge.*"

"Because I don't know the answer."

"A nice girl, very friendly. Well-behaved even if she was pretending to be someone else."

"Madame Vaton's convinced her daughter Evelyne—the real

Evelyne—is somewhere in Guadeloupe." Anne Marie was between the two old people. From time to time she guided the man's elbow.

"She didn't recognize the body? It's not a friend of her daughter's?"

"No, Madame Lecurieux."

"So who is this poor girl?"

"If I knew, I wouldn't be here asking you questions."

"I never dreamed she was lying to me."

"She was lying to you or Madame Vaton's now lying to me."

"Madame Vaton must have a photograph of her own daughter."

Anne Marie said, "The victim seems to have looked like Evelyne Vaton."

"You can smell the ylang ylang, *mademoiselle*?"

Anne Marie smiled, turning back to Monsieur Lecurieux. "I am forty-two years old, Monsieur. I am *madame*, not *mademoiselle*—I have two children."

"A bit louder," Madame Lecurieux said. "My husband is going deaf."

"The ylang ylang," the old man repeated.

"I can smell the ylang ylang, yes." Anne Marie raised her voice. She turned, addressing the woman. "I've been promising myself an Azzaro perfume for months—with an ylang ylang base."

"You like perfumes?"

Anne Marie nodded. "I just never get time to go shopping."

"I like the perfume you're wearing now." Monsieur Lecurieux smiled. "It's nice."

"Ideal for the morgue."

"A lovely tree, the ylang ylang—but its roots break everything that gets in the way." Monsieur Lecurieux's face was dark beneath the brim of the panama hat. "You remember the ylang ylang we had in Basse-Terre, Gerty?"

The woman squeezed Anne Marie's arm, and whispered, "I'll have to get him a hearing aid. He's getting worse."

"We had to cut it down, because it was bringing down the wall of the garage. You remember?" Monsieur Lecurieux chuckled to himself. The rimless glasses glinted in the reflection of the overhead lights.

"My husband's seventy-eight," Madame Lecurieux said, not without pride.

"You both look very young."

"My husband worked for forty years in the customs and I was a schoolteacher." Another squeeze of Anne Marie's arm. "I've had a good life—a job I loved and a good husband."

"How old's your daughter, Madame Lecurieux?"

She did not reply and Anne Marie repeated her question.

"Geneviève is thirty this year."

"Your only child?"

The woman nodded thoughtfully. "Thirty at the end of July."

They had reached the entrance of the hospital. The parking lot was filling up with evening visitors. Rain glittered on the roofs of the cars. Women along the sidewalk were selling flowers and roasted peanuts. A crowd had formed around a Toyota truck where, in the yellow light of a butane lamp, a man was slicing green coconuts with a neat movement of his machete. He was doing brisk business.

"Your daughter's a lot older than Evelyne Vaton—six years older."

"They worked in the same ward . . . before my daughter started doing the lab work."

"What sort of girl was she?"

"Who?"

Anne Marie gestured again toward the hospital. "You never noticed something strange about Evelyne? Something that might explain why she lied?"

Two men were working the red and white striped barrier at the main gate of the hospital entrance.

"Where do you have to get to, Madame Lecurieux?"

"My husband and I would rather walk. It's not far—my brother lives in the Assainissement. The exercise is good for us."

"I'll accompany you."

"You are a kind person."

Anne Marie laughed. "After the mor—the hospital, this warm air's like a tonic."

"And to think my daughter spends most of her time with dead bodies."

Anne Marie disentangled her arm and walked to where Trousseau sat waiting in the Peugeot. He had left the door open, and he was reading a copy of the Bible propped on his attaché case in the wan circle of light of the ceiling lamp. He had put on his half-frame glasses. When he raised his head from his reading—he reminded her of her law professor at university—she told him that he could leave.

"Won't be needing you this evening, Monsieur Trousseau."

"You don't need me, *madame le juge*? I can go home? Cook myself a meal?"

"Where's Richard?"

Trousseau smiled at her toothily. "They gave him something to make him sleep. On the journey back, he got very talkative. Couldn't get it all out fast enough. Seemed to think somebody wanted to kill him."

"Kill him? Why?"

"He even asked me if I had a gun. He's in the prison section with Docteur Lavigne." Trousseau went on, "Richard Ferly works at the Crédit des Outremers. Everybody thought he was on holiday, seeing his son in Italy. None of his colleagues associated him with the photograph in the *France Antilles*." Trousseau lowered his voice. "He has a history . . . been seeing a psychiatrist for years." He sniffed. "You know what these blacks are like.

"I don't think I do."

"Schizophrenia among blacks is more frequent than among other social or racial groups."

"Where on earth did you get that statistic? *The Watch Tower*?" Before he could reply, Anne Marie said, "*Palais de justice*, seven thirty tomorrow morning. Now hurry home before you starve to death."

"Tomorrow's Saturday."

"Seven thirty, with Lafitte and Parise."

"Saturday, *madame le juge*?"

"Without fail." Without another word, her *greffier* turned off the ceiling lamp, put the car into gear and made his way out of the parking lot.

Anne Marie rejoined the couple. Madame Lecurieux was smiling at her while her husband watched the passing traffic, the car lights dancing on his the lens of his spectacles.

"You really don't have to accompany us. I imagine you want to return to your family, *madame le juge*."

Anne Marie looked at the older woman and smiled. "How do you manage to look so young?"

"I obtained my *certificat d'études* in 1929," the woman replied with pride.

"If Geneviève is thirty, you must have had her fairly late in life."

Monsieur Lecurieux said, "Geneviève is our adopted daughter."

38

Doctors Without Borders

"Her company was agreeable. I spent my working life with children and it's still a pleasure to have young people around. We live a very quiet existence in Basse-Terre, my husband and I. There are times when the television . . ." She paused. "It'd be nice if one day Geneviève could return but I understand she must think about her career." Madame Lecurieux smiled reassuringly. "This girl was used to being with old people. We all got on very well. My husband liked her a lot. Didn't you, Clamy?"

"You didn't, Madame Lecurieux?"

She smiled. "Female intuition."

"What?"

"In the evening, she would go off to her room. The maid'd already cleared the table and my husband was already in bed. Before going off, Evelyne once or twice sat and talked but I bored her with my questions."

"In what way?"

"Clearly she didn't want to talk about my daughter."

"What did the girl talk about?"

"It's true we adopted Geneviève—but that was heaven's blessing. I like to hear about her, hear about her job, hear other people telling me how my daughter's getting on." An apologetic shrug. "I'd ask questions."

"What did the girl reply?"

"That Geneviève's a doctor, and that she was only a nurse."

"What did she tell you about your daughter?"

"She didn't tell me anything I didn't know."

They were returning to the city along the Boulevard Hahn. The yellow headbeams of Friday night traffic danced on the wet pavement and the spinning tires swished by. Anne Marie walked between the old couple, their arms now linked in hers, and she was reminded of the evening promenades with her family in Oran, before the violence put an end to innocent pleasures. "She talked about the hospital?"

Madame Lecurieux shook her head. "She's not an intellectual girl. Sweet and kind. And thoughtful. But her conversation tends to be limited. You must excuse me if I sound a snob . . ."

"What did she speak about?"

"Clothes—that sort of thing. Music—she was interested in *zouk* and all the modern music."

"Nothing about her life in Paris?"

"She has a boyfriend—I asked her about that. I think she's an only child." The woman tugged gently at Anne Marie's arm. "She's not really the sort of person I imagine being the friend of my girl."

"Because she's not the real Evelyne Vaton. What can you tell me about your daughter, Madame Lecurieux?"

"An avid reader. Geneviève has the combined curiosity of her two parents, even if she doesn't have our blood."

"When did you adopt her?"

"That's really not important. We brought her up as our child. It wasn't until she was twelve we told her the truth. She loved us too much to be upset." For a moment, the old woman was lost in recollection. "My greatest joy—you have your children, I am sure you can understand. Always brilliant at school. Geneviève went to the *lycée* in Basse-Terre and won all the prizes. Got a scholarship. The youngest qualifying doctor in her year. She spent a couple of years in Africa with Medecins sans Frontières."

"She has a specialty?"

"She hopes to be a hematologist—which now of course means that she does a lot of work in the lab. A shame, because Geneviève enjoys working with people and she loved doing the wards during the internship, but then the professor offered her a lab job—and what with AIDS and hepatitis and so on . . ."

"AIDS?"

"In Africa, she got depressed seeing the children die. She was in Uganda and she wanted to get back into research." A slight heave of the shoulders. "The professor'll get the Nobel Prize in time. Everybody says that about Professor Schondöffer's research on immunization. She's excited—but then that's Geneviève. Our daughter has to be doing things."

"Very intelligent." Monsieur Lecurieux's walking stick tapped on the sidewalk. They crossed the road, past the hot dog van, the sickly smell of burning grease and the crowd of young people waiting to be served. "We miss Geneviève a lot, don't we, Gerty?"

Anne Marie touched the back of his hand then turned back to his wife. "When did you last speak to your daughter?"

"Before Evelyne came out she telephoned to say she'd like us to put her up, that she worked in the same hospital, that they were best friends."

"You haven't heard from her since?"

Madame Lecurieux shook her head. "My daughter's in Réunion—in the Indian Ocean—for a conference. When I heard about the car being found, I phoned. Just to tell Geneviève what had happened."

"You spoke to your daughter?"

"There's a time lag. I still haven't been able to get through to her."

"Your daughter hasn't phoned you?"

"Geneviève tries to keep in touch, but I would so much like her to give up all this moving around to come back to Guadeloupe, once and for all. She could get a good job here at the hospital or in Basse-Terre. Get married and settle down in Guadeloupe. She's a pretty girl; the boys all doted on her when she was at the Gerville Réache high school. But she must hurry up if she wants to give us the grandchildren Clamy and I want. Time she had children of her own."

(Anne Marie's own mother had died long before Fabrice was born. Before Papa and the two girls left Algeria.)

They walked in silence on a carpet of flame tree petals. "It was the ylang ylang or it was a flame tree that we pulled down, Gerty?"

The two women laughed softly.

"So to answer your question . . ."

"I ask so many."

"I did notice something about Evelyne Vaton, *madame le juge*. About the girl calling herself Evelyne Vaton." A brief hesitation. "I'm not a person to pry—why should I? If Evelyne's my daughter's friend, I know I've nothing to worry about."

"What did you notice?"

"In the evening, she went to her room. She was always in a hurry. My husband was already in bed. She was always in a hurry to smoke."

"You don't approve?"

"Over the phone Geneviève'd reassured me that Evelyne didn't smoke."

Anne Marie shrugged. "She was away from home."

"I don't like to judge people and I know all the young people smoke marijuana now. You hear about it on the television—and it becomes fashionable."

"I'm terrified of my son taking to drugs."

"That's what surprised me."

"What?"

"Children can be difficult at adolescence—it's a time when they're discovering themselves. Girls in particular. You expect teenagers to experiment. To smoke, to drink, to try drugs. You don't expect that behavior from a grown woman who has the responsibility of children."

Anne Marie shook her head. "I don't understand."

"Evelyne Vaton had left her five-year-old daughter in Paris. Smoking marijuana—it's not what you expect from a mother, is it?"

39
Phone

The phone was ringing as Anne Marie ran up the stairs, past Desterres sitting next to a police officer and into the office. She slung her bag onto the table and grabbed the receiver. "Judge Laveaud," she gasped, out of breath.

"Anne Marie?"

"Yes?"

"I phoned your house and Fabrice told me you were still working."

"Just got back from the morgue, Lucette. Third time in two days. Hold the line. I'll turn on the light."

"You can't speak to me in the dark?"

Anne Marie set the phone down to switch on the ceiling lamp and closed the door. The police officer gave a resigned shrug and glanced pointedly at the watch on his wrist. "The dark makes me irritable—my children laugh at me about it," Anne Marie said as she lowered herself onto the chair. She kicked off her shoes.

"You work too hard, Anne Marie. Your job can always wait."

"The *préfet* can't. Nor can Arnaud."

"Fabrice and Létitia need you."

"I know, I know." Anne Marie sighed. "I'm going into the *lycée* tomorrow. Fabrice seems to be acting up and I want to know why."

"A way of compensating."

"Compensating for what, Lucette?" The evening air was cooling fast but Anne Marie was sweating. Her cold was returning; she was going to sneeze.

"Children need to know they're loved. Love is time, Anne Marie."

"It wasn't me who walked out on them," Anne Marie retorted.

"They need you more than the *préfet* or Guadeloupe needs you. Or Arnaud. There are other *juges d'instruction*."

"Is that what you're phoning me about, Lucette?"

"We must talk."

"Let me bring up my children as I think fit. I have a family to feed."

"You need your children just as much as they need you.

"Let me bring up my children as I see fit."

"You need your children for your own wellbeing."

"You should have had children of your own."

There was an awkward silence, then Anne Marie said, "I shouldn't have said that."

"Nearly eight o'clock on a Friday evening and you ought to be at home."

Anne Marie sneezed noisily. She put her head back and looked up, her eyes watering, at the ceiling with its yellow bulb and its familiar zigzags of damp. "I know, I know, I know."

"I need to see you, Anne Marie."

"What for?"

"You've already seen the woman?" A hesitation. "That name I gave you."

"I saw Madame Théodore yesterday."

Lucette Salondy hesitated again. "I haven't been totally honest with you. I'm phoning you from my office. Can you come over now? It's important."

Anne Marie laughed. "You're still at school at this hour?"

"I don't have a family to go home to."

Anne Marie lifted her head and looked at her watch. Nearly five minutes to eight. "There's somebody I've got to see. The *préfet* is breathing down my neck. Can you give me an hour, Lucette?"

Satisfaction in Lucette Salondy's voice. "Not too late, mind, and then we'll take the children for a pizza."

40

Handcuffs

He walked slowly into the room.

Anne Marie frowned, sneezed and took a Kleenex from her drawer. To the police officer, she said. "You can remove the cuffs."

He was dressed in green. He was wearing clothes identical to those of the previous day, except they were cleaner and better pressed. Green trousers, a safari shirt with epaulettes and short sleeves, a green *foulard* tied at the neck. Green canvas shoes.

"I'll probably have to arrest you."

"Don't feel it's an obligation." Desterres rubbed nervously where the handcuff had left a red mark on his wrist. "I'd rather go home."

The enlargement of Polaroid photograph lay on the top of the desk; it had been slipped into a transparent plastic folder for protection.

"We'd all like to go home." Again she sneezed. "It's late, I'm tired and my children are waiting for me. Please sit down, Monsieur Desterres."

"I want my lawyer."

"You're not under arrest, Monsieur Desterres."

"Then why the cuffs?"

"What cuffs?"

"This has gone beyond a joke."

"I agree wholeheartedly," Anne Marie concurred. "First I must ask you several questions." She pushed the folder toward him. "Questions that need to be answered."

Desterres smiled. "I wish to speak to my lawyer."

"What made you come and see me?"

"What am I supposed to do when two policemen appear at my front door?" He glanced sideways at the officer who stood behind him. "I've been five hours with cuffs on my wrists. You treat me like a common criminal."

"Yesterday—Thursday morning you turned up here of your own accord. Unsolicited and unaccompanied, you waited for over an hour to speak with me."

"I'd rather see you than the police." He rubbed again at his wrist. "Perhaps I was wrong."

"How did you know the girl had been murdered?"

He raised his eyebrows in surprise. "It was on the evening news on RFO."

"There was never any mention of the girl being white."

"I beg your pardon?"

"I've just been looking at a video of the evening news," Anne Marie lied. "There's no mention of the girl's race or color, yet you came here, telling me you'd seen the Vaton girl on Sunday morning."

"That is correct."

"The dead girl's not Vaton—and although she has pale skin, she's probably a local girl, probably mixed blood."

Desterres sat back, his body upright, and folded his arms. The handcuffs had left a slight weal.

"Well?"

"The television said a nurse from Paris had been found on the beach. I assumed it was the same nurse from Paris I'd spoken to on Sunday morning—only a few kilometers from the place where the body was found. I never said the woman was white. I thought she was a *Négropolitaine*." He added, "I could see she had West Indian blood."

"Evelyne Vaton doesn't have black blood."

He appeared surprised. "Then it wasn't Evelyne Vaton." Desterres held his hands with the palms outwards. "I'm merely repeating what the girl told me."

"There are things which you've not told me."

No movement of the eyes. "I've not lied to you."

The wind danced at the billowing curtain and outside there was the dull buzzing of a pneumatic drill. After years of neglect, Place de la Victoire was being renovated. (Soon there would be the municipal elections. Despite Berlin and *perestroika*, the Communists were sure to win, as they had won for the last thirty-five years.) The laborers were working overtime; night had fallen and after the rush hour, the cooling evening air carried the tang of the Atlantic.

He nodded toward the plastic folder. "I gave you the photo, *madame le juge*, and the bikini top. I was doing my duty."

There was more shouting from the ground floor and the clatter of heavy feet down the stairs.

"This isn't Evelyne Vaton."

"She never told me her surname."

"You didn't ask, Monsieur Desterres?"

"She was accompanied by the Indian." A movement of the epaulettes. "He called her Véli. That's how she introduced herself."

"We've found Richard, the Indian."

"He'll corroborate everything I've said."

"At the moment he's in the hospital."

"You've arrested him, too?" Desterres smiled, without taking his unblinking eyes from Anne Marie. "*Madame le juge*, Richard knows the woman was alive when she left my restaurant."

"You omitted to tell me you have a criminal record."

An impatient gesture. "There's no reason to keep me here."

"And your criminal record, Monsieur Desterres."

"Merely allegations."

"That is not what I read."

"There can be no criminal record, *madame le juge*, following the presidential amnesty of 1988."

"I don't give a damn about your past."

"I do." The eyes blinked three times in fast succession while he stared at her.

"I care about the murdered girl."

"Precisely because I have been maligned in the past that I immediately came to see you. I repeat: immediately." His lips were pressed together.

"You knew Rodolphe Dugain?"

Another flicker of his eyes. "Why do you ask?"

"Answer my question."

"I am interested in protecting this island's heritage. Dugain chose to think of himself as an ecologist but like all politicians he was more interested in power than ecology, more interested in himself than in nature." A shrug. "Now he is dead."

"You knew each other well?"

"When I stood for election, he gave me his support. Dugain wanted power—and, of course, money. Ecology was a means for him—not an end. My approach worried him. Couldn't understand what made me tick."

"What makes you tick if you're not interested in money, Monsieur Desterres?"

"I've never been poor—and I have no desire to be rich. I don't need to buy up apartment blocks and let them out at exorbitant rates. I can live well enough on what I have. Dugain belonged to the old generation—the generation that believes progress is a fast car, more tarmac and ugly condominiums on pristine beaches."

"Dugain didn't take the environment seriously?"

"The only thing Dugain took seriously was his power base. He was black and like all blacks, he felt he had to show that he was just as good, if not better, than anybody else."

"You don't consider yourself black?"

"The time will come when we mongrels will inherit the earth."

"Mongrels?"

"*Madame le juge*, look at all the people suffering from sickle cell disease. All they had to do was marry an outsider, and the danger of a genetic disease like anemia would have disappeared. I'm proud of being a mongrel—black blood, African blood. I also have English blood—and Corsican blood. I am not ashamed of what I am."

"Dugain was ashamed of what he was?"

"Show me someone from Martinique who isn't."

"Harsh words."

"Martinique likes to look down on Guadeloupe."

"*The gentlemen of Martinique, the honest folk of Guadeloupe?*"

"They consider us peasants."

"Why did Dugain get involved in the environment?"

"I never said Dugain was a fool, *madame le juge*." Desterres took a deep breath. "There was a time—before he began to smell power—when he was honest. Ten, fifteen years ago when no one had ever heard the word ecology, when politicians were vying with each other to fill the mangrove with concrete. Dugain was the first to speak out and he did useful work saving the mangrove around Pointe-à-Pitre." A pause. "Later he sold out, but by then he was spending money at the casino in Gosier."

"What money?"

"There's always money for politicians in our *département.*"

"Including yourself, Monsieur Desterres?"

"If money'd been my motivation, I could've gone into an alliance with Dugain and his pals." He paused. "My family is not *nouveau riche.* We've been here a long time after having moved down to Trinidad when Victor Hugues and the French Revolution set up their guillotine and started chopping off the heads of the aristocrats." He looked at her without blinking. "A jumped-up mulatto from Martinique."

"Victor Hugues?"

"Dugain'd done good work on the mangrove—and dined off that for ten years. The mangrove was excellent for his profile among the researchers at the university, and through them, with the Ministry of the Environment."

"You got Dugain to give a job to a young lady."

Silence.

"Mademoiselle Augustin—Marie Pierre Augustin—tells me you helped her get a job in Dugain's shop."

"She can also tell you why I helped her."

"You raped her."

"I've never raped anybody." He began to lose control of the immobile face. "Why do you accuse me of rape? Why not the Indian? He was with the damn nurse. Why don't you accuse him?"

"You helped Mademoiselle Augustin find a job with Dugain and now she has sufficient funds to travel to Brazil with her friend and to set up a little business in leather goods."

"I know nothing about that. With a male friend?"

Anne Marie nodded.

Desterres's blank face broke into a broad smile.

41
Millet

"Geneviève Lecurieux?"

Anne Marie watched carefully as he ran the back of his hand across his mouth. "You knew her? Before the meeting at Tarare beach, had you ever met Geneviève Lecurieux?"

"You think the nurse was Geneviève Lecurieux?" The unblinking eyes stared back at her.

"You are going to lie?"

"Why should I lie?"

"You're scared and because there's something you wish to hide."

"I've told you the truth."

"Monsieur Desterres, you knew it wasn't Vaton who was killed."

He raised his hand in a spontaneous gesture of protest. "I knew nothing, *madame*, and I still don't."

"You knew Evelyne Vaton was a friend of Geneviève Lecurieux."

He shook his head. "I haven't seen Geneviève Lecurieux in a very long time." A dismissive shrug. "She lives in Paris. She's a doctor, not a nurse. It was a young nurse I met on the beach. Along with the strange Indian. What has any of this got to do with Geneviève?"

"The murdered woman was staying with Geneviève's family."

"She said she was in Basse-Terre—nothing else."

"Vaton and Lecurieux work in the same hospital." A pause. "Lecurieux was with Richard and the murdered girl—but you didn't tell me." She folded her arms. "That's lying."

Although the evening air was now cool, there were large patches of sweat under the arms of Desterres's green shirt. Perspiration pearled his forehead. "As far as I know, Mademoiselle Lecurieux's in Paris."

"Perhaps you can tell me who you spent Sunday afternoon with?"

"I met the two people on Sunday morning."

"There was another woman, wasn't there, Monsieur Desterres?"

"No." He ran his tongue along the pale lips.

"You don't have an alibi for Sunday afternoon."

"I was in my restaurant."

"Until what time?"

"Until the last customer had left . . . eight, nine o'clock in the evening."

"The girl was murdered around midnight on Sunday night."

"She left with the Indian. I never saw her again."

He licked his lip again as he turned to glance at the police officer sitting by the door. The eyes were slightly bloodshot.

The ocean breeze wafted through the open window, tugging at the lace curtain.

"Well, Monsieur Desterres?"

"I've told you everything, *madame le juge.*"

"There was another woman, wasn't there?"

Desterres looked at her without speaking, without blinking.

"You've nothing to add?"

"You've already made up your mind."

Anne Marie opened her drawer. She took out the black and white photograph. Without looking at them—the closed eyes and the false tranquility of death—she pushed it toward him. "This is the woman in the morgue."

Taking the photograph he frowned slightly, but there was no hint of recognition.

"Do you know this woman?"

"Whatever I say," Desterres said, holding the photograph at a distance from his eyes, then looking up at Anne Marie, "I get to spend the night at the *maison d'arrêt.*"

Anne Marie made a movement of irritation with her hand. She pointed at the photograph. "Do you know this woman?"

"Geneviève has parents here, people who know her. This isn't her."

"Who is it?"

"The nurse who called herself Véli."

From the open drawer she pulled out a thick pad of lined paper.

"I think it's the nurse. I'd never seen her before and once she left, I never saw her again. She went off with the Indian. It's not Lecurieux. You're bent upon arresting me—so why bother asking me? Ask the other witnesses—the two gays on the beach."

"Who?"

"They saw me. A schoolteacher and another man—he's a technician at RFO by the name of Léonidas. Check with him—but you won't, will you, because it's me you want to put in the shit." Desterres emitted a rasping laugh as he handed the photographs back to her. "You'll regret the mistake, *madame le juge*."

Anne Marie looked at the photograph. A full frontal view— narrow hips and large breasts. The girl must have been pretty, a pleasant face and youthful body. Now she was dead. Dead and unclaimed in the city morgue. Repressing a sigh of empathy, Anne Marie placed the photographs back in the folder.

There was a mocking tone to Desterres's voice, "It certainly isn't Geneviève Lecurieux."

Anne Marie nodded to the policeman, who, catching her eye, stood up.

"Phone her—Lecurieux should be in Paris."

"Should be, Monsieur Desterres?"

"She's one of those women who aren't interested in men. There was a time—a long, long time ago—when Geneviève was interested in the environment." He paused. "Five, six years ago before she went off to Africa. I've had no news—she's probably pounding millet in Togo and getting back to her African roots."

Anne Marie took out the enlargement of the Polaroid—the photograph of Desterres, the dead girl and Richard. "You admit this is you?"

"Of course—and that is the nurse. And that's the crazy Indian."

"Crazy?"

Desterres smiled. "For an intelligent woman, you don't have much of an understanding of men."

"What do you mean?"

"Men resort to physical violence when they can't satisfy their needs in other, more persuasive ways. I may not be intelligent, I may not be rich and I have good reason to believe I'm not physically prepossessing—but rest assured, *madame le juge*, there's no shortage of women in my bed." He smiled. "At least, there used not to be, before we all started to worry about AIDS."

"Monsieur Desterres, you know this girl and I'm convinced you know what happened to her. You came to see me to protect yourself."

The policeman was standing behind Desterres and held the unlocked handcuffs in his hand.

42
Luc

"Luc, I was just about to leave."

"Glad I caught you."

"What did you want to tell me?"

"I'm not going to be available over the weekend."

"You told me that this morning."

"I wanted to hear your voice, Anne Marie."

"If you want to hear my voice, you can give me a ring during the week."

"Why are you so aggressive?"

"Your wife isn't waiting for you?"

"I missed you and now that I phone you, you start to attack me."

"Luc, I'm tired."

"I know you're tired and I want to be of help."

"That's why you accuse me of attacking you?"

"I want to help. I'm your friend, remember?"

"It's been a long day. I was in the morgue again this evening. I seem to spend my time talking to people whose company I could easily do without."

"You can do without my company?"

"Luc, why do you take everything so personally?"

"I'd like to see you."

"You have your wife."

"We've had this conversation before, Anne Marie."

"Precisely."

"I'd willingly get a divorce. You've only to say the word."

"Luc, let's not go into all that. Not now. Another time, but not now."

"You never want to talk."

"In bed, I recall it was you who refused to talk."

"At two in the morning I'm not really interested in the difference between male and female pubic hair."

"I can understand that, Luc."

"Can you understand I'm your friend?"

"Go home, Luc. I'm sure your wife'll be pleased to see you, and unlike me, she won't be aggressive. She loves your company and she isn't difficult as I am. She won't wake up in the night and make unreasonable demands. Perhaps she doesn't care about female pubic hair—and even less about male pubic hair. A good and loving wife, you don't want to lose her. She can give you all the warmth and affection an aggressive magistrate could never give you. Then in the middle of next week, if you really feel you want to talk to me—about pubic hair or my aggressiveness—you can give me a ring. But only if you feel like it. Goodnight, Luc, and have a pleasant weekend."

43

Corsica

The *procureur* had appeared out of the crowd. He smiled tensely and took Anne Marie by the arm.

The reflected light on a steel helmet reminded her of Algeria and she felt fear in her belly—fear that took her back to 1958.

The rue Henri IV had been sealed off to traffic. One or two cars remained, perched with two wheels on the sidewalk outside the school. The police had set red tape across the road to keep the hushed crowd at a distance.

The air away from the sea was warm and damp.

Bright beams were trained on the front of the school. Two men with machine guns and leather boots, heavily overdressed in the tropical night, their bodies bulky beneath the flak jackets, were like insects caught against the pink wall.

The center of the city had fallen silent, apart from the croaking threnody of the frogs. The crowd did not speak. From somewhere far distant came the wail of a siren and the approaching *clap clap clap* of a helicopter rotor blade.

One of the officers gestured and the two men moved sideways, out of the circle of light, toward the nearest of the CRS vans.

Bastia was in charge. He stood behind the Renault truck, holding the transmitter loosely in one hand, while in the other he had a hailer. He was not in uniform and Anne Marie noticed incongruously that he wore scuffed boating shoes without socks. He was blaspheming in his soft, Corsican accent.

Beside him, two unsmiling men had trained their rifles on the school. Another man had climbed onto the roof of the optician's.

"Tell Bourguignon to switch that damn light off." Bastia turned and caught sight of Anne Marie. "A rasta and he's already killed someone." He saluted perfunctorily.

"Who?"

"About five minutes ago there were was the sound of gunfire. Somebody crying and then another explosion."

"Who?" Anne Marie spoke with difficulty. A knot in her gut. "I was on the phone to Lucette about an hour ago," Anne Marie said.

"Lucette?"

"Miss Salondy—the headmistress. My sister-in-law. She's in her office."

Bastia rubbed his chin unhappily, looking at Anne Marie.

"Where's Miss Salondy now?"

Bastia pointed to the administration buildings where Anne Marie had been talking with Lucette, where the two women had walked across the yard, between the trees, beneath the pendulous, unripe mangoes swaying gently at the end of their long stalks. Where Anne Marie had been reminded of her school years in Algeria.

"The perpetrator's hiding there. He's armed—and he's already killed the janitor. Stabbed in the heart with a syringe."

Anne Marie ran a hand along her forehead. "Arnaud, give me a cigarette." Overhead, the helicopter hovered and cast down its cone of bright light onto the corrugated roofs.

"Stupid bastards," Bastia said, and rasped an order into the walkie-talkie.

"Can't be many people inside the school at the moment."

The *procureur* asked, "How are you operating?"

Bastia gave the *procureur* a brief glance, devoid of sympathy. "Waiting for you, *monsieur le procureur*." If he was being sarcastic, there was no hint of it in his voice. "I've sent three men in through the back, through the *boulangerie* in the rue Sadi Carnot. Equipped with tear gas and stun grenades but no night vision, I'm afraid. The helicopter's working as a decoy. At the moment we don't know what kind of firepower he's got and we don't know who he's got in there with him."

"Hostages?"

"He mixes his French with Dominican Creole. I can't understand his English. High on ganja or something. Up there"—he pointed— "behind the window. Screaming a minute ago, saying he was going to kill everybody."

"Is he going to kill everybody?"

"We tried to phone into the school but nobody's answering," Bastia said. "You can hear the phone ringing from here. Ignorant bastard probably doesn't know what a telephone is. Immigrants. Too many damn immigrants in this island."

"Where exactly is he?"

"There's the concierge and his family still in there. From what the Dominican seems to be saying, there are two women with him."

"You could drop somebody onto the roof."

"Corrugated iron, *monsieur le procureur*. If our rasta gets suspicious, he'll shoot through the ceiling."

"A risk we'll have to take."

"No point in losing a set of balls." Bastia grimaced at Anne Marie. The *procureur* asked dryly, "The *préfet*'s been informed?"

A rising note of irritation in Bastia's voice. "I don't know who's informed. I just try to stop the bullets."

"Give me that speaker," the *procureur* said, holding out his hand. "And get me the phone. We'll have to get him to calm down. Set of balls or otherwise. This is Pointe-à-Pitre—not Beirut. Or Corsica."

44
Aftermath

It was a modern, lightweight mask, but it was nonetheless uncomfortable, pulling at the skin of her face. Anne Marie had the feeling she looked like a snub-nosed black pig. She still had the taste of Arnaud's cigarette in her mouth. Her head had begun to spin.

She wanted to sneeze, to vomit. Above all she wanted to get away, escape from the noise and the smoke. Take off the bulletproof jacket and escape. Escape with Lucette, go somewhere safe.

The Cacharel skirt was filthy.

From where Anne Marie was standing, the Rastafarian appeared to be sleeping.

He was slumped on a chair and from between his long, delicate fingers, a copy of the *Bulletin Officiel de l'Education Nationale* had fallen to the floor. His skin was the color of tobacco and his hair hung around the sharp face in matted locks. Beside his bare feet was a woolen bonnet, grubby and knitted in the green, yellow and black of Abyssinia. A large bruise above one eye.

Blood on the wall, beneath the photograph of a placid and arrogant President François Mitterrand.

The entry hole in his singlet was scarcely perceptible. The bullet had disintegrated much of his lung and then splattered flesh and blood against the wall.

Two men were crouched down, tentatively touching the corpse.

They had opened the doors and windows but the air still swirled with the fumes of tear gas and cordite.

(Oran. The smell that in the end Papa could no longer endure. The smell of death that had driven Monsieur Bloch and his two daughters and the maid to France and Sarlat-la-Canéda.)

The young man's copper cheeks were damp. He had been dribbling like a child; saliva had run from the corner of his mouth and onto the dirty singlet. A singlet advertising But Baie-Mahault. The eyes were wide open.

Like a zombie, Anne Marie thought, a mindless zombie. Killing and now killed.

The *procureur* was standing beside Anne Marie, bulky in the flak jacket. He said something, but the words were meaningless. He had pushed the mask up onto his forehead.

Anne Marie knelt down beside the woman.

Lucette Salondy, too, was weeping. Her face was grey, drained of blood.

"She's going to die, isn't she?" Anne Marie wanted to gather the large body into her arms and drag her sister, her friend out into the fresh night air. "Going to die." Anne Marie pulled off the mask and immediately the gas began insidiously burning at her unprotected face, burning her eyes and her nostrils. "Why, for God's sake, why?"

Anger, frustration and a welling-up of hate.

Two men—they were not wearing masks but wet handkerchiefs were tied about the mouth—firmly elbowed Anne Marie aside so they could place Lucette Salondy on the stretcher. One set an oxygen mask to the grey face.

A flutter of an eyelid?

Another man wiped Lucette's forehead with a damp cloth.

Anne Marie coughed. "Will she be all right?"

Their faces were damp with tears and their eyes were red as they raised the stretcher. "Is she going to live? She's my sister-in-law." She added pointlessly, "The sister of the wife of my brother-in-law."

"You need some fresh air, *madame le juge.*"

Anne Marie impatiently pushed past the doctor—a friend of Bouton's—and followed the men out of the room, down the wooden stairs and out into the evening.

The fresh air did not stop the gas from burning her eyes, burning into the flesh of her nostrils.

"Care for something to calm you, *madame le juge?*"

"Don't die." She breathed deeply. "Don't die, Lucette, damn it, woman." The gas clung to her clothes and Anne Marie rubbed her face. Then she broke into a run, trying to keep up with the firemen. Her lungs were burning.

The doctor was saying something.

"Don't die, Lucette, please don't die," Anne Marie said over and again, angry, trembling, coughing and crying. A terrible sense of being here before, of having said the same things before. A sense of loss. Impending, permanent loss.

A red van stood waiting in the rue Sadi Carnot, its blue light turning.

The rear door was opened, the stretcher lifted inside and then one of the men held out his hand. Anne Marie took it and clambered aboard. "She's my sister-in-law," she repeated.

As the van started to move forward, a man put a woolen blanket over Lucette Salondy's body. At the same time, he glanced up at Anne Marie, sitting on the bench opposite him.

His eyelids were bright red and his cheeks smeared with tears. There was blood on the black knuckles. He did not try to smile but he handed Anne Marie a plastic bottle of water, a bottle that cyclists used.

45
Bloodshot

Saturday, May 19, 1990

The telephone rang.

The doctor's pill had taken its effect and while Anne Marie was sleeping, the children had dressed, eaten the breakfast that Béatrice prepared and gone off to school in a neighbor's car, whose imperious hooting had failed to disturb Anne Marie's drugged sleep.

It was nearly eight o'clock when Anne Marie finally opened eyes that were still hot and irritated. Too late for the telephone that had ceased to ring just as she picked it up.

"My God."

Anne Marie sat up slowly in the dark, chill bedroom and shook her head. She turned and replaced the telephone in its cradle. Her neck was stiff. The conditioner hummed.

She could still taste the cigarette in her mouth, a taste of ashes, and smell the tear gas on her skin. She ran her hand across her lips, then got up, flung open the blinds, went to the kitchen, put on the coffee and returned to the telephone.

All the lines to the hospital were engaged.

With her left hand, she flicked through the pages of the directory, trying to find another number for the hospital. *Centre hospitalier régional* Pointe-à-Pitre/Abymes.

Nothing.

The pleasing smell of percolating coffee came from the kitchen—normality, a smell that reminded her of her childhood.

Anne Marie sighed, then rang her office at the *palais de justice*. It took over a minute to get through.

"Why didn't you call me, Trousseau?"

"Is that part of my job?"

"I left a message."

"I just rang you."

"What's the news from the hospital?"

"I assumed you were sleeping."

"Lucette Salondy—my sister-in-law."

"You were with her until past midnight, *madame*."

"Tell me how she is." She could hear Trousseau's breathing. "Just tell me how she is. You've been to the hospital?"

"She's under sedation."

"Give me the number, will you?"

"Overweight and diabetic. I rang at seven o'clock. As soon as I found your message on the answering machine. She'll be in intensive care for some time."

"Why intensive care?"

"There may have been damage to the skull. When she fell, she struck the table with the back of her head."

"Who did you speak to at the hospital?"

"Perhaps you'd like to ring."

"I can't get through."

Trousseau laughed. "I called again about half an hour ago but there was no answer on Bouton's extension. Extension three-oh-seven. Ten minutes just to get them to pick up the phone in that place. Saturday morning and in the People's Republic of the City Hospital, it's an English weekend." The humorless laugh. "What they call decentralization. West Indies run by West Indians." A pause. "Give me the bad old days any day."

"No visitors?"

"Not until at least Monday."

"Lucette's not even sixty years old."

"You're going to take the day off, *madame*?"

It was some time before Anne Marie replied, "I'm not overweight and I'm not diabetic."

"You need the rest after last night."

"Are Lafitte and Parise there, Trousseau?" Again she rubbed her eyes. The hissing of the coffee machine.

(Nobody could make coffee like the Berber maid. She had helped Papa bring up the children after Anne Marie's mother died in 1955. Nassérine, with little Arabic and no French, spent her time toing and froing between the kitchen, the laundry and Papa's bedroom.)

"Before going over to Carnot, I was with Desterres. Trying to get a confession out of him."

"And?"

"Nothing—other than he knew Mademoiselle Lecurieux."

"You didn't arrest him?"

"On what grounds?"

Trousseau said in an aggrieved voice, "I'm only a *greffier, madame.*"

"If the autopsy's correct, there was no rape and there are no grounds for his arrest—whatever my friend Arnaud says."

"You seem to think I've studied the law."

"I'm going to the television station later today. According to Desterres, one of the gay men on the beach at Tarare can support his alibi. Léonidas—a technician called Léonidas."

"You seem to think I've studied law like you, that I have every Dalloz at my fingertips, that I'm party to the workings of our judicial forces. A *greffier, madame.* An Indian and a *greffier.* My wife may be a white woman like you, but I'm an Indian." Trousseau coughed and she could imagine him running his finger along the line of his moustache.

"You have a friend at the Pointe des Châteaux—she finds you very attractive, Monsieur Trousseau."

"Despite a night's rest, your sarcasm has lost none of its sting, *madame le juge.*"

"Olga calls you Alphonse."

"You know my name, *madame le juge.*"

"Nat King Cole?"

There was an indignant silence.

Anne Marie rubbed her face again. "Any developments from Lafitte and Parise?"

"Lafitte checked with Air France. Air France checked with the other airlines—American, LIAT, even the Venezuelans at Aeropostal. Nobody by the name of Vaton on any flight. The only reference is for the AF flight she came out from France on." A pause. "May fifth, 1990."

"So the Vaton girl is here somewhere."

"Perhaps she was murdered—or kidnapped—and then the dead girl took her credit card." He added, "Carte Bleue, supplied through the Banque Nationale de Paris, through the branch in the Place de la Nation, twelfth *arrondissement.* Parise's expecting a fax from Paris and details on what the girl bought."

"If the credit card was stolen, you'd've thought Vaton would inform the Carte Bleue." She rubbed her neck. "The dead girl knew Mademoiselle Lecurieux well enough to imitate Vaton—and stay with Lecurieux's parents." Anne Marie sighed. She still felt sleepy and dearly would have liked to lie down again. She rubbed more forcefully at her neck. "Hold the line." She went to the kitchen, put four spoonfuls of sugar into the black coffee—just like Papa. With age she was getting more and more like him, irascible and fixed in her ways.

"I'd better come in."

"You should rest, *madame.*"

"You can wait for me, Monsieur Trousseau?"

"For a charming woman like you? Of course, *madame.*"

"You flatter me."

"Not at all."

"I'll take a taxi." She glanced at her Kelton watch—there was more humidity beneath the plastic. "I'm going to the *lycée* and I should've finished by ten. Come and pick me up at a quarter past ten. At the *lycée*—you can drive into the school."

"There was a very young woman." The sound of his hand being placed over the mouthpiece.

"Who's there, Trousseau?"

His voice came back on the line, clear again, with the strong, nasal intonation of the islands. "I was hoping to get some breadfruit at the market for the weekend."

"Who's with you?"

"A young lady wanted to see you."

"What did she want?"

"To see you."

"Is she still there?"

There was the muffled sound of talking and then laughter.

"Who is she?"

"She left about half an hour ago, *madame le juge.* Said she knows

who the murdered girl was. She recognized the photo and said she'd
be back later in the morning."

"What young lady?"

"You ask her, *madame le juge.*"

Anne Marie knew better than to argue with Trousseau over the
telephone. "Buy your breadfruit, Monsieur Trousseau. But first get
hold of Bouton and find out what's happening to my sister-in-law." A
slight hesitation. "Intensive care?"

"She was out of danger last night by the time you left the hospital.
That is what I was told but I'm merely repeating what people want to
tell me."

She took a sip of the hot coffee. "A good woman, Lucette Salondy."

"Will you be wanting any breadfruit, *madame?*"

"Thanks for the compliment, Trousseau. A charming woman like me."

"Charming, intelligent and loyal."

Anne Marie smiled a weary smile into the mouthpiece. "This
charming, middle-aged woman with bags under her eyes and wrinkles
and the beginning a double chin and with sleeping pills and too
much coffee in the blood—she thanks you for the compliment."

"I was being sarcastic, *madame le juge.* Even Indians can attempt
humor."

46
Baimbridge

She took a local taxi into Pointe-à-Pitre.

The surly driver dropped her off at Baimbridge, on the edge of the ring road. Anne Marie should have told him to do something about the noisy exhaust pipe and the broken headlamps but instead she quietly paid her fare and turned toward the school.

The complex was now nearly thirty years old; the reinforced concrete had weathered with the years, but the architecture remained functional, French colonial and ugly. The metallic blinds were in need of repair and a coat of fresh paint.

Anne Marie had forgotten to ask the driver for a receipt but she was relieved to see that she was going to be on time for the appointment; it was the beginning of the break. An unbroken flow of adolescents—mostly West Indian with one or two whites—was streaming out of the buildings, heading for the vans and a mid-morning snack.

The main entrance to the *lycée* was cluttered with vans—similar to Olga's at the Pointe des Châteaux—selling sandwiches, candy and fruit juice to the pupils who jostled forward, holding out their money while shouting to attract the attention of the vendors.

Anne Marie went up the hill.

The sidewalk was blocked with parked cars—for the most part, middle-market five-seaters that teachers invested in; an occasional BMW, but mainly sensible, well-maintained Peugeots, Citroens and Fords.

The stream of pupils drew apart to let her past. One or two smiled in her direction.

Anne Marie found herself smiling, too. She wondered—and not for the first time—whether she had chosen the right career. Her father had always wanted her to be a schoolteacher. Since returning to Pointe-à-Pitre, Anne Marie had in fact given several courses at the faculty of law and enjoyed the experience.

But teach in a *lycée?*

Motivated, well-dressed and well-behaved adolescents. Eighteen hours' teaching a week. Three months' holiday a year and enough free time to be able to be with Létitia and Fabrice, help them with their school work. Teacher's children, as her father liked to remark, always made good pupils. And she would not be coming now into the school to discuss her son's wayward behavior.

As Anne Marie walked up the incline, she thought she caught sight of Fabrice in a small group of white boys. As she got closer, she realized it was not her son, but the boys, local or white, all looked very much alike in their casual uniform. Surfing T-shirts, long Bermudas, Vuarnet sunglasses on string and sailing shoes; one or two had gold rings in their ear lobes. A couple smoked.

She had been to the *lycée* a couple of times before and had an idea of where the staff room was. Unlike at Lucette Salondy's school, there were no mango or coconut trees here in Baimbridge, just shadowless asphalt, more cars and lots of young people milling around. The *lycée* was so big—nearly four thousand pupils, and judging from the adolescents about her, a majority of girls.

Anne Marie picked her way between the cars and entered the staff room. Nobody took any notice of her. A mix of whites and West Indians, no difference in the style of clothes, the way they spoke or held themselves. The same self-importance that had always irritated her in teachers, the result, no doubt, of their always being right in the classroom.

Anne Marie took a chair and sat down. A man looked up at her and smiled tentatively before returning to a pile of marking.

"You're the supply mathematics teacher?" A woman approached her.

"Madame Laveaud. My son is in *Première Scientifique* Eight. I have a *rendezvous* with Monsieur Siobud."

The woman nodded and returned to a group of teachers. Many

of them were smoking—not Marlboro or Peter Stuyvesant cigarettes but filterless Gitanes and Gauloises. Although the blinds to the staff-room were open and there was a breeze, the air swirled with pungent tobacco smoke.

Pretty young women—it was hard to be sure they were pupils—hovered at the doors, where teachers chatted with them and laughed. There was a relaxed atmosphere that appealed to Anne Marie. Nothing like the *lycée* in Oran or later, in Sarlat, after they had left North Africa for good. And certainly nothing like the *palais de justice*.

Perhaps Papa was right, perhaps she should have become a teacher.

"Madame Laveaud?"

Eighteen hours a week.

47
Proud

Anne Marie stood up and held out her hand.

She had met Siobud a couple of times before at parent/teachers meetings, but she would not have recognized him in a crowd; he was typical of the island's educated middle class. A small, fair-skinned man, well-dressed—designer jeans with a careful crease, Daniel Hechter shirt and a couple of pens clipped purposefully to the breast pocket. Short sleeves and dark forearms thick with hair. In his mid-forties, he had well-cut curly hair that was going grey. White socks, black leather shoes with metal tips. A flat gold watch, several gold teeth.

"You look tired, *madame*." He gave her a prompt smile and placed an attaché case on the table before shaking hands.

Despite a careful shampooing beneath the shower, she could still smell the tear gas in her hair. "I was at the *lycée* Carnot last night—and I wasn't wearing a mask."

"How exciting," he said without lowering his glance. "They say two people died."

Anne Marie nodded. "A man murdered the concierge."

"And the police murdered the man?"

"He was killed by a police officer—acting on the orders of the *préfet*."

"Wasn't tear gas sufficient to pacify him?"

"He was armed—a certain William Williamson. He'd already killed the concierge and the headmistress was being held hostage."

"I heard it was the independence people again."

"A petty criminal living in Boissard. We'd already deported him back to Dominica a couple of times."

"You say 'we,' *madame*."

"I'm an investigating judge."

"I should've remembered—your profession is in your son's *cahier*."

"The murderer's a rasta—dreadlocks and bare feet," Anne Marie said. "We've got no idea why he went berserk."

"A stand against Babylon?"

"The *gendarmerie* tried negotiating but his Dominican Creole was as unintelligible as his English. In the end . . ." Her voiced trailed into silence.

"In France, they complain about clandestine immigration, but the problem's worse here." Siobud clicked his tongue. "Too many Dominicans and too many Haitians."

"The highest standard of living in the Caribbean—only normal that people from the poorer islands should want to come and work in the French islands."

"And give birth in our hospitals." The man invited Anne Marie to sit down. As he took a chair opposite her, he produced a small box of Tampa cigars. "I've got nothing against Haitians and Dominicans. An immigrant myself—like most people on this island, I'm a racial hotchpotch. My mother was white, my father black, my grandmother an original Carib." He lit the cigar. "Hence my high cheek bones, of which I am inordinately proud. I have Arawak blood—my Carib ancestors must've eaten enough of them." He paused. "My children have your color."

"Off-white?"

Siobud laughed, showing his gold teeth and his small tongue flecked with a couple of minute shreds of tobacco. "You must think I'm racist to talk like this of color."

"One thing to define people by their color; it's quite another to judge them because of their color."

"You're an intelligent woman."

"A man always find a woman intelligent when she agrees with him." Anne Marie smiled sweetly. "There are two races on this earth: women and men. Unless of course you consider men a sub-race."

"You have a lot of interesting theories."

"A lot of experience." She continued, "About my son, Monsieur Siobud."

The pale brown face had blushed very slightly. "Fabrice Laveaud?" He chewed thoughtfully at the end of the cigar.

"You've been having a bit of a problem with him of late."

"You could say that."

"I'm not always at home to see that he does his work."

"And his father?"

"I divorced him more than eight years ago."

"Fabrice sees his father?"

"My ex-husband's been in France for over a year, which isn't a bad thing."

"Why do you say that?"

"You have children?"

Siobud nodded. "I have custody of my two sons."

"Fabrice's father isn't a good influence."

"Monsieur Laveaud?" The teacher sucked thoughtfully at the plastic end of the cigar. The cigar had gone out. "Laveaud—was he not the man from Pointe-à-Pitre . . . ?"

Anne Marie held up both hands. "My ex-husband planted a bomb on an airplane. He was fortunate enough to get a presidential amnesty when Mitterrand was elected."

He lit the cheroot. "When I was at the university in Montpellier, there was a Laveaud. Studying law, I believe." Speaking over a cloud of rising smoke, Siobud said, "You resigned, didn't you?"

"My administrative superiors chose to refuse my resignation, maintaining I was not responsible for my husband's actions."

"Something about a trunk being found on the beach?"

"My husband's friends had used my trunk to kidnap somebody." Anne Marie made the same dismissive gesture with her hand that her father used to make, but then she smiled. "At least I have two wonderful children."

"Better single than unhappily married?" He tapped ash from the cigar into an ashtray.

"Fabrice's a very good son—and a good brother to his little sister."

"You could have moved on, got another posting and gone back to France."

"My children are happy here."

"Never tempted to change your name?" Again the smile. "Your husband's name."

"It is also my children's name, and they have nothing to be ashamed of." She smiled, holding his gaze. "At least, as far as my ex-husband's political activity is concerned."

48

Baccalauréat

"Difficult?"

"Madame Laveaud, I have two sons of my own and I know it's not easy to bring them up single handed."

"In what way do you find Fabrice difficult?"

"Your son's an intelligent boy—that's not the problem. He does well without even trying."

"He likes English."

"I'm well aware of that. Good vocabulary that shows he reads in English and that he listens to music."

"My son watches a lot of American television."

"He could be the best in the class. It's not his work."

"It's his attitude?"

"His Spanish teacher agrees." A pause. "Your son doesn't want to be at school."

"He never goes out—apart from windsurfing. Fabrice hasn't got a girlfriend."

"Your son can scrape by on his native wit, but native wit's not sufficient in mathematics and in science. Your son doesn't want to make the necessary effort but chooses instead to be difficult."

"Difficult in what way, Monsieur Siobud?" There was a querulous tone to her voice.

"Sarcastic toward his teachers and his classmates. Your son's not a very popular boy."

She shook her head. "He has lots of friends."

"In class Fabrice's disruptive. Talking, not paying attention and preventing the others from working. There are times when he is elsewhere, daydreaming. At others, he tries to attract attention with puerile remarks. Puerile and obscene remarks." Siobud shrugged. "Which is why I asked to see you."

"At primary school and in *quatrième* and *troisième*, his teachers praised him. They praised him because he was so well-behaved."

"Madame Laveaud, your son's in a good class and all being well, he should sit his scientific baccalaureate next year. All being well but regrettably at the moment all's not well."

Somewhere a bell rang, signaling the end of the break. The staff room was now empty and they were alone.

"The clown of the class. Only nobody is laughing."

"I find that hard to understand, Monsieur Siobud."

"Your son can't afford to lose sight of his future."

People were hurrying along the corridors, beyond the metal blinds.

"You and I—professionally we're both dealing with human beings. Human beings don't always want to make life easy for us or for themselves."

Anne Marie nodded.

"Fifteen years here at Baimbridge—and before that I was in Paris. This is a good *lycée*. There aren't real discipline problems—and when there's conflict, we teachers know we can count on the support of the parents."

"You can most certainly count on me, Monsieur Siobud."

He smiled his appreciation before looking down at his hands that he had placed palm upwards on the table. "When children are difficult, there's always a reason. Nearly always the reason is . . ."

"Yes?"

An intake of breath. "A lack of affection."

"You're suggesting I don't love my children?"

"I'm not a psychiatrist, but in some way, Fabrice's not getting the kind of affection he wants." Siobud held up his hand. "When there's a divorce, there's often a sense of guilt. 'If Maman or Papa has left, it's my fault because I should've been able to keep them together with my love.'"

"If my husband left, it has nothing to do with my son," Anne Marie said hotly. "And it was a long time ago."

"Fabrice may know that—but he may not necessarily believe it."

"I know how my son feels."

"I know how my own boys feel—most of the time." A wry smile as Siobud lightly touched the back of her hand. "Girls are used to crying, to showing they're unhappy but boys are taught from an early age they have to be strong." Siobud sat back in the uncomfortable chair and folded his arms.

"Fabrice has always been very open with me."

"He's turning into a man. There are things he feels he can't tell you."

"Fabrice knows I love him."

Siobud lit another cigar, his eyes watching her from behind the grey smoke. "Sometimes, when we feel the love we want is not forthcoming, we try to provoke it. And if we can't provoke love, we try to provoke other reactions."

"Provoke?"

"The opposite of love is not hate. Hate's a kind of love, a perverted love."

"I love my son."

"Madame Laveaud, I don't have the presumption to say I know what your son thinks. I simply know from experience he's looking for a reaction."

"Why?"

"By causing a reaction, he knows he exists, even if the reaction is negative." A puff of cigar smoke. "Fabrice's making life awkward for me and for himself because his need for love isn't being answered."

"Absurd."

"He's trying to get himself hated." The grin of gold teeth. "Believe me, your son's succeeding."

49
Wife

"Something wrong, *madame le juge?*"

"Of course not." For the eighth time Anne Marie dabbed her forehead with a crumpled Kleenex. "It's hot."

Trousseau had been waiting for at the foot of the hill, sitting in the Peugeot with the door open, reading his illustrated scriptures while occasionally looking up as pretty adolescents left the *lycée*. "Back to the *palais de justice?*" Sunlight bounced off the dark polish of the car's roof.

"Yes."

Nothing wrong other than her son was turning into a juvenile delinquent and that it was her fault.

"Where do these young people get the money from? They can't all be rich but they are all so well-dressed." Trousseau shook his head. "With that kind of money, I could've built myself a villa. In my day, my parents could scarcely afford my books. We wore the clothes handed down from one brother to the next. Eight brothers—plus two girls. We were always clean, mind."

She knew her face was still flushed. "Does the name Siobud mean anything to you?"

"When we were kids, everybody laughed at us because we wore rags, because we had to walk the three kilometers to school. My poor father, God rest his soul, never learned to read and write. Like all the Indians, he had to wait until 1928 before they decided to make us French citizens."

"You know anything of the Siobud family, Monsieur Trousseau?"

"I know nobody." He ran a finger along the thin line of his moustache before rising from the seat and opening the car door for her. "You seem to forget that I'm a *greffier*."

"Siobud?" Anne Marie repeated coaxingly as she slid into the rear seat.

"I don't walk the corridors of power. I keep my own company—it's the best way to avoid problems. The inhabitants of this island enjoy interfering into your affairs, always asking questions and telling lies. They'll even put a curse on you, because they're jealous of your success." He closed the rear door quietly and then took his place behind the steering wheel.

"Well, Monsieur Trousseau?"

"A family from Pointe-à-Pitre, isn't it?" He tapped his chest. He was wearing the same frayed shirt as yesterday. "I've lived in Paris, *madame le juge*, and I know what it's like to live in a big city."

"Of course."

"You seem at last to be aware of the lack of respect your race has shown toward the black man."

"Have I ever shown you a lack of respect?"

"Siobud—try writing it. Or if you prefer, try writing it backward . . . D-U-B-O-I-S."

"I fail to understand."

"You understand perfectly. The superiority of the white race must manifest even in our family names."

"How?"

"When Victor Schoelcher set the black race free, names had to be found for people who'd been little more than beasts of burden. What better way of reminding us how ridiculous we were than by giving us ridiculous names?"

"Dubois written backward?"

Trousseau sighed. "Look in the telephone directory and you'll find names like Nirélep and Noslen, Trébor and Succab, Cirederf, Nomis and Divad. As well as Nègre and Pasbeau, just to inform the world we're black and ugly."

"Do you know Siobud? "

The heave of an exaggerated sigh. "The father had a printing business in rue Moretenol."

"The Siobud who teaches English at the *lycée?*"

"One of those families where the father has enough money to have many children and several mistresses." He turned in his seat to look at her. "Wasn't he married to a white woman?"

"Who?"

Trousseau again ran the finger along the line of his upper lip, and Anne Marie knew he was no longer offended. "The Siobud who teaches. There's a son who works at the dispensary and another at the agricultural institute. A daughter who died in childbirth and whose husband returned to France with the newborn baby and was remarried within a couple of months." His shoulders jerked in soundless amusement. "The Siobuds—they all married whites."

"Love's blind, Monsieur Trousseau."

"Not color blind." He grinned maliciously. "The man you're talking about—Michel Siobud. Small—he was at university in Montpellier studying languages and that's where he met his wife—a woman several years his senior who speaks English."

Anne Marie nodded. "What do you know about him?"

Trousseau put the key into the ignition but did not turn it. "Typical mulattos."

"Pointe-à-Pitre's full of typical mulattos. Guadeloupe is full of typical mulattos."

"Stuck-up and self satisfied. The Siobuds worshipped the whites, despising anybody with a skin that's a shade darker than their own." A dry laugh as he plucked at the dark hair of his arm. "Better than me because I'm black."

"You're not very tolerant yourself."

The eyes flared. "People like the Siobuds've always despised us coolies. Michel's problem is simple. He's a runt."

"I beg your pardon."

"One meter sixty and the blackest skin in the family. With an inferiority complex like that, you can see why he needed to marry a white woman."

"Because he loved her?"

"To gain some self-esteem."

"You married a white woman, Monsieur Trousseau."

"You used to see them in Pointe-à-Pitre, shopping or going to the cinema or in the smart hotels. He was so proud of his wife."

Anne Marie found herself laughing. "What was a coolie like you doing in the smart hotels?"

"Siobud's wife towered head and shoulders over him." He added, "They even held hands in the street and everyone knows West Indian men don't hold hands with their women in public."

Anne Marie asked, "He didn't have mistresses—like his father?"

Trousseau shook his head. "It was his wife who went off, apparently to be with Dugain—but I never believed that."

"Dugain? To be with Dugain, Monsieur Trousseau?" Anne Marie repeated, incredulous.

He grinned widely, looking at her, his arm over the back of the driving seat. "Perhaps you know her. She didn't like the name Siobud—I can understand that. She left him—she even left the children—and reverted to her maiden name."

"How should I know her?"

"She left him with the two boys." Trousseau went on, "It was Dugain who got her the job—a job with an American courier service."

"Madame Théodore?"

Trousseau looked at her and laughed. "That's right. Mademoiselle Théodore."

50

Breadfruit

As soon as he closed the door, the car smelled of overripe breadfruit. A sickly smell made more nauseating by the closeness and heat within the car. Anne Marie lowered the window. More nauseating than Madame Vaton's *eau de cologne*.

"The conditioner's on." Trousseau drove, his illustrated Bible open beside him on the front seat, his thin hands on the wheel.

"You found your breadfruit."

"Nothing wrong with breadfruit." Trousseau stopped for the traffic lights at the Baimbridge roundabout. "I own land in Trois-Rivières. I grow pineapples and I have livestock." He laughed. "When the revolution comes, I'll be able to look after myself."

"What revolution?"

He snorted disparagingly.

The lights changed and the Peugeot surged forward. Wind through the window pulled at Anne Marie's hair. "The hurricane last September put paid to all talk of independence. National solidarity—Guadeloupe can't do without the help of mainland France. Your compatriots were only too glad when they saw professionals flying out from France to get the island back on its feet. Revolution? It's a thing of the past. Six years ago there were riots but it didn't take your compatriots long to see that Faisant's hunger strike was bogus."

"A white teacher had chosen to kick a black pupil in the pants. Monsieur Faisant wanted to denounce French colonial injustice."

"In this *département*, schoolteachers strike children all the time. It is like cockfighting—totally illegal elsewhere in France."

"Young people need discipline, *madame le juge*."

"Discipline that is meted out solely to black children, Monsieur Trousseau. West Indian teachers never strike white kids because they're afraid of the reaction from us white parents."

"Being hit never did me any harm and in my time, young people respected their teachers. I knew I was going to get the same treatment at home, first from my mother and then from my father."

Anne Marie fell silent. They were approaching the city and she looked out of the window at a pack of dogs sniffing at the rubbish spilling from an overturned garbage bin.

"I have land here—and my wife owns property in France. At the first hint of independence we'll be on the first plane out."

"I thought your wife was in France, Monsieur Trousseau."

"There are times, *madame le juge*, when I can't help feeling you're just like the people of this island—in that you seem obsessed by the details of other people's lives."

"Part of my profession." She leaned forward and tapped him lightly on the shoulder. "Well?"

"Well what, *madame?*" Trousseau half turned in his seat.

"The pretty young woman I'm supposed to be meeting."

"Very pretty." Trousseau nodded in acquiescence. "She said she'd come back to the *palais de justice*." Trousseau went on, "You really must come down to Trois-Rivières one day. I'll make you pork tails with breadfruit. You'd like that. You spend too much time with people of your own race."

"At the moment, my most pressing problem's my son. According to his teacher, Fabrice's a clown at school."

"That's what Michel Siobud thinks?"

"He says I should spend more time with my children."

"I've been telling you that for years. It's never too late to get back to the Bible, *madame le juge*."

"A lot of people have been giving me advice—and I don't listen." Anne Marie leaned forward and again she tapped him on the shoulder. "Why does this girl want to see me?"

Trousseau did not reply.

"Well?"

"You like breadfruit, *madame le juge*?"

"Monsieur Trousseau, please, just for once answer my question. What does this pretty girl want to see me about?"

He glanced at her in the driving mirror. "Docteur Bouton rang before I left. He wanted to speak with you, *madame*."

"Why won't you answer my question about the girl? I'm not interested in Docteur Bouton."

"Mademoiselle Salondy's out of danger."

"You told me that on the phone."

"They're keeping her in intensive care. Docteur Bouton said you might be able to see her tomorrow. He gave his home number which I duly wrote down and left for you on your desk." He turned to glance at her. "You really must try to smile, *madame le juge*. These last few days, you've had a permanent scowl on your face."

"I didn't see you smiling at the Pointe des Châteaux yesterday."

"Siobud teaches your son?"

"You don't think I've got reason to scowl with my sister-in-law in the hospital and my son turning into . . ."

"Into what, *madame*?"

"And a *greffier* who can't answer a straight question." She added hastily, "I'm not sure I like your friend Siobud."

"Friends? I've got better things to do with my time. I have my garden in Trois-Rivières and I have my pigs and my wife owns a hotel in the tenth *arrondissement* so I don't need friends. And if I did have friends, believe me, there are a lot of people I'd prefer to a jumped-up mulatto."

"That's what everybody says about Dugain."

"Mulatto runt."

"Monsieur Trousseau, I sometimes suspect you're a racist."

"An Indian who marries a white woman? An Indian who has four children who have all completed their university education and who all have jobs?"

"Pork tails with breadfruit—that sounds appetizing," Anne Marie mused aloud as she stared out of the window. They approached the city and she did not want to quarrel.

"I suppose you're allowed to eat pork, *madame le juge*."

Anne Marie sighed noisily.

Shacks, concrete and wood, corrugated iron roofs, new cars and abandoned wrecks. They went past the ghetto of Boissard on the edge of the city. A violent ghetto, full of clandestine immigrants.

Ten years that the mayor had been promising a renovation of Boissard, but there was still no sidewalk, still no shade. Just puddles after the rain, packs of mongrels, pigs and cats. A few chickens. Rusting refrigerators and the bald trunks of coconut trees that had lost their fronds the night of Hurricane Hugo.

Trousseau spoke. "Docteur Bouton might need to send Mademoiselle Salondy to France."

Again the fear in Anne Marie's belly. "Why does he want to send my sister-in-law to France?" Her knuckles turned grey as she gripped the door handle.

Trousseau's lips parted to reveal his teeth. "Docteur Bouton added that everybody at the hospital was counting on your support."

"Why send my sister-in-law to France?"

"The sister of your ex-sister-in-law, *madame le juge.*"

"Can't they treat her here?"

They had reached the main boulevard and Trousseau's attention was taken up by the traffic. Saturday morning and the city was filled with shoppers before the weekend. "To the *palais de justice, madame?*"

"Monsieur Trousseau, why can't they treat Lucette Salondy here?"

"The young woman said she'd be at the *palais de justice* before eleven at the latest."

"I don't know any young women. At least, not any young woman that's alive. "

"And dead?"

Anne Marie said, "Let me out here. Something I need to do. Trousseau, I'll be along in a minute."

"One other thing, *madame le juge.*" The car had turned into the rue d'Ennery behind the church. Trousseau double-parked in front of the hat shop. "The Indian Richard—you can see him at the hospital. Doctor Lavigne rang to say Richard'd woken up and eaten. Quite lucid."

"I wish I were lucid." She got out of the car, the door banging against the high curb. "Tell your girl to wait for me. See if you can get anything out of her. Get her name, for example. Do your understanding older man routine."

"It's not a routine, *madame.*" Trousseau waved and there was the rattle of the exhaust pipe as the Peugeot pulled away from the sidewalk.

51

Chez Camille

As always, the hat shop was open, with its wares of broad brims, felts and its panamas, but there were no customers. Outside the church, already repaired after Hugo, the women selling imported carnations as well as mountain flowers from Martinique—lobsterclaw and anthuriums—were doing a brisk weekend trade. Solange, an imposing woman who had whored in Paris for twenty years, accumulated a fortune and two very dissimilar sons, gave Anne Marie a friendly wave from under the wide parasol and blew her a kiss, accompanied by a manly laugh.

It was a bright, dry morning in Pointe-à-Pitre. The breeze was hot and car fumes made Anne Marie's eyes prickle. The head cold had cleared up.

Anne Marie always enjoyed the jostling crowd in the rue Nozières, the Dominican women with their displays of Dettol, Morgan's pomade and carbolic soap, the open shops, the Syrians standing on the sidewalk, trying to entice customers over crackling public address systems. Every other shop sold clothes, from dull emporia with stocks of pith helmets, blue overalls and rubber boots to the franchise boutiques of Cédixsept, Benetton and even Rodier.

This morning she scarcely noticed the activity about her. She needed another coffee. Strong coffee and a moment to gather her thoughts.

Anne Marie went into Chez Camille.

Thoughts about Lucette Salondy, about her son. About the Pointe des Châteaux. About her job, her life and the future.

Kémel Yacoub was from Beirut, a Christian who had opened a Middle Eastern restaurant and snack bar in the colonial center of Pointe-à-Pitre. The bar gave onto the rue Alsace Lorraine, a hundred meters from the *palais de justice*. Only two tables, spindly legs and a plastic surface that was occupied by skewered raw meat, piles of Duralex plates and cutlery in preparation for the next meal.

The Lebanese cedar tree and the red and white flag were ubiquitous. Levantine music came loud and unmelodious from an old cassette player, perched on the counter. Not an attractive place—even if you ignored the flies and the grime.

Anne Marie sat down at a table and ordered a coffee from the girl who nodded and turned away in silence, dragging her sandals across the floor.

Michel Siobud was right, of course: it was Anne Marie's fault. Fabrice was turning into a problem—and she had not noticed a thing because she was spending too much time on the job.

Children need to be loved—and they need to know they're loved. Love is time, Anne Marie.

"Turkish coffee, *madame?*"

Anne Marie turned, surprised. "My head feels like putty. I took a sleeping pill last night."

"I know just how you feel—and I've never taken a sleeping pill in my life." He laughed; she could smell his breath of Bastos and rum.

"You were waiting for me, Monsieur Lafitte?"

He shook his head and she knew he was lying.

Anne Marie wiped her forehead with a paper napkin as Lafitte slid onto the spindly seat beside her. His discomfort in Chez Camille was almost palpable. "You'd care for some Turkish coffee? This is the only place in Pointe-à-Pitre you can get it."

L'Escale was Lafitte's kind of bar. There he could drink his rum at any time during the day and smoke his Bastos while keeping an eye on the entrance to the Commissariat. L'Escale was a bar frequented by policemen, more often white than black, and by their women, more often black than white. The sort of place where Lafitte would feel in his element.

He must have been waiting outside the *palais de justice*, hiding behind the copy of the morning's *France Antilles* that he now held in his hand. He had seen her get out of the Peugeot and followed her. He had watched her go into the open-fronted bar.

He grinned without looking at her. "I suppose it's a bit early for an *apéritif.*"

"You can always have a beer."

He looked at the rasping tape recorder. "I didn't know Arabs drank beer."

"Not all Arabs are Muslim and not all Muslims are practicing Muslims. The proprietor is a Christian. Like you and me."

"Something very cold," he said, and dabbed at his forehead. "You've seen this?" He grimaced as he threw the newspaper onto the table. On the front page was a photo of the murdered girl, her eyes closed in death. The headline announced, THE IDENTITY OF MUTILATED WHITE WOMAN REMAINS A MYSTERY.

"There was never any mutilation."

"Mutilation sells papers." He paused. "Isn't that what Arabs do to their women? Mutilating them—cutting into their parts?"

Anne Marie quickly read the article. "Where did they get this photo from?"

"The *procureur*, I suppose."

"I thought I was in charge of the enquiry."

The girl brought the bronze pot of black coffee on a tray. She set it down on the table, along with a dish of lumpy brown sugar and a glass of water. "And a Kroenenburg for my friend," Anne Marie said.

"She doesn't look like an Arab." Lafitte watched the girl disappear.

"She's from Pointe-à-Pitre."

"Thank goodness for that."

"Lots of black Muslims, Monsieur Lafitte. Just as there are a lot of black Christians and Jews." She gave him a tight smile. "I thought you'd worked in Africa."

"Five years in New Caledonia but that was years ago," he said. "And to tell you the truth, I prefer the West Indies."

"You surprise me."

"The people are more civilized," Lafitte replied. "You saw the *procureur?*"

"He didn't mention anything about distributing her photo to the press." Anne Marie shook her head. "I was at Baimbridge and haven't seen anyone other than Trousseau."

"Trousseau didn't tell you then that Parise has found the murderer?"

A car went past in the street, between the dense rows of parked vehicles, hooting irritably at pedestrians.

Anne Marie poured coffee from the small pot. Her hand did not tremble.

"*Madame le juge.*" Lafitte watched her carefully. "Parise's found the murderer."

She returned his glance. "Sure you don't care for coffee?"

"You don't look terribly excited, *madame le juge.*"

"Over the moon."

For a moment his eyes held hers. "The heat's off us, *madame le juge.* You, me, the *gendarmerie.*"

"You mean this Pointe des Châteaux dossier is out of my hands?" Anne Marie said flatly, "Now that is good news."

"The *procureur* says the murderer's identified—and now dead."

"I can get back to family and to living my life?" Not without malice, she added, "I can take up the Dugain dossier without everybody frightening me off?"

He squinted at her from behind a cigarette. Today he was smoking filterless cigarettes. "The Dominican killed the girl . . . the dead Rasta."

"William Williamson?" A spoonful of sugar.

"He was living in Boissard, sharing a shack with a couple of Dominicans like him." Lafitte nodded. "Small time dealers. Ganja and occasionally cocaine from South America via St. Martin. Petty thieves. The *gendarmerie* searched the place early this morning."

"William Williamson tried to kill Lucette Salondy. I was at Lycée Carnot last night and I stayed with her until past midnight at the hospital."

"Since the riots of eighty-five, Boissard is *gendarme* territory." Lafitte gave a charitable smile. "Better equipped than us."

"What did they find?"

"Parise did one of his dawn raids. Flak jackets and tear gas—and of course, the TV journalists from RFO. You know how they love to dress up. It comes from seeing too many American films. Can't help feeling our friend Parise believes he's Mel Gibson. You'll see him on the local news this evening." He added, "Mel Gibson, or perhaps Danny Glover."

"On the *procureur*'s orders?"

"An arsenal of weapons. Knives and a couple of guns."

"I don't see the connection with the Pointe des Châteaux."

"They also found pieces of women's clothing, *madame le juge*, which is proof enough for the *procureur*. The dawn raid was his idea—and he got what he wanted."

"Proof of absolutely nothing." Anne Marie shook her head. "Guns and clothing by themselves do not constitute proof. Arnaud must be out of his mind. We don't know the cause of death at the Pointe des Châteaux. We don't even know who the victim is."

"The Dominican's an escaped convict." Lafitte raised a finger, the nail yellow with nicotine. "Serving five years in Roseau, Dominica." He paused as the girl brought him a chill can of beer on a tin tray. He paid for Anne Marie's coffee.

"Five years for what?"

"Rape of white American tourists in Dominica." Lafitte shrugged philosophically. "Getting himself killed was probably a good idea. For us all. Particularly for your friend."

"Friend?"

"Your very good friend Arnaud."

52

Air France

"There was no rape or even attempted rape. Discoloring on the inner thighs and round the vaginal area. Bouton insists bruising occurred after the time of death—bruising that was probably intended to look like rape. You were there at the autopsy, Monsieur Lafitte. You know there were no signs of penetration."

Lafitte pulled back the ring on the can of beer. "There were traces of sperm."

Anne Marie shook her head. "There's no definite proof of sexual activity prior to death. At least, not until we've heard from Pasteur."

"Without wishing to contradict you, *madame le juge,* at the autopsy Docteur Bouton seemed to think there was sperm."

Talking about death in the brightness of Pointe-à-Pitre, Anne Marie repressed a shiver. "Possibly—but that's not what he wrote in the preliminary report." She paused. "I left early. I didn't get round to signing the *procès verbal.*"

"I wouldn't worry about it. The electric saw is never much fun."

"I do worry about it. When we get this thing to court, I don't want to have my case thrown out for a flaw in procedure."

"If we get this thing to court." Lafitte pulled on his beer, putting his head back. His eyes lingered on the serving girl who was back behind the counter. Then he turned to Anne Marie. "You were right about Desterres. With the timely death of the Dominican, the pressure is off you to arrest Desterres."

"It was you who wanted me to arrest him."

"An arrogant bastard."

"Because he's educated?"

"A long time ago I learned not to trust politicians."

Anne Marie remarked, "There was no way I could arrest Desterres. Even without William Williamson, Richard's going to corroborate Desterres's story." She hesitated. "In a way I agree with you . . ."

"With me, *madame le juge?*"

"Desterres is hiding something."

"You're getting to be like a policeman." Lafitte grinned. "You believe in gut feelings?"

"You mean female intuition?"

"Call it what you want."

"Just one thing I believe in, Monsieur Lafitte: justice. I don't believe in intuition, whether it's masculine or feminine. Intuition can send the wrong person to the guillotine."

Lafitte said regretfully, "No more guillotine, *madame le juge.*"

She set the cup down. "You saw Parise this morning?"

"For a few fleeting seconds. Flushed with his success in Boissard— he dropped in just to show that he hadn't forgotten us little people." Lafitte nodded. "At the *palais de justice* where your *greffier* told me you wouldn't be there."

"And the Institut Pasteur?"

Lafitte wiped his damp lips with the back of his hand. "I beg your pardon?" Pearls of sweat were forming along his forehead.

"Anything from the Insitut Pasteur? We still need a cause of death."

"Parise didn't say anything because he was too busy basking in the glory of arresting six dealers—all Dominicans. Our *procureur* is over the moon."

Anne Marie clicked her tongue. "All very well for the *procureur* to find rapists. No shortage of them, I'm quite sure. The computer came up with more than sixty for the last two years. But that's not why this woman died."

Their eyes met. "Why did she die?"

"I wish I knew, Monsieur Lafitte. I really wish I knew—because if I did, then I could get back to living my life—without having the *préfet,* the Tourist Office, Arnaud and everybody else breathing down my neck."

"They all seem happy enough with the Dominican."

Anne Marie said, "I can only guess why the girl was murdered, but I'm pretty sure it wasn't for sex. If I knew who she was, I might be able to find out who killed her."

The intelligent eyes looked at her. "You have an opinion, *madame le juge?*"

"What woman would want to pass herself off as Evelyne Vaton? The dead woman used Vaton's driving license and her credit card. She stole her money—and then impersonated her. Impersonated Vaton for over a week—even stayed in Basse-Terre with the parents of Vaton's friend in Paris." Anne Marie shook her head. "Monsieur and Madame Lecurieux came to the morgue to identify the corpse."

"And?"

"Nice people—old fashioned. They had no difficulty in recognizing the girl staying with them. The girl they thought was Evelyne Vaton. The girl they thought was a friend of their daughter's."

"You want me to contact their daughter?"

"Geneviève Lecurieux—their adopted daughter—is in Réunion for some medical conference. I got Trousseau to send a fax to Saint-Denis in Réunion." Anne Marie glanced at her watch. "Eight hours between here and there. As yet, she's not made contact."

"What can she tell you?"

"Seems strange Vaton and Lecurieux should be friends but she should send the girl to stay with her parents rather than coming on holiday with her." Anne Marie paused for a moment. "Vaton's here somewhere in Guadeloupe."

Lafitte's self-assurance had returned. He grinned from behind the can of beer. "Unless . . ." A cigarette smoldered in the same hand that held the beer. Moisture had beaded the sides of the can, making fine tracks of condensation and running onto his yellow fingers. His eyes were red and the smile patronizing. He continued to appraise the girl behind the counter.

Anne Marie did not hide her irritation. "Unless what, Monsieur Lafitte?"

"Unless it wasn't Vaton."

"Of course it wasn't Vaton. No reason for Madame Vaton to lie about her own daughter. Or at least, no reason that I can think of." Anne Marie hesitated. "The real Vaton has a five-year-old child. If

Bouton'd seen traces of childbirth on the dead body, he'd've mentioned it."

"Unless it wasn't Vaton on the plane from France."

Anne Marie frowned unhappily.

"Unless the driving license and the credit card were stolen before the flight."

Anne Marie poured a second cup of coffee from the battered pot. The flow of coffee was comforting in its normality.

"*Madame le juge*, if the victim was using Vaton's credit card here, she might just as well have been using it for her air ticket. It's not as if she had to go through customs. Between here and Paris, all flights are internal. There's no point where the ticket is checked thoroughly against a passport."

"I suppose . . ."

"If the woman could steal Vaton's credit card, she could have stolen her passport as well." Lafitte grinned. "Perhaps we ought to check how the ticket was paid for."

53

Palais de Justice

A beautiful girl, according to Trousseau.

Apart from a couple of pupils from the *lycée* who sometimes went windsurfing with Fabrice, Anne Marie did not know many girls.

Anne Marie did not know many people at all. Acquaintances, yes, and a lot of contacts, but socially she had never mixed in Guadeloupe. There was never time and she had always avoided the social functions she got invited to. In the early years, her only friends had been the family-in-law. Since the divorce, Jean Michel's family had disappeared, partly in solidarity with Jean Michel, but mainly, Anne Marie suspected, out of embarrassment at the way things had turned out.

Two cracks in the wall of silence from the extended family-in-law were M'man Jeanne and Lucette.

Lucette had remained a good friend and a cheerful voice only a phone call away. During those awful months after the divorce, it was Lucette who had listened sympathetically to Anne Marie as she poured out her feelings over the telephone. Feelings of resentment and betrayal and self-doubt. And above all, a terrible loneliness.

Most probably, Anne Marie would have aborted without Lucette's common sense advice. There would never have been Létitia, her little Létitia.

"Before going home this evening, I'll go and see her. I've got to get up to the hospital to see the Indian. Lucette should be out of intensive care."

"Who, *madame le juge?*"

"My sister-in-law—Mademoiselle Salondy." Anne Marie knew she owed a lot to Lucette Salondy. "Do you know any beautiful girls, Monsieur Lafitte?"

"I beg your pardon?"

"According to Trousseau, there's a pretty young woman who wishes to talk to me."

"Pretty girls?" Lafitte rubbed his chin. "Apart from you, *madame le juge?*"

Anne Marie smiled at his spontaneity. "How's your wife?"

"My wife?" Lafitte sounded surprised. "As well as can be expected."

Anne Marie glanced at him but said nothing. With Lafitte walking beside her, she entered the *palais de justice*. Out of the sun the air was cool, and as they went toward the stairway, she heard the familiar plop of a terrapin falling back into the water of the pool.

Up the stairs.

Anne Marie had always loved the *palais de justice* with its airy, tropical lines, its grey-green stone floors and the beige paint. Although made of concrete, there was something Moorish about it that appealed to her North African sensibilities. The law courts had been built in the 1930s with money received from the Germans in war reparations. The building had the functional layout of architecture that exploited the trade winds and even on the hottest days of the hurricane season, it somehow remained cool within the *palais de justice*.

Lafitte reached the door first and opened it for her. She stepped past him and immediately noticed the perfume. Not the smell of Bastos and beer on Lafitte's breath, not the smell of Trousseau's overripe breadfruit in a plastic bag on the floor, but the fragrance of jasmine essence.

Trousseau was sitting at his desk, his arms folded and a proprietary smile on his face. He got up, stepped forward, one hand on the door handle, and shook hands with Lafitte. The satisfied grin was for Anne Marie.

Anne Marie put her bag on the desk and lowered herself onto the chair. The smell of jasmine was pleasant.

The effort of climbing the stairs had brought more pearls of sweat to Lafitte's sallow forehead. He wiped his face with a handkerchief. "I'll be wishing you a pleasant weekend, *madame le juge*," he said. "I'll check with Air France for the ticket."

Lafitte nodded and quietly closed the door.

Anne Marie waited until they could no longer hear his footfalls on the stairs.

Marie Pierre Augustin was looking at Trousseau. "A policeman?"

He glanced from one woman to the other and ran a finger along his moustache. "Lafitte's keeping tabs on you, *madame.*" He seemed pleased with himself.

"Lafitte's a lonely man," Anne Marie replied.

"Keeping tabs because he's worried what dirt you'll dig up on Dugain—and the SRPJ."

"He's one of these men who like to appear macho and yet desperately seek the reassurance of women." Anne smiled at Marie Pierre. "They're lost without us."

54
Cane juice

Anne Marie could hear the fall of Trousseau's fading footsteps on the stairs outside her office.

"You told me you were married."

Marie Pierre nodded. "I married in Paris and we came out here. A big mistake."

"Getting married?"

"Jean Claude wanted to return to the islands."

"Jean Claude's your husband?"

A thin smile. "Don't ask me where he is now because I don't know and I don't want to know. All my life I've belonged to someone— someone who has owned me, someone who's told me what to do. Not for my sake, but for their sake." She folded her arms. "At last I'm free."

"You live with a man. That's what you told me yesterday afternoon."

"I am free."

"You didn't want children?"

She was wearing a white lace-edged bustier showing the flawless ebony of her shoulders. "I was only eighteen when I married."

"A lot of women have children at eighteen."

"No point in bringing a child into this world if you can't look after him. Children cost a lot of money."

Anne Marie nodded. "Money and time."

"I received very little of either. I was born in Martinique and when I was five, my mother took me to Paris to be operated on while my father stayed on in the Caribbean. Like all men, he wasn't capable of living by himself. He needed a woman . . . a woman to iron his shirts and to keep him warm in bed. So he found another woman." She attempted a smile. "We remained in France. We were living with an aunt, Maman got a job working in a hospital and I married the first man I met."

"Who brought you back to the Caribbean?"

"Jean Claude had grown up in France. He was twenty-three and a sergeant and they wanted him to go to officer school but he left the army because he was desperate to return to Guadeloupe. Fed up with France, fed up with the bad weather, fed up with the whites. As you're white, *madame le juge*, you can't understand. You can't understand what it's like to live every day of your life in a country where you don't belong."

"Like you, I had to emigrate to France."

"Your father went off with another woman?"

"He didn't have to."

The girl frowned but Anne Marie felt no need to elucidate.

"We came to Guadeloupe and Jean Claude set up a garage and I got a job working in a beauty parlor. A good job." A glimpse of even teeth between the parted lips. "There's more to life than blow brushing."

"Not if you're happy."

"I've never been happy . . . happy like other people."

"A home, a job, a husband—that's sufficient for most women."

The girl unfolded her arms and picked up the glass. She drank some more cane juice. "Jean Claude'd been five years in the army and he'd worked as a mechanic. When we were engaged, we talked about what we were going to do. Jean Claude was full of theories. '*The islands are rich—with all those civil servants and their fat salaries.*' In France—we were living in Asnières—the garage he was going to open in Guadeloupe, that was all he could talk about and I believed him." She paused, breathing in. "You'd have thought that with my father I'd have learned my lesson, that I'd learned to be wary of men, but I am afraid you'd have thought wrong. Once we got here, it didn't take long for things to unravel. He set up his garage and he started getting clients but when people brought a car in with a flat tire, of course he would repair the carburetor and give it a wax polish. A perfectionist,

Jean Claude, but he was surprised when they complained about the bill." She heaved her chest. "Nothing went right."

In the distance, the passenger ship gave a last, long hoot, before heading north. Antigua, St. Kitts, St. Martin, St. Thomas.

(Trousseau had brought drinks, cane juice and a bottle of mineral water. Then he had smiled knowingly as he left the two women.)

"We'd sunk all our savings into the garage—and it scarcely paid for the overalls. Jean Claude couldn't bring himself to admit it was his fault. He should've cut his losses and pulled out, got a job, but he was looking for someone to blame. The fault of his family, it was the fault of his compatriots. Everybody's fault but his own."

"Sometimes it was the fault of his wife?"

"You're married, *madame le juge?*"

"I was."

"White men are supposed to be better. They're supposed to listen to their wives, treat them like equals."

"All men are selfish. The only difference is how well they hide their selfishness."

For a moment Marie Pierre did not speak. Her hands were now motionless on her lap; a couple of crumbs from the croissant had fallen to the floor of the office. "We were staying with a cousin. He has a house at the top of a hill opposite the university. A nice enough place. A couple of cats, a pig and some chickens. I like being with animals. But I needed to get away. To a place of our own. I was still in love and it wasn't our home. There was no privacy."

"And there wasn't any money?"

"Jean Claude grew more and more bitter. He started accusing me of not being like other women, of not caring about children, but there was no chance of my getting pregnant as long as there was no money coming in."

"You had a job."

"Thank goodness." For a moment she hesitated, running the long, thin fingers across her forehead. "Jean Claude's a good man—he isn't violent, he never hit me or anything."

"Why should he hit you?"

"I am not always the easiest person to live with." An unexpected smile. "There are some things—things that men want—that I don't . . ."

"Yes?"

"I don't enjoy that sort of thing. I try to—but I don't enjoy it." The smile had vanished. "Then one fine day I lost my job—the woman hair dresser took on a girl without any qualifications because she was cheaper. I hate being unemployed, being left to sit with my thoughts. I looked everywhere. I even put adverts in the paper and went to people's houses. But I didn't have a car. Jean Claude couldn't understand what I was going through. 'We can have children,' he kept saying, 'that'll give you something to do.' Pretty soon I couldn't bear being alone in the house with him so I found a job selling encyclopedias. Door-to-door selling, going into the projects and trying to sell twenty volumes of some cheapjack encyclopedia—*Creole Cooking* or *The History of the Black Woman*. Selling useless books to people who could scarcely read."

"You could've returned to France?"

She suddenly noticed the crumbs on the short red skirt and brusquely brushed them away. "We had each other—and there were times when I felt close to Jean Claude. The magic had gone out of our married life—but he was a friend—my best friend. He can get carried away by an idea, and then for a few weeks he puts his heart and soul into it. Always working on some crackbrained idea for making money." A smile stretched the deep gloss of the lipstick. "Jean Claude's stubborn." A flash of her white teeth. "I'm stubborn, too."

"You left him?"

"When he started getting involved in politics. Suddenly everything was the fault of the whites. He'd spent most of his life in France, many of his friends were whites, friends from school and his days in the army. Then . . ." She stopped and shook her head. "He felt he had to explain why nothing was working out. Explain to everybody, but above all to himself." She added, "We no longer slept together."

"Nothing like parenthood to get a man to concentrate on finding a job."

"Perhaps."

"Why did you leave your husband?"

"Jean Claude never made bombs—I don't think he was involved in anything like that. I certainly hope he wasn't but he started reading political books and West Indian stuff. I remember there was a book he talked about—*The Wretched of the Earth*, written by a man in

Martinique. He started browsing through all the Caribbean encyclopedias I was supposed to sell. Even at night, in bed, he would talk politics. Marx—you know Karl Marx?"

"You were in the same bed?"

"The same bed—but I didn't like him touching me. Not any more. After a while, he gave up."

Anne Marie allowed herself to smile. "I used to be like that."

"You didn't like sex?"

"I was a Marxist a long time ago."

"Bad enough when all he could talk about was the garage, but the politics was worse and he'd get angry with me. I couldn't stand his denigrating the whites because I could remember the white doctors who'd been so good to me when I was little. He'd tell me I was a woman, that I was politically immature." She breathed out, her nose pinched. "I'd roll over and try to go to sleep and when finally I did fall asleep, he would hold it against me and say I was stupid and unaware of what was happening in my own country. So when people came to the house—intellectuals, people at the university—he'd never introduce me to them. I was supposed to make the drinks and then disappear."

"You disappeared?"

"He came to our house twice."

"Who?"

"We didn't have a television and so I didn't recognize him. Later, when I saw his program, it came as quite a surprise. I don't know why he wanted to see Jean Claude—I have no idea of what they were planning. This was about two years ago, about the time there were still bombs going off. It was so obvious they were flattering Jean Claude and that they wanted something. They were running circles round him and Jean Claude just lapped it up—he loved to be told he was intelligent. It was Dugain. Nobody knew it—it was a secret—but I can assure you Dugain was in the independence movement and I wouldn't be surprised if he was behind some of the bombs."

55
Lovers

"You recognized her?"

"My friend Agnès Loisel."

Anne Marie looked at the photograph and she could feel bitterness swelling in her throat. "Why didn't you tell me before?"

"I never knew she was dead."

"You didn't know, Marie Pierre? You read the papers, you listen to the radio."

"I didn't know it was Agnès." She pointed. "Not until I saw that photograph."

Anne Marie turned the *France Antilles* over, hiding the grim face of death. "When did you last see Agnès?"

"When Dugain kicked us out in February."

"You never saw her again after that?"

A grudging nod. "I chose not to talk to her."

"I thought you were good friends. Isn't that what you told me yesterday?"

"We were," Marie Pierre said. "When I needed someone, she was good to me. Agnès was very good to me. She took me in and looked after me."

"Your husband was also your friend—you just said so."

Marie Pierre snorted angrily. "Jean Claude had become unbearable. In his opinion I was just a stupid woman—and all I wanted was to escape but there was nowhere to go."

"Under the bedsheets is where reconciliation normally takes place between a man and his wife."

"Agnès had a little place at Sainte-Anne. It was small but for me, it was like moving into a palace. We were happy together."

"You no longer loved your husband?"

The face clouded. "By then there was another woman."

"A lot of men have another woman. That's something we learn to live with."

Unexpectedly, like the sun breaking through clouds, a smile lit up Marie Pierre's face. "If Jean Claude had other women, I really didn't mind. It would give him something to do during the day and then he could sleep at night instead of pestering me. He didn't love me—the garage had made him too bitter for that."

"A man needs tenderness. By refusing him your body, you were refusing him your love."

Marie Pierre looked at her hands, she looked at her red skirt, at the matching fingernails, she looked at the empty plastic cup on the table. "There was another woman."

"So what?"

"A woman in my life."

56

Car Grease

"Things'd reached the point where I could no longer stand the feel of his hands on me. Hands still dirty with car grease. Fingers that he wanted to put inside me."

"A lot of women enjoy sex."

"I'd have left him anyway."

"If they didn't enjoy sex, Marie Pierre, they wouldn't put up with the pain of childbirth."

"Agnès made me realize I owned my body." She hesitated. "Agnès set me free and now she's dead."

"How did Agnès set you free?"

"A little girl, obeying orders and doing what I was told, desperately trying to please everybody and forgetting about myself. Agnès was right: I'd spent my life being a good little girl, letting people touch me, letting people use my body when I didn't want it. That's what Jean Claude couldn't understand. He was like everybody else, like Maman, like the teachers at school. He couldn't see I was a human being because as far as Jean Claude was concerned, I was there for his satisfaction—not a mind, not a living person but just a docile body with the right number of orifices. Just a body in the same way that I was a body for my mother. A little body to be kept clean, to look tidy—we were the only black people in our street in Paris, and it was all so terribly important what the neighbors thought."

The pretty face frowned in thought. Finally Marie Pierre brushed at her cheek and looked up at Anne Marie. "With Agnès, I knew it couldn't last. I don't really know if I like that sort of thing."

"What sort of thing?"

"Between two women—it's not normal, is it?" Marie Pierre tried to smile. "When Agnès touched me—I know this sounds silly—it was magic. Agnès was an explorer—a discoverer who discovered what wasn't even there—what had been lying hidden for twenty years. It was like . . ."

Outside from the streets came the sound of Pointe-à-Pitre on a Saturday morning—the sound of traffic, the sound of the Dominican women shouting their wares, the sound of the breeze in the royal palm trees of Place de la Victoire.

"Like being born again," the girl said simply. A tear was running down her cheek.

"When she went off with her boyfriend, you murdered her, Marie Pierre?"

"How could I want to kill her? The person who'd helped me see what had happened to my soul?" She shook her head. "The boyfriends'd always been there. There'd always been men buzzing round her like dogs on heat, long before Olivier. I always knew I couldn't give her all she needed."

Anne Marie found herself smiling. "That's nothing to be ashamed of." She screwed the plastic cap back onto the mineral water.

She looked at Anne Marie. Traces of her tears had reached the deep red lipstick. "For six months we were happy."

"Who murdered her?"

"It's not natural, is it?"

"Love is natural but love makes big demands on us—and as often as not, we're not up to them."

"It was so nice—but it couldn't last and in the end Agnès left me in the same way Papa had left me."

"Why did she leave?"

Marie Pierre caught her breath. "She was going to Paris and it was me who told her to get pregnant. With Olivier, it wouldn't be difficult, she'd just need to monitor her temperature. I told her we'd bring the child up together and that she didn't need a man."

"What did she say?"

"She laughed and she said her child must have a father." Marie

Pierre added after a moment's pause, "Perhaps if I'd had a father, a real father, I'd have waited, instead of marrying the first man who promised freedom from my mother. Perhaps I wouldn't have married a man who was just another brick in the wall." She looked at the hands on the red skirt. "Perhaps I could've given my husband what he needed."

"You have a boyfriend now."

She shook her head. "A business relationship."

"Marriage is business—love and romance are the icing on the cake, Marie Pierre. Only it's not a cake. Bringing children into this world and looking after them—it's hard-nosed business."

"There's not much a woman can do by herself. You need a man just so that the others will leave you alone." Marie Pierre fell silent.

"Agnès Loisel and you broke up because she wanted a child?"

"A woman needs a man—just as a whore needs a pimp."

"Just as a flower needs sunshine." Anne Marie leaned forward across the desk and touched the girl's arm. "Did Agnès go off with her Olivier?"

"I don't know."

"Yes, you do."

"How do you know I know?"

"Because you want me to help find the person who killed your friend."

Marie Pierre looked at Anne Marie for a moment without speaking.

"Well?"

"She found a job in a hotel in Paris. I hadn't seen her since the time Dugain gave us the sack. I was still angry. I hadn't wanted to leave her house in Sainte-Anne but Agnès kicked me out and she said unkind things which hurt me a lot."

"Such as?"

A shake of her head, as if trying to rid it of unpleasant memories. "I should've gone looking for her but instead I got involved in the leather goods and with Jaime—he's from Colombia and he has a lot of contacts in South America."

"You manage to sell that stuff?"

She looked up at Anne Marie. "We do the hotels and the beaches—the tourists are looking for souvenirs, and there's virtually nothing authentic from Guadeloupe. I don't make much money but it pays the rent. I'm from Martinique, remember, and I don't have any family here—apart from Jean Claude and he's got another woman now. The job gives me a semblance of normality and at last I can get my ideas in order and take charge of my life." She started to cry again. "The idea I could do something by myself, without relying on anybody, the idea I could survive without having to seek permission from other people—that's what I owe to Agnès."

"You never saw her again?"

"She went to France."

"Who murdered her?"

Marie Pierre spoke softly. "She sent a postcard with the Eiffel Tower."

Anne Marie ran a hand along her forehead. "Who killed Agnès Loisel and then left her body on the beach at the Pointe des Châteaux?"

"Agnès didn't save my life, *madame le juge*. Agnès created it. Agnès was my true mother and the man who killed her is a very evil person."

"So who killed her, Marie Pierre?"

The girl looked up at Anne Marie. Her dark eyes were wet. Even in her distress, she was beautiful, more beautiful than any sculpted goddess. She was beautiful, human and alive.

"Who killed her?"

"You must ask Olivier."

57
Ashanti

A slight shrug of the smooth shoulders. "He'd been to the house to see Jean Claude but like most men, I don't think he really looked at me. I was part of the furniture and he had come to talk politics with my husband."

"I thought Dugain liked pretty girls."

"They were all men there, talking politics, Jean Claude, Dugain and a couple of teachers from the university. They didn't take any notice of me and my job was to serve, to bring them drinks and then stay out of the way."

"When you were working for him, Dugain showed interest in you?"

"I showed no interest in him."

"He touched you?"

"He wouldn't have dared."

Anne Marie sat back in her chair. She held the pen between her fingers and absent-mindedly played with the screw-cap. "How exactly did you get the job?"

"Through Desterres."

"And how do you know Desterres?"

"What woman doesn't know Desterres?"

"He tried to rape you?"

"He liked me."

"In what way?"

"In what way do you think, *madame*? He found me pretty and perhaps he thought I was available."

"Desterres's married."

"Married and divorced, with grown up children. Children of your color. Desterres's wife is from Terre de Haut—with that light skin they have in the Saints."

"Like Agnès's skin?"

Marie Pierre nodded. "Agnès could have passed for a white woman."

"Her father was white?"

"Agnès never knew her father. Her mother remarried when she was still a little girl."

"You have the sort of skin that Desterres liked?"

"All mice are grey, *madame le juge.* You seem to think at night, when the lights are out, black men worry about color. You seem to think even in bed they prefer white women. But, if anything, when black men want to enjoy themselves and to work up a sweat, they prefer the negress's rump."

"If Desterres preferred black women, why did he marry a woman with light skin?"

"Black girls give pleasure but the light-skinned girl gives status." Marie Pierre no longer frowned. "Why do you think my father left my mother? By going off with somebody else, he was going to find a better wife? He was looking for status, and as soon as he could, he dumped my mother—she has the same skin as me." Marie Pierre pinched the flesh of her own arm. "We are descended from the Ashanti in Africa but what did my father care? He found his *chabine*, for all the good it did him."

"If what you say is true . . ."

"Of course it's true."

"If black men don't marry black women, how did you manage to marry so young?"

The lustrous lipstick widened with her smile. "I was in France, *madame le juge*, where black girls are the exception, not the rule. In Paris there are none of the complexes that go all the way back to the time of slavery and before. When I was in *collège*, I had a white boyfriend. Thierry—he was very sweet."

"You should've married him."

"And spend the rest of my life in the suburbs of Paris? Metro, job, bed." Marie Pierre shook her head. "More to life than that—and I didn't want to end up like my mother, worrying what the neighbors'd think. Paranoid over a spot on my dress or a scratch in the varnish on the front door."

"Instead you got married, returned to the Caribbean and discovered life was no better here."

The carved goddess shook her head again. "Here in the West Indies—there are a lot of things wrong. The men are immature and spoiled mama's boys but at least I belong." She paused. "You, *madame le juge*, why don't you return to Paris and to your people?"

"Why did Desterres use influence to get you the job?"

"I met him once when I was selling encyclopedias. Desterres was friendly and I knew perfectly well what he wanted. I wasn't going to risk my marriage with a lecher like Desterres, an arrogant bastard who throws his money around to impress women. Desterres believes that every woman has her price."

"Why did Desterres get you the job with Dugain?"

"To impress me."

"He came to your house and he offered you a job?"

"That was later—that was when I had moved out and I was living in Sainte-Anne. He dropped by."

"You were staying with Agnès?"

Marie Pierre nodded.

"He proposed a job to you both?"

"At first just to me. He wanted to get between my legs and he thought he had a better chance now that I no longer was living with my husband. Perhaps Dugain had told him he was looking for a couple of women to run the shop in Abymes."

"Who told him where you were living?"

"No idea." Marie Pierre paused. "I don't know and I don't care. He got me the job—and he got nothing in return."

"Desterres knew Agnès?"

"It's through me he met her."

"At her house in Sainte-Anne?"

"Of course. Where else?"

Anne Marie turned the copy of *France Antilles* back over, with the poorly reproduced photograph of Agnès Loisel. She tapped the photograph with her pen. "Monsieur Desterres swore to me that he'd never met this girl."

58

Coquetry

Her problem, Anne Marie knew, was that she was obsessive. Once she had decided to do something, she could think about nothing else. Anne Marie's obsession with work had blinded her to the demands of her children. High time she was obsessive about them, about Fabrice and Létitia. No child of hers was going to turn into a juvenile delinquent. Fabrice was going to get his baccalaureate and later he would go on to be a teacher, just as his grandfather had always wished.

She should have gone home but instead accepted Trousseau's invitation and they went to a small, inexpensive restaurant on the boulevard. "At least I can be sure of getting something to eat," Trousseau said in an aggrieved tone as they crossed the Boulevard Chanzy.

"Any news from the hospital?"

"You can see Richard at two thirty, *madame*. Lavigne says he's been sleeping."

She was, Anne Marie realized, very hungry. Hungry and determined to resolve the killing of Agnès Loisel as soon as possible. "And the news from Lucette Salondy?"

Trousseau said, "I didn't see Bouton. Richard's been sleeping ever since he got to the hospital." He tapped the side of his head. "Something about his synapses, according to the doctor."

"You told me it was blacks who were prone to schizophrenia." She ran her finger along her upper lip. "Richard would appear to belong to your race, Monsieur Trousseau."

The features hardened. "I fail to understand the implication, *madame le juge*."

She glanced at her Kelton watch. "We've got an hour to eat." She pulled the hard, wooden chair from under the table and sat down. "After seeing Richard, I can go home."

"Schizophrenia's more common among people of African origin than among other racial groups. You seem convinced I'm a racist but unlike many white people, *madame le juge*, I have no time for the theories of racial superiority."

"Of course not, Monsieur Trousseau."

"No race has the monopoly of any one disease. Just as no one race has the monopoly of intelligence. Or of the truth although there are people who believe they are the elect of God."

"On Saturdays, my son goes windsurfing with his friends. Perhaps I'll get time to drive down to the beach—Fabrice'd like that. Perhaps even, if you're free this afternoon, you'd like to drive me."

"The elect of God respect the Sabbath."

"Could you drive me?"

"Down to the beach, Madame Laveaud?" Trousseau was about to say something. Instead he adjusted his tie. "It'd be a pleasure."

"You're very good to me."

"The beach?" Trousseau raised his eyebrow. "The case is solved?"

"Desterres was lying. He knew the dead girl."

"You now know who she is?"

"One of the girls employed in Abymes by Dugain. Through her boyfriend she took Dugain to the work inspectorate because he wasn't paying national insurance."

"There's a connection between the two deaths?"

"Two deaths?"

"Dugain's suicide and the murder at the Pointe des Châteaux?"

They were served by a plump girl in a yellow dress. She took a ballpoint pen from where it had been set, aerial-like, in her chignon, and wrote down their order on a note pad. She knew Trousseau and there was banter between them in Creole. She was young enough to be his daughter.

Anne Marie ordered a *planteur*. She felt she deserved something strong but then as she let the liquid linger in her mouth, the tang of rum reminded her of Lafitte and she was very glad that she was with

Trousseau. Lafitte with his nicotine-stained fingers and his cynicism. Lafitte, the European growing old in the tropics.

Dear, irascible Trousseau.

Perhaps he read her thoughts. Trousseau gave her a bright smile as he drank the soursop juice. They sat in a breeze at a table on the edge of the sidewalk, looking from time to time at the steady flow of shoppers, heading home, weighed down with plastic bags. Mainly women with little children in tow. Children from the countryside, the girls with beads in their plaits, the little boys overdressed for the hot streets of Pointe-à-Pitre.

On the other side of the boulevard rose the city hall, its concrete architecture now pleasantly weathered by age. It stood before an open plaza and beds of flowers in a concrete base. The mayor had conducted a couple of weddings during the course of the morning and the last lingering guests stood, laughed and had themselves photographed in their white dresses and their silk suits. Like petals, pink confetti was strewn everywhere, shifting with the trade breezes, crossing the busy boulevard and even entering the small restaurant.

For *hors d'oeuvre* they ate spiced blood pudding garnished with tomatoes and garlic salad that the serving girl placed on the table—madras tablecloth, which was protected beneath a sheet of plastic—with a disparaging but amused remark for Trousseau that Anne Marie failed to understand.

"The case is solved?"

"Which case, Monsieur Trousseau?"

"You know the murderer of the girl?"

"The *procureur*'s decided the Dominican was the rapist—because along with guns and drugs, the *gendarmerie* found women's clothing in his shack in Boissard." She shook her head. "He'd been sentenced for rape in Dominica—rape of American tourists."

"Perhaps he did rape her."

Again the click of the tongue—a West Indian habit she had picked up and could not put down. "Monsieur Trousseau, the bruising was after death and the girl wasn't murdered on the beach. The body was brought down to the beach in the last stages of rigor mortis."

"What makes you say that?"

"In three days the dogs would have started ripping the body to pieces." Anne Marie sliced the blood pudding. "The fishermen would have noticed something."

"That doesn't mean the girl wasn't raped."

"We now know who the dead girl is."

"That's why you sent me away?" He sounded hurt.

"The girl wanted to be alone with me. It wasn't anything personal. The presence of a man would've made things more difficult."

"Most women find my company reassuring."

"There are certain things . . ."

"I should like to remind you my wife's a white woman like yourself. I'm not one of these macho men who consider women as mere objects."

"Monsieur Trousseau, in our years of collaboration, I've had ample time to appreciate your innumerable qualities."

He did not repress a smile of satisfaction. "The dead girl had nothing to do with Evelyne Vaton?"

Anne Marie looked across the road, at the plaza between the town hall and the Centre des Arts. The last guests had disappeared. The photographer was packing his cameras into a satchel. He had parked his station wagon on the sidewalk.

It was some time before Trousseau finally asked, "Well? The connection between Evelyne Vaton and this girl."

"Agnès Loisel." Anne Marie felt strangely relaxed. Her cold had disappeared and she could sense she would soon be free of the Pointe des Châteaux murder. She could take time off, perhaps even leave Guadeloupe for a month. Travel with the children, visit her sister in Lannion, get away from the tropical heat. "I'll need to talk to this Richard in the hospital."

"There's a connection?"

"Afterwards I'll look in on Lucette."

"The black girl was able to identify the dead woman, *madame le juge?*"

"Marie Pierre recognized her photo in the *France Antilles*. No doubt she already had her suspicions before she came to see me." Anne Marie added, "They used to be very good friends at the time they were working for Monsieur Dugain."

"She knows why Agnès Loisel was murdered?"

"No."

"D'you have any idea?"

"Agnès Loisel enjoyed the company of women as much as she enjoyed the company of men."

His open jaw revealed a tongue covered with blood pudding and sweet corn. "That pretty girl, that Marie Pierre—you're telling me that she and this Agnès . . ."

"I'm not telling you anything."

Trousseau ran a finger along his lip. "A lesbian?"

"Lesbians tend not to be murderers—or at least, it's not the sort of thing I've experience of."

"Hence the lack of signs of rape, *madame le juge*. Not so easy for one lesbian to rape another."

Almost against her will, Anne Marie laughed. "That is not what I meant."

"What did you mean?"

Anne Marie held up three fingers. "I now know Desterres's been lying since he first came to see me. Contrary to what he claimed, he must've known Agnès because he'd met her when he went looking for Marie Pierre who was living with Agnès Loisel. Desterres was lying and that's why I need to see Richard."

"Doubt if you'll get much out of Richard."

"Richard was with the girl when she met up with Desterres. Perhaps Desterres and Loisel were working together at something. Perhaps they were putting on an act for Richard."

"What on earth for?"

"Quite possibly Desterres and Agnès were pretending not to know each other."

"Eat your food before it gets cold. More water?" Trousseau filled the glasses with sparkling Matouba water.

Anne Marie held up two fingers. "The second problem's the camera."

"What camera?"

"Desterres gave me the Polaroid. Why would a bona fide tourist carry a Polaroid?"

"To take photographs." Trousseau said, "In my humble opinion."

"A Polaroid's not the sort of thing I'd take on holiday. Many years ago I had one—clumsy and expensive and the quality of the pictures could never do justice the vivid greens and turquoises of the

Caribbean. The only advantage is you get the photographs straight away."

"Perhaps that's what this Agnès wanted."

"Most tourists don't want to be lumbered with big cameras. Photos are something you look forward to, once you've returned to the grey skies of Paris. Tourists tend to have small Japanese compacts."

"And the third thing?"

"The bikini." Anne Marie held up her index finger.

"What about it, *madame le juge?*"

"You yourself said it might have been left to decoy us. Think for a minute, Monsieur Trousseau. You're a man who understands women."

"It is not I who says so."

"What's the major trait of West Indian women?"

"You mean their coquetry?"

"Precisely." Anne Marie smiled. "In the last ten years, who's the West Indian girl who wears a bikini?"

"They all do."

"Not as close to the weaker sex as I believed."

"All women wear bikinis."

"Like Brigitte Bardot?"

"Precisely."

"You should go to the beach more often, Monsieur Trousseau. West Indian women prefer one-piece suits."

"I am more interested in a woman's mind than in her body." Trousseau added, after a brief silence, "Vaton was a *Négropolitaine.* She wanted an even tan, perhaps."

"Suntan or otherwise, it is something we must look into—perhaps compare the number of bikinis with swimsuits in the postal catalogs. That should give us an idea."

"You don't go along with the *gendarmes*' theory?"

"Either way, I'll need to see the bikini—both parts. For the moment that's all we've got on Agnès Loisel." She set down knife and fork on the plate. "You know, the Americans have psychological profilers."

Trousseau was not looking at her.

"They have professional psychologists and sociologists who move in on the crime scene and who try to work out the identity of the murderer by studying the methods he uses. Instead, in the French system, it's the *juge d'instruction* who must leaf through the postal catalogs."

"You don't think it was the Dominican who murdered Agnès Loisel?"

"What do you think, *monsieur le greffier*?" Anne Marie asked and was about to raise her glass of mineral water when a shadow was cast across the table. She looked up.

59
Downtown

"How's my sister-in-law?"

"I used to be your wife's sister-in-law. But that was before the divorce, Eric. My husband and I divorced many years ago."

Eric André stepped through the open bay window and into the restaurant. As he bent over to kiss Anne Marie on either cheek, she could recognize his after-shave. In his hand, he held a plastic bag that advertised Lacoste sportswear. He was immaculate in an oxford shirt, black trousers and casual leather shoes. "You'll always be my sister-in-law."

"That's what worries me, Eric. You know Monsieur Trousseau, my *greffier?*"

He appeared unaware of her sarcasm as he shook hands with Trousseau, who was eating lentils and salted cod. "André, director of the Tourism Office," Eric presented himself.

"A pleasure," Trousseau nodded, scarcely looking up from his plate.

"I'm sure we've met before." Eric looked at the Indian. "Statistically, everybody has met everybody in this island. With the population at a third of a million and only two decent streets in which to shop, we must ultimately end up bumping into each other. What the guide books call Pointe-à-Pitre *intra muros.*" Without being invited, he pulled back a varnished chair and sat down at the wooden table beside Trousseau. He looked about with satisfaction at the wood paneling of the open dining room, the scraggly potted plants, the advertisements for beer and Capès Dolé mineral waters. "I hear this's a good little restaurant. I have friends at the Social Security who have lunch here regularly. Cheap and good. Was thinking of having it put onto one of the gastronomic lists."

Anne Marie said, "Not the best food in the world."

"Then I can put it on one of the tourist lists." His boyish smile was strangely at odds with the deep voice. "My friends at the Social Security won't be too pleased to have tourists trekking in here. People on this island want the tourists' money—but not the tourists."

"I thought you were thinking of leaving the tourist industry, Eric. What with a hurricane and people getting killed on the beaches of our archipelago."

He looked at Anne Marie for a moment before giving a wide smile. "Best to keep several strings to your bow."

"And politics?"

Eric André made no attempt to hide his irritation. "Certain things it's best to be discreet about. I've told you that before."

"Something to drink, Eric?"

"They do coffee?" He looked at his flat, gold watch. "I'm in a hurry."

"Why did you want to see me, Eric?"

He smiled. "I didn't even know you were here."

"I was with Lucette Salondy last night. There's nothing to worry about—just that she's diabetic and overweight." The server had brought Anne Marie a plate of conch. Eric André ordered a coffee and Anne Marie started to eat.

"You're working today?"

"Lucette's a relative of yours, too, Eric."

"Only by marriage."

"Like you and me. I'm sure Lucette Salondy'd appreciate a visit."

Eric said nothing. Beside him, Trousseau ate noisily, sucking at the fish bones caught between his teeth.

"Getting anywhere, Anne Marie, with the murder of the Pointe des Châteaux?"

"There is reason to believe the rasta who died raped and killed the woman."

It was Trousseau who spoke. "You were saying there was a connection between the dead girl and Monsieur Dugain, *madame le juge?*"

Trousseau was the soul of discretion and he knew the paramount importance of secrecy when the *juge d'instruction* was preparing a case.

"I beg your pardon, Monsieur Trousseau."

"Not very tender. Yet it's the specialty of the house." Trousseau did not look at her. With his fork in his fist, he pulled at the salted fish. "You think there's a connection, *madame le juge?*"

"Not the sort of thing I care to talk about, Monsieur Trousseau. There are certain things—"

"You know that Dugain was favorable to the Ilet Noir project?"

"What Ilet Noir project?" Anne Marie asked coldly.

"A couple of years ago there was a lot of talk about a refinery. Texaco or one of those American companies wanted to set up a refinery here, on the grounds it'd be cheaper to ship in crude oil from Venezuela than buying it already refined. But the idea of a refinery at Port Louis was not popular. You can understand—a threat to the tourist industry in an island where the future lies in tourism." He raised his eyes, lowered his fork onto the plate and ran the paper napkin along the thin line of his moustache. "Your brother-in-law would know more about it than me." He shrugged with humility. "I'm just an ignorant *greffier.*"

"Not necessarily a bad idea," Eric André said. "I personally think it's a good idea. It'd bring down the energy cost in the island. After all, we have to import all our energy."

"I haven't got any energy left—not with this conch."

Eric André looked at her and gave a perfunctory smile. His glance went from her back to Trousseau. "I must be along."

"And your coffee?"

"You drink it, Anne Marie."

"You knew Dugain was involved in the Ilet Noir project, Eric?"

It was Trousseau who spoke. "He wasn't involved, *madame le juge.* At least not in the sense that he supported it."

She frowned.

Trousseau looked up at Eric, who was now standing. "Has there been a decision yet?"

Eric André observed an embarrassed silence.

"A bit of an outcry at the time, as I remember, Madame Laveaud. You don't remember?"

"Must've been when I was in France."

"Dugain was never more than a whore. He saw the way the wind was blowing, he saw people'd be hostile to a refinery off one of the prettiest beaches." Trousseau turned back to Eric André. "There should be a vote quite soon at the local assembly and I doubt if the refinery'll go through. Thank goodness. Another one of those projects where the *békés* see their interest—and couldn't give a damn about the island."

Eric André said lamely, "It'd bring down the petrol prices, which would bring down costs in general." He placed a hand on Trousseau's shoulder. "Prices are our number one obstacle in the tourist industry. We can get the tourists in from Europe or North America because the airfares are cheap but where we lose out is on the high cost of living. Everything here's some fifty percent over the French price." He again glanced at the flat wristwatch. "I must be off." He placed a ten-franc coin on the table.

"And what do I tell Lucette Salondy?"

"Tell her I'll be along. It's just that I'm very busy at the moment."

"Politics, Eric?"

Eric André did not reply. He had already melted into the crowd hurrying along the boulevard sidewalk.

60

Carnation

They got out of the car and walked up the hill to the main hospital building. Saturday afternoon was a popular time for visits, with children free from school.

She was still angry with Trousseau, but since he had not given any sign of wanting to take his Saturday afternoon off, she said nothing. She was glad to have him with her.

Trousseau meanwhile whistled tunelessly under his breath, occasionally breaking off the private melody to pick at his teeth.

Anne Marie bought a large bunch of red carnations from a woman sitting on a wooden stall.

The prison section was at the back of the new hospital, in old colonial buildings that bore the scars of time and several earthquakes. The walls had been painted a dark ochre that had lost its texture. A row of coconut trees bent in the wind, their fronds creaking noisily.

A couple of male nurses were smoking in the shade of a tree. Neither man seemed to notice Anne Marie as she hurried past. One, who was wearing a round white cap, called out to Trousseau, who laughed and replied in Creole.

They entered the low building and walked along a corridor, past a trolley with its load of kidney dishes and steel utensils. There was a smell of ether and sea breeze. As in many buildings in the tropics, the ground floor was open to the elements. There were no doors and instead of windows, there were regular gaps in the brick wall through which Anne Marie caught sight of the Atlantic, silver and sullen at this time of the day. Although the hospital was some distance above sea level, and although it was exposed to the trade winds, Anne Marie felt hot and very sticky.

"He was embarrassed, wasn't he?"

"Who, Trousseau?"

The *greffier* turned to look at her, surprised by the curtness in her words. "I did not know Eric André was a relative of yours."

"Used to be." Anne Marie spoke flatly. "He married one of my ex-husband's sisters."

"He quite likes you."

"Just one of his problems." She looked at him. "What do you know about Ilet Noir?"

Trousseau gave a small smile, ran his finger along his moustache and was about to say something when a man called out, "Madame Laveaud?"

They stopped.

The man held a microphone and there were earphones around his neck. Sitting on a bench behind him was another man, a television camera placed on the lap of his tennis shorts.

61

Harassment

"I have nothing to say."

"Why not?"

Anne Marie recognized him because he frequently presented the local news at 7:30. "I have nothing to say for the moment."

"Is it true, *madame le juge*, that the murderer of the Pointe des Châteaux killing has been identified?"

"No comment."

"If you have already identified the murderer, why are you here in the penal section of the hospital?"

"Why are you here, gentlemen?"

"Has the murderer been identified?" The man who held the microphone had a round face; the curly hair had started to move back from the high forehead. It was the first time that she had seen Jean Paul Grégory in the flesh. Without makeup and studio lighting, he appeared fatter than on the small screen. Fatter and even more complacent. His skin was damp with perspiration.

"No comment."

"Is there is a connection between last night's siege at the Collège Carnot and the murdered girl?"

"No comment."

Trousseau was standing beside her. He held her flowers in one hand. He now placed himself between the journalist and Anne Marie.

"Is it true the slain Rastafarian had a criminal record?"

The lisping voice and self-satisfied tone made her angry. Anne Marie held up her hand. "You must be very careful."

"Did the rasta have a criminal record of sexual violence?"

She tried to move forward. "You're interfering with the course of justice."

The reporter unexpectedly pushed hard against Trousseau, who was forced to step back. Trousseau said something in Creole—something vulgar that Anne Marie had heard in the mouths of irate detainees.

The cameraman in shorts with earphones around his neck switched on an overhead lamp that he held out at the end of a perch. The sudden light was blinding. Anne Marie brought her hand to her brow to protect her eyes.

"Do you intend to arrest Richard Ferly?"

"Please let me past."

"Are you going to arrest Richard Ferly?"

"You must go."

"Why do you intend to arrest Monsieur Richard Ferly if the murderer of the Pointe des Châteaux's already been identified?"

"I'm an investigating judge involved in official business. Get out of my way."

"Are you aware that Monsieur Ferly has already undergone psychiatric treatment?"

She could feel her heart thumping against her chest. "Take your microphone out of my face and turn off that light."

"Is it true, Madame Laveaud, that Mr. Ludovic Desterres, a well-known ecologist and also a politician . . . is it not true, Madame . . ."

From somewhere a man in white had appeared.

"Is it not true, Madame Laveaud, that Ludovic Desterres's lodged a complaint against you and against the *parquet* for unlawful arrest?"

He had tortoiseshell glasses and he was gesticulating. A stethoscope danced on his chest. He was accompanied by the two nurses who had been smoking beneath the tree.

"Has Monsieur Desterres brought a complaint of harassment and false arrest against the *parquet?*"

The doctor cursed noisily.

"Why don't you answer the question, *madame le juge?*"

The bright light went out as suddenly as it had come on, and Anne

Marie found herself being bundled into a small office, her arms pinned to her sides by the man in white.

Anne Marie saw that the frayed black tie had worked its way round to the left, under Trousseau's stiff collar. With illogical relief, she also noticed that Trousseau was still holding the carnations.

62

Les Messieurs de la Martinique

"I never arrested him."

Trousseau was sweating profusely in his dark suit. He now straightened his tie.

"I really don't see how Desterres can accuse me of wrongful arrest."

"I'm sorry about that, *madame le juge*. The journalist is a bastard from Martinique and next time I'll use my stethoscope." The doctor held out his hand. "I'm Lavigne, and if I'd known you were coming, I'd've been waiting with a machete." He added, "Didn't know the television people could be so aggressive."

Her heart was still thumping. "First time it's ever happened to me."

"I thought the journalists at RFO were civil servants like everybody else. Why the need to behave like paparazzi? You know what people from Martinique are like—they like to think they are more gentlemanly and more French than us honest folk of Guadeloupe."

"The Pointe des Châteaux killing," Anne Marie said simply. "Bad for business and bad for the island—white girl killed on a black island."

"And perfect for the decentralized media," Trousseau remarked. He wiped his forehead with a grubby handkerchief.

Anne Marie smiled at the doctor. "Thanks for rescuing me."

"As for your visit . . ." Lavigne folded his arms against his chest; a pack of cigarettes peeked from the chest pocket. "I don't think Monsieur Ferly's going to be of much use to you. At least, not for now."

She presented Trousseau and the two men shook hands. Lavigne nodded. "Monsieur Trousseau and I've already spoken over the phone."

"Apart from Trousseau, nobody knew it was my intention to come here," Anne Marie said thoughtfully. "I mentioned to Lafitte I hoped to speak with Richard but I didn't know I'd be coming until Monsieur Trousseau told me we could."

"*Madame le juge,* it will not do much good trying to speak to him."

Anne Marie took a deep breath. She looked at the doctor, who was still standing with his back against the door, as if afraid the journalists would attempt to break through with their microphone and overhead lighting. Like monsters in a science fiction film. Anne Marie ran a hand through her hair and smiled gratefully at the doctor.

Then she looked about her. The room smelled of ether. The louvered blinds were made of glass, high in the wall. It could have been any small ward in a tropical hospital—the beds, the cotton blankets, the white cabinet, the chipped paintwork—if it were not for the bars against the high windows.

The beds were all empty.

"Richard Ferly may hold the key to the killing at the Pointe des Châteaux."

The doctor turned and gestured for her and Trousseau to follow. They went down the ward and into a small corridor. Lavigne put a finger to his lips, bent forward and quietly unlocked a second door that opened into a small room.

The air was very cold. A conditioner buzzed high in the wall. The blinds had been drawn. The room was dark except for narrow slants of thin afternoon light squeezing through the closed louvers.

"Ferly?"

"*Madame le juge,* your star witness's sleeping."

"There's nothing wrong with him?"

"Nothing that sleep can't repair. Lots and lots of sleep."

"I need to talk to him, doctor."

"I don't want him woken up."

Anne Marie placed her hand on the doctor's sleeve and looked up at him. Doctor Lavigne had an intelligent face, freckles and thick lips. He was not from France, she now realized, but a Creole and despite his remarks, he may well have been from Martinique. A gentleman from Martinique. "Richard Ferly's the last person to have seen the murdered woman alive. If I'm to arrest the right person, I must speak to him."

"Then come back on Monday."

"Monday?"

Docteur Lavigne added cheerfully "Perhaps you and your *greffier* would care for a drink?"

63
Sigmund

"Mild schizophrenia."

"Does that mean Richard's capable of murdering?"

Lavigne smiled. "I don't think I can answer your question, *madame le juge*, because I don't know the patient sufficiently well. From what I've been told, Richard seems a mild sort of person and not at all aggressive."

"Schizophrenics can be murderers?"

"Six percent of prisoners in high security are schizophrenics, but more often than not, their anger, their rage is directed against themselves."

"Suicide?"

"One in four attempts suicide." Lavigne added, "One in ten succeeds."

It was strangely quiet in the long, empty ward. Docteur Lavigne sat on the bare mattress of a bed. From time to time, Anne Marie's eyes went from his face to the paint at the bedpost—paint that had been chipped away. By handcuffs, no doubt.

"You must understand my problem, Doctor."

"You must try to understand my position." He took a cigarette from the pocket of his jacket and lit it. "Another drink?"

She shook her head, but Trousseau went to the refrigerator and poured himself a second glass of mineral water.

"Is Richard capable of having murdered the young woman at the Pointe des Châteaux?"

"Anyone is capable of murder, *madame le juge*. In the right circumstances. Murder can be the instinct for survival breaking free from the norms imposed upon us by a civilized society. We're all animals."

Trousseau coughed noisily.

"Darwin tells us all species seek survival. Without the desire to survive, there's no life. Life must procreate in order to live."

Trousseau coughed again, even more noisily. He had returned to his plastic chair. Drops of moisture glistened on his straightened tie.

"We don't know whether animals have moral codes but we humans do have codes. You and I, *madame le juge*—there are things we do, not because we need to do them but because our group has told us to do them."

"Like murder?"

"Like not murder. Murder—in terms of group survival—isn't a very good idea. Nor is incest. That's why we created subjective rules which in time have taken on a force of their own."

"What's this got to do with Richard?" Anne Marie asked.

Lavigne laughed, and she liked the way the corner of his lips moved upwards in amusement. She also liked his long, delicate fingers. He must have been in his early forties, with his hair greying at the temples and the first wrinkles coming to the corner of his eyes. He did not wear a wedding ring. "The human brain's a highly sophisticated piece of machinery. A Porsche among Renaults."

"Mine feels like a Mobylette scooter."

"Whereas you can put your Porsche on a jack and send in the mechanics, nothing's so easy with the brain." He laughed to himself. "Removing a bad plug's less dangerous than lobotomy."

"Lobotomy for Richard?"

"Richard's an autonomous human being. He can live his life perfectly well. When he came in, he told me he had a doctor and I've been in touch with Docteur Finlande."

"If Richard can run his life perfectly, why was he hanging around on the beach at Tarare, unshaved and unwashed? It's normal for a bank employee to wander around in swimming trunks and a camera? To judge from his breath, he hadn't eaten for several days." Anne Marie crossed her legs and sat back. The synthetic leather of the upright chair was uncomfortable beneath her skirt. "Docteur Lavigne, I'm sure Richard's a lovely person—kind, good and affectionate—but I need to know whether he killed the woman Agnès Loisel."

"You know how she was killed?"

"Not yet."

"Schizophrenics tend to retreat into themselves. Like you and me . . ." Lavigne paused, glanced at Trousseau. " . . . and like your *greffier*, they're capable of murder. But the schizophrenic's not the sort of person capable of plotting ahead. His is the sudden, explosive rage of restrained forces suddenly being set free."

Trousseau said, "On the way back from the Pointe des Châteaux, he talked about killing."

"Killing who?"

"He wanted a Kalashnikov and said there were twenty or thirty people in Pointe-à-Pitre who needed to be eliminated—people who talked about him, who were plotting against him."

Lavigne turned back to Anne Marie. "In a state of acute stress, his idea of violence and revenge's not very sophisticated. More Rambo than Macchiavelli."

"Most people don't go around talking about killing other people."

"That fat journalist who was sticking his microphone into your throat—you don't think with a gun in your hand, you could've pulled the trigger?"

"Stop putting ideas into my head." She smiled, almost against her will. "I'm taking the children to church tomorrow."

"You'll be going to confession, *madame le juge*?"

Trousseau coughed again. Anne Marie turned and frowned. Trousseau drank more water. Her *greffier* stood up, setting the battered carnations into an empty coffee tin. He took a comb from his pocket and started to comb his hair, looking into the mirror.

"You go to confession, *madame le juge*?"

"Haven't got time."

"To go to confession? Or you haven't got enough time to confess everything?"

Anne Marie wondered whether the *béké* doctor was flirting with her. "Docteur Lavigne, I've never murdered anybody."

Lavigne inhaled on his cigarette, put his head back and watched the blue-grey smoke swirl toward the ceiling. "Richard's a mild sort of character. Indeed, Finlande says he's personable, when he doesn't slip into one of his depressions."

"What do you know about him?"

"In his late thirties. Richard Ferly's held down a good job in a bank for over ten years. He draws up financial reports and is well-educated and literary. His director . . ." A slight bow of the head. "The bank's run by a cousin of mine from Martinique. The director's got no complaints other than the occasional absence, but all absences are accompanied by a medical certificate. Lately they've been more rare. Some surprise at the bank when Richard disappeared without warning. Nobody saw the connection between their well-mannered colleague and the Indian of the Pointe des Châteaux killing."

"He'll lose his job?"

"That depends largely on you, *madame le juge*." Lavigne smiled. "If you feel you'll have to arrest him for murder and rape, I don't think my cousin at the Crédit des Outremers will be able to keep him on for very long."

"What set Richard off on this depression?"

"He'd been hearing voices like Joan of Arc."

"The maid of Orleans was a schizophrenic?"

"Would you have stayed in Orleans if you thought the English were going to burn you at the stake?"

"I ceased being a maid a long time ago."

"Hearing voices and having the impression people are plotting against you are frequent symptoms of schizophrenia. But with Richard it'd got to the stage where he couldn't endure staying in his house. Had to get out into the open to places like the beach. He lives in the city center and he was being woken at nights by the sound of talking. According to his doctor, what Richard believes to be the figment of his imagination was in fact taxi drivers making a din outside his house in the night and the noise was preventing him from sleeping. Once Richard started to lose sleep, he'd lose touch with reality—an objective sound his mind would transform into devils and demons plotting things against him. He'd lose sleep, he'd cease to eat—and started spinning out of control."

"Out of control when he met the girl at the Pointe des Châteaux?"

"No idea—I can only tell you what I know about Richard. He grew up in Paris, where I assume he felt slightly out of things because of his color."

"He never married?"

"Richard doesn't have much respect for himself. Although he would appear to be attractive to the opposite sex—and he has a good job but he's never lived with a woman. He told his doctor he isn't interested in local girls—only in white women."

"He assumed Loisel was a white woman?"

"Finlande maintains Richard loses interest in women who show any interest in him. He's had lots of affairs—even with pretty, young girls—but he lives alone."

"Wouldn't be the first man to be afraid of responsibility."

"It's more like the old joke—the man who won't join a club that accepts riffraff like himself." The doctor shrugged. "Richard was asleep on his feet when he was brought in. He showered and went straight to sleep without eating. He woke up during the night and was given a steak and yam *purée*. I managed to chat with him for twenty minutes." Again Lavigne breathed heavily on the cigarette. "He's been sleeping ever since."

"He'll be awake by Monday?"

"He's not on medication, *madame le juge*. Times when Richard took thorazine, but Finlande doesn't think it's necessary now—just plenty of sleep and a regular diet. It's not the first time he's lost hold on reality. His father died several years ago. With people like Richard, behind the death of the loved one lurks the realization he's going to be left alone in the world. The death of the loved one opens the prospect of years of solitude to come."

"What triggered the present crisis?"

"He was probably already beginning to slip from reality when he met this woman at Tarare." Lavigne paused. "Once he recovers the lost hours, once he gets a square meal under his belt, he should be as right as rain. He'll probably wake up, feeling refreshed, and having forgotten everything about his days of wandering." A resigned smile. "Sigmund Freud always believed schizophrenia was chemical in its origins. Even the modern drugs—the Americans are getting very good results with Clozapine—require psychological backup. I don't think there's any clear cut line between physical and mental—they run into each other and interact."

"It's possible his emotional problems were triggered by a woman? It's possible Richard already knew Agnès Loisel." She took a copy of the Polaroid photograph from her bag. "Look at this photograph: there's an almost possessive look on Richard's face."

"If you say so."

"You say humans are like animals. What do animals do when they think they're going to lose something? You've tried to withhold a dog from approaching a bitch in heat? Agnès's pale enough to pass for a white woman and he's a handsome man—with a good job."

"So?"

"There's an affair between them . . . until she discovers the man she wanted to fall in love with was far from mentally stable. What does she do?"

Trousseau spoke. "She tells him it's over."

"What does Richard do—faced with the prospect of the years of solitude opening up before him?"

Neither Trousseau nor Lavigne said anything.

"Like an animal—if he can't have it, he certainly won't let any one else have it. Particularly if that other person is a rich mulatto like Desterres. He does the only thing that can assuage his anguish."

"Richard Ferly murders the girl." Trousseau ran a thoughtful finger along his moustache.

64

Morne

She was anxious at the thought of seeing Lucette.

"At least the journalists from RFO have gone, *madame le juge.*" Trousseau was grinning as he walked beside her. They had to go down the hill before taking the road up the opposite morne that led to the hospital. The air had cooled as the sun moved slowly westward.

"What's the time, Monsieur Trousseau?"

He tipped the bunch of flowers downwards to look at his watch. "Half past three."

"I hope I can get to the beach before the wind drops. Last time Fabrice sulked because I was late again."

Trousseau said, "I suppose you're still wanting me to take you home."

"That would be very kind of you."

"I know what's expected of a *greffier.*"

"You're good to me, Monsieur Trousseau." She looked at him and despite the tumult of feelings in her chest, Anne Marie could not stop herself from smiling. "I'm surprised your wife doesn't want you with her on a Saturday afternoon."

"*Madame le juge,* you know full well my wife's in France. My youngest boy, Ronny, has just finished at the university and is looking for a job. My wife wants to be with him."

"Must be very difficult for you, Monsieur Trousseau. I know you're attached to your family."

"Madame Trousseau doesn't really like this island." He was slightly out of breath from walking. "Unlike you, she's never really tried to fit in."

"You feel I fit in?"

"You do your best."

"Is that a compliment?"

"There's no need for compliments."

"You have in the past reproached me for my disdain toward the darker races."

"I would never presume to reproach you with anything. I know for a woman, ours is a macho society."

"You never talk to me about your wife."

"You don't normally ask me to work on Saturday afternoon."

Anne Marie smiled. "I won't be asking you to work tomorrow. I've decided to spend the day with my children for once. I'll take Létitia to church. She's been rather religious lately—and I don't know whether it's for her first communion or just for the pleasure of wearing a new dress." She added, "My daughter's discovered the joys of dressing up."

"My wife returned to Paris six years ago."

Anne Marie turned. "You never mentioned anything."

"As much as I respect you, *madame le juge*, and as much as there's considerable sympathy between you and me—sympathy that's been built up over our years of collaboration, fruitful collaboration together . . ."

"You can be very long-winded at times."

"Despite our collaboration, I don't feel it's a deontologically desirable to allow my private life to invade my professional one."

Anne Marie nodded.

"Which is why I have never told you about my divorce . . ."

"Divorce?"

"Strictly in confidence, *madame le juge*."

"I thought you were the happiest of married men."

He had raised the bunch of flowers and his face was partially hidden by the bright carnations. Trousseau hesitated before speaking. "My ex-wife and I both have high regard for each other, of course, and we both love our children very dearly, but Madame Trousseau cannot live here in Guadeloupe and for the moment I've no desire to return to Paris. You see, Madame, as much as I respect the French way of doing things, I feel a lot more at home here in the islands."

"You get to see the children?"

"The two oldest girls are married and have their own families. Ronny's the last one. I miss him because he enjoys working in the garden at Trois-Rivières. We phone of course."

"You live alone?"

"I cook my own produce." Trousseau was smiling, but there was melancholy in his brown eyes. "You really must come to Goyave and I will prepare a meal for you—a dish of pork and the breadfruit you so despise."

They had reached the entrance to the hospital. Anne Marie was about to give Trousseau's arm a reassuring pat when the glass doors opened silently before them and Dr. Bouton was there, smiling from behind his round spectacles.

"Carnations, *madame le juge?* You really shouldn't have."

"I've come to see Lucette Salondy," Anne Marie said as Bouton kissed her on both cheeks. His skin was cold and felt like that of a lizard's against her cheek.

"Lavigne told me you were on your way."

Anne Marie said, "How is she?"

"Lavigne told me you now believe this Richard Ferly's the murderer."

"How's Lucette?"

Dr. Bouton took her by the arm and they went toward the large lifts. Almost immediately, the steel doors drew apart and as they stepped inside, Dr. Bouton hit one of the buttons. The lift moved gently upwards.

"Lucette's going to be all right?"

It was very cold inside the hospital.

"I'd hate to be in one of these things during an earthquake," Dr. Bouton said, his eyes—or perhaps the rims of the glasses—twinkling.

Anne Marie put her hand to her belly; she could feel the tenseness of her muscles. "How's my sister-in-law, Docteur Bouton?"

Bouton looked at her, then at Trousseau. Anne Marie could recall how much she had loathed him when he had told her that she was pregnant with Létitia. For a while, he had played with her, like a clever cat playing with a mouse. He had knowledge she needed and he enjoyed the power that knowledge gave him. Anne Marie returned his stare. "Well?"

He raised one shoulder. "You knew of course that she had sickle-cell disease?"

"What?"

"You needn't worry about last night—that was nothing more than an unpleasant shock. Her system's resistant enough to deal with that but I'm afraid Mademoiselle Salondy doesn't look after herself. From birth she's been anemic—and she's now diabetic."

"Lucette . . ."

Dr. Bouton looked at Anne Marie with his alert smile. "The poor woman's carrying more weight than's good for her and I'm afraid she's not very careful about her diet." He lowered his voice. "Surprised her doctor didn't tell her to lay off the alcohol. I get the impression she has a more than healthy fondness for white rum."

"That's not the impression I have."

The illuminated roundel in the panel indicated they had reached the twelfth floor as the doors slid open. Dr. Bouton stepped aside to allow Anne Marie out of the lift. "You should be able to speak to her for a few minutes. She's no longer in intensive care, but she does need rest so it wouldn't be a good idea to upset her."

"Why should I upset her?"

Dr. Bouton placed his hand on her sleeve. "I won't have time to see you afterwards, *madame le juge*, because I'm invited to a *souper dansant*. However, I wanted to tell you . . ."

"Yes?"

He held his hands down in front of him, like a falsely contrite child. Because of the temperature in the hospital he was wearing his double-breasted cashmere cardigan. A bogus escutcheon, an English regiment perhaps, at the chest. "I wanted to tell you there's still no word from Pasteur, other than that they can find no trace of anything in the woman's body."

"The woman?"

"The woman we thought was Vaton. I believe she's now been identified. I'm extremely embarrassed not being able to identify the cause of death. However . . ." He held up his hand in a deprecating gesture that irritated Anne Marie. "I'm willing to stake my professional reputation her death wasn't violent."

"If it wasn't violent, how was she killed?"

"Pasteur's sent blood samples to Paris. Normally they'd wait a week, but neither they nor I think we're going to find anything. The girl'd been dead for more than three days. In that time, the chemical components started to break down. If she didn't meet with a violent death, the most probable explanation—a healthy young woman in the prime of her life, who was seen to be happy and healthy on the Sunday morning—the most plausible explanation is poison or drugs. Unfortunately by the time I got my hands on her, there wasn't much left in her stomach. There were old traces of syringe marks, but that doesn't prove anything. However—and if you are right about Richard, this may well be a nail in his coffin—I'm convinced the girl didn't die on the beach."

"Why not?"

Again the patronizing smile of a man who can share or withhold knowledge. "From the beginning I was convinced the body'd been carried to the beach, *madame le juge*, on the Wednesday morning. If we accept she died on Sunday night and the corpse was found on Wednesday by the fisherman, there seems no reason why animals shouldn't have started tearing the body apart. Of course, there are times when a body can give off a smell that frightens animals away—but a smell'll never frighten away all animals."

"More or less the conclusion I had come to, Docteur Bouton."

He nodded, trying to conceal mild irritation. "Livor mortis would suggest the corpse wasn't moved after death. You no doubt remember livor mortis seemed to indicate the woman'd collapsed onto her back and had remained in that position."

Unexpectedly, Trousseau spoke from behind the bunch of flowers. "Perhaps she'd died in bed."

"Excellent, Monsieur Trousseau," Bouton exclaimed, beaming at the *greffier*.

"Which would mean," Anne Marie said thoughtfully, looking from one man to the other, "the bikini on the beach was left there deliberately." She spoke slowly. "The bikini was left there so we'd associate her with the young woman Monsieur Desterres'd met and photographed at Tarare."

65
Diabetes

She was glad to have Trousseau beside her.

(Dr. Bouton had accompanied them as far as the closed door, then turning on his heel, had gone off down the corridor, his shoes echoing off the linoleum against the bare walls.)

Anne Marie took the flowers from Trousseau and entered the small room. It was on the north side of the building, bright but without the heat of the sun. It gave on to the hospital park, the boulevard and, beyond that, the ghetto of Boissard.

There were flowers everywhere, yellow chrysanthemums, balisiers, varieties of roses and many bouquets of carnations. They had been placed on tables, on chairs and on the floor.

In the middle of the room was a single bed, anchored to the floor by various tubes and leads. At first, as Anne Marie approached, she could scarcely see her sister-in-law. The large body had sunk into the mattress and the small head was lost in the depths of a plump pillow.

Trousseau took the flowers from her hand and walked over to a small sink.

With a pounding heart and the muscles taut in her belly, Anne Marie stepped forward. She thought Lucette Salondy was asleep. The face had lost its color and the mouth was slightly open. A double loop of plastic piping ran across each cheek into a nostril. There was a saline drip, an opaque bag hanging from a metal pillar and leading to Lucette's arm, concealed beneath the cotton blanket.

The head turned, the eyes opened and there was recognition. With relief, Anne Marie saw the sunken face slowly break into the familiar smile.

Lucette said something. Anne Marie had to lean forward to hear the feeble, sibilant voice.

"They thought they could kill me." It was as if a brace had been set onto Lucette's teeth.

Trousseau left the flowers in the sink beneath a running tap and he now brought a chair for Anne Marie to sit down. She kissed Lucette's forehead, noting the faint smell of tear gas, placed her hand on Lucette's shoulder and slowly lowered herself onto the cold chair. "Nobody's going to kill you."

There was a slight wince of pain.

"You should be out of here before long."

"No pizza."

"What?" Anne Marie leaned forward.

"Supposed to be taking the children for a pizza, you and I, and look what happens to me." A smile and Anne Marie realized that the sunken cheeks and the sibilant pronunciations were because Lucette's false teeth had been removed. "Instead I end up here."

"You need to rest, Lucette."

"They told me the Dominican was killed."

Anne Marie nodded.

"You were there, *doudou*?"

"I came—but when I reached the school the police had cordoned it off."

"You saw?"

Anne Marie had seen very little. She had seen one of the men in a flak jacket stand up on the opposite roof as he aimed and fired the canister of tear gas. She had seen the other CRS move forward toward the office, but the action had been indoors, out of view. With the swirling tear gas, her eyes had started to water and she was no longer watching. No longer able to watch. It was some time later Bastia had approached her and given her a mask. She had followed him— strangely nonchalant, he was smoking a cigarette—into the small office where the Dominican's lung had been blown apart. Blood on the wall, beneath the photograph of a placid, arrogant President Mitterrand.

"I got there later."

"You came with me in the ambulance?"

Anne Marie said, "They gave you something to sleep."

"Then he's dead?"

Anne Marie nodded.

Silence in the room, apart from the sound of the running tap and Trousseau's arranging the flowers in a vase. Anne Marie's offering seemed insignificant alongside the other exuberant bouquets.

Lucette smiled a toothless smile. "Like a cemetery in here."

"The doctor says you should soon be out."

"I want to sleep."

"You must sleep, Lucette. I just dropped by to see how you were."

"You accompanied me last night, didn't you? That was good of you. You are a good person, Anne Marie."

"Tomorrow I'll come with Létitia and with Fabrice, if you like."

Slowly, as if it were valuable and fragile porcelain, Lucette turned her head on the pillow and Anne Marie felt that she had never seen her sister-in-law look so old. "Bring Létitia?"

"You'd like that?"

"Kiss me, Anne Marie."

Anne Marie leaned over Lucette. She could smell the unhealthy breath, just as she could smell the skin of her sister in law, the faint whiff of tear gas, blood and death. As she was bending, Lucette caught Anne Marie's hand. "Perhaps it's His judgment on me."

"Whose judgment?"

"God's angry with me."

"If He is, tomorrow my daughter will light a candle and say a prayer for you."

"You're a disbeliever, Anne Marie, and I'm an old and jealous woman."

"Lucette, just think about getting some sleep. Then we can get you out of here."

"It's God's punishment." For a sick woman, she had a strong grip. Anne Marie looked at the freckled brown hand that clasped her own. "I should never've told you about the Théodore woman."

Anne Marie frowned. "Madame Théodore?"

"Keep your voice down, my sister."

"You never told me anything about Madame Théodore."

"A jealous old woman. My fault, I should never have allowed myself to love Rodolphe—but that's an old story."

"Rodolphe Dugain?"

There was a long pause. Lucette looked at Anne Marie and her bloodshot eyes were damp. "An old, old story."

"Love Rodolphe Dugain?"

"There could never be anything between him and that white woman but I was jealous—just as I was jealous of Liliane when she married Rodolphe all those years ago. I never forgave her—although, for heaven's sake, the poor thing's suffered for her presumption. It's just that . . ." She had started to cry.

"You and Rodolphe Dugain, Lucette?"

"Oh, I always suspected the truth. I knew what he was like—but if he'd wanted to, I'd have married him and even later, a lot later, when the Théodore woman was running after him, even then I was jealous. An old, old woman, with already one foot in the grave and one foot macerating in white rum, I was as jealous as a silly adolescent."

Lucette had lowered her voice and Anne Marie had her ear almost against the toothless mouth.

"In my pride I always felt I could've changed him." She snorted softly. "I could have made him love me."

"Dugain was a womanizer, Lucette. You could never have changed him."

"Womanizer?" Perhaps she coughed, perhaps she laughed. "Rodolphe Dugain was a homosexual—right to the end, it was the pretty boys he liked. Why else do you think he killed himself?"

66

Tails

"It's very kind of you, Monsieur Trousseau."

She sat in the back of the car. Perhaps because he could feel her unhappiness, Trousseau drove carefully.

"I'll come tomorrow with the children. It would do Lucette a world of good to see them—she's always been fond of them. More fond than their own grandmother."

"She mentioned Rodolphe Dugain to you?"

"She's afraid of being stuck in the hospital."

"Your sister-in-law is overweight."

"Is that breadfruit?"

Trousseau turned in the seat. "I beg your pardon?"

"Your breadfruit smells absolutely terrible."

"The plastic bag's torn."

"You intend to eat something that smells like that, Monsieur Trousseau?"

The *greffier* was offended. "I can't smell anything." He coughed loudly and leaned forward, placing his hands carefully on either side of the steering wheel. "She mentioned Dugain? You were whispering between yourselves like adolescent girls."

Anne Marie opened the window. "It's worse than the Vaton woman's *eau de cologne.*"

They had come to the edge of Sainte-Anne, and the Peugeot hissed smoothly along the *boulevard maritime.* It was not yet five o'clock and there were bright sails skimming over the turquoise waters of the Atlantic. Along the sidewalk, the itinerant vans had parked and were preparing their evening trade of drinks, pizzas and crêpes.

"So you can drop the whole affair?"

"Affair, Monsieur Trousseau?"

"You're going to drop the Dugain thing?"

"We still haven't found the murderer of Agnès Loisel."

"Your friend the *procureur*'s happy to blame the dead Dominican."

"One, Arnaud's no more my friend than you are."

"Very flattering, I'm sure."

"And two, he hasn't said anything to me. Until he does, I'm still in charge of the dossier."

"You're going to let Dugain drop?"

The breadfruit in the boot must have been in an advanced state of putrefaction. Anne Marie raised her wrist to her nostrils, seeking a hint of van Cleef and Arpels. "Why for heaven's sake does everybody want me off the Dugain dossier?"

"For your own good, *madame le juge*."

"I'm old enough to know how to look after myself."

They had come to the end of the village and the road narrowed as Trousseau took the slow incline that led to the turning for Ffrench.

"And I don't understand, Monsieur Trousseau, why you felt it necessary to be so aggressive toward the Director of the Tourist Office. I don't suppose it occurred to you that as my brother-in-law, he merited a minimum of courtesy."

"They go off to France, these West Indians, they get some little *diplôme* and then when they come back to the islands, they wear double-breasted suits and they think they can lord it over us."

"Eric André's my brother-in-law."

"Ex-brother-in-law, *madame le juge*."

"Brother-in-law or ex-brother-in-law—that's got nothing to do with you." Anne Marie was suddenly very angry. "Lucette Salondy's my ex-sister-in-law. That doesn't stop me being worried for her."

"Eric André's a phony. A crook and a phony."

"You mustn't say those things about my brother-in-law."

"What do you want, *madame le juge*?" Brusquely Trousseau brought the car to a halt beneath a billboard advertising a nearby *discothèque*, now in an advanced state of abandon. Creole cows gazed calmly.

"What on earth do you want?" He pulled angrily on the handbrake and turned to face her. "Just answer that."

"I think my family deserves respect."

"You want a sycophant? You want somebody to tell you just what you want to hear? Or do you want a friend? Can't you see that André was behind the death of Dugain?"

"Eric murdered Dugain?" Anne Marie laughed in disbelief.

"As for the breadfruit, *madame le juge*, it's not for human consumption. It's for my pigs at Trois-Rivières. And don't say I haven't already invited you to come and eat pig tails and breadfruit at my place."

67
Sharks

It was a small beach next to the Méridien hotel. Trousseau parked the Peugeot on the edge of the unsurfaced white road, between the open Méharis and Japanese four-wheel drives.

The trade breezes were blowing noisily through the palm trees that seemed to lean into the wind. After the lush green of the countryside, the coral beach was almost blinding in its whiteness, even at this late hour of the afternoon. The sun was fast moving toward the Soufrière and the West. In another half hour, the wind would drop and the sailboards would be brought onto the beach, taken down, packed up and set back on the awaiting motor vehicles.

There was no sign of Fabrice, nor of his distinctive fun-board, with its yellow and mauve sail.

"You should've told me a long time ago, Monsieur Trousseau."

"I thought you knew." He ran a finger along his moustache. "After all, he's your brother-in-law."

"I scarcely ever see my ex-brother-in-law. I hadn't seen him in ages when he phoned me last Wednesday night." Anne Marie shrugged. "I assumed it was over the Pointe des Châteaux murder." Instinctively, she looked eastwards toward the Pointe des Châteaux. At a distance of over ten kilometers, the concrete calvary was clear against the limpid afternoon horizon.

"Instead he spoke to you about Dugain?"

"He's intending to go into politics."

Trousseau laughed. "I don't think he's got much chance."

Beneath the palm trees there was a small white shack, clean and freshly painted. Plastic tables and chairs were set out on the powdery sand. Anne Marie made her way toward a free table in the shade. The customers were beach types, European men and women for the most part, with matching blond hair and tanned backs. Their beautiful young skin would soon be losing its elasticity from over-exposure to the sun. Even with Fabrice's mixed parentage, Anne Marie insisted he wear a T-shirt while windsurfing. She knew the treachery of the sun and was reminded of it every time she looked in the mirror.

"André's not a doctor. He doesn't belong to the old class of West Indians who went to France to finish their studies or flew there in the days of the Lockheed Constellation. Not a doctor, not a pharmacist, not that category of people the population likes to respect—people who understand that in return for a personal vote, there's a personal favor to be repaid. Your ex-brother-in-law's a wolf in wolf's clothing. If he hadn't gotten a job at the Office of Tourism he'd have been a teacher in some godforsaken junior high on the Côte-sous-le-Vent or in one of the islands, Désirade or Marie-Galante. He belongs to that class of second-raters."

"Like me, Monsieur Trousseau?"

"*Madame le juge*, you have many failings, but you're not second rate. You have professional probity—perhaps too much."

"Not sure whether I should take that as a compliment."

"You still have your illusions—perhaps that's all you've got left." Again Trousseau ran his finger along the line of his moustache. Then he straightened his tie. "You're part of that generation of white do-gooders."

"Thank you."

"You came out to the Caribbean with the best of intentions. The post-1968 generation in tie-dyed T-shirts and clogs, you ran around in bell-bottom jeans and Renault 4Ls and you paid the air-duty to read *Le Monde* every day. And you married into the local population, just to prove that you were free of prejudice."

"I met my husband in Paris."

(Jean Michel used to have an old Panhard coupé, and in the afternoons, the car could be seen cruising up and down the Boulevard Saint-Michel, along the rue de l'Odéon and as far as the rue

Monsieur-le-Prince and the Luxembourg gardens. The roof was always down, despite the chill spring weather of Paris, and the back seat was packed tight with grinning friends from Martinique and Guadeloupe, with bright teeth and short hair and American Army raincoats. Invariably sitting beside Jean Michel was a blonde girl, with skin of alabaster and a scarf round her head like the actress Pascale Petit.)

"It comes to the same thing. Don't think I don't respect you, *madame*. Quite the opposite. There are times when I think you choose not to see the opportunism of my compatriots—after all these years. The opportunism of people like Eric André. You insist on seeing the best in him."

"Blame the tie-dyed T-shirt and clogs."

"What's worse, he'll probably get away with the Ilet Noir project. Use influence he has as director of the Tourist Office and he'll make a lot of money. While my island"—Trousseau tapped the table—"yet again, this poor Guadeloupe'll be pillaged and made poorer. Just so that Eric André can wear his Lacoste shirts and run around in a Mercedes."

"Why was Eric responsible for Dugain's death?"

"Dugain was a bastard—but I don't think he sought money."

"He committed suicide because he'd been embezzling."

"No one believes that, *madame le juge*."

"What do you believe?"

"Dugain was concerned about the environment."

"Like Desterres?"

"Desterres is like your brother-in-law." A derisory snort. "A shark—only he's better educated and there's been money in Desterres's family for years. A vulture—but less of a vulture than Eric André." Trousseau started to laugh. "Having lighter skin, Desterres's got less of a complex about himself."

A girl in a swimsuit took their order: mineral water for Trousseau, iced tea for Anne Marie. Trousseau glanced admiringly at the girl's long white thighs. When she was out of earshot, Anne Marie said, "You, too, are a bit of a shark."

"My pigs at Trois-Rivières—that's all I'm interested in."

Anne Marie sighed. "Lavigne's probably right—we're animals."

"Sharks?"

"Mice—we're like mice in a maze, Monsieur Lafitte. And the cheese we're all looking for—we're all frantically sniffing out—is sex."

"Speak for yourself, *madame le juge.*"

"Power, money, influence—all substitutes for our libido."

There was still no sign of Fabrice on the horizon. Anne Marie was not particularly worried, but she never liked it when he went beyond the protection of the barrier reef, eight hundred meters out into the sea. A calm sea could suddenly turn into swelling breakers.

"Putting your analogies aside, if I may for a moment . . ." Trousseau waited until the girl had brought the drinks. "There must have been some sort of blackmail being used on him."

Anne Marie leaned forward and poured tea into the glass. "On him?"

"On Dugain. Didn't you read about it? A couple of years ago—it was in the papers."

"Probably when I was in France for the in-service training course. A month in Châtelrault."

"The *préfet* set up a council of wise men to deliberate over the whole Ilet Noir affair. At the time, they said it was an American consortium, Texaco or Esso. In fact it was Elf Aquitaine that wanted to install a refinery off the coast of Port Louis, bringing the crude oil up from Venezuela. It would've meant a lot of jobs and it would have meant housing petroleum engineers coming out from France. Well-paid professionals from the mainland. The mayor of Port-Louis was for it—and so of course was the Office of Tourism."

"But Dugain wasn't?"

"Precisely, *madame le juge.*"

"And Desterres?"

The *greffier* said, "I can't remember but I do remember Dugain going on television and doing a series of programs about the possible danger of oil spills. His special interest'd always been the mangrove—which never endeared him to the building lobby, anyway. Especially when you remember half of Pointe-à-Pitre is built on mangrove. Even the sugar fields in Grande-Terre were originally mangrove—they were drained by the English when they controlled this island."

"Then what happened?"

"In return for Quebec and Canada, the English handed this island back to the French at the end of the Seven Years' War. A bit of a shame, really, because we could've been English and you'd be drinking tea."

"I am drinking tea. What happened over the Ilet Noir dossier?"

"Demonstrations—you're sure you weren't here, *madame le juge*? To keep things calm, the *préfet* called for an enquiry but the review body still hasn't submitted its report. Dugain was on the television, he was on the radio, he was in the papers—and then suddenly silence as if his power had been switched off. Strange."

"Why?"

"Why did he suddenly shut up?" Trousseau looked at her. "I'm only a *greffier* of course."

"Even so, you have an opinion."

"I know about sharks—and I know about the money to be made from setting up a new industry in a place like this, where forty percent of the population is unemployed. Government handouts—that's what we live on. A lot of money to be made out of Ilet Noir. And Dugain was treading on a lot of people's toes."

"They silenced him?"

"The blackmail worked."

"If blackmail worked, then there was no need to kill him," Anne Marie said.

"*Madame le juge*, they *suicided* him."

"Suicided?" Anne Marie said and gave a start as she felt a coldness on her shoulder, as cold as death itself.

Fabrice, hair wet and the torn T-shirt clinging to his chest, bent over and kissed his mother. "For once you're not too late." He stroked her hair. "I'm starving."

68

Nylon

"Maman, please help me iron my dress for church."

"Can't you see I'm watching television, Lélé?"

The local news was taken up by the siege in the rue Schoelcher. The cameramen had reached the scene late because they had been covering a basketball match at the hall *bicentenaire*. Shots of the ambulances and police vans outside the Collège Carnot. Anne Marie recognized herself as she was being helped into one of the red ambulances. She saw that she had put on weight, particularly around the buttocks. Too much sitting and not enough exercise was turning her into one of Trousseau's steatopygous women.

Following the siege and the dawn raid on Boissard—more pictures of *gendarmes* in bulletproof jackets—the journalists had interviewed the *préfet* in his office in Basse-Terre. Ill at ease under the television lights, speaking in a marked Provençal accent, he assured the viewers the enquiries would follow their course until the murder of the Pointe des Châteaux was properly resolved.

"Our *département* can return to normality, thanks to the prompt intervention of the forces of order. The difficult and unpleasant experience of the last few days is now behind us, just as Hurricane Hugo is behind us, so let us look to a brighter future. We cannot allow the gruesome murder of a tourist to prevent us from getting back on our feet. My compatriots understand the future prosperity of the *département* is largely dependent upon tourism for it is tourism that brings in more wealth than either the banana or the sugar industries. We must all strive to improve this island's image among our potential customers and friends, in Europe as in North America. We must all, I repeat, make a very big effort." He smiled wanly into the camera. "The *parquet* has not yet closed the Pointe des Châteaux dossier and if the man who died last night during the unhappy events at the Collège Carnot is the perpetrator of the senseless murder of the young tourist, I must nonetheless warn my compatriots against the temptations of xenophobia. Our republic has a long tradition of welcoming foreigners, and it is not because of an individual act of folly that we will hold all foreigners responsible. Witch hunting is not a French tradition and I solemnly call upon the people of this island to treat the foreigners among us with the same republican fraternity we show to our own compatriots, friends and family. *Vive la Guadeloupe. Vive la France.*"

"Please help me iron my dress for church."

There was nothing from the hospital, although the newscaster, a round-faced man in a silk jacket, said that Mademoiselle Salondy was out of intensive care. Smiling into the camera, he mentioned that an employee of the Crédit des Outremers was helping the investigators.

No mention of Desterres.

"Please, Maman."

"There's nothing wrong with your dress."

"It's creased."

Béatrice had gone home for the weekend and Anne Marie refused to be bullied by her daughter, so with a theatrical sigh, Létitia had set up the ironing board, plugged in the steam iron and began to iron the dress. "What's the point of having a maid if she can't iron clothes properly?" To get pressure on the fabric, she had to stand on a footstool. She made a clicking sound of disapproval with her lips.

"It's not for you to criticize Béatrice. She has enough on her plate with you two. And don't tisk. It's ill-mannered, Lélé. I've already told you that."

"Yes, Maman," Létitia replied diplomatically and sighed softly.

The television link-up with Paris was later than usual.

Anne Marie sat in the armchair. Fabrice came in from his bedroom, the Walkman clipped to his belt. He wanted to watch Ushuaïa.

They had quarreled in the car and Anne Marie had even shouted.

She had told him about her conversation with Siobud. Like his sister, he had made a clicking sound of disapproval and then laughed.

"Not a laughing matter, Fabrice."

"Siobud's pathetic," he had said, dismissing the matter.

"The clown of the class?"

Worse still, Trousseau had taken Fabrice's side. Now between Anne Marie and her son there reigned an uneasy truce.

Fabrice sat down cross-legged at her feet. He had broad shoulders and was fast turning into a man, with a man's body, although he did not yet need to shave. She could feel the reassuring warmth of his body against her leg. He was still hot from his exposure to the sun and his hair smelled of the sea.

The clown of the class?

"What time do we have to be at church, Lélé?"

"I bet Patricia wears a necklace."

"Patricia Petit?"

"Oh, Maman," Létitia replied with mock exasperation. "You know Patricia Petit's an Adventist. She doesn't go to church."

"Patricia who?"

Létitia placed her hand theatrically on her hip. "I'm talking about Patricia Ganot. You know her. Her father works for Air France and he spoils her and she can go to Miami whenever she wants." She lowered her voice, for greater effect. "You know she came to school with nail polish?"

"And what did the mistress say?"

"Sister Marie didn't say anything because she's as blind as a bat, but I don't think it's right, do you, Maman? It's not right for little girls to wear nail polish."

Fabrice spoke without taking his eyes from the television. "You wear lipstick."

"No I don't," his sister replied hotly.

"Is that true, Lélé?"

Létitia asked innocently, "What, Maman?"

"You wear lipstick?"

"Maman, you know what Fabrice is like."

"Answer my question."

"He loves to make trouble." She had returned to her ironing and was concentrating.

"Please answer my question, Lélé."

"What question?"

"Do you wear lipstick?"

Another sigh. "Only once, Maman."

"My lipstick? Lélé, I've already told you not to go into my bedroom. You are not to rummage in my drawers. You're still a little girl and I don't want you wearing makeup. It doesn't suit you."

"Yes it does."

"Don't answer back."

"Patricia wears lipstick."

"You are not Patricia. You are Létitia Jeanne Laveaud. You're my little girl and you're not yet ten years old. As long as you live under this roof," Anne Marie said, and she could hear her father in her own words, "and as long as you eat at my table, you'll do as you are told and you shall not wear lipstick. Do I make myself clear?"

"But Maman . . ."

Anne Marie glared. "Mademoiselle Laveaud, do you understand?"

"Yes," Létitia said, hanging her head, but as soon as she thought her mother had turned away, she made a silent snarl of antipathy in the direction of her brother, then stuck out the pink triangle of her tongue.

"If you want to paint your face up because you want to act or you want to play with your girlfriends here in the house, I don't mind—but you mustn't use my cosmetics. I pay a lot of money for that makeup. We can go to the Prisunic on Wednesday and I'll get you some children's makeup. But you won't go out of the house with it on."

Létitia was now quietly smiling to herself, as if she had just recalled a private joke.

"You mustn't play with my things, Lélé. Try to understand. You mustn't play with my clothes or with my shoes or with my makeup. It's very important—because I must always look my best for work."

Létitia set the iron down on the board, having decided to change the subject. "Maman, why do you always put on that strong perfume when you know you're going to the hospital?"

"After church tomorrow, we're going to see Tatie Lucette at the hospital."

Létitia crossed her arms in disapproval. "I don't want to go."

"You're her favorite."

"There's nothing wrong with her. They just said so on television."

"When you were in hospital, Lucette came and saw you and she brought you a present every day."

"She's fat."

"You can't be nice to her just because she's fat?"

"She likes kissing me and cuddling me."

"I like kissing and cuddling you. You're my favorite mongoose—even though you're spoiled and you run rings around everybody and you wear my shoes and you wear my lipstick and you tell fibs."

"I don't."

"If you're not careful your nose will grow."

"It already has," Fabrice observed wryly.

"And if you're not careful this very minute, you're going to burn that dress. Lélé, look, look!" Anne Marie hurriedly pulled herself from the armchair and took hold of the iron. "Goodness, child, you've set the thermostat for cotton." Anne Marie barged her daughter off the stool. Squirting the white dress with a fine spray of water, she hurriedly ironed out the remaining creases. "Ten years old and you can't tell the difference between cotton and nylon."

"All because you don't want to help me," Létitia said in an aggrieved tone. "And I'm still only nine."

It amused Anne Marie to let her daughter think she had not seen through Létitia's stratagem. Any trick in the book to get Maman to iron the difficult parts.

Then the phone rang and Létitia ran to take the receiver off the wall. Anne Marie glanced at the Kelton. "Who phones at this time of night?"

Létitia held the telephone to her ear and frowned.

"Who is it, Lélé?"

"It's your friend."

"What does he want?"

Létitia held out the phone in silence.

"Time you were in bed, Létitia Jeanne Laveaud," Anne Marie said, turning off the iron with one hand, and taking the receiver in the other. "Is that you, Luc?"

"Anne Marie?" The line was poor.

"Stay here." Fabrice was suddenly standing beside her, his tanned fingers pulling at her sleeve. "Don't go out tonight, Maman."

The fear of abandonment in his eyes reminded Anne Marie of his father.

69

Sermon

The priest gave his sermon, speaking into a microphone that rose like a steel tulip before him in the pulpit. He spoke slowly, carefully pronouncing each word, as if addressing a class of dull theologians. Anne Marie was not listening. She stood between her children, near the back of the church, close to one of the iron pillars.

The church had been quickly restored and renovated in the few months since the hurricane. It was now full of flowers, slanting light, people and the smell of incense. Candles flickered in the small lady's chapel. Near the front of the church, there were several wheelchairs.

The priest droned on and the oblong loudspeakers, perched on the pillars, repeated his words. Anne Marie held her daughter's hand.

Létitia's hand was small and the fingers were sticky. She was wearing neutral nail polish. Anne Marie had put her foot down about the makeup and had insisted her daughter remove the rouge before setting off for church.

Her anger was largely pretense. Anne Marie did not find Létitia's love of makeup strange or even precocious. As a child, Anne Marie herself had always enjoyed dressing up, putting on exotic clothes from Maman's wardrobe that smelled of mothballs. With her sister, she had produced plays—normally romantic adaptations of Cinderella. Papa had delighted in the amateur dramatics provided the plot was fairly straightforward and the histrionics did not go on too long.

The priest—a bishop from Cayenne—was talking about tolerance.

Anne Marie tried to concentrate but her attention began to wander. She thought about her life, about the mother she had scarcely known, about her children. She thought about the phone call from Luc. She had noted the look of disapproval on her daughter's face as Létitia handed her the receiver. The same look of disapproval—wrinkled nose, lips rounded and open to reveal her teeth—that Létitia had made when Fabrice had started to tell tales.

(Létitia had nothing to be afraid of. Anne Marie had no intention of allowing Luc to enter her life. It was not that Anne Marie did not like him, or indeed the fact that he was already married.)

In Africa, the bishop was saying, Jesus was presented as a black man. But Jesus was every color, because He was the Son of God. Since man was made in the image of God, the bishop said, we could assume that God was an Asian, was an African, was a European.

Anne Marie glanced to where Fabrice sat quietly on the mahogany pew beside her. Perhaps with his mixture of race—West Indian father and Jewish grandfather—he was a true representative of God on Earth.

Smiling at the thought, Anne Marie looked about her, at the old ladies in their *glacé* straw hats, the men sweating in suits and ties. Here assembled in St. Peter and St. Paul was the bourgeoisie of Pointe-à-Pitre—or at least, that bourgeoisie that still went to church.

Pointe-à-Pitre.

It was here, she realized, here in this provincial, tropical city on the edge of the mangrove, that Anne Marie had taken root. She was like a plant, she told herself, and her children were the branches. They were branches of mixed parentage—and it was here, in this French city 6,750 kilometers from Paris, this city with its strange mixture of African and European, that they belonged.

"In the name of the Father," the bishop said and crossed himself. With retarded synchronization, the congregation repeated his words, bowing their heads and crossing themselves.

Anne Marie's children belonged here, and no matter how much she liked Luc, he was European. He could never understand her children. They were her children and to get any more involved with him would be a betrayal. It would be a refusal to recognize their identity, it would be a betrayal of the people and of the island that Anne Marie had grown to love.

She lowered her head and slowly crossed herself.

Létitia tugged at her elbow. "Afterwards, we can go for McDonald's."

Anne Marie made a silent prayer. For the dead, for family and friends. Then a few minutes later, Judge Laveaud and her children stepped out into the sunshine, Létitia resplendent in her white frock, Fabrice in black T-shirt (Def Leopard) and Reeboks.

St. Peter and St. Paul stood silently in their sunlit niches; beside them, the four evangelists. On the far side of the square, the flower vendors were doing brisk business. Not wanting to talk to anybody (her ex-husband's parents lived in the nearby rue Alsace-Lorraine), Anne Marie took her children by the hand and headed toward the rue Nozières.

"What a pleasant surprise!"

He must have been sitting at the front, near the altar. He was wearing a pale lightweight suit and beige shoes with matching socks. His hands were placed on the handles of a wheelchair. He looked admiringly at Anne Marie. "I didn't know you came to St. Pierre and St. Paul."

A West Indian woman was sitting in the wheelchair. She sat to one side, trying unsuccessfully to adopt the fetal position. Despite the heat, she was covered with a blanket. Red shoes with bows like those worn by Minnie Mouse stuck out from beneath the blanket at an improbable, oblique angle.

"My daughter's preparing her Confirmation, Monsieur Lafitte."

Létitia stepped forward and demurely held out her hand. Lafitte bent forward and kissed her on the forehead.

"I believe you've already met my son, Fabrice."

They shook hands. "A long time ago, *madame le juge.* He has now grown into a fine young man."

"Who doesn't take his studies at school very seriously, I'm afraid."

"With the intelligence of his mother," Lafitte said, "I'm sure he has excellent marks."

The congregation was slowly disappearing into the cars parked along the neighboring streets. It was nearly midday and the faithful were in a hurry to get out of the sun, to get out of their Sunday best before heading off to the beach or to the hills.

Anne Marie took her children by the elbow. "Monsieur Lafitte, it's been nice."

The policeman smiled, his breath tinged with beer. "You've never met my wife, have you?" He placed his hand on the shoulder of the chairbound woman.

There was no smile of acknowledgment in the immobile face. There was no movement of the bulging eyes. Just a hand that trembled.

"Madame Lafitte."

70

Fast food

The McDonald's was in the main street of Pointe-à-Pitre, and with its beige, synthetic décor, it reminded her of an ageing computer. The building had in fact just been renovated.

Anne Marie hated hamburgers, but today she was spoiling her children in return for their having agreed to accompany her to the hospital.

(She had read somewhere that junk food was one of the solutions to anorexia. Children who did not want to eat could often be persuaded to wolf down a Big Mac, French fries and a giant Coke. Anne Marie would have preferred anorexia. She wondered whether Papa would shudder at the gastronomic suicide or whether he would be delighted to see his grandchildren eating with such gusto.)

They sat by the window on the first floor. Anne Marie had ordered a cane juice. The smell of grease alone was sufficient to spoil her appetite. Létitia and Fabrice ate noisily. There were still traces of rouge on Létitia's cheeks, although Anne Marie had carefully purged her daughter's face of makeup.

Rouge or ketchup?

Létitia had poured ketchup onto the hamburger and now it ran from the sides of the bun onto her fingers. Fabrice pretended to eat with more delicacy, but his taste and appetite were identical to his sister's.

"You promise me you will make an effort, Fabrice?"

"Siobud doesn't understand anything, Maman."

"That's not for you to say."

"The old bore spends his time giving us vocabulary."

"He's your teacher and you must listen to him."

"Siobud says I speak with an American accent but I'm only repeating what I hear on CNN and BET. Lots of words he doesn't understand."

"Of course he understands."

"When I put my hand up, Siobud ignores me."

"Fabrice, you go to school to learn."

"The other teachers don't complain about me."

"That's not what he said. The math teacher—"

"Math is difficult, Maman. In math, I know I need to learn. And the math teacher is nice. He made all the fuss when the headmaster slapped Alexandre."

"Who's Alexandre?"

"The *béké* in my class."

"The headmaster slapped a white pupil?"

"The headmaster hits everyone, Maman—particularly the girls." Fabrice shrugged. "Siobud is a pain in the ass."

"Mind your language in front of your sister."

"My sister's not a pain in the ass?" Fabrice gave her a disarming smile. "She's Miss Pain 1990."

While her brother's attention was elsewhere, Létitia took some of his fried potatoes.

"Siobud spends his time talking about slavery and he thinks he is cool but the guy's racist and he doesn't like me because I can speak good English and for him I'm a white. He made us watch a Spike Lee film over four lessons and I told him I was part Jewish and that Jews are like everybody else and that his film was crap. He got angry and said Portuguese Jews invented the triangular slave trade. He likes to pretend he's a musician but Siobud's never heard of zydeco. He knows nothing about American music."

"What's zydeco?"

"A kind of music, Maman," her son said, taking a couple of French fries from Létitia's basket.

"Don't," Létitia said, slapping him with ketchupped fingers. "And anyway, Fabrice's got a girlfriend and that's why he doesn't like his English teacher, because the English teacher has favorites."

"You've got a girlfriend, Fabrice?" Anne Marie asked, setting the juice down on the plastic tabletop.

Fabrice started to blush. He turned toward his little sister. "You should mind your own business, Mademoiselle Sait-tout. Mind your own business or I can tell Maman what you said to Béatrice about Luc."

"Fabrice, your girlfriend's in your class?"

He ignored the question by lowering his head and raising the remains of his hamburger.

"What's her name?"

"The other teachers don't complain about me."

"She's in your class?"

"Except Néron," Fabrice acquiesced, "and he's an old fart who reads the racing results when he should be teaching."

"Don't talk like that in front of your sister."

"Néron wears the same shirt to school for three days."

"You've really got a girlfriend, Fabrice?"

"Néron's breath smells because he never brushes his teeth."

"Fabrice, you're not answering my question." Anne Marie frowned. Her little boy.

("Eight years and two months—eight years, two months and ten days."

The white beach was scattered with dry sponge. Fabrice's naked back was hot beneath her hand. "You should put on a T-shirt." She looked around for a beach mat, a towel and some clothes. There was nothing.

"That's right, Maman. Eight years and two months and ten days."

"What on earth are you talking about, *doudou*?"

"If you had to walk to the moon. You remember, don't you? That's how long it would take." He folded his arms with satisfaction.

Anne Marie kissed his forehead, which tasted of salt; grains of sand glistened in the hairs of his eyebrows.

"Papa helped me—we used the calculator in the hotel. But that's without sleeping.")

"If you really must know, the girls in my class are so pathetic. They sit at the front and they flirt with the teachers."

Létitia nodded. "That's why he doesn't like Monsieur Siobud. Because of Rita."

"Rita, Fabrice?"

He raised his voice. "Your daughter tells lies."

"I don't tell lies, Fabrice. I heard you on the phone and I heard you talking to your friend and you said that you didn't like Monsieur Siobud because he sends Rita to the blackboard just before the bell goes."

"I never said anything of the sort."

"Oh yes, you did. You were talking to Patrice Ganot and you said Siobud keeps your Rita behind after the end of the class and then he talks to her. I heard you, Fabrice—don't lie to Maman. You said you were going to let the air out of the tires on Monsieur Siobud's car because he's a sex maniac and because he's already invited Rita to the beach and she's not even seventeen."

71

Useless

Hinitil, the cane row terrier Létitia had found on the beach and brought home, was a good guard dog and once he started barking, it took a long time for him to fall silent.

Hinitil and all the neighboring dogs were asleep when Anne Marie heard knocking on the door. At first she thought it was Béatrice and turned the sound of Frédéric Mitterrand down and got out of the armchair.

"That you, Béatrice?"

A man's voice.

"Who is it?"

"I need to talk to you, *madame le juge*."

Her heart beat faster.

"We met yesterday, *madame le juge*." It was an educated voice. "Could you please let me speak to you? I know it's late but I have something which I need to tell you."

There was a spyhole in the unvarnished wood, but looking though it served no purpose because the outside light had blown a long time ago and Anne Marie had forgotten to have it repaired.

"Tell me tomorrow."

"I need to talk to you."

"Who are you?"

"I need to talk to you about the dead woman."

"Who are you?"

"You don't know my name, *madame le juge*. I work for the television."

Carefully she opened the door and the light from behind her lit up a man—a West Indian wearing a pair of white tennis shorts and a V-necked T-shirt. He wore a golfing eyeshade and as he moved his head and his eyes came into the light, Anne Marie recognized him.

"You saw me yesterday, *madame le juge*."

"The technician?"

"My name is Léonidas—Lionel Léonidas, the cameraman. We came to interview you in the hospital annex."

"Then you'd better come in." She removed the chain from the door. "Come in if you're not going to stick a microphone down my throat."

He was small and slim and as the man stepped past her she could smell suntan lotion.

"Who is it, Maman?"

"You go back to bed, Fabrice," Anne Marie said, turning to her son, who stood in the kitchen doorway. He had his hand behind his back and was in his pajamas.

Léonidas entered the room.

"Are you all right, Maman?"

"Go to bed, Fabrice."

"Do you mind if I sit down?" Léonidas asked and without waiting for a reply, he lowered himself not onto the armchair but onto one of the high-backed wooden chairs. He was an attractive man—she had scarcely noticed him at the hospital because the bright lights had prevented her from getting a good look.

"Care to join me in a drink?" Anne Marie nodded to the almost empty glass on the chair arm. "*Rhum vieux*."

"Nothing." He shook his head. He had soft hair, almost blond, and he could have passed for a European with a deep tan. He was wearing green boating shoes. "Unless of course you'd have a verbena tea."

"Nothing could be easier."

"Very kind, *madame le juge*."

Anne Marie went into the kitchen and poured water from a bottle into the electric kettle. Fabrice was standing in the doorway and he made her jump. He whispered the question, "Who's the man, Maman?"

"From the television," she replied and noticed that there was a carving knife on the draining board. "Now go to bed."

When she returned to the sitting room, Léonidas was watching the television. "I can't understand a word he says."

"Who?"

"Professionally, it's very well put together—slick and fast in the way that the English do their documentaries, but I just can't understand a word Frédéric Mitterrand's saying. My fault, I suppose." He gave a wide grin. "Seven years of *lycée*, another four at university studying communication technologies. Only normal it should be beyond me."

"You studied in France?"

"*Madame*, I'm sorry to come knocking on your door at this hour of the night."

"I was about to go to bed, actually."

"Not really the done thing, barging in on the privacy of a *juge d'instruction*."

"How did you know where I live?"

"A few enquiries at the television station. But I don't want to take up your precious time."

"You'll drink the verbena now that you're here."

"You see, I'm a homosexual. Don't ask me why, because I don't know. Perhaps if I did, that might change things. Believe me, when you're different from other people, life can be pretty grim." A wide smile. "No, I haven't come here to give you a dissertation on homosexuals."

"Why have you come here?" Anne Marie sat down in her chair, without taking her glance from his regular features.

"A piece of information that might be of use to you."

"That you're gay?"

"I've heard about you, *madame le juge*, people say you're decent, so you can understand why I've come to see you privately."

"Not really."

"You've lived in this island and you've adapted to the customs of the place. You know how small-minded the people of Guadeloupe can be. You're probably from Paris—you grew up without knowing the neighbor on the other side of the hallway and you know things aren't like that in Guadeloupe. Not here. Privacy, having a place to yourself, having your own personal space that no one will intrude upon—that's not part of our culture. You've seen the vulgar graffiti on the walls and you know the meaning of the word *maco*."

Anne Marie frowned and glanced in the direction of the bedroom.

"To be curious, that's what *maco* means. The worst insult you can use—and yet everybody here is *maco*. People need to know what you're doing." He really was very attractive. Léonidas smiled his broad grin and she saw he was not looking at her.

Anne Marie sat up in the armchair and turned. Fabrice had entered the room, carrying a tray with a pot of boiling water.

"The verbena tea, Maman."

She thanked her son, who set the tray down on the coffee table and then left the room, accompanied by the glance of Léonidas.

"A nice boy," he said.

"You take sugar?"

"At the *lycée* I imagine."

"Fabrice?" She nodded. "Not a very good pupil, I'm afraid. Really far too interested in the girls."

The smile slowly disappeared from the regular features. "You understand my need for discretion, *madame le juge*."

"Discretion's a word that people like here, Monsieur Léonidas, but it's a virtue that few seem to practice."

"Precisely what I was saying."

She poured the tea into a cup and handed it to the man. "What exactly was it you came to see me about?"

"I've just come back from Tarare beach. I go there every week. I have a friend now." He paused.

"What are you trying to tell me?"

"Every Sunday I go to Tarare, sometimes by myself, sometimes with a friend."

"Last Sunday you were not alone?"

"No, I was not alone."

"That's why you've come to see me? Here, at my house in Dupré, at nine in the evening?"

"There's a man you've been seeing at the *palais de justice*. His name is Desterres and I don't think he likes us very much."

"Us?"

"He hates gays."

"I thought it was just investigating judges he didn't like."

"Like most homophobes, Desterres's afraid of finding out he has more in common with us than he'd like to admit. Desterres wouldn't be the first—Adolf Hitler was a repressed homosexual."

"You're not a repressed homosexual?"

"I've come to terms with my sexual preferences," the man answered simply. "Please don't judge me, *madame*. Just because I do with other men precisely those things most men do with women doesn't mean I'm any less a human being. You know about the evils of racism and of exclusion." He made a delicate movement of his hand before raising the porcelain cup from the tray.

"I don't want to hurry you, Monsieur Léonidas, but tomorrow is a busy day."

"Desterres's happy enough to take our money when we go to his restaurant—Mère Nature—but as a rule, we don't go because the welcome isn't friendly. He feels we lower the tone of his beach." Again the disarming grin. "I suppose in a way we do."

"Go on, Monsieur Léonidas."

"Which presents the problem of bodily functions."

Anne Marie frowned.

"Rather than visit Desterres's restrooms, having our dignity and a toilet roll, we tend to go into the bushes to answer the call of Mother Nature."

"You mean defecate?"

"I mean shit." A bland smile. "Last Sunday, it was about three in the afternoon and I'd been swimming and the chill of the sea water must have triggered a form of colic—something I'd eaten for lunch."

"How very interesting, Monsieur Léonidas."

"I left my friend on the beach."

"Your friend who is . . . ?"

"That doesn't concern you." He licked the edge of the Limoges cup. "I went into the bushes. There's a kind of isthmus behind the beach and on the far side there's another, stone beach. You can't bathe there because of the rocks and there's not much shade. There, in the low bushes, I went to answer nature's call and I overheard these people."

"What people?"

"Desterres—he speaks with that Anglicized accent of his but I didn't recognize the other voice."

"You could see them?"

"I was squatting down, *madame le juge*."

"I can understand that."

"A woman's voice."

"What were they talking about?"

"They couldn't hear me shitting and I couldn't hear what they were saying."

"That's why you've come to see me?"

"It was the murdered girl Desterres was talking to." Léonidas nodded slowly. "I recognized her photograph in the newspaper a few days later."

A long pause; the television droned softly in the corner. The hum of the air conditioning from the children's bedroom.

"You're certain it was in the afternoon?"

"After lunch—I'd drunk some wine that went straight through me—"

"Murdered girl? Desterres says the woman left in the morning, before midday."

"*Madame le juge*, it was the afternoon."

"Which would suggest Desterres is a liar."

"Desterres's life is a lie. He is afraid to face up to the truth of his own sexuality."

"You actually saw the girl?"

"Crouching's not an observation position, but, yes, I saw her, *madame le juge*. No more than a peek—but it was her and I heard them shouting. The wind carried their voices in the wrong direction but I assure you they were quarreling. They'd left the beach to get away from the tall black fellow with the camera."

"You know him?"

Léonidas shook his head. "If I'm here now, it's because I realize what I witnessed may be important. I want to help. She may have been a bitch—but she didn't deserve to be murdered."

"A bitch?"

"They were quarreling and that's when she laughed at him—or at least, that's what I thought from where I was."

"You didn't hear what they said?"

The technician shook his head. "He shouted at her and she just laughed." He added, "Desterres lost his temper."

"He struck her?"

Léonidas shook his head again. "No."

"What did you do?"

He drank the herbal tea in a ladylike sip. "I wiped my ass."

72

Silhouette

Monday, May 21, 1990

The *France Antilles* was on Trousseau's desk. There was a sheet of paper in the typewriter, the illustrated Bible lay beside the newspaper, the window of the office was open and the curtains danced in the morning breeze.

Anne Marie felt serene. She had taken yesterday off to be with her children and it was a wise decision.

She placed the Texier bag in her drawer, picked up the *France Antilles* and sat down. The front page showed a grubby picture of the siege at the Collège Carnot. The headlines announced the death of the assassin of the Pointe des Châteaux.

"You're late, *madame le juge.*"

She smiled at her *greffier*. Trousseau returned the smile and slipped something into his pocket before shaking her hand.

"I overslept but fortunately the neighbor was able to run the children into school for me." She looked at her watch; it was not yet half past eight. "I stopped at the Prisunic on the way in."

"You're going on with the enquiry?"

"I haven't yet been informed the *parquet* considers the case closed." She frowned. She could smell the pungent odor of fish. "Even if it were, I'd still come into work."

"Take a few days off."

"I've got bags under my eyes?" She leaned back in the chair, stretched and yawned simultaneously, without putting her hand over her mouth. "Do you have any news for me, Monsieur Trousseau?"

"You're really continuing the enquiry?"

"That's what was asked of me." Anne Marie ran a finger along her upper lip. "I was given the case and I won't close it until it's solved."

"Like the Dugain dossier?"

"Monsieur Lafitte was supposed to be here at seven thirty. I told him I'd be wanting to see Marie Pierre's boyfriend. No reason why Lafitte shouldn't be here on time." Anne Marie clicked her tongue in irritation, just like her children. "Unless he's privy to the *procureur*."

"There's this, *madame*." Trousseau held up a typewritten sheet of paper. "A report from Pasteur concerning the bikini."

Her face brightened. "And what does it say?"

"Nothing."

"Two pages of typescript to say nothing?"

"Government scientists are paid by the syllable." He held the type-script at arm's length to get it into focus. "A size M bikini, of a type easily available in several supermarkets for a price ranging from eighty to two hundred francs. Trademark Silhouette, made in Turkey, cotton and synthetic mixture. Matching top and bottom. Analysis of the fiber suggests that top and bottom were bought together, although the top has been washed with a powerful detergent."

She took the report from his hands and ran her finger down the text. "Matching top and bottom, probably bought together," she read aloud.

"Which is what I said, if my memory serves me right," Trousseau said. He sat down behind the typewriter and took a half-eaten sand-wich from his pocket.

"What you said, admittedly, Monsieur Trousseau, but that doesn't mean it makes sense."

"If you feel what I say's senseless, I should perhaps be quiet." Trous-seau bit into the sandwich.

"What you say is always full of sense," Anne Marie acknowledged. "The bikini doesn't make sense. A West Indian woman's not likely to buy a bikini—I told you that on Saturday. A French girl coming on holiday wouldn't've waited until she came out to the Caribbean before buying a bikini."

"Then why sell bikinis in the supermarket?"

"I stopped at Prisunic on the way in just as they were opening. There are very few bikinis and when I asked the girl at the counter, she said they didn't sell very well at all."

"Who buys them?"

"Mainly Europeans."

"You see, Madame, it could've been a woman from the mainland who bought it. And," Trousseau said through a mouthful of half-masticated mackerel, "it's quite possible the bikini was bought in France. There's no big difference in stock between here and France—just we don't have their seasons."

Anne Marie opened the drawer and pulled out the copy of the Polaroid. Agnès Loisel on the beach, between Desterres and the Indian. "You're overlooking one thing, Monsieur Trousseau."

"Wouldn't be the first time."

"According the Institut Pasteur, it's a matching top and bottom." She tapped the photograph. "Look at the girl. What do you notice, Monsieur Trousseau?"

"Nice pair of breasts."

"You like big breasts?"

"You know, *madame le juge,* that I see more in a woman than her body."

"Precisely what Olga the van lady said at the Pointe des Châteaux, I believe."

Before he could allow himself to be offended, Anne Marie continued in a hurry, "Her breasts are firm but they're also large. Now look at her hips. What do you notice?"

He took the photograph and held at the end of his outstretched arm. "Boyish."

"Big breasts and narrow hips. Don't you understand, Monsieur Trousseau? A girl with that kind of anatomy—she'd never think of buying a bikini off the peg. And most certainly never in a supermarket; the bottom would be too big—or the top too small."

73

Passport

There was a knock at the door and a pretty girl came into the office. She wore the laboratory coat of a pharmacist, flat shoes, and surprisingly, stockings. She addressed Trousseau. "Are you *le juge* Laveaud?" She had jet-black hair that was short, straightened and brushed back.

"I am," Anne Marie said.

The girl turned and smiled sheepishly. "Your friend sends you these prescriptions." She held out a thick manila envelope that Anne Marie took. "He asks you to phone him as soon as you can."

"Thank you, *mademoiselle.*"

The girl walked out of the office, leaving a faint odor of castor hair oil and formaldehyde that was then lost to the stronger smell of mackerel and peppers.

Anne Marie opened the envelope.

THIS IS WHAT YOU'RE LOOKING FOR? The note, pinned to a wad of grey photocopies, was not signed.

"Good news, *madame le juge?*"

There were no prescriptions.

Her finger ran down the pages. The date was at the top of each page, next to the heading LABORATOIRES ESPIÈGLE.

"Good news, *madame le juge?*" Trousseau asked and again Anne Marie ignored him.

It was on the third page, dated July 1988, that Anne Marie found what she was looking for. The typed entry had been encircled by a ring of yellow marker on the photocopy, with an arrow in the margin.

"You're an angel, Luc," Anne Marie said under her breath and slapped the desktop.

Trousseau looked at her in surprise.

Anne Marie winked at him and picked up the phone. She dialed the number from memory and, after a few moments' wait, said to Trousseau, who was now concentrating as he slowly typed at the Japy, "Monday morning and in the People's Republic of the Tourist Office, it's an English weekend—they still haven't come in for work."

Trousseau ignored her.

Somebody lifted the receiver.

"I should like to speak with Monsieur Eric André."

"Monsieur André is in a meeting."

"Then you'd better call him."

"That won't be possible."

"I'm calling you from the *palais de justice*. I am *le juge* Laveaud. Kindly bring Monsieur André to the phone immediately."

There was a clunking noise as the telephone was set down and then Anne Marie heard the sound of the woman's high heels. Thin legs, high heels and fair skin—Anne Marie intuitively knew the type of girl Eric André would employ as a receptionist.

"Is that you, Anne Marie? You're calling at a very inconvenient time. I've got a couple of mayors here with me—"

"You told me you were going to New York at the end of the week for a conference."

"So what?"

"Might be a good idea, Eric, if you sent someone else in your place."

"What are you talking about, Anne Marie?"

"I don't suppose you went to see Lucette Salondy."

"I've got better things to do than to traipse off to the hospital just to see an overweight sister-in-law. Now, Anne Marie—"

"You've got time to take another sister-in-law out to the restaurant? Or perhaps I'm not overweight?"

"I'm very busy this morning, Anne Marie," he said tersely. "You're playing games."

"I'd prefer it if you didn't leave the *département*. Not for now."

"A threat, Anne Marie?"

"I don't need to make threats."

"You're withdrawing my passport? Is that what you're saying?"

"In a manner of speaking."

"I'm your brother-in-law." Worry was sapping the self-assurance. "You don't mean what you're saying."

"Precisely because you're my ex-brother-in-law I'm contacting you, Eric. I'm trying to save you embarrassment. You're in a delicate situation."

"You're threatening me?"

"For your own sake, it's best you don't leave Guadeloupe. I'm not asking you to hand in your passport—not yet."

"Anne Marie, you're not acting rationally."

"You knew Rodolphe Dugain was suffering from a viral infection, didn't you, Eric?" She ran her finger down the photocopied sheet that lay on her desk. "Ever since the month of July, 1988. You knew it was a secret he had to keep quiet at all costs."

There was no answer, just the click as her ex-brother-in-law hung up.

74
Gambetta

It was nearly nine o'clock when Lafitte came into the small room. He was out of breath and he looked tired, as if he had not slept. "I'm sorry I'm late."

"Have you located the boyfriend?"

There was no reaction on his sallow face.

"The dead girl's boyfriend—I asked you to bring him in."

"His name is Olivier Rullé and he works in a bank." Lafitte took the chair opposite Anne Marie. "He wondered whether it would be possible for you to go over to his office at the Crédit des Outremers."

"Crédit des Outremers? Then he knows Richard Ferly?"

"Possibly, *madame le juge*. I'm not sure they work in the same branch. I managed to get hold of him only a few minutes ago, and he'd like you to see him in the rue Gambetta—if you don't mind. Otherwise," Lafitte went on, "to ring him on this number and he'll come over." He added lamely, "He works on the computers."

She took the number. "A West Indian?"

"I don't know where he's from—I've only spoken to him on the phone. He doesn't speak with a local accent." Lafitte propped his elbow on the edge of the desk. "I've got some very good news."

"That'll make a change." From behind the typewriter, she heard Trousseau's soft laughter but she chose not to look at him. He was still sulking.

Lafitte held up two fingers. "Two bits of news."

She made a gesture for him to continue.

"Lecurieux phoned."

"From Basse-Terre?"

"Geneviève Lecurieux's been in Mauritius for the last few days and that's why she didn't contact us any earlier. She's only just got back to Saint-Denis in Réunion. Eight hours between here and there—she contacted the SRPJ at four o'clock this morning."

"What did she say?"

"Say?" A slight movement of the shoulders. "Nothing that I'm aware of. Baptiste was on phone duty—he took her number. She can be contacted at the Novotel until tomorrow—tonight in Guadeloupe time—when she flies to Paris."

"No mention of the Vaton girl?"

Lafitte grinned with satisfaction. "They've found her."

"Who?"

"Evelyne Vaton, *madame le juge.*"

"Who's found Evelyne Vaton, Monsieur Lafitte?"

"Carte Bleue have found the girl. The credit card people've found Evelyne Vaton."

Anne Marie took a deep breath. "How on earth did Carte Bleue find her?"

"Evelyne Vaton phoned in yesterday to say her Visa card'd been stolen."

"Evelyne Vaton?"

Lafitte nodded. "She's in Paris and she phoned to report her credit card was missing."

Anne Marie looked at her watch, then looked at the Air France calendar that sat on her desk. She laughed with incredulity, raising her glance to Lafitte. "I find that very hard to believe, Monsieur Lafitte. You're telling me Evelyne Vaton's Visa card was stolen, she's alive in Paris and it's only now she discovers she's lost it?"

Lafitte ran his fingers though the short hair. "That's why I'm late, *madame le juge.* I was phoning through to their twenty-four-hour service. It's not far from the airport at Roissy. Evelyne Vaton's indeed alive and well and living in Paris. Visa card and driving license and most probably her identity card were stolen—were being used here in Guadeloupe."

"It's only now she realizes it?" Again the snort of incredulity. "What did Carte Bleue say?"

"It might be wiser if you phoned yourself, *madame le juge*."

"Wiser in what way, Monsieur Lafitte? I'll have the damn woman arrested, you mean."

"What for?"

"Answer my question, Monsieur Lafitte. You've done useful work—now kindly tell me what Carte Bleue said."

"Evelyne Vaton lives in Paris in the twentieth *arrondissement*."

"Twentieth?"

"She changed apartments fairly recently."

Anne Marie sat back in her chair. There was an awkward silence. Trousseau pretended not to be following the conversation, but his two-fingered typing had ceased. He did not look up from the keyboard.

When Anne Marie spoke, she was repressing anger. "You mean to say the police in Paris didn't check? They didn't go to Vaton's home? Despite the search request you sent out?"

Lafitte took a Bastos from his shirt pocket.

"Don't smoke in this office and please explain to me why your SRPJ colleagues in Paris didn't go looking for this Vaton woman at her home address. Isn't that precisely what I asked them to do?"

Lafitte took an embarrassed, deep breath. "When the mother came out, we thought it was Evelyne Vaton who'd been murdered."

"And since then, Monsieur Lafitte?"

He was looking at the floor. "I don't know."

"You must know." Anne Marie could hear the hectoring tone in her voice, the same tone her father used when she came home from school with poor marks in mathematics. "You must know, Monsieur Lafitte. I put you in charge of the *police judiciaire* enquiry at this end."

A long, difficult silence in the small office. The trade winds played at the curtain and from beyond came the sounds of Monday morning on the Place de la Victoire.

"You really must know, Monsieur Lafitte, because if you don't know, who does?"

Lafitte spoke with his head to one side. "Evelyne Vaton told the people at the Carte Bleue one of her handbags'd been stolen—and that she hadn't noticed it."

"Evelyne Vaton, living in Paris, hadn't noticed her credit card had been stolen? You don't find that difficult to swallow, Monsieur Lafitte?"

He did not speak.

"Evelyne Vaton was booked on the Air France flight for the fifth of May—and the ticket must've been bought several days earlier." Anne Marie tapped the calendar. "Today's the twenty-second. Nearly a month—and she doesn't miss her credit card?"

"A lot of people have credit cards but don't use them, *madame le juge.*"

"And her driving license?"

"When did you last look at yours?" Wounded pride in his voice. He had started to stammer. "You know how women can change handbags."

"Still the misogynist, I see." Anne Marie clicked her tongue in irritation—just like Létitia. "You know what this means, Monsieur Lafitte?"

Their eyes met.

"It means lots of things—and I don't think I like all the implications." She caught her breath. "I'll have to make a report."

"Because of Madame Vaton—"

Anne Marie cut him short. "Madame Vaton knew her daughter was alive. She came out to the Caribbean on false pretenses and on a free ticket. We needed somebody—a relative—to identify the corpse." She looked at the police officer. "Madame Vaton knew her daughter was alive."

"Do excuse me, *madame le juge,* if I interrupt." It was Trousseau who spoke. "Madame Vaton is supposed to be returning on this evening's flight, *madame le juge.*"

Anne Marie turned to look at him. There was a sense of cold anger in the pit of her belly. "Well?"

"Madame Vaton's asked for permission to stay on in Guadeloupe. She's moved out of the hotel and has gone into a guest house in Gosier."

"A free holiday in the Caribbean at the expense of the Ministry of the Interior? Weren't you telling me she was a good woman, Trousseau?"

"Even a humble *greffier* is entitled to his opinion." There was no humility in his voice.

"A good, Christian woman?"

"My opinion, *madame le juge.* If I'm wrong, it wouldn't be the first time."

"A selfish, frigid monster and I couldn't understand why she appeared so unaffected by her daughter's death. The cow, the scheming cow—she knew her Evelyne was alive."

Trousseau chose to remain quiet.

"I'll have her arrested," Anne Marie said while her fingers ran through the Air France calendar.

"Madame Vaton?" Lafitte shook his head. "You've got no proof she was aware of her daughter's whereabouts, *madame le juge.*"

"I don't give a damn about Madame Vaton. She can rot, Monsieur Lafitte. She can rot." An icy smile came to her lips. "With her religion and her hypocrisy and her Savior, she can rot."

Trousseau straightened his worn tie.

"I want Evelyne Vaton to be brought in on the first plane—and I need to know whether the Lecurieux woman is involved as well."

"You're going to arrest Evelyne Vaton, *madame le juge?*"

Anne Marie grinned tightly. "Why not?"

"Evelyne Vaton wasn't in Guadeloupe. Evelyne Vaton never came out here and so she can't be guilty of Loisel's death."

Anne Marie said, "I never mentioned murder."

"Then on what grounds, *madame le juge?*"

"Fraud and attempted fraud," Anne Marie replied. Seeing the puzzled look on both men, she burst out laughing. "And, Monsieur Lafitte . . ."

"*Madame le juge?*"

"I want Desterres—now. With or without his lawyer, with or without handcuffs."

75

Half a Dozen

He wore a bow tie and had an infectious laugh.

Olivier Rullé stood up and pushed the sunglasses up on to his forehead. He shook hands with Anne Marie and Trousseau, then invited them to sit down on the anthracite settee.

"Something to drink, perhaps?" Before they could answer, he gestured toward the computer. "Sorry to ask you to come here but we're very busy. I'm the only person in the house who knows the intricacies of the program."

"You are an accountant?"

"For my sins."

"You know why we're here?"

"Something to drink?" There was a small refrigerator recessed into the wall, beneath an old engraving of Pointe-à-Pitre. He opened the door and took out a bottle of Contrexéville. The outside of the plastic bottle was misted.

"My *greffier* and I have just had coffee."

Olivier Rullé nodded and poured himself a glass of water that he drank thirstily before returning to his desk. He typed something onto the keyboard and the computer went blank.

"You know Agnès Loisel's dead, Monsieur Rullé?"

"I do now." He smiled but there was whiteness at the corner of his lips.

"When did you find out?"

"I thought Agnès was in France. She came to see me a couple of months ago and asked me to lend her the money for the air fare."

"One way?"

"I didn't ask." He shrugged. "Like everybody else in this island, I get to see *France Antilles* and I watch the RFO news in the evening—the job demands it of me. Like everybody else, I read about the killing at the Pointe des Châteaux, but I never for a moment associated it with Agnès. As far as I was concerned she was in France."

"Then how did you find out?"

"From Marie Pierre."

"A friend of yours?"

"A friend of Agnès's." He caught his breath. "*Mêm bitin, mêm bagaï.*"

"You speak Creole, Monsieur Rullé?"

He smiled. "My grandmother's brother was President of Haiti—many, many years ago. My mother's from Lyon, but I grew up here."

"*Mêm bitin, mêm bagaï,*" Anne Marie repeated. "Marie Pierre and Agnès Loisel are the same sort of people? 'The same booty, the same baggage?'"

There was a long silence while Rullé looked at her. Anne Marie was sitting on the low settee, her bag at her feet, her notepad open on her lap. Trousseau was also taking notes.

"Off the record, *madame le juge.*"

"What?"

"I'd rather what I said was off the record." His glance went from Anne Marie to Trousseau and back to Anne Marie. "Later, if you wish, I can make a statement." He grinned. "Unless, of course, you're intending to arrest me."

"Did you murder Agnès Loisel?"

"It'd be difficult to pin her murder on me, since I was in Martinique until last Tuesday—working on the head office computer."

"Any idea of who murdered her?"

There was sadness in his smile. "There was a time when I was fond of Agnès. A year ago, I'd have married her with my eyes shut. I proposed marriage, you know."

"And?" Anne Marie slipped the pen into her bag.

"Agnès's a hard person. Hard on other people, but above all, hard on herself."

"What makes you say that?"

"I went out with her for over six months. The kind of girl I find attractive, and although I know quite a lot of women, Agnès was different. Probably all in my head, I know. I'd have married her and if she'd've accepted, I'd have thought myself lucky. Wife, children, family—the full catastrophe and I'd've been overjoyed."

"Why did she turn you down?"

"She'll never live with anyone—not with me nor with anybody else—because Agnès Loisel's trying to run away from herself."

"You knew she was a lesbian?"

An awkward silence descended onto the room. On the other side of the rue Gambetta, through the curtains, Anne Marie could see the ugly cement wall of the Commissariat.

"I'm not sure she's a lesbian."

"She lived with Marie Pierre."

"Agnès liked men, she liked the company of men. It's just that she didn't like sex."

"Why not?"

Olivier Rullé shrugged and the jovial, round face was now reflective.

"You never had sex with her, Monsieur Rullé?" It was Trousseau who asked the question.

Olivier Rullé looked at Anne Marie.

"Answer the *greffier*'s question," Anne Marie said softly. "Did you and Agnès ever make love?"

He took a deep breath. "At first."

"What happened?"

"Stupidly I thought I could reach out and touch her heart even though those first times we made love, she clearly didn't enjoy it. That much was obvious." He ran a hand across his forehead. "So I tried other things. The women here, they often say West Indian men are only interested in their own physical satisfaction, so I tried kindness and I tried to be gentle, body and soul."

"To no avail?"

"After a while, she wouldn't let me touch her any more. She'd moved in with me, into my flat in Gosier and I tried everything, but the strange thing was, when I was allowed to caress her—intimate caresses—Agnès'd start scratching herself. She scratched her thigh, she scratched her shoulder, her arm, as if she was trying to trigger off another sensation in her brain—an alternative sensation to the pleasurable one I wanted to give her. It was as if . . ." He stopped short.

"What?"

"She was unemployed. She had no money—and she had absolutely no qualms about taking mine. We went to the cinema, we went to the restaurant. She had expensive tastes but in return, there was nothing. I paid for everything—and in return, I had a block of ice lying beside me in my bed."

Trousseau ran his finger along his upper lip.

"Friends said she was a whore but that's not true and even if it were true, I wouldn't have believed them. When you're in love, you hear what you want to hear, you believe what you want to believe. Agnès wasn't a whore." He snorted with false amusement. "A whore's better than that. You get a service from a whore. You pay her money and in return she does her business."

"I imagine so," Anne Marie said.

"Agnès took everything without ever giving anything back. She was using me but I had my pride and I thought the problem came from me."

"You never asked her about her past?"

"She lied. Told me her parents lived in Martinique when in fact her mother lived with a man in Abymes."

"Why did you stay with her if she was a liar?"

"Those were things I found out later. I thought I could get her to love me. I thought her selfishness was an act, a pretense, a way of protecting herself. If only I could get through that outer barrier, then she could be a real woman, the kind of woman I wanted to love."

"Agnès didn't have real emotions?"

"Just two things she was interested in—clothes and traveling. Once we went to Martinique together and I had promised to take her to Tarpon Springs."

"Where?"

"Tarpon Springs in Florida. My mother has a sister there who married a Greek fisherman. He owns the biggest sponge company in America."

"But you never went?"

"We quarreled and Agnès went off to Sainte-Anne. She found a little concrete shack there and later Marie Pierre moved in with her. In a way, her departure was a relief—in physical terms. We'd lived in my flat, we'd slept in the same bed but never a centimeter of skin. Agnès would always go into the bathroom in her nightdress and come out fully dressed. Yet for all that . . ." Olivier Rullé faltered.

"Yet for all that?"

"In a couple of months I will be thirty-one. A grown man of thirty. Agnès gave nothing and she took everything but when she moved out, it was as if I'd died. A grown man and at night I was a little boy crying into my pillow."

76

Threat

"Did Agnès Loisel take drugs?"

He shook his head. "She wasn't like that." Olivier Rullé had moved from his chair and now sat on the edge of a large mahogany desk. "She spent her time preening herself—like a cat that incessantly licks itself. She wasn't vain or anything. She didn't admire herself in the mirror. She was careful about what she ate, about her weight and three times a day, she'd disappear into the bathroom for ten minutes to clean her teeth. She had several toothbrushes—and got me to buy her more." He shook his head. "Funny, isn't it?"

"What's funny?"

"I'm not particularly generous by nature. Like most people, I'm selfish and I used to think women were less selfish than men but that was before I met Agnès. She only had to ask for something—a new dress or a pair of pretty shoes or a necklace—and I'd give it to her. I'd take her to the shop and buy precisely what she wanted. Yet that didn't stop her going off and finding a flat of her own, going out to work and living with Marie Pierre."

"She left Marie Pierre, too."

"Agnès needed a man—she liked men, but she couldn't keep one. A man'd've meant sharing her body. And Agnès couldn't bear having anybody touch her."

"That's not what Marie Pierre said."

The light skin seemed to flush. Then Olivier Rullé let out a sigh. "Perhaps not."

"A woman who doesn't like men?"

"Agnès liked being with me. Just she didn't want me to touch her."

"You never asked her why?"

He was silent for a moment. "Agnès was not a stupid girl and she respected knowledge. I think that's why she went to bed with me in the first place—attracted to intellectual men."

"You're intellectual?"

"I'm not a bricklayer, *madame le juge.* I make no claims to being intelligent but I have my *baccalauréat.* Whereas Agnès had nothing— nothing. She couldn't even spell. Basic things; things most people learn by the time they're in *cours élémentaire,* by the time they're eight or nine. She couldn't spell and she never learned to spell my name. I suspect she was dyslexic."

"Why?"

He raised an open hand as proof of his bewilderment. "Agnès was a prisoner of her ignorance. She talked of going to university—but she'd left school without a diploma, even if she pretended she had her *certificat.* Agnès Loisel could never be happy. She said it herself. There were times when she could be very realistic."

"And you believed her?"

"Women don't tell lies in bed."

Anne Marie laughed.

"Unlike you, *madame le juge,* I slept with the girl."

"Because you slept with her, she didn't lie?"

"No hope, no ideals and certainly no human warmth. When I asked her if she wanted to have children one day, she looked at me as if I were talking a foreign language and when I told her that other women had children to cherish and to love, Agnès simply replied it was a bad idea to love."

"Why?"

"I talked about all those things. Love, affection, caring for other people—things you take for granted, things you learn at your mother's knee—and Agnès just laughed. Tapped her forehead and gave me her pretty smile and said I was crazy and then she'd turn away. No point in loving anybody, she said, because afterwards you'd only be disappointed. Everybody'll let you down; sooner or later, everybody will disappoint you." He put his hand to his face and rubbed it. "Isn't it strange?"

"What?"

"A warm bed, a mother's kiss. You take it all for granted. Then you grow up, you get a job, you become a man. You go out into the world and without even being aware of it, you're looking for affection. I can't live without it—I need to give it and to take it. In a way, I'm envious of Agnès."

"She doesn't sound a very enviable person, Monsieur Rullé."

"Agnès could never cry as I cried over her. When she hurt me, when she failed to turn up, when she turned her back on me—I was like a whimpering child again."

"You seem to have got over her."

"She's still part of me."

"Agnès's dead."

"Agnès shared my life for several months, she moved into my life and now she's dead and that . . . And that . . ." Again the young man rubbed his face.

Neither Anne Marie nor Trousseau spoke.

"And now it is too late because she's dead." Olivier Rullé got up and returned to behind the desk. He ran the back of his hand against his nose.

"Did she take drugs?"

Trousseau coughed, crossed his legs, straightened his tie.

"She was addicted to clothes. She could spend hours poring over the 3Suisses catalog. She wanted to be pretty, at all costs, and she loved to wear good clothes. Obsessed with lingerie—she got me to buy La Perla and Aubade that cost a fortune. That's why she looked after her body. After all, with men she couldn't know the kind of bodily satisfaction that other women enjoy."

"Where are her parents?"

His thoughts were elsewhere. The eyes focused slowly. "Her mother's still here but Agnès refused to talk about her."

"And the stepfather?"

"A violent man—and a drinker." He held up his finger. "Why do you ask me about drugs, *madame le juge?*"

"Perhaps Agnès took an overdose."

"What makes you think that?"

"We have no cause of death. We suspected rape—but forensic tests say the bruising on her body occurred after death and not before it. And there were no traces of sperm."

"Times when I think that I was almost capable of rape. I was frustrated—frustrated by her refusal at any sort of intimacy."

"You didn't rape her?"

"I'm lucky, *madame le juge*. My parents love each other—a marriage made in heaven. If they can spend thirty years together without ever resorting to violence, I don't see how I can justify violence on a woman—on a woman or indeed on anybody." His smile was wise, but there were now wet traces down his cheek. "One of my rules—perhaps the most important—is that to deserve respect, you must give it. Violence's the antithesis of respect." He went to the refrigerator and took out the bottle of Contrexéville. "Sure you wouldn't like something to drink? Coca-Cola?"

Anne Marie shook her head.

He drank swiftly. "Drugs." Olivier Rullé looked at Anne Marie and her *greffier*. "She hated herself—deep down in the stoniness of her heart, she hated herself. Her selfishness was a kind of revenge."

"Why would Agnès Loisel hate herself?"

"Agnès never knew affection. Nobody had taught her to love herself. No matter how hard she tried to be selfish, way down there was self-loathing."

Trousseau coughed again.

"The first time we ever went to bed together . . ." His voice trailed away.

"Yes?"

"It's not important."

"What happened the first time you went to bed with Agnès?"

He smiled sheepishly. "She's dead, isn't she? It doesn't really matter."

"What happened?"

He sighed. "It was as if there was no life in her body. Letting me do with her body whatever I chose. She was elsewhere . . . as if her soul was hovering above her and calmly watching what was happening. When a man touches a woman, there are normally responses."

"I hope so."

"When I took off her top—I remember quite clearly, she was wearing an ochre-colored Naf Naf top. I took it off and there were marks, lots of marks. I asked her about them but Agnès shrugged and didn't answer. Scars that must have been a couple of weeks old; ugly blemishes on her beautiful skin."

"What caused them?"

Rullé looked evenly at Anne Marie. "She must've done it to herself with burning cigarette ends. Trying to punish herself. Or perhaps even trying to escape."

"Escape?"

"Her life was an escape. She ran away from me for Marie Pierre, she ran away from Marie Pierre to go to Paris. At sixteen she'd run away from home. Agnès was running away from life. You ask me if she took drugs. The simple answer is no—Agnès enjoyed nice clothes and nice jewelry too much, but I think that there were times when . . ." He put a hand to his eyes.

"Go on."

"Other girls talk about babies, about life, about the future. Agnès talked about death. She talked about it a lot; she wanted to escape. Not the occasional joint or a bottle of whiskey. What Agnès wanted was the final curtain, fast, painless and for keeps. That was her style, *madame le juge*. Escape from life, escape from the threat of love."

77
Hawaii

Détection, 9.xii.1989

. . . not in Detroit or Chicago, but surprisingly in Duluth and to a lesser extent, Atlanta.

However, one of the most interesting cases of dumping, as the practice is now called by North American enforcement agencies, comes not from one of these urban centers but from the relatively rural environment of Maui in Hawaii.

One morning in 1986, Mrs. Carnegie reported her daughter missing to the local police. At about the same time, a member of the public informed the police that he had found the documents belonging to Miss Daphne Carnegie scattered across the road outside his house. Called to the scene, police officers found the car of Miss Carnegie, abandoned and out of gas.

The previous evening the young woman had been at Maui Community College (see photo) until 8:30. She had never turned up for her rendezvous with her boyfriend at a nearby mall for nine o'clock.

Her boyfriend waited patiently for half an hour, then phoned the girl's house at ten o'clock from a local bar. Mrs. Carnegie's mother informed him that the young woman had not yet returned home. The boyfriend waited until the early hours of the morning, finally returning home at two in the morning.

The body of Miss Carnegie was found three days later, naked and in a state of decomposition, in a cane field. The corpse was autopsied immediately at Oahu, where the forensic physician could identify no cause of death. There was semen in the vagina but no signs of violence. Toxicology tests proved negative, and the police authorities were faced with the riddle of a healthy young woman, just twenty years old, dying without any apparent reason.

The semen was not that of the boyfriend, who had already been arrested. He was released when his alibi was corroborated by several customers of the shopping mall bar.

The death of Miss Carnegie remained an unsolved mystery for two years, until the arrival of New York forensic pathologist, Dr. Baden (see Détection *N° 203, 257), who suspected a case of dumping.*

According to Dr. Baden, the toxicology tests in Hawaii were good as far as they went, but they did not go far enough. Dr. Baden knew urine could not give satisfactory answers and that cause of death would be found in autopsy tissues. After death, the body's enzymes continue to break down cocaine, hydrolyzing it into benzoylegonine, which is even harder to find than cocaine. In testing for benzoylegonine, only the best equipment can give satisfactory results. Thanks to North American efficiency, Dr. Baden was in luck. Although Miss Carnegie had now been dead for over two years, the decomposed tissues had never been destroyed because the case had not been solved.

Dr. Baden sent sample fluids to the director of the Chemical Toxicology Institute in Foster City, California. This private laboratory specializes in drug identification and, in particular, the body's metabolism of cocaine. Using ultramodern equipment, the California institute was able to identify benzoylegonine in the sample.

And thus, the so-called murder was explained. For some reason, Miss Carnegie had not met up with her boyfriend but had spent her time free-basing, i.e., inhaling cocaine among friends, most probably at a party. Unfortunately, the young woman killed herself with an overdose. Her friends, not wanting to go to the police and risk arrest for the use of illegal drugs, found themselves encumbered with a corpse they did not know how to get rid of.

Consequently, they hastily dumped the body in a cane field and tried to disguise Miss Carnegie's death as a murder. Without Dr. Baden's vast experience, her mysterious death would have been attributed to a sexual predator.

A similar case, closer to home, is the embezzler of Saint-Michel-en-Grève (Côtes d'Armor) who was found naked . . .

78

Winning Team

"You read *Détection*, Luc?"

"You want me to put the *New England Journal of Medicine* in my waiting room?"

"You buy *Détection* for all the anxious mothers in your waiting room?"

"My secretary brings it in for me."

"Strange taste for a secretary."

"Her husband reads it, Anne Marie."

"That's how you saw this article?"

"One of my patients. You don't seem pleased. I thought you wanted to get this thing out of your hair."

"I've still got tear gas in my hair and I worry about Bouton."

"Don't worry about Bouton."

"It's not going to be easy to tell him. You know what he's like—a prima donna of the electric saw. He won't like me telling him his job."

"Bouton's arrogant but he's competent. Nobody else would accept to do the autopsies at the rates the Ministry of the Interior pays. For Bouton, an autopsy's an act of love."

"A cold lizard. If that's his idea of love, I wouldn't like to be in bed with him."

"Talking of which . . ."

"Lizards?"

"I missed you over the weekend, Anne Marie."

"I was with the children."

"It would have been nice to see you."

"Thanks for the photocopies."

"What photocopies?"

"The blood tests from Laboratoires Espiègle."

"I know nothing about any photocopies. Furthermore, I can assure you, *madame le juge*, that if I had access to the medical records of any patient, I would not be entitled to communicate them without the customary legal requirements. I am duty-bound to respect the professional oaths that I made upon taking up my career as a doctor and pediatrician. Can I see you this evening?"

"No, Luc."

"I miss you."

"I'm very grateful for all your help."

"We could take the children for a pizza and I'll get a divorce."

"I don't want you to get a divorce, Luc. Please don't make me angry when there are people looking, I need support."

"I give you my support."

"You're a good man."

"I'd like to have children of my own."

"I'm not going to embark upon motherhood again."

"I love you, Anne Marie."

"I'm forty-two."

"I'd love to be part of your life, be with you. The joys of married life—the smell of your smile, the touch of your perfume."

"A *juge d'instruction* can't have a sense of humor. It's no good trying to make me laugh. I'm afraid, Luc . . ."

"Afraid of what?"

"I don't want to see you any more."

"I love you, Anne Marie."

"I love my children."

"You don't love me?"

"I have two children who don't want to share me with another man."

"I'm attached to Fabrice. He needs a masculine presence in the house."

"You really don't understand?"

"Understand?"

"The masculine presence in the house is Fabrice and that is enough for me and my daughter. Fabrice, Létitia and Anne Marie—it's a winning team. We don't need anybody else, Luc. We don't need you."

79
Terrapin

As she placed her hand on the banister Anne Marie heard the familiar plop of a tortoise falling back into the water of the pool.

"You've been crying, *madame le juge?*"

She spun round as the woman stepped out of the shade. If it had not been for the cigarette between her fingers, Anne Marie would not have recognized Madame Théodore. Out of her American uniform, she looked older and very tired. "Your makeup's smudged."

Anne Marie said nothing but turned toward the lavatories on the ground floor of the *palais de justice.*

"I told you to take a lot of vitamin C for that cold."

It was Monday afternoon, which meant divorce; estranged couples—haggard, betrayed wives and weary husbands not wanting to look at each other. Anne Marie had to barge between groups of lawyers, chatting and sweating in their black gowns. She entered the staff lavatory and went to the mirror. She saw the reflection of Madame Théodore coming up behind her. Anne Marie turned on the tap and ran cold water onto her hands.

"Why have you been crying?"

"That's nothing to do with you." Anne Marie spoke into her cupped hands, pale beneath the water.

"I know what it's like to love someone and know there can be no future."

"I couldn't care less." Anne Marie washed her face, then wiped it with a Kleenex from her bag. She noticed, incongruously, a sheet of a Dalloz law book lying on the grubby tiling of the floor. "I suppose you've come looking for me and I don't suppose it's to give me marriage counseling. I certainly hope not."

"To apologize," Madame Théodore said simply.

"Because you lied to me?"

She leaned against the edge of a chipped sink. "Because I could've been more honest."

"More honest and saved me a lot of trouble? Saved me from alienating myself from my colleagues?"

The other woman said nothing. She put a cigarette to her lips and inhaled without taking her eyes from Anne Marie.

"You knew Rodolphe Dugain was homosexual, didn't you?"

"Probably."

"You knew or you didn't know?"

Madame Théodore said flatly, "Rodolphe liked me and I liked him. I liked being with a man who didn't feel the need to touch me."

Anne Marie said, "I hear your husband likes teenage girls," and immediately regretted the remark.

The wrinkled face seemed to age. "You've met my husband?" Madame Théodore was wearing jeans and a yellow silk blouse, neither of which was flattering to her middle-aged body. "You've met my husband, *madame le juge?*"

"He teaches my son at the *lycée.*" Anne Marie picked up her bag, opened it and took out the lipstick case smudged with Létitia's fingerprints. She quickly applied red to her lips, a red that matched her eyes. "You must excuse me. There's somebody waiting for me."

Madame Théodore stepped in front of Anne Marie, blocking her way. "I came to see you. I wanted to apologize—but I discover you're not interested in the truth."

"A time and a place for everything. You could've told me the truth last week. You could've told me Dugain was homosexual."

"I told you there was no sex between us."

"With good reason. You don't like sex—and Rodolphe Dugain was gay. You could've told me Rodolphe Dugain was being blackmailed because of his tastes in young men."

"I just knew he was depressed."

Pointedly, Anne Marie looked at her watch, "You didn't know he was being blackmailed to keep quiet over the Ilet Noir project?"

"I know nothing about Ilet Noir." Madame Théodore shook her head. "Rodolphe didn't talk about that. He never talked about politics, or even about his television programs."

"Oh, really?" Anne Marie interjected sarcastically.

"You know what he talked about?"

"I don't think I care."

"Death."

"Now he's getting some practical experience."

"He wasn't afraid of dying, but he talked about death. And he talked about his children and his wife; he said he didn't want them to suffer. He was trying to protect them because he loved them very much."

"You knew he was ill, didn't you?"

Madame Théodore put a hand to her face. The cigarette between her fingers glowed as she inhaled. The eyes held Anne Marie's.

"He was sick with AIDS and if you'd told me he'd killed himself because of it, you'd've saved me a lot of time. Saved a lot of bother for a lot of people but instead you come to see me now, here in the *palais de justice*, because you're afraid what might happen to you. You're afraid that—"

"AIDS? Rodolphe had AIDS?"

Anne Marie brushed past her, out into the patio of the *palais de justice*, where the terrapin were basking beside their turquoise pond.

80

Zorro

"No lawyer, Monsieur Desterres?"

Desterres held a leather case under his arm. He was dressed in green. Green trousers, a safari shirt with epaulettes and short sleeves, a green *foulard* tied at the neck. Green canvas shoes. He was sitting forward on the chair, his narrow shoulders stooped. "I thought we could come to some kind of understanding."

She laughed.

"I don't see what's funny."

Again Anne Marie laughed. "The wonderful thing about you politicians is you have no understanding of the machinery of justice. I'm a functionary of the state—and unlike politicians, I'm afraid I can't make the rules up as I go along."

Desterres turned his head to look at Trousseau who was sitting behind the typewriter, engrossed in his illustrated Bible. "I can be of use to you."

"I know that, Monsieur Desterres. Otherwise I wouldn't have asked the police to bring you in." She put her bag in the drawer and sat down. "More to the point, can I be of any use to you?"

He looked at her.

"You're facing several indictments. Eight years, at least. Obstruction of justice, fraud, attempted fraud, non-assistance to persons in danger." She gave him a bland smile. "You might have to put your political career on to the back burner for a few years. More if I can prove you murdered her."

"Can you ask your *greffier* to leave the room?"

"I can't change the rules just to suit you, Monsieur Desterres."

"*Madame le juge*," he said flatly, "I thought you wanted to know the truth."

"Why this sudden change of heart?"

His fingers pulled at the end of green *foulard*. "You understand the meaning of loyalty."

"I understand you're scared."

"Please ask this gentleman to leave the room." The eyes looked at Anne Marie attentively, glinting slightly in the oblique afternoon light.

Anne Marie glanced at the Kelton; it was nearly three o'clock. When she looked at Trousseau, he had raised his head and was smiling at her. In silence he ran his finger along the line of his thin moustache. "Would you mind, Monsieur Trousseau, leaving the room for a few moments? You realize it's highly irregular, but I believe Monsieur Desterres here wishes to communicate some information of a highly personal and confidential nature."

"My pleasure, *madame le juge*."

"Don't go far as Monsieur Desterres will be making a signed statement and I will need you here."

"Can I get you something to drink, perhaps, Madame?"

She shook her head. "You are most kind, Monsieur Trousseau."

Trousseau grinned, hitched up the crocodile belt and left the room, closing the door silently behind him.

"Why, Monsieur Desterres?" Anne Marie rose from her seat and switched on the ceiling fan. Then returning to the desk, she sat down and folded her arms against her chest. She looked at the man.

"Why what?" His face was immobile, devoid of emotion.

"A respected member of the community, you're a politician with convictions, you're concerned about the future of the *département*. Not the sort of person to act rashly. Intelligent, informed, politically committed. Before breaking the laws of our Republic, you're the sort of man to weigh the pros and cons most carefully. Why did you decide to get involved in a cheap attempt at fraud?"

"Fraud?"

"Wasn't that the idea? The bikini and the Polaroid photograph? That's what it was all about, isn't it? Ready identification, proof of Vaton's identity. The silly girl was going to disappear, drowned off the beach at the Pointe des Châteaux. But she needed to leave proof of her death so her child would get the insurance."

Desterres said nothing.

"Well, Monsieur Desterres?"

"I hadn't thought of that."

"Of what?"

"Insurance."

"It never occurred to you? The whole point of the foolish exercise—Agnès Loisel pretending to be the Vaton girl and then pretending to be carried out to sea and drowned? That never occurred to you?"

"I was doing her a favor."

"Vaton?" Anne Marie laughed harshly. "You don't even know her."

"Geneviève."

Anne Marie's smile vanished quickly. "Mademoiselle Lecurieux?"

Desterres's unblinking eyes remained on Anne Marie as he slowly nodded. "An old friend."

"That's not what you told me last time. You called her a boy scout."

"Geneviève's a boy scout—always has been, but she's a good person."

"She's your friend?"

A movement of acquiescence.

"As I recall you said you met her six years ago, that she went off to Africa to pound millet and get back to her African roots."

"Precisely." Desterres crossed his legs. He was wearing green socks. He had placed the case on the floor; his hands were folded on his lap. "A long time ago she was interested in the environment. That was before she got involved with Medecins sans Frontières, when she was still living here in Guadeloupe. She was interested in protecting the environment—and I got to know her." The eyes blinked once. "I'd hoped in Africa she'd find a husband."

"Instead you discovered she was a lesbian."

"I don't think Geneviève Lecurieux's like that."

"Everybody has sexual desires, Monsieur Desterres."

"Including investigating judges?"

Anne Marie leaned forward on the desk, her elbows on the wood. Overhead, the fan swirled calmly. With her index finger she tapped the wood. "I really don't think, Monsieur Desterres, that your present position allows you to indulge in light banter."

"Geneviève Lecurieux phoned me from Paris a month ago." Desterres spoke calmly.

Anne Marie reverted to the more comfortable position, sitting back in the chair with her arms folded. Her eyes felt hot and tired.

"She intended to visit Guadeloupe for two weeks. She said she'd be coming to Tarare. She's always liked me—the last boy scout." The face remained immobile. "Later she phoned to say she had to go to Réunion for a congress, but that her friend would be coming out. Coming out alone."

"Evelyne Vaton?"

He nodded. "Geneviève asked me to take her under my wing. Evelyne was a young, working single mother and a holiday in the West Indies would do her a world of good. She told me Evelyne's father was originally from Basse-Terre. She also said . . ."

"Single mother? That's not what her mother told me."

"It's what Geneviève said. She asked me to be kind to her. Evelyne'd suffered at the hands of her boyfriend . . ."

"And that she was a lesbian?"

"You seem to have a thing about lesbians, *madame le juge*. Perhaps you're one yourself." He shrugged. "Geneviève Lecurieux, Agnès Loisel, Evelyne Vaton—I don't know if they're lesbians. I don't know if you're lesbian. Nothing would surprise me and really, it's got nothing to do with me."

"You're just a loyal, disinterested friend? Zorro to the rescue of these poor, unhappy damsels?"

He looked at her coldly, then let out his breath. "You are a woman, *madame le juge*, and like most women, you're profoundly misogynistic."

"Really?"

"You have little time for the other women who fall by the wayside. You're the perfect woman, the perfect professional, the perfect mother but unfortunately, some women don't always have such an easy time of it. It's not always easy to be a woman."

"Is that why you've been accused of rape?"

"Most women want to be loved by a man and nearly all women are willing to make sacrifices because they feel it's worth putting up with someone who is selfish, who snores and who spends all his money on Gauloises or his Renault Twelve, who has folds of skin coming over his belt top, who doesn't wash, who is going bald, who has bad breath."

"My word, you're a feminist."

A cold smile. "Most women shut their mouths and make do with what they get. But women like Geneviève—women who with their good looks should be able to take the pick of the bunch—something frightens them and they look for affection elsewhere."

"You generalize."

"Geneviève finds love by being a boy scout, by going out to Africa and by helping the starving children. Vaton has a child on which to shower affection. And Agnès looks for love between the legs of other women." He held up his hand. "It's not for me to judge them."

"That's why you helped Loisel—because Geneviève Lecurieux phoned you? I find that very noble."

"I make no claim to being noble. I simply try to be loyal. There are people who've helped me—and there are people I try to help. I was expecting Evelyne Vaton to come out from Paris and instead it was Agnès who approached me."

"You knew Agnès, didn't you?"

A slight nod of the head. "I'd met her once, when Dugain sent me looking for the black girl."

"Marie Pierre Augustin?"

"Dugain had gotten involved with her husband, an ex-para-trooper who was trying to set up a garage opposite the university. Dugain had a thing for young black men but unfortunately for him, young black men rarely had a thing for an aging Martinique mulatto like Dugain." The eyes were turned toward Anne Marie. "The young man got Dugain to give his wife a job and Dugain sent me to find the wretched woman at Dupré and that's where I met Agnès." The eyes blinked. "A bitch."

"What makes you say that?"

"Agnès used me. She knew I was expecting the Vaton girl—I'd even phoned Geneviève's parents in Basse-Terre—and she came out with this complicated tale about Evelyne Vaton. Something to do with a bank manager in France who was making her life hell."

"The father of Evelyne's child?"

"I should've phoned Geneviève but she'd already gone off to the Indian Ocean. So I agreed to help Agnès set up the disappearance. She had Vaton's credit card and . . ."

"Monsieur Desterres, you expect me to believe you when you say you helped this woman set up her disappearance but you had no idea that the motive was fraud?"

"Believe what you like."

"No." Anne Marie banged her hand against the desk. "I'm not interested in beliefs. I want the truth."

Desterres suddenly and quite unexpectedly started to laugh.

"I don't see what's funny."

"You, *madame le juge*. You think you can frighten me but I'm not scared. I don't want to go to prison. You seem to think you can bully me into sharing your own petty values. You can't understand, can you?"

"You are a noble person, Monsieur Desterres, genuinely interested in helping your friends."

"If I wanted money, you honestly think I'd run a crummy, run-down restaurant on a nudist beach? You think I'd fight for the environment?"

"Dugain made money through the environment."

"Believe what you choose to believe, Madame Laveaud. There's no point in my telling you I was trying to help a friend of Geneviève's. So I won't bother." He shrugged one shoulder. "However, you'll believe me when I tell you I regret ever having met Agnès Loisel. The woman was supposed to spend the day at the Pointe des Châteaux, running into the sea from time to time, getting herself noticed. Instead, at about eleven o'clock, she turned up at my place at Tarare with that stupid Indian banker in tow and with her silly Polaroid camera."

"These girls all have a thing for bankers."

"What could I do? She didn't want to go ahead with the plan. It was her plan all along. Hiring the car, using Evelyne Vaton's credit card to buy the camera and the cheap bikini, even lying to Geneviève's parents. Her plan—a plan she'd worked out with Vaton—and now she'd roped me in, she got cold feet. I told her to go back with the Indian to the Pointe des Châteaux."

"Did she?"

"We took a few photographs and then she went off before midday, but within couple of hours later, she turned up again at Tarare."

"You lost your temper with her?"

The eyes looked at Anne Marie. "Wouldn't you? She'd left the car in the parking lot at the Pointe des Châteaux. The Indian had disappeared and I couldn't run her back and she refused to walk the three kilometers again. Said she was tired. Tired and sun-sick."

"She stayed in your restaurant?"

"Nobody saw her there. She lay down and she fell asleep immediately. Heaven only knows how because during the day it's unbearably hot inside. That's where she slept, at the back. And that's where she killed herself."

"With an overdose?"

Desterres shrugged.

"You didn't do anything?"

"I thought she was asleep."

"The girl overdosed on cocaine and you thought she was asleep."

"A little less arrogance, *madame le juge*. Loisel'd pissed me off. She'd used me and when I agreed to help her and her lover friend, for heaven's sake, she started acting up. Of course I thought she was asleep. I wanted her to be asleep so I could drive back to Pointe-à-Pitre."

"At what time?"

A hesitation. "After dark—at about seven. I went home but I left a message for her—there was food in the refrigerator and I left the key."

"You forgot all about her?"

"I didn't give Mademoiselle Loisel a second thought until Tuesday morning, when I found her dead. Dead—beneath a swarm of flies. Dead for over a day." He looked at Anne Marie. The eyes blinked a couple of times is succession. "What else could I do but dump her and her bikini on the beach?"

"You didn't have to go through with the Evelyne Vaton rigmarole."

"Perhaps not."

"Why did you come here, telling your lies?"

He shook his head. "How was I to know you could see through my inventions?"

"You panicked?"

"I didn't panic, *madame le juge*. I felt ashamed of myself. Agnès had pissed me off and I'd wanted to punish the bitch and I knew perfectly well what I was doing when I left her there alone on an isolated beach.

I knew what I was doing—I was even proud of myself. I wanted to teach the wretched woman a lesson."

"She died?"

"By her own hand."

"Your fault."

"She was a stupid, egotistical bitch but she wouldn't have died if I'd stayed with her. If I'd looked after her, if I'd just looked in on her—a young woman in the bloom of her life. Agnès would still be alive and instead I allowed her to die alone and abandoned." He picked up his attaché case. "You'd better call in your *greffier, madame le juge*. There are some things I don't like to admit in front of other people. Like all West Indians, I'm proud—possibly because deep down I'm not so sure of myself after all. Agnès Loisel was a scheming, selfish bitch, no doubt, but she was a human being and she was alive. Like you and me, she was alive on this earth." Desterres clicked his fingers. "Now she's gone. Gone forever because of my male pride."

81

Invitation

A lie.

"The masculine presence in the house is Fabrice and that's enough for me and my daughter. Fabrice, Létitia and Anne Marie—it's a winning team. We don't need anybody else, Luc. We don't need you."

A lie that she believed at the moment of speaking. In the smart restaurant that gave onto the harbor, she had been so sure of herself, convinced she could survive alone, convinced she did not need him. Him or indeed anybody else.

A lie because there had always been a man in her life. Papa, Jean Michel and then for the last four years Luc.

A winning team?

Only once had Anne Marie been alone. It was when she was pregnant with Létitia. After the discovery of the trunk, Jean Michel disappeared. Almost overnight, the man who had sworn his everlasting love in the Jardins de Luxembourg had moved out of her life and Anne Marie was overcome by a grief worse than when Maman had died. Fabrice was staying with his grandmother and Anne Marie took to her bed and for two days, she stayed in her room and wept until there were no more tears. On the third day, after having slept for nearly fourteen hours, she was woken by Létitia moving in her belly. Lying on her back, Anne Marie stared at the ceiling and she knew then a moment of intense euphoria. She would never be alone again.

"We don't need you, Luc."

After the frugal yet expensive meal she had left the restaurant She was not going to give him the satisfaction of seeing her cry.

The winning team.

The afternoon had been unbearably long and now, at last, she was home with her children and Béatrice was clearing the table. The television was turned on to the evening news from RFO and there were traces of pineapple yogurt on the tip of Létitia's nose. Fabrice was reading a surfing magazine under the table.

The telephone rang and Anne Marie felt relief flood through her. Relief and guilt.

Létitia slipped out of her chair and ran to pick up the handset. Apart from Luc, very few people had her ex-directory number.

Fabrice spoke softly, almost inaudibly, without looking up. "Maman, stay with us tonight."

"For your brilliant conversation, Fabrice?"

He raised his eyes in hurt silence as his sister handed Anne Marie the telephone. "A man," Létitia said.

"*Le juge* Laveaud?"

She held the receiver to her ear.

"Anne Marie, I hear you've been upsetting some important people."

"Good evening, Arnaud. How are you? How's your wife? How are the children?"

"I thought you decided to let the Dugain dossier drop."

"Important people? What important people?"

"Your brother-in-law."

"I didn't know Eric André was important."

"You asked for his passport."

"Dugain committed suicide."

"Then you needn't bother Eric André, need you?"

"As you wish, Arnaud." She looked at Fabrice. "Now, if you don't mind, I should like to get back to my supper. Unless of course—"

"Quite frankly, I don't give a shit about André—an upstart with more ambition than brains."

"Then why the phone call, Arnaud?"

"You know who killed her?"

"Her?"

"The Pointe des Châteaux girl? You know how she died?"

Anne Marie stood up and took the telephone into the kitchen, closing the door behind her. Béatrice was stacking plates into the washer.

"An overdose of cocaine—she was staying with Desterres. At least, that's where she died—in his bed at Mère Nature."

She could hear the *procureur* light up a cigarette. A Peter Stuyvesant. She could almost smell the nicotine of his breath over the line.

"You're going to arrest him, Anne Marie?"

"We'll need the Vaton girl from Paris." She added, "As I understand it, the murdered woman and Vaton were having an affair and they wanted to get out of Paris and were thinking of going to Canada to start a new life. They wanted to set up their little *ménage à trois*—Vaton, Loisel and Vaton's little baby. But they needed money—insurance money, so Loisel accepted to impersonate Vaton and pretend to drown at the Pointe des Châteaux."

"Instead she killed herself with an overdose?"

"Precisely, Arnaud."

"Good work." Again the sucking sound of his cigarette. "You've been quicker than I thought. A lot quicker than I feared. You have proof?"

"Desterres's made a statement."

"But no arrest?"

"Desterres lied to me, he set us all up with the Vaton thing and he deliberately went ahead with the mysterious disappearance."

"Why?"

"The idea cocaine was being used at his restaurant." Anne Marie caught her breath. "He's a strange person—a cold fish, but I believe he has a sense of honor. At least I'd like to think so. Something about him that makes my flesh creep, but at the same time . . ."

"A lot of people make your flesh creep."

"You noticed?"

"No arrest, Anne Marie?"

"I can wait."

"Probably a good idea."

"Arnaud, I'd like to remind you that a few days ago you were pressing me to arrest Desterres."

"That was before the Collège Carnot thing and before the Dominican got himself killed. Fortunately we've come out of the Carnot siege fairly well."

"Sometimes I wonder who you work for, Arnaud."

"Guadeloupe was in a state of high anxiety following the girl's death and in next to no time we identified the culprit—who also happened to be a foreigner." He gave a brief, smoker's laugh. "That can suit us all a lot."

"Can suit you, Arnaud."

"The *préfet*'ll be only too happy to impose more stringent rules on immigrants. The mayor of Pointe-à-Pitre can count on central funding for the renovation of the ghetto at Boissard—and kicking out the Dominican rastas and dealers. Not a bad thing. Even you will agree that can't be bad. And . . ."

"You want me to forget about Desterres? Arnaud, is that what you're saying?"

"Bastia, Parise and the *gendarmerie* have come out of all of this like Vestal Virgins rising from the dog shit. Good for their public image—because nobody really likes the *gendarmes* but now everybody—black and white alike—is glad our gallant *gendarmerie* can restore peace and security to the *département*. Security so that we can get on with our lives. Security for the tourist industry."

"And Desterres?"

"You've done a good job."

"Desterres, Arnaud?"

"Do as your conscience dictates. We all have complete faith in your professionalism and your common sense."

"Thank you, Arnaud."

"Of course, you'll be destroying Desterres's career as a politician."

"I'd thought of that."

"You'll be making a lot of enemies among the forces of order. Parise's very fond of you—you've done some good work in coordinating our police forces. Good to see you getting on so well with the *gendarmerie*."

"I like Parise."

"It'd be a shame to squander the good rapport you've built up. Quite honestly I don't think the *préfet* would necessarily be upset if Desterres got on with his life."

"There's the problem of bruising, Arnaud."

"What bruising?"

"Desterres doesn't have an alibi for the evening. According to

Bouton, the cuts to the lower part of her body and the bruising occurred after death—and Desterres was the only person to see her."

It was as if she had not spoken. "Anne Marie, the ball's in your court. Desterres can be useful for the future wellbeing of this island. Our present *préfet* is not too keen on the way the shoreline is being transformed into hotel beaches and the *département* needs some kind of ecology movement now that Rodolphe Dugain is dead . . ."

Anne Marie laughed.

"You're going to be reasonable," Arnaud said cheerfully.

"Reasonable?"

"Act as you think best. As the investigating judge, you have complete freedom."

"Of course, of course."

"I'm glad you agree with me."

A long silence over the line.

"Well?"

"Well what, Arnaud?"

"Do you agree with me, Anne Marie?"

"A favor I need to ask you."

She heard him breathe on the cigarette. "I'm listening," he said tentatively.

"I need a holiday."

"A holiday? At this time of the year?"

"I would like to get away, take the children to France, take them to see their aunt in Brittany."

"Something we could discuss over a meal, perhaps."

"I need to bring forward my administrative vacation."

"You want to leave Guadeloupe for six months, Anne Marie? You're joking, of course."

82

Les Bonnes Gens de la Guadeloupe

Tuesday, May 22, 1990

"You're looking for me?" Her face appeared tired, the eyelids dark. There were wrinkles about the soft brown eyes. She had placed a pile of dossiers on the table.

Anne Marie moved toward the large desk. "How are you, Madame Dugain?" The plastic cube containing various pictures of Lucette Salondy's relatives had not been removed, but had been placed next to the green telephone.

For a moment the expression was blank, devoid of emotion, while the eyes searched Anne Marie's face. "The *juge d'instruction?*"

Anne Marie held out her hand. "I'm Madame Laveaud. We met last week."

Madame Dugain took the proffered hand coolly, keeping her distance. Then Anne Marie sat down on the other side of the table.

A photograph of Mitterrand hung on the wall between a framed poster of the Declaration of Human Rights and a calendar from a local garage. The cables leading into the light switches were unconcealed and had been tacked into the wall with staples. "I have just been to see Lucette Salondy."

"Lucette Salondy's my cousin."

"Then we are related, Madame Dugain." Anne Marie tried to smile. "Lucette is my sister-in-law—or rather the sister of an ex-husband."

"How is she?"

"I didn't get to see her." Through the open shutters, Anne Marie could see the blossoming flame tree. "She's gone into a coma, I'm afraid."

Madame Dugain leaned her head wearily against the headrest. "Oh."

"The doctor said it's the sugar in her blood." Anne Marie nodded slowly. "I think she is going to die."

The two women were alone. There was silence in the headmistress's office. Somewhere children were singing. In another building a class burst into muffled laughter.

"I don't think your cousin wants to live anymore."

"There are times when I think Lucette loved Rodolphe as much as I did—as much as I do." Madame Dugain looked at Anne Marie. "And now she's going to leave me. She's going to die, too."

"When I came to see you last week, I spoke to her. She was talking about her retirement and she sounded very cheerful. Excited about her plans for the apartment on the beach. Excited about being more involved with my children. But she was acting out a *rôle*—that's the impression I got."

"Lucette's too old to act." Liliane Dugain folded her arms against her chest. She was wearing a white blouse. A necklace, matching gold earrings. Her black hair had been pulled back into a tight bun. "She should've married and had children."

"The pupils here were her children."

"She loved them with all her heart. I feel like an impostor, sitting here in her office. But what else can I do? The *rectorat* sent me a telegram telling me to fill in. My God. I do hope she comes back." Her lipstick was a matte red. White, regular teeth.

"Why did your cousin never marry, Madame Dugain?"

"There was a man. A long, long time ago. When I was her pupil here, Lucette was a beautiful woman and there was more than one boy in my class who had a crush on her—and a girl I could mention, too—with her almond eyes and her beautiful skin."

"Why didn't she marry?"

"I don't know who it was. Somebody from Martinique, I think, somebody who was already married."

"She could have married an honest man from Guadeloupe."

In a small glass jar, there was a solitary anthurium.

Madame Dugain smiled. "Lucette would have made an excellent mother."

"Children need to know they're loved. Love is time, Anne Marie."

"I beg your pardon."

Anne Marie said, "Lucette felt I wasn't spending enough time with my own children." She leaned forward and tapped the side of the plastic cube. "My daughter." Children in white dresses, holding flowers and squinting into the sun. Létitia stood at the edge of the group. She looked at the camera with her head to one side. She was holding a bouquet of tropical flowers. Inquisitive, self-assured eyes. "The apple of her aunt's eye."

Coldly, Madame Dugain asked, "And my husband?"

Anne Marie did not speak, her eyes still on Létitia.

"My husband was not a criminal."

"I never said he was, Madame Dugain."

The eyes flared with brief anger. "He was hounded to death."

"You knew he was ill."

"Ill?"

"He took his life." Anne Marie touched Madame Dugain's arm. "The dossier will be allowed to drop because I don't think any good can be achieved by continuing. Your husband was under great stress."

"Ill?" Her eyes were damp, the corners of her mouth twitched. "My husband and I were happy. He wasn't ill. There was nothing wrong with Rodolphe. He was hounded to death by people who were jealous of his success." She looked at Anne Marie defiantly. "We'd been married for seventeen years."

"Yes."

"He loved me—and he doted on his children. He doted on all the children, those he had with me and the children from his first marriage in Martinique."

"He didn't want to upset you," Anne Marie said. "Some sort of cancer—or at least, that's what the doctor told me."

"Rodolphe loved me and he loved the girls." A shrug. "Two lovely children. I married someone who was many years older than me, *madame le juge*. That kind of age difference isn't so very common but I was lucky. I wanted a companion, a friend and I married a wonderful man. Somebody who could have been my father. You see, between Rodolphe and me there was total equality. My husband was a kind, good, highly educated man, someone who respected women, who not only gave me two lovely daughters but also gave me the best years of my life."

"Your husband didn't want you to see him losing his hold on life."

"Rodolphe loved life"

"He didn't want his wife and children seeing him turn into an old and sick man."

Somewhere an electric buzzer sounded, followed almost immediately by the sound of scraping chairs and the scuffling of feet as the pupils left their desks at the end of the lesson.

(Anne Marie was reminded of her school years in Algeria.)

"Rodolphe and I were very happy, *madame le juge.*"